Emma Hornby is the author of *A Shilling for a Wife* and *Manchester Moll*. Before pursuing a writing career, she had a variety of jobs, from care assistant for the elderly to working in a Blackpool rock factory.

She was inspired to write because of her lifelong love of sagas and after researching her family history; like the characters in her books, many generations of her family eked out life amidst the squalor and poverty of Lancashire's slums.

Emma lives on a tight-knit working-class estate in Bolton with her family.

Discover more about Emma and her books at her website: emmahornby.com

www.penguin.co.uk

Also by Emma Hornby

A SHILLING FOR A WIFE
MANCHESTER MOLL

and published by Corgi Books

THE ORPHANS OF ARDWICK

Emma Hornby

CORGI BOOKS

TRANSWORLD PUBLISHERS
61–63 Uxbridge Road, London W5 5SA
www.transworldbooks.co.uk

Transworld is part of the Penguin Random House group of companies
whose addresses can be found at global.penguinrandomhouse.com

First published in Great Britain in 2018 by Bantam Press
an imprint of Transworld Publishers
Corgi edition published 2018

A CIP catalogue record for this book
is available from the British Library.

ISBN 9780552173254

Typeset in 11/13.25pt ITC New Baskerville by Jouve (UK), Milton Keynes.
Printed and bound in Great Britain by Clays Ltd, Elcograf S.p.A.

Penguin Random House is committed to a sustainable
future for our business, our readers and our planet. This
is made from Forest Stewardship Council® certified paper.

MIX
Paper from
responsible sources
FSC® C018179
www.fsc.org

6 8 10 9 7 5

For my grandma, who had more than a little of Cook May in her. And my ABC, always x

For each man knows the market value
Of silk or woollen or cotton . . .
But in counting the riches of England
I think our Poor are forgotten.

Adelaide Procter, poet and philanthropist

Chapter 1

December 1860

'LOOK, SEE? SEE the pictures in the clouds? It's a cat and horse dancing a jig! Tha sees it, don't thee?' asked Pip hopefully.

The small boy followed her finger towards the darkening sky and squinted at the scudding mist. He sucked noisily on the thumb planted firmly in his mouth. Moments later, he turned his huge blue eyes, shiny with miserable tears, towards her. He shook his head. 'Hungry, Pip. Terrible hungry.'

His pitiful cries tore at her. Careful not to put her feet into the stagnant pools of human filth which filled the stinking floor of the communal privy they were crouched in, she eased her stiff legs out from under herself and wriggled her cold toes to coax some life back into them. Then she wrapped her arms around the tiny boy by her side and drew her shawl more tightly around them both. He snuggled into her thin chest and within seconds, the bodice of her ragged dress was soaked with his tears.

'Hungry. Hungry!'

Pip shushed him softly. 'Quiet, lad, else owd Betty will hear and we'll be for it then. Didn't she warn only last night what she'd do if she found us sheltering in here again?'

'Ram her clog up our arses and kick us into next Sunday, Pip.'

A wry smile touched her lips. 'So you see, you must be quiet, like. Try to sleep and in t' morning, we'll go and hang around Mr Hoggart's bakers, see if we can't persuade someone to take pity on us and buy us a stale bun. What d'you say to that? But it's late, now, so you must sleep. That's it, you keep close to me for warmth, there's a good lad.'

Half a minute later, the boy's voice cut through the gloom again: 'Can't sleep. Too hungry to sleep. Guts like that, Pip.' He clenched and unclenched his small fists in imitation of his cramping stomach. 'It hurts. It hurts.'

Before Pip could soothe him, a second lad sitting apart from them nearest to the broken door cut through the youngster's whimpers. 'Go to kip, Bread, for Christ's sake. There's nowt to be done till morning so just you shut up.'

Pip cast him a frown. 'Don't be harsh with him, Simon. He's only a babby. He feels it more than us. And will tha stop calling him Bread? I told thee from the start, I'll not address him by that. It's an altogether stupid thing to call a body. His new name's Mack. Call him Mack.'

The dark-haired boy turned his scowling face away and flicked his shoulders in a shrug. 'Aye, well. Bread, Mack, call him what you will. I ain't mithered. Just keep him bloody quiet, will thee? He's getting on my nerves.'

Silence fell and the three children settled down for another long, cold night stretching ahead.

The Sunday late hours were empty of sound and for this, they were grateful. Weekends were the devil's own holidays; the drunken, raucous goings-on of the slum dwellers once their wages were in their eager palms was a battle the children endured with quiet grimness week in, week out. Weekdays were not so bad. Folk had to be up early for work the following day and generally the narrow, cobbled streets and lanes were free of drama.

Soon, Mack's breathing steadied into a regular rhythm and Pip released a soft sigh of relief. This life was hardship enough at her and Simon's ages – though just how old the lads were, she couldn't rightly say, had never asked – but for the small one beside her, it was torture. Only this morning, she'd had to bite back tears when she'd attempted to check Mack's feet. He'd been having trouble with them for weeks and when he'd stumbled, wailing in pain and unable to take another step, she'd knelt before him to investigate. The rotten remnants of his old boots, she'd soon discovered, had seemed to become one with him. She'd tugged at the crumbling leather but his screams had halted her attempt and, heartsore for this poor child she'd come to love as a younger brother, she'd had no choice but to leave them be. The boot looked to have fused to his bare flesh and, short of tearing the skin from the bone, there was little she could do. He'd have to try and ignore the pain, and she'd told him so.

No, a life on the streets wasn't one they endured easily. Yet what was the alternative? The workhouse? Her lips tightened in determination. Never, never. She'd sooner finish her days all bone and frozen to the marrow in the gutter than pass through those doors. They all would. That place with all it stood for was the scourge of the poor's nightmares. Man or woman, old and young, fit or weak – each knew how easily their fortune could change and the prospect of the poorhouse could be upon them in the blink of an eye. They would take these grey, filth-ridden cobbles any day, thank you very much.

3

'Is he asleep?'

Pip looked over the top of Mack's fair hair towards Simon. His face was in shadow, hiding the worry she knew would be in his eyes – was always there for this boy they both fretted over, however much Simon tried to hide it. She nodded. 'Aye. Best get some shut-eye ourselfs. We want to be up and out of it afore sunrise, else we'll be for it. Betty will have a blue fit if she happens upon us when she comes to empty her chamber pot in t' morning.'

'Owd bitch, she's nowt else.'

'Aye, well.'

'I'd like to tip a pot of piss over her ugly bull head as she did to me. See how she'd like that, rotten cow.'

Carefully, so as not to disturb Mack, Pip felt the air in the darkness until her fingers brushed the coarse material of Simon's jacket. She pressed his shoulder. 'Get some sleep, lad.'

Simon brought his knees up closer to his chest and pulled his too-large cap low over his eyes. His teeth began chattering; cursing quietly, he folded his arms around himself tightly.

'Shuffle up here against me and Mack. You'll be warmer that way.'

After a moment's silence, he answered her gruffly. 'Nay. I'm all right.'

Pip smiled to herself. Within minutes, the older lad's even breathing matched Mack's and just as she knew he would, as he did each night, Simon snuggled closer in his sleep. His head found her shoulder over Mack and she brought her shawl around him, encompassing the three of them beneath the woollen folds.

A chink of grey moon winked down from the inky sky through the holes in the roof, as though watching over them like a caring mother. Suddenly, soft brown eyes and hair to match, framing a pale face, flitted like fog through Pip's mind, bringing to her chest a drum of pain. With a small sigh, she closed her eyes.

The morning of Christmas Eve had not yet touched the wintry sky with light when the three children slipped through the tumbledown door and into the bitter coldness of Lomax Street. Sounds of movement, as folk began to rouse for the day in Betty's lodging house adjoining their shelter, had trickled through to them moments before and, rubbing the sleep from their eyes, they had wasted no time in scrambling up to melt away undetected.

In less than an hour, the streets were teeming with people and carts and despite the poverty which was their lot, the people of Manchester seemed to have a slight spring in their clogged step this day. Early festivity hung in the sharp air and passing folk greeted each other with more nods and smiles than usual, their normally pallid faces ruddy with cold, their breath hovering in white clouds around their shawl- and cap-covered heads.

Sprigs of dark green holly dotted with ruby berries adorned shop doors and windows, and even the harnesses of horses passing by, and a thin sprinkling of powdered frost had settled on the stones of the roads. The temperature looked set to plummet further later and the droves of women who would venture out to Smithfield Market tonight to grab knocked-down vegetables and, if they were lucky, a small chicken or goose for the following day's fare, would be blue with cold by the time they returned, shivering, to their hearths.

But at least they had a fire to go home to. At least they

had a family, a place to lay their head of a night, a sense of belonging. For Pip, Simon, Mack and countless others, Christmas was the same as any other day – stark and empty. Though it did differ ever so slightly from every other day of the year in one sense: it served to heighten their awareness that they were not like the fortunate plenty who, though they suffered terrible hardships themselves in this chimney-choked, smoke-clogged, sad-coloured industrial city, at least had each other. To be alone in the world was the most destroying reality of all.

Mind, I'm not alone, am I? Pip reminded herself, glancing left to right at the two boys walking either side of her. A smile touched her lips. *Not now. Not with these lads of mine. Life wasn't worth the bother not a few short months past but now – now it is. Now, I face the days easier. And the nights, too . . .* Aye, the nights. They were the worst.

The horrors involved with destitution were only too real. The bleak outdoors, during both the sunlit and twilight hours, were no place for the vulnerable, particularly children. Threats and abuse were commonplace. Dogs, traffic, not to mention harm posed by the elements, to name but a few of the dangers. Then there were the older kids, and sometimes adults with tendencies to turn vicious with drink, who thought nothing of lashing out at them with words, also clogs and fists, for no other reason than that they existed – even as they huddled in doorways, sleeping. Or they would wake – indeed had more than once – to find they had been spat or urinated on. Such mindless cruelty made no sense to them.

'Bun, Pip? You promised. Bun?'

She took Mack's hand, then motioned to the small baker's up ahead. 'Aye, look. We're nearly there, lad.

And see, there's a few kindly looking wenches by the door. You remember what to do?' she added through the side of her mouth as they drew nearer.

Mack nodded and, from necessity and practice, instantly developed a perfect rolling limp. Sticking out his bottom lip, he set it quivering expertly.

'Good lad. Come on.'

Simon, with his usual scowl and hands thrust deep in his trouser pockets, held back. Catching his eye, Pip flushed, sensing his disapproval. Using Mack to garner sympathy didn't sit easy with him and she shared his sentiments completely, but there was nothing else for it. The youngster reaped better results – his size and obvious need was enough to melt most hearts.

'Spare a penny, missis?' Holding out a hand palm upwards, Mack thrust it towards the women in turn, whimpering to each as he did, eyes brimming with tears, 'Please? Please? Please?'

Pip caught their sorry stares and pitying sighs but it was clear they wouldn't be in luck. These women looked almost as much in need as they themselves. Their ragged shawls and patched, discoloured skirts looked as though they would crumble to dust from their persons should a strong wind blow their way. Nonetheless, she stepped forward – it didn't hurt to make sure.

'Please, me and my brother, here, ain't eaten for days. We're poor orphans and shall perish if we don't put summat in our bellies soon.'

'Eeh, lass . . .' The tallest of the women looked over them with a shake of her beshawled head. 'I've a houseful of my own back there in the same boat.' She jerked her chin in the general direction of a row of smoke-blackened houses up the street. 'They're wanting, an' all, and if I can't feed my own, I sure as bleedin' hell

7

can't feed youse.' Her companions murmured agreement and her eyes softened. 'Sorry, lass, lad.'

With a bleak smile and a nod, Pip shepherded Mack around and away.

The three children huddled by the roadside for a while in silence, looking this way and that, eyeing all who passed, alert to any opportunity. Should a slightly better dressed body cross their path, Pip and Mack would hold out a hand, the practised beseeching slipping from their cold lips, but today it didn't seem to be doing the trick. Tears dripped down Mack's grubby cheeks when again their begging, this time of a pair of working men, yielded no result, and biting back tears of her own, Pip drew him against her.

'Don't fret, now, there's a good lad. Someone will surely—' She broke off with a frown as she glanced left at the older boy. Simon was staring intently at a boot mender's across the road, and following his gaze, Pip shook her head. His attention was on an elderly man counting coins in his hand. When he returned them to his trouser pocket, Simon's eyes swivelled to meet hers, and again Pip shook her head. Since she'd joined the lads' company, she'd put a stop to that right away. She'd been raised to know stealing was wrong. Begging was one thing – at least they were asking and folk had the chance to decide whether to part with their brass. To take it from them without their knowledge was just plain wicked. Hungry or not, she wanted no part in that kind of thing.

Simon made to move forward and she clutched at his sleeve. 'Nay, lad. Please, not that. Summat will turn up, you'll see. Not that. It's wrong, Simon.'

He turned blazing eyes on to her. 'Aye? You think, d'you? Does it favour that folk are tripping over theirselfs to hand over a copper or two? Wrong – huh! Don't talk to me about wrong. This here?' He motioned to the three of them with an angry flick of his hand. '*This* is wrong. Frozen stiff? Stomachs twisting with hunger? Bowing and scraping to every passing bastard without so much as a glance in return from most, never mind owt else. Nay. *I'll* get us some brass, my way. It's seen me through this far, ain't it, and kept that one alive the past year, an' all,' he added, nodding down at Mack.

'But . . . that's not what good people do! And *you're* a good person, Simon. You are, I know it.'

For the briefest moment, his dark eyes softened. Then the hardness returned to them and his lips tightened. 'Good people stand no chance against a world so bad. The sooner tha realises that, Pip, the better for thee.' He freed his arm from her hold and crossed the cobbles.

'Spare a penny, kind sir?'

Watching helplessly, filled with sadness as Simon closed in on his victim, Pip barely registered Mack speaking. The deep-voiced answer, however, caught her attention immediately. She turned, hope fluttering in her breast, to face a tall, slim gentleman. And a gentleman he clearly was. The cut of his cloth, tall black hat and shiny gold-tipped cane spoke volumes of his wealth. Yet it was the interest in the pale green eyes as they assessed the youngster that set her pulse racing with excitement. He hadn't ignored Mack's plea, hadn't flapped a clean and manicured hand in dismissal before strolling on his leisurely way. He'd stopped to listen, and he was smiling.

'A penny, you say?' the man asked in a soft, articulate voice. He reached out a hand and touched Mack's chin in a slow caress, and his gaze deepened further. 'I think I can do better than that, boy.'

Mack's eyes were as big as saucers. His mouth spread in a dazzling smile. 'You mean it, sir?'

'I do. However . . .' The man patted his breast pocket with a click of his tongue. 'I appear to have left my purse in my carriage. It must have fallen out during the drive and will be lying on the seat as we speak, you mark my words.'

'Oh!' The child's face fell. 'Oh, sir!'

'Don't take on so, young one. This small problem is easily rectified. What say you come along with me while I collect it? My driver is waiting but a street away, after all.' He held out a hand, smiling when Mack responded eagerly, and closed his slender fingers around the tiny ones. 'Come. You deserve a few shillings, I think.'

The boy squeaked excitedly. 'Aye?'

'Oh, at least.'

Shooting Pip a joyous grin, Mack trotted off happily. With a smile of her own, she followed but after a few short steps, the man turned to look at her. His face showed surprise, as though he'd only just noticed her existence.

'Yes?'

'I . . .' She blinked down towards Mack. 'He's with me, sir.'

'Oh. I see.' He cast her a tight smile. 'No need for you to trouble yourself, girl. The boy and I shall collect the money ourselves. We shan't be long.'

She hadn't time to respond; before she could utter another word, he guided Mack through a dark and narrow alleyway up ahead. Pausing by the mouth of the opening, she watched the figures walk away. Of their own accord, her teeth moved to chew at her lower lip. Slowly, her excitement was beginning to wane and for reasons she couldn't fathom, a feeling of foreboding

10

trickled through her. But she was being daft, wasn't she? He was a gentleman and he'd spoken kindly. He was going to give them a few shillings – aye, at least, he'd said – and they would be all right, then, wouldn't they? They could buy some grub and a hot drink, and Mack would stop crying for a while. And they would even have the pennies for a kip in a lodging house tonight instead of the cold flagstones they usually called their bed. Then why did she have this queer rolling in her stomach, as if something was amiss?

'Mack.' The whisper fell from her lips and her chest constricted. *Mack!*

'What about him?'

Pip whipped around to find Simon behind her. A relieved breath escaped her. 'Simon. I don't know . . . Something doesn't feel – feel right, and . . .'

'What d'you mean?' He flicked his gaze down and around. 'Where is he? Where's Bread?'

She pointed to where the two shapes had almost disappeared in the distance. 'There were a gentleman. And – and he promised to give Mack some brass, told me to wait here—' She gasped as, with a growled curse, Simon charged past her and set off at full speed down the entry. 'Simon, wait! What—?'

''Ere, you get away from him, you filthy bastard, yer!'

Hot on Simon's heels, Pip gasped again as he threw himself at the flabbergasted gentleman, sending his tall hat bouncing to the muck-strewn ground. 'Let go of his hand, Bread. D'you hear me? Do as I say – let go of it, now!'

'What is the *meaning* of this?' Blustering with fury, the man held on tighter to Mack. 'You young street monkey, I'll dash your brains out!' With his free hand, he raised his cane and brought it down across Simon's back. 'You dare to behave like that to one of your betters? I'll knock you back into your place, my boy. I will, all right!'

The change in the man's demeanour had Pip rooted to the spot in shock. Venom now screamed from the once kind eyes and spittle had formed at the corners of his twisted mouth.

The blow had stolen the wind from Simon's lungs; coughing and groaning on his hands and knees, he raised his head. 'You get on out of it or so help me, I'll do for you,' he brought out breathlessly. 'I know your game, all right. I've come across enough of your sort in my time.'

The man, though still stiff-lipped with anger, blanched at Simon's words and Pip was filled with confusion. Just what had Simon meant by that? She herself had sensed something was afoot, it was true, but hadn't been able to put her finger on why. Simon, however, seemed to know exactly what was going on and she could tell he was correct in his guess; the man's face confirmed it. When the lad staggered to his feet, she turned to him with a frown. 'Simon?'

Ignoring her, he addressed the man again. 'Let him go.'

'Nay, Simon.' Mack stuck out his chin in a pout. 'I want to go with the gentleman. He's going to give me brass and I'm hungry. I want to, I want to!'

The older boy's eyes never strayed from the man's. 'Let him go,' he repeated through gritted teeth.

After a long hesitation, throughout which the man glared down on Simon with such fury in his eyes it seemed he would pounce and murder him on the spot at any moment, he released the youngster's hand. Mack made to grasp it again but he thrust him away towards Simon and Pip. He stooped and lifted his hat. Then he

12

pointed a long, pale finger at Simon. 'I never forget a face,' he murmured. 'You'll do well to remember that.' He struck the ground with the tip of his cane, turned on his heel and strode off.

When he'd disappeared, Simon visibly sagged. He closed his eyes and breathed deeply.

'I hate you, I hate you!' Mack beat at Simon's chest with his small fists. 'You sent the kind gentleman away and now we're still hungry and it's all your fault!'

Simon caught the child's shoulders and shook him none too gently. 'Enough, d'you hear? We don't need brass off divils like that.'

'Divils like what? What d'you think he intended, lad?'

Simon flashed Pip a withering look. 'I don't think, I know. Christ sake,' he added quietly when she frowned, still in confusion, 'do I really have to spell it out? Some folk have an appetite for young flesh. Like to do things . . . touch where they shouldn't. He were one of them.'

'You mean . . .?' Colour rising, she shook her head slowly.

'Aye. By hook or by crook, they'll do owt for a taste of it. They . . . hurt people, and think nowt of it so long as they get what they're after.'

She studied his face for a moment. His eyes were empty of emotion, his mouth set as though in stone, and sadness filled her. She opened hers to ask if he spoke of this from experience but, as though sensing her intention, Simon swung about and made for the street again. She and Mack followed in silence.

As though matters were not bad enough, moments later the leaden clouds decided to release a steady drizzle of rain. Stamping their feet to coax some warmth into them, they looked about. Already it was late afternoon and the sky was losing its light. Not that much sun ever did manage to penetrate the thick blanket of noxious smoke from thousands of industrial and domestic chimneys. This, coupled with the winter months, seemed to encase the residents in perpetual gloom.

Designed to tempt Christmas customers, the surrounding shop windows were a feast to the eyes if, for the three of them at least, nothing else. Pip tried not to look but it was impossible. Saliva filled her mouth and her stomach growled in response. Plump birds for those with extra brass to spare, and cheap offcuts of meat and sheep heads for those who didn't, winked back from behind the thin panes. Big and small loaves, wheels of cheeses, brown and white eggs and colourful vegetables, fruit and figs and nuts and sweet pastries . . . She wrenched her gaze away with a low moan.

'I feel queer, Simon.' Mack gripped the older lad's arm to stop himself from stumbling. His face had turned a worrying shade of grey and his eyes were glassy. 'Need to . . . sit down.'

Without a word, the older lad supported him across the cobbles and eased him down to the ground to lean against the cold bricks of a towering warehouse. Mack closed his eyes and Simon glanced around with narrowed ones.

'It's the hunger, that's all, Mack,' Pip told him soothingly, stroking the top of his head. 'The dizziness will pass.'

'Aye, and it'll be back soon enough.' Simon's gaze now held an expression of desperation. Again, he scanned the street from end to end in search of opportunity. 'We can't go another day without grub. We need brass.'

'Did you . . .?' She had to force the words out through

14

her disapproval. However, Mack was in a hopeless state; she must ask. 'The owd fella whose pocket you set your sights on . . .?'

Simon shook his head. 'I couldn't get close enough. I think he guessed what I were about.'

Pip gave a sigh of relief, yet it was tinged with despair. Just what *were* they to do? Not a morsel had passed their lips since yesterday morning – and then but a hunk of dry bread apiece from a driver as payment for watching his horse while he ran an errand. As soon as he disappeared, they had cupped their hands into a rusty pail in the corner of his cart and drunk as much of the cloudy water meant for his beast as they could stomach. It had placated their cramping guts for a short while and the bread kept the gnawing at bay for a time longer, but all too soon familiar hunger had crept back, as it always did. Now, they were nearing breaking point. She herself felt weak; her head hurt and her mouth was parchment dry. Although he didn't show it, Simon must feel the same. He was bigger than her and Mack, and so too was his appetite.

The gentleman from earlier flashed into her mind and she sighed sadly, recalling the happiness his promise had brought. Yet her hopes of hot food and a warm bed had soon been dashed. Did some people really do . . . *those* sort of things . . . with children? Not that she disbelieved Simon, but still, it was difficult to think on it.

Her eyes swivelled round to the tiny boy huddled on the flagstones and anger sparked in her breast. Simon had said the man would have hurt him. How could anyone think of taking advantage of a child's desperation to satisfy their own depraved needs? And a *gentleman* at that. You couldn't trust anyone, could you?

15

Not no one, not really. And especially not mams. For mams left you, just as hers had left her. She'd gone and died, leaving Pip all alone. And she missed her, in ways she couldn't even describe. And these lads; their mams had left them, too. Did they miss them? Pip wondered. They must, surely. Mind, they never mentioned them. As always, Simon kept his feelings to himself, and Mack was likely too young to remember his mam much. Pip didn't speak of hers, either. What was the point? It hurt and she was gone, for ever. Best not to dwell on things that couldn't be changed.

'I reckon our best bet is the market, later,' Simon was saying now. 'Whether Bread will be up to the walk, mind . . . Well, he'll have to be, won't he? He'll not get his belly filled else.'

Pip brightened slightly. Smithfield Market *would* surely tip up a few of its spoils. Thousands flocked there each week, and Christmas was busier still. Surely someone would take pity on them there? Thoughts of the hot chestnuts, pigs' trotters and pie sellers had her mouth filling with saliva once more. Or perhaps busy traders might require a helping hand with something? They could earn a penny or two that way. And if all else failed . . .

She bit her lip guiltily. The heaving, bustling space would be crammed with carts and stalls piled high with every manner of foodstuff you could imagine – if Simon managed to swipe something, then just this once, she'd turn a blind eye. Aye, for Mack, for he needed something in his stomach soon, it was clear to see. He'd only grow sicker otherwise; surely the good Lord would understand?

'If nowt else, there'll be plenty of skenning sods falling from the taverns the night,' Simon continued, as though reading her thoughts. 'Whether you approve or no, their pockets will be lighter by the time they reach home, an' all. Needs must, and you don't get much needier than that,' he muttered, jerking his head towards Mack, who was still propped against the wall and had fallen into a fitful sleep.

Pip was silent for a moment, then, 'Happen we can find ourselves somewhere warm and dry to kip around there? A stable, mebbe?' she said. A slow smile spread across Simon's face and she grinned.

'Aye, well. It was good enough for the Holy Family, eh? Mind, I reckon Bread's a bit big to pass as Jesus.'

Pip giggled. '*Mack*, Simon, not Bread. Remember? And anyroad, that would make us Mary and Joseph – and we're not big enough!'

''Ere, happen three wise men will visit us in the night bearing gifts.'

'Eeh, I hope they fetch grub,' she breathed dreamily.

'Aye, a couple of cakes or a nice chop.'

The children cast each other a soft smile and lapsed into silence once more.

A plump girl of seventeen or eighteen emerged from a confectioner's up the street, a laden wicker basket over each arm and a small pile of brown-paper packages in her hands, and they watched her idly. When she drew level, she caught them staring and her eyes turned thoughtful. She bobbed her head in a nod.

'You, boy.'

Simon touched his chest. 'Me, miss?'

'Aye, you. Come here.'

Pip watched his thin legs skitter across the road. Folding her arms, she frowned. What they spoke about, she didn't know – Simon nodded several times and turned to point to her and Mack, but he and the woman were too far away for Pip to hear what they were saying. When finally he turned, his eyes were alive with excitement. He ran back to Pip and in a breathless rush, said, 'That one wants me to carry her purchases home. She's a maid in a house up Ardwick Green, said as how there would be a few coppers in it for me.' He motioned to Mack, who had roused and was yawning and rubbing his eyes. 'Help him along, will thee, whilst I see to her things. Come on afore she changes her mind.'

Pip's heart gave a flutter of happy relief. 'Eeh, that's a bit of good fortune, eh? Is it one of the big residences, aye?'

Already turning back to the road's edge, he shrugged. 'Must be if it's up that end. Just think, happen she'll take us into the kitchen. I'll lay it on to the cook, like; if she's owt about her, she'll surely find us a plate of summat. Come on!'

Pip highly doubted this but nonetheless nodded. The promised brass would be welcome enough. Aye, more than welcome; she could almost taste the grub that they would be able to buy. Mack leaned on her heavily and she supported him with an arm around his shoulders.

Luckily, their destination wasn't such a distance off. It lay just across the River Medlock, which formed a boundary between it and Manchester proper. It was where the most powerful and important men in the city lived, the rich factory owners and cotton merchants, she knew that much, but she'd never ventured across before; had no reason to. Besides, folk of her ilk were not welcome in vicinities in which the genteel made their homes. Should a police officer spot them loitering around streets such as those, they would be accused of being up to no good and hauled away quick smart. They had a good excuse today, though. The maid, here, would back them up should the need arise.

18

The female in question surveyed them with undisguised distaste as they approached, and Pip felt herself flush with shame. They must look a dreadful sight. Their clothes and bodies were filthy, their hair lank and matted, and all of them were far from bug free. And it was evident that wasn't all they had going against them when the maid held a hand to her nose with a shudder of revulsion.

'Mother of God, you lot stink summat awful!'

''Ere, miss, I'll take them,' Simon said, his tone flat.

He held out his arms and the woman relieved herself of the baskets with a thankful grunt. She then plonked the packages into his hands, turned and with a flick of her head, barked, 'Well, come on, then, and hurry up about it. This way.'

Chapter 2

THEY PASSED ALONG London Road in silence, the maid walking a few steps ahead. Pip's eyes travelled the length of her, and her own ragged appearance in comparison struck her acutely still. From the neat hat, adorned with sprigs of artificial winter berries, perched atop the clean brown hair, down to the trim jacket, pinched in at the waist, and long, dark skirts with no tears or patching in sight, which swish-swished as she moved – to Pip's eyes, she looked glorious. Black-booted feet peeped out from beneath and their small heels met the frosty flagstones with a gentle click at each impatient step.

Pip was certain that it must be wonderful to be a domestic, wear clothes and boots such as those and live in a fancy house with meals on tap – and a regular wage into the bargain. Oh, *she* wanted to be a maid, she did. She opened her mouth to address the woman, ask her how girls went about being taken on, but thought better of it. Her stiff back and earlier reaction to them set her in an intimidating light. Pip knew she wouldn't take too kindly to being spoken to by a vagrant like herself. Happen Simon would know? He knew about most things; she'd ask him later, she determined with a nod.

Lost in thoughts of the three of them one day soon working side by side in a beautiful home – surely there would be positions for the lads, too? – Pip was brought up short when Simon suddenly halted in front of her. His breathing was heavy and twin spots of colour stained his cheeks. His heavy cargo, coupled with his weakened strength due to lack of sustenance, were taking their toll.

'Shall I help?' she asked, holding out her free hand, but he shook his head.

Wincing, he stretched his back muscles then sighed when the maid, turning and seeing he'd stopped, snapped at him to get a move on. He straightened, gritted his teeth against the pain, and continued along.

By the time they had crossed the river over Ardwick Bridge and reached the corner of Tipping Street, Simon looked as Mack had earlier: pallid faced and fit to collapse. Here, with obvious reluctance, the servant allowed him to pause briefly to catch his breath. He readjusted the baskets' handles over his arms and they were off once more, their tired feet tripping over themselves to match the strides of the maid as she passed on through Downing Street.

They emerged into a broad and leafy road. Now, it was Pip who stopped dead in her tracks. Despite the relatively short distance from the slums of Ancoats they had just left, it was a cavernous difference, as though stepping into a whole other world.

Like the affluent areas of Higher Broughton and Cheetham Hill to the north, the attractive spot of Ardwick, situated about a mile south-east of the centre of the city, was a fashionable and wealthy suburb. With each passing second, the very air itself had seemed to shift. A clean-smelling breeze drifted in to wrap around their lungs like a silken shroud. Pip drank it in greedily in great gulps and gazed about.

Differing shades of green had replaced the uniform

grey she was used to. The bricks of the magnificent Georgian terraces, as yet unmarred by chimney smoke, were not soot-blackened red but retained their bold hue. No damp and decrepit dwellings here. No mills belching out their noxious filth on these privileged few. Such businesses were to the owners as to the workers they employed: their bread and butter. However, that didn't mean they desired to live near their premises – far from it. They wouldn't soil *their* lungs with the pollution they created – unlike their less fortunate workers who, ironically, lived and toiled in such conditions to make their masters the vast wealth which enabled them to enjoy this luxury.

Most of the better class rarely came into contact with 'lowers'. Conveniently, they took the shortest route to their businesses of work each day and back again, bypassing the squalor of the other world and all it entailed, blissfully ignorant and blind to it all.

Another striking change here was the sound. Birdsong took the place of the crash and din of daily life that was Pip's home. More notably, there wasn't a public house in sight. No gin palaces and alehouses choking every inch. Not a murmur of lewd voices or thud of traffic. No drunken fights in these streets, no beggars and thieves and streetwalkers. Life-worn men with dead eyes and empty pockets, and ragged women sporting the usual Saturday-night black eye – where were they? Or screaming babies, and stick-thin children with jutting cheekbones, claw-like hands forever wanting of a crust? Stray and skeletal cats and dogs that roamed and foraged in the rotting refuse that littered *their* tumbledown streets? The stench and the horror and the hopelessness?

Not here. Oh no. Not here.

Tightening her hold on Mack, Pip walked on.

The maid halted before five or six spotless steps which led to a narrow-fronted, three-storey house of red brick with sandstone dressing. Sparkling sash windows, behind which hung thick, dark-green curtains, dotted the exterior. Beyond two grand columns, and beneath a round-headed entrance, stood a pale blue door with a well-polished brass knocker in the style of a lion's head.

'This it, then, miss?' asked Simon, more than a little impressed despite his fatigue.

'That's right. I'm sure I can manage from— Ay! And where the divil d'you think you're going?' the woman added in a hiss, wrenching him back by his collar as he made to climb the steps. 'You bold bloody article, yer. The main entrance indeed – huh! Is it a fine gentleman you think you are, now? It'd be the back way for the likes of thee – me an' all, mind, for that matter. But as I said, I can manage from here, thank you very much.' With a sniff of disdain, she relieved him of his burden and turned for the rear of the house. 'Now be gone, all of you. Go on, go.'

'But . . . Wait!' Simon hurried after her. 'The coppers, miss, remember? You promised me a few coppers—'

'Ah.' She halted and a sly glint appeared in her eyes. 'I did. Mind, that were afore I knew you weren't up to the job. Took me twice as long, it has, the journey, because of you. Huffing and puffing and stopping every two minutes. I'm dreadful late thanks to thee and will be for it should the master find out. Nay, tha deserves nowt.'

Pip and Mack stared back in open-mouthed horror and disbelief. Simon, on the other hand, turned puce with rage. 'Why you snidy, rotten piece . . . I honoured

23

my end of the deal fair and square, and you know it. You planned this from the off, didn't you? You had me lug that lot all this way and never intended paying up, did you? This you're spouting, it's just an excuse so you don't have to cough up.'

'Get out of it, you bundle of vermin, afore I—'

'I ain't shifting, no bloody how, till I gets what's owed!'

The woman and boy glared at each other. Suddenly, up ahead, the unmistakable clump of a policeman's heavy boots cut through the darkening street. Simon turned wary eyes in his direction, and the maid gave a smug sniff. Further words were not needed – both knew who had come out of this victorious. The children couldn't risk her summoning the constable over, and she knew it. She, a neat clean woman employed in a respectable household, and they ... Whatever tale she'd have a mind to concoct, the policeman would take her words as truth over theirs any day of the week.

Pip shivered. It would be the worst for them. They would likely be hauled away to the cells, she reckoned – or worse, the workhouse. She willed Simon to back down and come away out of it. To her relief, he seemed to hear her silent pleas. With a last, hate-filled look at the maid, he swung on his heel and walked away.

With a self-satisfied laugh, the maid headed towards the rear of her residence and the traders' and domestics' entrance, as she'd earlier mentioned. The urge to run after her and give her a good hard kick on the leg had Pip's heart banging with the struggle to desist. Just what were they to do, now? Why couldn't they ever catch a break, just once? Why did the world and everyone in it seem to be against them, *constantly* against them? she asked herself and tears pricked her eyes. She shot a quick glance ahead and was just in time to see the constable turning off into nearby Rusholme Road, and her despondency lessened somewhat. She gave Mack's shoulder a gentle squeeze, then she and the youngster hurried after their friend.

Simon led them across the wide roadway to the heart of the neighbourhood facing: Ardwick Green, a private park for residents of the surrounding houses that fronted it. Fenced with cast-iron railings, the oblong enclosure was, to their eyes, a garden of paradise. Gazing through the bars, Pip half expected to glimpse Adam and Eve amongst the foliage; she'd never seen anything like it in her life. This vast expanse of nature and beauty for such a fortunate few!

Like the gardens of the houses, the park was ornamented with shrubs and hawthorn, and planted here and there with tall trees. A large glacial erratic – the boulder looked as if it had been a feature almost from the beginning – stared back at them coldly.

Despite Pip warning that they were not permitted to enter and would be in awful trouble should the constable happen in this direction again, Simon made through the gate. The fight seemed to leave him in a rapid gust. He plopped on to the rotting carpet of leaves beneath a craggy poplar, rested his back against its grey trunk and closed his eyes.

'It was foul of her to con you like she did, lad, and after you breaking your back carrying that lot up here. Mind, it'll be all right,' Pip soothed, addressing his bowed head. 'Summat will come up, you'll see. We've the market to try yet, remember? Aye, there'll be spoils to be had there, I'll be bound.' He didn't respond, and she squatted beside him. 'Don't fret so, Simon. We must keep trying, is all.'

'I'm tired. I've nowt left inside. Nothing, nothing.'

She'd seen him down once or twice in the months she'd known him. But nothing like this. All strength and hope had abandoned him, leaving his body boneless, to curl in on itself. He looked broken. This latest cruelty was the last straw, it was clear, and Pip didn't know what to do. Simon was the strong one of the three. He was the decision-maker, the one who picked *them* up when they were in need of support. To see him like this was more than a little frightening. They needed him, she and Mack. They needed him to be who he usually was. She bit her lip and looked about uncertainly.

A serpent-shaped pond, running the length of the Green, lay in the centre of the grassy promenade, its dark waters glistening silver-jade beneath the early moon. Shuffling across the bank to the water's edge on his knees, Mack dipped forward and plunged his cupped hands beneath the glassy surface. He drank, repeated the action twice more, then shuffled back to snuggle between Pip and Simon.

Gaslights beyond were brought fizzing to life and the windows of the houses glowed with soft light. The children sat on, the unwanted yet familiar guests of cold and hunger along with them.

The rumble of private carriages and clop of hooves sounded in the distance. Then another carriage, and another; likely relatives arriving to join their wealthy families for the festivities. Doors were opened by uniformed maids, and impeccably dressed gentlemen in tall hats and velvet-collared, broad-tailed coats and matching waistcoats over fine lawn shirts drifted inside the comfortable homes. Close behind were their ladies in wide hoop skirts trimmed with flounces, cloaks in plaid or lined with fur of brown and dark grey secured around their shoulders. Elaborate bonnets tied beneath the chin in wide bows completed their dress, while delicate hands were hidden snugly in matching muffs. Sometimes, a nursemaid followed with their plump, cherry-cheeked charges, immaculate in pale-coloured frocks or breeches. The occasional servant in tow, noiseless in well-trained fashion, took up the rear.

Peeking through the shrubs, Pip watched the elegant processions in wonder. And she'd thought that maid's attire was special! She shook her head, dumbstruck. Compared to these fine people, her apparel had been as plain as they came. Suddenly, as though the mere thought of the nasty piece in question had conjured her up, there she was, emerging from the direction she'd disappeared in earlier, an empty wicker basket over her arm and a face like thunder. Had she forgotten something when making her purchases and been ordered out again? Pip wondered. Ha – serve her right, too! Mind, the smaller domestic trotting behind her would likely bear the burden of the carrying this time, no doubt.

She nudged Simon. 'Look who it ain't. It's that bad piece.' As she spoke, the pale blue front door of the house where the maid was employed opened. A gentleman and two ladies emerged.

Following her gaze, Simon's demeanour changed. The maudlin look left him and cunning from years of necessity returned to his eyes. He rose. Without a word, he strode across the Green. Before Pip had time to catch her breath, he swung through the gate and headed for the two groups – who were almost level with each other now, going their different ways – step purposeful, head high.

'Miss? Miss?'

27

To say the maid was surprised was putting it mildly – her face was a picture. Holding Mack's hand, a nervous Pip watched on from a distance. Just what did Simon plan? Fancy him confronting her like this – in front of her fine employers, too! By, but he was brave. Braver than herself, that was for sure.

With a nervous lick of her lips, the maid looked to the gentleman and ladies, who had halted to turn curious stares on the urchin standing close by. 'On your way,' she told Simon quietly, though anger sparked from her eyes. 'You've no business begging around here—'

'I'm not begging, miss. I've come asking on the brass you owe me, is all.'

Her lips bunched in embarrassed fury. 'Brass? Brass? I don't know what—'

'Do you know this . . . boy, Hardman?' cut in one of the ladies with a haughty lift of her chin.

'Nay. Certainly not, Mrs Goldthorpe. I've never clapped eyes on him in my life.'

'Aye, she does.' Simon nodded. 'Swindled me out of some coppers, earlier, she did. I lugged a load of purchases for her and she promised—'

'Oh! Liar.'

'The only liar's thee and I reckon your master deserves to know what a black-hearted divil he has amongst his labour force—'

'Silence at once!'

They all jumped at the authoritative voice of the gentleman, whose face had turned a dull purple. He paused to flash a smile and touch his tall hat to an affluent-looking couple walking by, who gazed with undisguised disgust at Simon and horror that he should be in their acquaintance's company, before addressing them again, his colour higher still. 'What is the meaning of this outrage? How dare you accost my servants and my family in this manner with your wild accusations! Be gone instantly, you young criminal, before I have you locked in prison.'

'Sir, she lies!' But Simon's protests fell on deaf ears. The gentleman and his lady friends were walking away, although one of the ladies looked back several times as though she wanted to say something until the gentleman, taking her arm firmly, hurried her along. 'Please, we need the money she promised for grub. Bread's poorly sick and—'

'You heard,' the maid shot over her shoulder as she too made off in the opposite direction, a look of such sly smugness on her face it had Pip's head swinging in anger. 'Get gone, you smelly slum rat,' she finished in a hiss before hurrying on, the young servant in her company running to catch her up.

Moments later, the street was once more deserted.

Slipping out of hiding, Pip and Mack made towards Simon, standing ramrod straight in the road. His face moved not a muscle when she touched his shoulder. 'Oh, lad. Let's get out of here, eh?'

Still, he didn't respond.

'We'll try the market instead as we planned—'

'I ain't shifting till I gets what's owed.'

'But Simon, it's useless! You heard what they said—'

'Aye, I did.' His eyes were steely, his mouth a mere line. 'I've had just about enough of folk like her the day and beyond. *Enough*, d'you hear?'

'Lad—'

'I'll get what I'm due, all right, one way or t' other.'

'Where you going?' Dragging Mack along, Pip hurried in Simon's wake as he marched to the house. He glared at the door, nodded once and stalked off towards

29

the rear entrance. Once more, Pip followed. Sickly foreboding ran through her; she tried again: 'What are you
about? Lad, what—?'

'There.' Simon jerked his head to the wide step by
the back door. 'See that? I ain't shifting from it till I gets
my brass. She must pass through yon door again some
time – I'll bombard her till she coughs up. She ain't getting away with this, Pip.'

'But Simon, prison, remember? The master said—'

'He'll not spot me back here, has no reason to venture this way.'

'But . . . lad, this is madness. We can't stop here for
ever.'

'You don't have to, nay.' For a brief moment, his face
softened. He looked down at the boy who was shivering
by her side, then back to her. 'Take yourself and Bread—'

'Mack.'

He rolled his eyes. 'Take yourself and *Mack* back to
Ancoats. Try your luck at the market, and afterwards
find shelter for the night nearby. Stick to the vicinity. I'll
come and find you once this Hardman divil's paid up.'

At this, Pip was emphatic. 'Nay. We'll not without thee.'

'Just do as I say. The lad needs grub in his belly—'

'Aye, as do we all. D'you know what we need more,
mind? To stick together. If you go, we go. If you stay . . .'
She shrugged then motioned to the step. 'Best make
ourselfs comfy, ain't we?'

Slowly, his mouth stretched in a wry smile. 'Best foot
forward, then. No whingeing, mind, when your arse
turns frozzen; it was your idea to stay, remember?'

With a smile of her own, she nodded and shepherded
Mack across to the length of scrubbed stone.

They hunkered down with grim purpose. Pip re-
arranged her shawl to encompass the three of them in

its meagre warmth and with simultaneous sighs, they huddled together.

Glancing at the gold-lit windows of the adjoining house, she released another long breath. 'Imagine dwelling in such places as these, though, lad?' she murmured.

'Aye,' Simon agreed quietly.

'It'd be fair heaven, it would. I ain't never known the like.' She flicked her eyes to either side. 'By, even the step here's cleaner than the inside of most lodging houses back round our way. Faults aside, I'll grant the maid that: she knows her way with a scrubbing brush all right.'

After some moments, he grudgingly nodded agreement. 'By, even the door's as clean and shiny as a new pin. As for the knob,' he added, reaching up a hand to the polished globe, 'you can see your face in it.'

'Must take some toiling to run a house such as this, it's true, but Simon, I'd do it for nowt. I would, 'onest,' she told him with feeling.

'Pip . . .'

'Nay, really,' she insisted. 'I'd not want wages, I'd not. Just to dwell beneath a roof such as this would be payment enough—'

'*Pip.*'

At Simon's excited tone, now, she turned towards him. His bright wide eyes caused her brow to crinkle. 'Lad?'

'Unlocked.'

'What is?' She followed his gaze up. Clutching the knob, he twisted his hand and ever so slightly pushed; sure enough, the door eased inwards half an inch. Light streamed through the crack to fall across their disbelieving faces.

'Unlocked,' he repeated. 'The bleedin' thing's *unlocked*!'

31

Chapter 3

A HUNDRED SIGHTS, sensations and smells hit them all at once as they peered, heads pressed together, around the door.

The long room was empty of sound, bar the soft rumble of the huge fire burning merrily to their right. Taking in at a glance that no persons were present, Simon moved tentatively inside. He'd taken half a dozen steps before Pip regained her senses. She shook her head with a gasp.

'Lad, nay! We shouldn't!'

He gazed around the kitchen without answering. An enormous, six-foot cooking range shone gold-black in the glowing light of lamps dotted along the walls – this, his eyes fixed on and as though in a trance, he headed across to it. Several iron cooking pots, containing what, Pip didn't know, threw out the most glorious aromas, mingling with the heady scent of beef roasting behind the small oven door to the side. A wave of saliva burst inside her mouth, almost choking her. Swallowing hard, she forced her feet to remain on the doorstep; for two pins, they would be across the stone floor if she wasn't careful, she just knew. In her starvation state, the strength it took to resist was agony.

'Have you ever seen the like?' breathed Simon, glancing at her over his shoulder.

'We must go. Come away, lad, come away,' she begged, wringing her hands. She turned her head to scan the black night outside. 'Eeh, if someone should arrive—'

'They'll not. Didn't we see them leave with our own two eyes?'

'Aye, but . . . What about the rest of the household; other servants and suchlike—'

'What a sight! By, it's kings and queens lives here, I'm certain.' He motioned to a tall, silver stand on the side. Neatly arranged on its four circular shelves was an array of fancy cakes and biscuits in differing shapes and sizes. After a moment's hesitation, Simon reached out a hand. He selected a sugar-dusted square of sponge and slowly carried it to his mouth.

Watching him close his eyes and the lines melt from his face as he chewed, Pip couldn't help whispering, 'What's it taste like, lad?'

'Oh, heaven.' He shook his head. 'Merry Christmas, Simon,' he murmured, looking every inch as though the festive day had indeed come early for him – all his Christmases at once, even. 'Oh, Pip, come and try some. Fetch Bread.'

A soft moan escaped her. Her toes twitched in her patched boots, itching to go to him, as though they had taken on a life of their own. When she spoke, her voice was little more than a croak. 'But it's stealing.'

'Call it payment for me lugging them baskets and parcels earlier.'

'Aye,' but that's the maid's debt, not the master's.'

He moved to select another cake. 'Don't make no difference. They're all part of the same establishment, ain't they? And he weren't mithered to hear what she'd done, was he, so bugger him. Anyroad, you reckon they'll miss a few ruddy morsels? Look around you, Pip.

33

They're hardly wanting, are they? Nay. But we are. We'll perish unless we eat soon, that's the truth of it. For all your good intentions, morals don't fill bellies. Now, hurry afore they return. We'll have ourselfs a bit of grub and be away without anyone knowing the difference.'

Pip bit her lip until her eyes watered. She sighed, and sighed again. Then she roused Mack, took his hand and crept into the house.

The little boy rubbed his eyes with his knuckles and blinked around in confused amazement, mouth agape. Simon beckoned him over but Mack didn't seem to notice. His attention was on the fire's leaping flames. He stood before it and as his freezing body absorbed the heat, he flopped like wet card. He curled up on the hearth mat, put his thumb in his mouth and fell fast asleep.

Pip turned fearful eyes to Simon then made to rush to wake the younger boy, but Simon stopped her.

'Leave the lad, let him enjoy the warmth. We'll rouse him in a minute when we're leaving.' He nodded to a fat black teapot atop the dark-wood table running down the centre of the room. 'I'll pour us a quick sup. You grab yourself a bit of grub. We'll take some with us for Bread.'

Pip put out her hand, drew it back, then reached out again quickly and plucked an orange-coloured biscuit from the stand. Simon was returning with a cup from the dresser as she popped it into her mouth and he'd just begun pouring tea when the green baize door at the opposite end of the room swung wide.

Like scorched cats, they bolted beneath the table.

Hell's fire, we're for it, now! Pip panicked, and worried tears stung behind her eyes. Then she spotted Mack through the shelter of the chairs, still sleeping soundly, and her breath caught. *God alive, the lad!* She glanced to Simon, who shook his head in shared realisation. Moments later, however, they both frowned in surprise when two feet crossed the threshold.

Clad in small, lemon-coloured slippers, they were those of a child, it seemed, only a few years older than the sleeping boy they had been fretting over seconds ago. The frilly hem of her white nightdress swished softly as she skipped across the room. To Pip and Simon's relief, she failed to spot Mack and instead made directly for the silver stand they themselves had been busy at. Chomping sounds, as she devoured cake after cake, filled the space between them – then a gasp escaped her as, again, the door opened. This time, there was no escaping the fact that this new visitor was an adult. The large boots beneath the long, snowy apron stopped abruptly; Pip's insides twisted with fright and she gripped Simon's hand tightly.

'Miss Lucy, well, I'll be . . .! I thought you were ill in your bed, child. What the divil are you doing down here, I ask you?'

Warm giggles rang from the girl. 'Hello, Cook. Oh, isn't it exciting; it's almost Christmas! Mama has promised me a new doll with a red dress and ribbons to match. I just knew it. Didn't I wish for just such a thing, Cook? Remember, this morning, when you let me stir the Christmas pudding mixture? Clockwise, you said, with eyes closed for good luck – oh, it worked! And I'm to be allowed to stay up a whole hour later tomorrow to play games in the drawing room!'

Definite amusement coated the cook's response. 'Is that so? Well, you know, the sooner you go to sleep, the sooner it'll be the morrow. On that note, why ain't you away in the nursery as you should be? Where's Finch, I should like to know?'

'I gave her the slip.'

'You did, did yer? Ay, I see your game, miss!' the cook exclaimed, as though she'd spotted the girl's crime. 'You made the whole thing up about being sick, didn't you, you imp, so you could skip the outing with the others and pilfer my baking. Well, have you ever known the like! You just wait till your parents hear about this.'

'Oh! Please, Cook, don't tell!' the girl beseeched, then stamped her foot, adding haughtily, 'I forbid you to. That is an order.'

The woman hooted with laughter, and Pip and Simon exchanged a surprised look – a servant laughing at a superior? A rum set-up this was! – before turning their gazes back towards Mack. How in the world these two hadn't spotted him yet . . .

'Listen 'ere, young 'un. Don't come all that, here. It might work with that sop Finch but it'll not wash with me. I take orders from none other than the master up yonder, so just you think on.'

'Humph!'

'And "humph" to you, an' all!' shot back the cook, and she and the girl burst into laughter. 'Now, you get yourself back to the nursery afore everyone returns. Go on, aye, take another ruddy cake along with thee. You selected one? Right, come along, then— Eeh!'

At cook's astonished squawk, Pip and Simon held their breath. *Mack. She'd seen him. Lord, what would become of them? The house would have the law on them for certain!*

'God in heaven above, what's this I'm seeing?'

Following the servant's gaze, the girl's gasp barely broke through the crash of blood pounding in Pip's ears. 'Simon . . .' she mouthed. He simply stared back, wide-eyed with helplessness.

'Is it a person?'

36

'Well, of course it is – what else would it be?' Cook murmured, as though to convince herself. She inched forward, the girl following, clinging to her skirts. Reaching out a tentative hand to the bundle of rags that was the young boy, she prodded his shoulder. He moaned softly and she sprang back. 'It is, it's a child!'

Simon's face was the colour of bleached bones. He extracted his hand from Pip's, then before she could stop him emerged from beneath the table. Biting back a cry, she scrambled after him – then stopped dead when the cook whirled around towards them.

For half a minute, the four of them stared at each other in stunned silence, a mixture of expressions creasing faces both young and old. At length, Simon took a hesitant step forward.

'Missis . . . We can explain.'

'Holy Mother, I don't believe what my eyes are seeing . . .' The cook swung her head from them to Mack then shook it slowly.

'Are they savages, like in my storybook upstairs?' cherub-faced Miss Lucy squeaked, grip tightening on the servant's skirts, eyes wide with fear.

'Hush, child.'

'They are, they are! I'm certain of it,' she cried, shuddering in horror at them, and Pip lowered her gaze in shame. 'Oh, they'll dash our brains out, eat us alive—!'

'Enough, now. Savages, indeed. Books will rot your head, I've allus said so. These here are but poor urchins, and children just like yourself.'

The words had held a pitying note; Pip's heart lifted slightly. She flicked her eyes back up.

'Now then. What's the meaning of this? Come on, spit it out.'

In a quiet rush, Simon explained about the maid who

37

had swindled him, how the door had been unlocked and, due to their desperate state, they had been unable to resist the opportunity of filling their bellies. 'Only a bit of grub, mind,' he insisted, eyes solemn. 'We'd not have swiped nowt else, 'onest. We were fair wanting, is all.'

'Sounds like you've had the misfortune of meeting Jess Hardman, the housemaid. There's none below stairs with a more vicious streak than her. Mind, that's no excuse for this. Housebreaking it is, that's what!'

Simon crossed the space, roused Mack and pressed him behind him protectively. 'Little 'un's not used to the heat, were overcome by it, is all. He meant no harm, neither. Will tha let us leave, quiet like? We swear we'll never darken yon door again. Please,' he finished on a whisper.

Cook scratched her chin in contemplation then put her hands on her hips and frowned. 'I've a good mind to alert the master here and now to give the three of youse the horsewhipping you deserve.' She scrutinised the room for a moment. 'Mind, it don't favour you've caused any damage and nowt looks to be missing . . .'

'Oh nay, missis.' Pip shook her head. 'We'd do nowt like that, not in a week of Wednesdays, never.'

'Hm. Well.'

'Can we go now?' asked Simon, already inching to the door with Mack.

'Hold up.' Cook studied them. 'What did you manage to scran afore you were interrupted?'

Pip and Simon exchanged guilty glances.

'One of them dainty cakes over there. All right, two,' Simon muttered when the woman lifted an eyebrow.

Pip raised her hand. 'And I took a biscuit,' she murmured, eyes downcast, adding before she could stop herself, 'By, it were heaven.'

Cook preened slightly. 'And so they should be, I'd say. Been at my baking since dawn's break, I have. What about the little mite, there?'

'Nay, Bread ain't had a scrap. He dropped to sleep the moment we entered.'

'Bread?' Miss Lucy gave a soft snort. 'Cook, that boy's name is Bread!'

'Nay, it's Mack, really. Simon forgets,' Pip told them.

'And what do you go by?'

She straightened her shoulders. 'Pip,' she told the cook proudly.

Again, Miss Lucy turned to the servant in amusement. 'That isn't a proper name, either!'

'Aye, it is,' Pip responded boldly then quickly changed her tone for fear of overstepping the mark with one of her betters. 'What I mean is, it's what Mam called me.'

'Where is your mama? Mine, along with Aunt Josephine, has accompanied Papa to see his friend, who lives nearby beyond the church. Is yours away making visits, too?'

A pang of pain struck inside Pip's chest. In a sense, her mam was, aye. Away, that was. And near a church, too. Well, in the church's boneyard, anyroad.

'I stayed behind because I'm unwell – well, I *told* them I was unwell but really, I'm not!' Miss Lucy added, grinning. 'I wanted to stay here; it's far too cold to venture out, even with my new fur cloak and muff. Besides, I don't much care for Mr Sutton-Shaw,' she continued in her sweet, articulate voice. 'It also meant I could sneak down here to the kitchen for more of Cook's delicious cakes. I stole some, too, like you!' She laughed up at the servant, who rolled her eyes heavenwards. 'Finch, that's my nursemaid, says I'm not to have any because I'm fat.'

Cook clicked her tongue. 'Finch said that?'

Nodding, Miss Lucy prodded her admittedly chubby midriff. 'However,' she finished to Pip, 'I've bested her; she believes I'm in bed! Ha!'

Pip smothered a giggle with her grubby hand. This lass wasn't like the gentry you heard about. She wasn't stiff and abrupt or unwilling to speak kindly with them because of who she was and, more to the point, who they were not. She was nice, and real bonny to boot. 'You're funny,' she told her shyly.

'Thank you, Pip. I've always thought so. My name is Lucy. You may call me *Miss* Lucy,' the girl stated without a trace of self-importance.

Simon made a derisive noise in his throat that only Pip caught, but she didn't share his sentiments. Miss Lucy wasn't being priggish, just herself. This was how she'd been raised, taught. Such was life.

'Aw, Pip. Ay, my feet – oh!'

They all looked down at Mack's rotten boots. Tears had filled his soft blue eyes as he whimpered, shuffling on the spot.

'All right, lad,' she told him quietly. Glancing at Simon, she motioned to the door.

'Can we leave, missis?' the older lad asked the cook yet again.

'What's this about his feet?'

'It's nowt—'

'Awful sore, missis,' Mack spoke over Simon, nodding to the cook.

The woman was silent for a long moment, then, 'Where d'you plan on bedding down the night? It's per-ishing out there.'

They stared back silently. Her guess was as good as theirs.

'Well?'

'We normally kip by the baker's shop on London Road when the weather's 'specially bad. Heat carries from his ovens and warms the flagstones outside, like. Happen we'll try there.'

'Or not,' Simon said quickly, shooting Pip a warning look. 'We ain't decided yet.'

'I don't plan on sending a search party of police after youse, lad, don't fret,' the cook assured him with a hint of sadness. 'I were enquiring, is all.'

'Aye, well. Like I said, we ain't decided—'

'Miss Lucy! There you are.'

Cook turned sharply to the baize door. Quickly, she positioned her wide bulk in front of the orphans, blocking them from the view of the tall, angry-sounding woman who had appeared.

'Why, you wretched child. You had me worried sick! Why aren't you in your bed? Just you wait until your mama—'

'All right, Finch, there's no harm done,' Cook interrupted her. To the child, she added, 'Go on, now, Miss Lucy. We'll keep this to ourselfs, eh? No one needs know.' Ever so slightly, she jerked her head back, indicating Pip and the lads behind her.

Catching the double meaning, the girl flashed a wink. 'Oh, yes. Thank you, Cook.'

Unaware that anything was other than it seemed, Miss Finch bristled. 'Indeed we shan't forget this, oh no! That child has disobeyed me once too often. I'll be informing her parents of this the moment they return. I specifically told her to—'

'Aye, all right, you do that, then. I'm sure they'll be interested to learn of your slapdash ways.'

'What?'

Cook bobbed her head in a nod. 'You heard. You

were meant to be watching your charge, missy. Dozing by the fire again, were you? Aye, thought as much. If you did what you're paid for, this wouldn't have occurred. Tell them, aye, for you'll be doing us all a favour – you'll be out on your ear and halloo to that!'

Glancing up at the back of the cook's head, iron-grey curls peeking from her frilled white cap, Pip wondered anew at this seemingly fearless woman. She spoke to both servants and superiors as she pleased and didn't care a fig. Eeh, she liked her, she did!

After a charged silence, Finch's voice sounded again, tight with rage. 'Come along, Miss Lucy.'

'Goodbye, Pip. Goodbye, Simon, Bread. Merry Christmas,' the girl breathed on a soft whisper then skipped to the door.

'And another thing.' Cook's words stopped Finch in her tracks. 'Don't be filling Miss Lucy's head with tales that she's fat. You leave the child be, you hear? Anyroad, if you want my opinion, you'd do well to get some flesh on them bare bones of yourn.'

'And finish up with a girth as wide as yours? No thank you!' shot back the nursemaid before ushering the girl out; the green baize door swished shut and all was still.

'Huh! Bold piece.'

Nudging Pip, Simon inclined his head to the back door. The three of them had almost reached it when the cook turned and, seeing what they were about, stopped them with, 'Hang on. Here.' She crossed to the small oven, pulled the long handle and opened it wide. She brought out a steaming joint of glistening, dark-brown meat. 'Take a slice apiece along with youse. Little 'un there's had nowt, you said. Sure, I can't see you go – of a Christmas Eve to boot – without giving alms.'

The children glanced at each other, mouths moving

into small smiles. Eeh! This woman was kindness itself, she was. A real-life Christmas angel. By, meat! Proper stuff, an' all, not the slink (premature or stillborn calves) or broxy (diseased sheep) they were used to, when fortunate to cadge scraps off charitable house-wives from the surrounding streets back home.

'The master's son and his wife, Miss Lucy's parents, have invited friends around for a small feast and drinks the night. No mind to me and the rest of the staff, already up to our eyes in it with preparing the banquet for the morrow's dinner. Oh no, they think nowt of that so long as they get their jollio. They'll not notice a few morsels gone, I'm sure,' Cook muttered as she sliced generous pieces of beef. All the while, her eyes flicked over them, lingering on little Mack with definite sor-row. She made for a drawer in the enormous dresser, took out some brown paper and tore off a large square. On to this she laid the succulent cutlets and folded up the sides, wrapping them tightly.

'For us, Pip,' whispered Mack; she nodded excitedly. His eyes widened. He clutched his hands to his chest in rapture. Grinning, he swung his head to Simon but the elder boy had moved to open the door.

Half indoors, half out, Simon's gaze darted towards the servant then back to the street, as though he believed this was some big trick and expected to be pounced on by a constable any moment. 'Need to go,' he mumbled to himself, picking agitatedly at the sores around his mouth.

'Oh, now just one minute . . .' Nodding, the cook headed for a far door set in a recess, saying over her shoulder, 'I've a blanket I can spare that youse can take along. Just hang about while I fetch it. You've the need of it more than me, that you have. Now wait a minute.'

She disappeared and they heard her tread on bare stairs as she ascended to what must be the domestics' sleeping quarters.

'Grab that grub and let's get gone.' Pulling his cap low against the cold, Simon moved outside.

'But the cook said—'

'I'm not hanging about here any longer. I don't fancy having my collar felt, nay, I don't.'

'But Simon, the blanket . . . We could do with it; it's turning more bitter by the hour out there. Anyroad, she'll not tell on us. She said so, didn't she?'

'And what if the nobs arrive back and catch us here?'

'You weren't mithered on that when you entered in the first place,' Pip shot back quietly.

'Aye, well. I were angry, then, weren't I? I weren't thinking straight. I'm grateful to the owd 'un; she's norra bad sort, but . . . You think a mere skivvy's word would mean owt against that of her betters should they return? It'll be their decision whether to get the law on to us, not hers. And there's the girl – mebbe she's blurted all to the hard-faced one, Finch, the minute she got upstairs. Word could have been sent to the station while we've been stood here. Happen a team of police are on their way this second to apprehend us! What?' he asked when Pip frowned. 'How do you know? They could be and—' He broke off as footsteps from the street outside drifted on the air. 'Oh heck. Now see we must be away. Come on!'

Despite the trickle of fear running through Pip, still she hesitated. It felt wrong to just leave without at least thanking the cook. She glanced to the door the woman had gone through, willing her to return, and was rewarded when her footfalls sounded again. Moments later there she was, a thick blanket folded over her arm.

'Here we are then— Oh.' The cook paused and cocked her head and the children whipped theirs towards the street. Voices could be heard approaching the front of the house, a female's softer one followed by that of a male, strong and refined.

'The master!'

Cook answered Simon's hiss with a shake of her head. 'He's ill in his bed upstairs. That there you hear is the master's son – Mr Philip.' Saying the name, she sniffed, as though she'd just detected a bad smell.

'Miss Lucy's father?' asked Pip.

'That's right.'

'We need to leave, *now*. Happen the servants . . .'

'Them two will be a time returning yet. Don't fret, lad. They'll not catch you leaving. Aye, and happen it *were* time you were leaving, young 'uns,' she finished, nodding.

And yet, after handing over the paper parcel and blanket to Pip and shepherding them to the door, the woman sighed several times, as though reluctant to set them free into the cruel winter night. She looked up to the jet-black sky from which fell a slight but cutting rain, then brought her kindly round face back to them. 'Ain't there anyone . . .?'

'We've no one, missis,' murmured Pip.

'Norra single soul?'

'Nay.'

Cook sighed again with a shake of her head.

'Ta ever so.' Pip motioned to the treasures in her hands. 'And a merry Christmas to thee, Mrs . . . Cook.'

'Aye. Ta.' Simon mumbled agreement.

'Ta, thanks!' mimicked Mack, his excited gaze flicking to the wrapped meat. 'Eeh,' he breathed, mind clearly on the delight to come, as if he were the richest lad in the world. Then he took the cook's plump hand in his small ones, dipped his head and pressed his lips to the back of it in a kiss. 'Very merry Christmas.'

As one, the children walked away. Before turning for the main street, Pip looked back in time to see the cook shutting the door and thought she spotted her wiping her cheeks, but couldn't be certain. She felt like crying herself. Why, when they had these heavenly gifts of food and warmth – she should be skipping with joy, shouldn't she? – she didn't know. *Or perhaps that's the reason?* she asked herself. Aye, people's generosity towards them always amazed her. After all, no one had to give them anything, did they? And yet some did, for no other reason than that they wanted to. They knew they would be getting nothing in return, and yet still some gave through sheer kindness, nothing more.

The image of the gentleman from earlier, who'd led Mack away down the alley, flitted in her thoughts and she shuddered. Well, almost everyone had kindness in mind. So long as they were watchful, and had Simon, here, to protect them from such evils, they would be all right. Glancing at the older boy with a soft smile, she followed his lead unquestioningly.

Simon stopped by the Green's railings and looked about.

'Will we still go to Smithfield Market?' Pip asked and was glad when he shook his head. She was tired and doubted Mack would be up to it.

'I don't fancy that trek, now. Happen we'll shelter down 'neath a tree, here, the night? What says thee? We'll be safe enough; no one's likely to catch us and we can be away in the morning afore anyone's risen from their beds.'

Pip was too weary to argue. 'All right.'

They found themselves beneath the aged poplar as before. They huddled close for warmth and after wrapping the blanket around their legs, Pip tore open the warm parcel. The meat's delicious smell exploded up their nostrils and they released a collective slow breath. Taking a piece each, they devoured them ravenously. No one spoke for a long while. The only sounds were the slurping and smacking of lips as they sucked every last trace of meat juices from their hands. They took it in turns to run a finger along the grease-soaked paper before popping the digit into their mouths, unwilling to waste a single drop and reluctant for the feast to end. After drinking their fill from the lakelet, they eased back against the tree trunk and snuggled beneath the blanket with contented sighs.

From somewhere along the street, the melodic strains of 'O Come, all ye Faithful' from a group of carollers carried on the night. Then the singers moved on and stillness closed in on them. Mack tucked his head beneath Pip's shawl, like a bird seeking comfort under its mother's wing, and she fastened an arm around his shoulders. Within seconds, he was snoring softly.

'Not so bad the night, eh, thanks to this,' she whispered after a while to Simon, indicating the blanket.

'Aye,' he murmured back.

'Reet good of that cook, weren't it, lad? I like her. Oh, I do. And Miss Lucy. She wished us a merry Christmas; did you hear?'

He nodded.

'She were nice in t' end, an' all. Weren't she?'

'Aye,' he said again after a pause. 'Suppose she were.'

47

Chapter 4

IT FELT LIKE she'd been asleep for hours but in reality it could only have been one, if that. Lamplight still showed at several windows of houses overlooking the park; not everyone had retired for the night yet; it couldn't be so late.

Why had she wakened? Pip didn't know. Simon and Mack were still slumbering soundly either side of her. She peered through the darkness and saw nothing. Shrugging, she closed her eyes again. Suddenly, by the bushes close by, a snuffling sounded; heart beginning to thump, she peeped once more over the blanket. She was deliberating whether to waken Simon when the unmistakable shapes of two large dogs materialised as her eyes grew accustomed to the gloom. She released air slowly in relief. Moments later, there came what sounded like a rodent's muffled squeak. The hounds bounded away across the Green and silence swooped back.

It seems I were wrong – even the rich do have their share of rats, she thought, then bit her lip and tucked her legs up under herself, hoping the dogs had caught it. Folk weren't the only beings that the pains of hunger touched; the furry pests thought nothing of taking a nibble at you, given the chance.

'Psst! 'Ere, youse.'

Pip had nodded back to sleep when the voice came close to her ear. A hand shaking her shoulder accompanied it. She sat bolt upright with a gasp. 'Wha . . .? Who—?'

'You Pip?'

Surprise and confusion chased away a little of her fear. She squinted up at the speaker – a plain-looking girl not much older than herself – and stammered, 'A . . . aye, yes.'

'You've to follow me. Cook says.'

'Cook?'

'That's right, at Bracken House. I'm Tabitha – Tabby to my friends – the scullery maid there. Rouse t' other two and come with me.'

'It's a ruse,' Simon stated when Pip woke him and explained what was happening. 'They've got the law on us, that's what! Well, they ain't nabbing me—'

'Have we bloomin' heck.' The maid chuckled. 'Give over, lad. You're talking daft.'

'Then what's she after?'

'I don't know, do I? I'm only the messenger. Neither will youse till you go check.'

As was their habit, Pip and Mack looked to Simon to make the decision.

He thrust his hands in his pockets and stared hard at Tabby. 'You certain she said to fetch us?'

'Aye.'

'There's no funny business afoot?'

'Nay.'

'And definitely no police awaiting us?'

'Course there ain't. Ay, you're the one from earlier, ain't you, what confronted Hardman on our way out?' she stated, nodding understanding now. 'What did you

49

do, call on Cook after we'd gone, for she seems to know youse somehow? When the master's dogs sniffed youse out minutes ago and I ran back to tell Cook there were trespassers in the Green, she reckoned she knew who it'd be right away.'

'The dogs what were chasing the rat, they're the master's?' asked Pip.

'Rat?'

'Aye, I heard it squeak.'

Tabby's mouth spread in a grin. 'That weren't no rat; that were bleedin' me! Frickened the liver from me, youse did.'

'Sorry . . . The gate were open. We never broke in or nowt.'

The maid pulled a guilty face. 'Ay, I must have forgot to lock it behind me after walking the dogs this morning . . . Good thing I spotted youse, else I'd have been for it off Mrs Goldthorpe, and no mistake.' She eyed Simon, one brow raised. 'So, youse coming along with me or ain't you?'

He breathed deeply with indecision and Pip touched his sleeve. 'Let's go see, eh? It can't do no harm.'

Tabby turned and walked away. He dithered a moment longer. Then he motioned to Pip and Mack and followed the scullery maid into the street. After locking the gate, she popped the key into her apron pocket and, checking they were following, headed for Bracken House.

Pip had almost forgotten the giddying assault on the senses the kitchen evoked; stepping back inside the bright warm room, her heart lifted instantly.

''Ere they are. Now look at youse, frozen and soaked to the bone.' Cook beckoned them towards the fire. 'Come on, let's be having you.'

'But . . .' Pip's gaze strayed to the green baize door.

'Missis, what's this about?' asked Simon.

'Laddo thought you had the police waiting.'

'Is what Tabby, here, says true? Tsk! Now I said earlier you needn't fret on that; didn't I say?'

Pip and the boys stared back silently. Then just what *was* going on? Why had the cook asked them back?

'Don't go worrying on that lot,' Cook stated, flicking her head to the door that led to the house proper beyond. 'The family don't venture in here. Well, besides Miss Lucy, given the opportunity. That one's the exception to the rule.' The woman smiled softly. It was evident she held deep affection for the child. 'Nay. This is servants' territory. You'll not be discovered. I've spoken on matters with Tabby, here.' Cook nodded to the girl now busy garnishing a platter of cows' tongues at the table. 'She'll not breathe a word. Will you, lass?'

'I'll not.' She smiled over her shoulder.

'Finch you saw earlier, she never shows her phizog down here usually. The night were a rarity owing to Miss Lucy's antics,' Cook continued. 'She takes her meals in the nursery with the child and sleeps in a room adjoining hers, has no cause to mix with us. Nor would she be welcome to,' she added with a sniff. 'That leaves the housemaid, Hardman, who you've already had the misfortune of crossing paths with. Don't fret on that one, mind. I'll see she says nowt or feel the full weight of my wrath. Bar the washerwoman Mary Stubbs, who calls twice weekly to collect and fetch back the laundry, us four make up the domestics employed here. This residence houses but a modest sized family, you see – just the five of them – without need of an army of folk at their beck and call. Youse understand all that?'

The children shared confused looks. It was Simon

who asked, 'Why you telling us all this, missis? Why have you asked us back?'

'Cook has her whims like this,' the scullery maid offered mildly. 'Took a stray cat in last month, she did, but it grabbed and gobbled a chicken she'd spent all day preparing and cooking and she slung it out.' She released a snort of laughter then shook her head. 'Oh, I'm not saying you're strays, like—'

'I should think not, Tabitha Newby!' cut in the older woman. 'These here are flesh and blood people just like yourself and me. Anyroad, that scraggy chancer were an ungrateful divil. Fed it fresh meat off the bone, I did, for nigh on a fortnight and it goes and pilfers the family's dinner? Oh no, missy, I weren't having that! This, now, is altogether different. These here are God's children. I'll not have it said that Mabel May don't perform her Christian duty should the need arise,' she proclaimed, prodding her puffed-out chest. 'As Lord Jesus hisself once said: *It's more blessed to give than to receive.*'

At this, much to Pip's astonishment, Tabby fell about laughing. Holding on to the back of a chair, she wiped her eyes, wet with mirth, with the back of her free hand. 'Christian . . .? Why, you ain't graced a church door in all the years I've know you, yer great untruth-teller!'

'Aye, well . . . Moral duty, then, flappy tongue!'

Again, Pip shared a confused look with Simon and Mack, unable to believe, to hope . . . Did this mean . . .? No, surely not! Surely the cook, here, wasn't suggesting they could stay at this house? However, her next words confirmed it and sent Pip's heart thumping in her chest:

'Now, here's what we're to do. You'll wait in my own room upstairs. Tabby shall show you to it. There, you stay till I shouts you. There's a mammoth amount of work to be had afore the night's through – the family have yet to have their Christmas Eve feast. Then there's the fare for the morrow's dinner and a million and one other things to prepare besides . . . But, no matter about that, no matter. We'll manage, allus do. Come along, then, that's it. Tabby, you lead the way, lass. Shake a leg, now.'

Instead of obeying, as Pip and Mack were about to, so lost were they in shock to argue, Simon backed towards the street door. Eyes narrowed, he shook his head slowly. 'Now I've asked enough and got nowt for my troubles,' he said quietly. 'I'd like some answers, missis, for I'll be damned, I've norra single idea what's occurring, here. Where are you expecting us to go to exactly, and why? Why are you doing this? *What* are you doing?'

'Taking youse in,' Cook proffered simply. 'Well, the night, at least. You think I'd sleep well in my warm bed knowing I'd cast three kiddies out into the bitter cold – of a Christmas Eve, an' all? Nay, now don't you fret and don't ask another question, for time's not on our side. Go on with Tabby, now. She'll see you well till I'm freed up, later.'

'But . . . the master,' Simon persevered as the scullery maid made to lead him towards the far door to the servants' quarters. 'Happen he were to discover—?'

'He'll not.'

'And Miss Lucy? Mebbe she's already—?'

'Nay, not her,' Cook interrupted him again. 'Young she may be but daft she ain't. She'll hold her tongue, I'm certain. Nor have you need to worry about her parents, Mr Philip and *Madam*.' Cook dropped the last word off her tongue with a roll of her eyes. 'Neither, for that matter, poor Miss Josephine, the master's daughter.'

'Aye, but if they *did* . . .?'

'Aye, well. Anyroad, they've no reason to, really, and

it's only right they don't. For as Jesus also said: *Beware of practising your righteousness before other people in order to be seen by them, for then you will have no reward from your Father who is in heaven. Thus, when you give to the needy, sound no trumpet before you, as the hypocrites do—'* At Tabby's guffaw, Cook shot her a stern look and continued: *'in the synagogues and in the streets, that they may be praised by others. Truly, I say to you, they have received their reward—'*

'*But when you give to the needy, do not let your left hand know what your right hand is doing, so that your giving may be in secret. And your Father who sees in secret will reward you.*'

All eyes swivelled to Pip, and for a moment she was confused. Then she realised it was she who had interrupted the cook, finishing the verse she knew so well, without thought, and her cheeks flamed red. 'I . . . I'm sorry . . .'

'What says you, child?'

'I . . . That . . . *But when you give to the needy—*'

'I heard it.' Warmth filled the cook's eyes. 'What I mean is, you know the Bible by heart?'

Pip nodded. 'Well, mostly. Mam read it to me each night. That there were her favourite bit.'

The lads were staring at Pip in surprise. Even Tabby had stopped her teasing of Cook's hypocrisy on religious matters, and was nodding her head, smiling.

Cook looked as if she'd ask more but changed her mind, saying instead, 'Ay, the master will like that. A reet God-fearing man, is he.' She'd spoken softly but in the next moment seemed to shake herself and her words were delivered with purpose. 'Well, lad?' she asked of Simon. 'Tha looks to be the decision-maker amongst you. What's it to be?'

All eyes were now on the older boy. Cook raised an eyebrow, Pip followed suit, and with a sigh that seemed

54

to come from the bottom of his cracked boots, his shoulders sagged in defeat. With a flick of his head to Mack, he took up the lead behind Tabby and the four of them left the kitchen.

No one spoke as they mounted the bare and narrow, well-scrubbed stairs, which seemed to go on for ever. Then they circled a sharp bend and climbed an identical set; up, up, towards the very top of the house. The candle that Tabby held high in front of her barely illuminated their path and Pip held on to the bottom of Simon's jacket, more for security than from fear of losing her footing. Likewise, behind her, Mack had balled his fist around the edge of her shawl. Suddenly, they were brought to an abrupt halt when Tabby paused at the top of the stairs. Before them ran a short landing with four doors leading off into the gloom. She nodded to the one nearest.

'That there's Cook's domain. Come on, then,' she said mildly with a quick smile. Before opening the door, she motioned to the others. 'This one's mine,' she told them of the neighbouring room. 'Next one along is Hardman's – hell's teeth, here's a warning you'll do well not to forget: don't go wandering into that 'un by accident! I've made the mistake of entering her bedroom only once afore and bore a fat lip for nigh on a week to prove it!'

Pip wondered to whom the last room belonged but didn't dare ask. She was certain that one wrong word or action and the three of them would be slung quick sharp back on to the street. She wasn't taking the chance. Just what on earth they were doing here now, she hadn't the faintest idea, but she for one wasn't about to burst this unbelievable dream. They were in a house; all three! They were to *sleep* in this house. Had you ever heard the like! Cook must have a fever of the brain, or been struck with some other mode of illness that was affecting her thinking, surely? She'd said one night, but that alone was more than nothing. By, it was. It was the grandest gesture they had received in . . . well, ever. Pip wouldn't forfeit this opportunity for anything. Nay, not she.

The scullery maid shepherded them into a fair-sized room and closed the door. She disappeared and moments later, murky light flickered forth from a candle atop a small bedside chest as she lit it from the one she held. 'Right, then. As Cook said, we've work to do so youse stay put here till she's ready for you.' She nodded to a neatly made bed against the far wall. 'Sit yourselfs down, take the load off. Lord hisself only knows when we'll be for finishing up downstairs the night. Mr Philip brought guests back – Mr Sutton-Shaw besides the rest – for drinks and songs. We can't greet our beds till the family's in theirs. You're likely in for quite a wait.'

Gazing at the pristine, cream-coloured coverlet and matching frilled-edged pillowslips adorning the cook's bed, then looking down at her filthy skirts and the lads' equally soiled trousers, a trickle of shame-filled horror ran through Pip. Tabby was heading back to the door and she hurried after her. 'Please. Is there anything we can use to protect the bedding? Some sacking, mebbe? Our clothing, you see . . .'

'Oh.' The girl tapped her lips, eyes thoughtful. Then she shrugged. 'It'll not matter, I'm sure. Cook will understand. Just sit yourselfs down,' she added over her shoulder, 'sit yourselfs down.'

The door clicked shut and the children were alone.

For a long moment, no one moved. Neither did they, despite the scullery maid's reassurances, make towards the bed. It didn't seem right; they felt it as though of one mind. They simply stared around them. Besides the bed itself and the chest alongside, the room held a plain-top desk and hardback chair set beneath a window, from which hung cream and pale-green striped curtains, the material rough-looking but pretty. A dark-wood wardrobe and set of matching drawers stood by the opposite wall. On top of the latter was a large, navy and white washbowl and pitcher, a fluffy flannel folded neatly, a hairbrush and a bottle of something – toilet water by the look of it – as well as a small wooden box with flowers carved into its lid.

Above was an only slightly cracked oval mirror. In the top right corner, held in place between it and the wall, was a portrait smudged and grimy with age. Hesitantly, Pip stepped nearer for a quick peep. She saw on closer inspection that it depicted a young girl with long ringlets wearing a plain frock, and a cheery smile just visible beneath a too-large bonnet that cast the rest of her face in shadow.

'Cook's child?' murmured Simon over her shoulder.

'Aye, mebbe.' A frown touched Pip's brow. 'I wonder where she is now?'

Simon didn't have opportunity to speculate. 'This room's like a magic room in heaven, like what angels have. Ain't it, Pip?' breathed Mack.

She glanced down and smiled. 'It is.'

'Are we going to live here, now, for ever and ever?'

'Nay, lad. Just the night. But 'ere,' she added quickly when his face fell, 'just think, a night beneath a sound roof! And the morrow, afore we leave, happen Cook will send us on our way with a few scraps again, eh? We'll find somewhere new, somewhere warm, like, and dry, and we'll snuggle together and eat our feast and sing songs, for it'll be Christmas when we waken. That'll be nice, won't it?'

He shook his head, his bottom lip wobbling, and she hadn't the strength to try and persuade him further, for her own eyes were stinging at the prospect of leaving here in a few short hours. She hugged him close and sighed. Then she motioned to the rag rug by the bed and the two of them settled down upon it, Simon following after some seconds. The blanket from the cook earlier, tucked under her arm, she now wrapped around them.

'Feet hurt. They hurt bad.'

Again, Pip sighed. 'I know. I know. Try and snatch some sleep, good lad.'

His pitiful griping continued for some minutes and just when Pip had exhausted all avenues of comforting words of distraction, Simon spoke quietly.

''Ere, Bread, look.' He pointed to the window where the curtains hadn't yet been drawn, and to the dark sky beyond, stained in places with grey cloud. 'You see? See the pictures? I reckon that's a fish wearing a top hat. What says thee?'

Pip could have hugged him. He could be thoughtful when he chose, loved this little lad deep down as much as she, however he tried to mask it. Their eyes met over the top of Mack's head. She gave him a smile and he responded with his usual, ever so brief one.

'I see, Simon, aye!' Wide-eyed, Mack nodded. Then he yawned and snuggled into Pip's shoulder.

Again, she and Simon shared a look. Then as one, they too closed their eyes and settled down for what they knew would be the warmest, safest, most cosiest sleep any of them had known in a long, long time.

*

The queer knowledge a body experiences when it's being watched, as though the spy's eyes are burning holes into your flesh, plucked Pip from her light doze. Under the cover of her shawl, through the hazy light of the near-spent candle, she saw Cook's figure in the doorway. For a long moment, it remained still and, half afraid to move unless the woman had changed her mind and might order them from this room and house, so did Pip. Then the woman turned and disappeared. Pip heard her knock at Tabby's room next door, then voices trickled through from the landing beyond:

'You certain about this . . .?'

'I've just been looking on the poor blighters sleeping. The rotten shame of it . . . Aye, I'm certain.'

The scullery maid's soft sigh floated on the air. 'Well, it's your call, I suppose . . .'

'That's right. Besides, you know how matters are, of my standing in this house. And neither Mr Philip nor that wife of his will alter my decision. The master will see to that once I've put him straight.'

'Aye.'

'Thing is, they're filthy and likely verminous. And that poor youngster has some problem with his feet, is pained, it's clear to see. It'll need addressing sooner rather than later if they're not to infest the whole house and us along with it.'

Curiosity momentarily left Pip as she felt embarrassment burn her cheeks. Then Cook spoke again and it returned, drawing her brows together in a puzzled frown:

'Now I know you must be dead on your feet, lass, as am I, after the day's toil. And I know it's all the sleep we can snatch that we need right now, for the morrow shall be busier still. But I'd appreciate a helping hand if you're for lending it? Them sorry mites in there are more in need than we at this moment in time. What says you?'

Tabby answered without hesitation. 'Aye, I'll help, Cook. It's no bother. What d'you want me to do?'

'The house is all abed bar Hardman— Oh, here she comes, now.'

The voices ceased and Pip heard the tread of the maid in question on the stairs. No words were exchanged between her and the other two servants, pleasant or otherwise. The housemaid walked straight past them and the room, and seconds later, her door opened then banged shut behind her.

Cook's voice, when she resumed her conversation, had dropped to a whisper, likely so Hardman wouldn't hear, and Pip was unable to catch the words. Then Tabby's light step descended the stairs to the kitchen and Cook appeared once more in her bedroom doorway. This time, she entered and closed the door behind her. She crossed the room to stand before the children, and again simply stared at them for a time. Then she sighed, stooped and spoke quietly:

'Waken, children. You hear me? Come on, that's it, poor divils. Rub the sleep from your eyes and come with me. I'll not keep you long, then you can rest easy again. That's it, lass,' she continued softly when Pip finally raised her head. 'And you, lad, aye,' she added to Simon, who had bolted awake. 'Fetch the little one. Quiet, now. Come along.'

Without another word, the cook hurried them down to the kitchen, Simon and Mack stumbling along behind Pip, dumb with tiredness. When they entered, the scullery maid paused in her task of dragging a bath before the fire to smile. Cook indicated the table, and

Pip and the lads sat. They watched, silent with confusion, as the woman and girl filled the tin tub with the bubbling contents of a mammoth pot on the fire. They then added cold water from a pail nearby. Cook swished a hand through to check the temperature, nodded satisfied, then hung a large towel on the wooden rack above the mantel to warm. Then she put her hands on her hips and turned to the children.

'Right, then. Who wants to go first?'

Pip and Mack glanced at each other then to Simon. No one spoke, astonishment holding their tongues.

'How's about biggest to smallest? That way, I can spend more time on the little 'un once you two are done, see what's the trouble with his young feet?'

Again, silence. Cook jerked her chin questioningly.

Simon finally found his voice. 'You want me to get in there?'

Cook nodded. 'That's right.'

'No offence, lad, but you smell like summat the dogs have coughed up,' piped Tabby, then shrugged when Cook gave her a stern look. 'Sorry, but it's true!'

Simon, proud to a fault, was always quick to take umbrage; biting her lip, Pip awaited his temper. It never came. Neither did he question Cook's motives. He gazed in disbelief, then a look passed over his face, something akin to understanding mixed with excitement. He rose. Within seconds, his clothes were in a heap around his feet.

Pip blushed scarlet, Mack giggled, but Cook and Tabby appeared unfazed.

He crossed to the bath, lowered himself into the steaming clear waters and lay back with a long sigh.

'There, that's it,' Cook said mildly. 'Though by hell, it's fortunate me and the lass, here, are from farming

61

stock and have seen it all afore from the beasts of the fields, else you might have given us a merry fright.' Then she took quick stock of his emaciated, dirt- and sore-riddled body and the amusement faded from her eyes. She nodded to Tabby, who handed Simon a flannel and small block of soap. 'Scrub yourself good and proper, now, good lad.'

Pip still had no notion of why all this was occurring but Simon seemed to, and if he trusted this was for the good then so did she. He always knew best. As he did as he was bid, the cook and scullery maid took his clothes to task. Cook filled a broad wooden pail with more water, grated in flakes from a different bar of darker soap and after working up a lather, plunged the clothing in. She then rubbed into them a foul-smelling disinfectant, likely to kill the lice, paying particular attention to the seams.

'Tabby? Stockings off, lass.'

Once in her bare feet, the girl hopped into the pail and, holding on to Cook's shoulders for balance, proceeded to perform an on-the-spot jog, pounding the grime from the clothing with each step. Working quickly, they then transferred the suddy garments to another pail waiting nearby filled with clean water and rinsed everything thoroughly. One by one, they took an end of each item, twisted it between them into a sausage shape to wring it out before placing it beside the towel to let the heat from the flames do its part.

When Cook disappeared with Simon's boots and a brush, presumably to clean them of the years' worth of muck, and Tabby, on instructions from the older woman, made through the green baize door for the house proper and the master's dressing room, Pip sidled up to the bath.

Dropping to her knees, she rested her elbows on the cold metal rim. 'What does it mean, Simon?'

He stared at her and ran a hand through his damp hair. 'I think she's for inviting us to stay on.'

'You mean . . .?'

'Aye.'

Her breaths came in short gasps. 'How d'you know?'

'Why else go to all this bother?'

'But . . .? I mean, how will Cook pull this off? Surely the household will notice us? Hardman for one definitely will—'

'By, I've missed a reet good tub soak. A dip in t' River Irwell on occasion ain't the same, somehow.' He sank further beneath the water.

Normally, he held steadfastly to making no reference to his past. However, he'd spoken with such feeling, Pip couldn't help asking, 'Aye?'

He stared straight ahead as if he hadn't heard her. Then he closed his eyes. 'Let's just see how matters play out, eh? Anyroad, the cook looks to know what she's doing.'

Pip studied his face for a moment, now a lovely shade of cream with pink cheeks from the cleaning he'd given it. He looked calm. And contented, aye, a side to him she'd never known before. Usually, he was on edge, furrow-browed and quick-eyed, almost feral, alert to possible opportunity or danger, as were they all. You had to be, had to look after your own well-being just to survive when you had no one in the world to do it for you. 'Is that what you want, lad? To stay?'

His head snapped around to face her. 'Don't thee?'

A note of worry lingered behind his eyes and she smiled. 'Aye, aye.' She knew his thoughts ran as hers did – they were a trio and would always be. Where one went, the other two wouldn't be far behind. They couldn't be separate beings, now, after everything they had faced together, the protective love they had for one another. The very notion was inconceivable.

''Ere, and me!'

She turned to grin at an offended-looking Mack sitting swinging his legs, thumb planted firmly in his mouth. 'Course and you, daft boy. Lord, just think of it!' she added, looking back to Simon and grasping his wet shoulder. 'Us, *here*, together—!'

'What's together?'

Pip scrambled to her feet at the cook's voice, the woman having returned without their noticing. 'Nowt. Nowt, Cook.'

'You ready next, lass?' she asked, motioning to the tub, and Pip nodded. 'And how are you getting on, lad?' she asked of Simon.

'All right. Ta.'

'Good. Now, where is that girl . . . Ah, here she comes. Come on, dawdle-Lil,' she told Tabby as she entered with a bottle in her hand.

'All right, all right. I had to take my time, didn't I, couldn't be dashing about the house at this hour!' The girl handed the bottle over. 'The master didn't hear me. He's sleeping soundly.'

'Good lass. Aye, glory be to God, that glass of mead he took with his meal will help him rest easy the night.'

'I don't know how he sups that stuff. The alcohol part, aye, I like, but honey . . .?' Tabby pulled a face. 'It's foul, that's what.'

'Aye well, the master likes it, so less of your mealy-mouthness,' Cook said over her shoulder as she crossed to Simon, and didn't see the tongue that Tabby poked out at her back, nor her grin, but Pip did. She and the scullery maid shared a smile.

64

Simon was eyeing suspiciously the bottle Cook held. 'And what's that when it's at home?'

She pulled out the cork, sniffed the contents and nodded. 'Head back, lad.'

'Nay, not likely. You ain't pouring no poisons on me.'

'Don't talk daft. This 'ere's but a little borax and olive oil mixed with water, will cleanse that raggedy mop of yourn. And ay, if it's good enough for the master's luscious locks, I'm sure as ninepence it's swell enough for thee!'

Pip was amazed. Surely any other servant in the land bold enough to make free use of their master's possessions without so much as a by-your-leave would be out on their ear if caught. Yet the cook didn't seem fazed by the prospect in the slightest. Just what was the deal, here, beneath this roof? She'd never heard anything like it.

'Aye, this is the pleasant part,' continued Cook, liberally soaking his hair. 'It's the delousing next, my lad – vinegar and water followed by the comb.'

Tabby was hovering nearby with the towel and when Cook had finished with Simon's head, amidst his growls and grumbles, she tossed it to him then reached on tiptoe to pluck down his clothes. She wrapped a rag around the handle of a flat iron that had been on the heat, spat on it, sending it sizzling like bacon in a pan, and quickly smoothed it over each garment with a deftness that belied her tender years.

When Simon had crossed to the corner of the room to dress, Cook and Tabby set about the tub with a fresh batch of water. Pip swallowed hard – her turn next. She couldn't recall when she'd bathed last and, if she was honest, she was a little afraid.

'Off with 'em, lass.'

Pip's fingers automatically travelled up to clutch at the bodice of her dress.

'No time for modesty, lass. Left untreated properly, you'll infest the whole house. All right, all right,' Cook added kindly, lifting her eyes to the heavens, 'the lads, here, will look away, I'm sure. That ease your fretting?'

Pip nodded, yet still bit her lip uncertainly, making no attempt to undress. Then she caught a reassuring nod from Simon across the room and relented. 'Aye, Cook. All right.'

Whatever her worries, she needn't have harboured them. The moment she slithered in and the silky waves hugged her skin, she quivered out a blissful sigh. By, it felt like a summer sun's embrace, it did. The heat made her eyes grow heavy but the desire to wash away the grime pushed through and as Cook and Tabby gave her clothing the same treatment as Simon's, she scrubbed herself with gusto. Then Cook was approaching *her* this time with the bottle from the master's room.

Eyes closed, she allowed the deft fingers to cleanse her matted locks. The touch felt comfortingly familiar and a wonderful sense of remembrance took hold of her. She envisioned her mother, her dark head tilted in smile, her soft hands undertaking this very action before the fire in the small room they once called home. From a far-off place, she heard her mother's gentle humming of long ago, saw in her mind's eye her mother envelop her in the scrap of towel, lift her from the water and sit hugging her before the flames until she was dry. They would talk and laugh quietly and after she was dressed, her mother would run a brush through her hair, exclaiming gently in admiration of its loveliness, before plaiting it neatly . . .

'Ay, lass, I'm not hurting thee, am I?'

Dragged from her memories, Pip glanced up at Cook's concerned face. It was then that she noticed the fat tears she hadn't realised she was shedding running down her cheeks and dripping into the scummy waters. Forcing from her mind the woman she missed with every part of her, she rubbed at her eyes quickly. 'Nay, Cook. It's just the steam, like,' she lied.

'Well, you might have cause to say otherwise in a minute, for it's the vinegar next, lass, so brace yourself.'

The liquid greeted the sores on her scalp with an acid handshake but Pip bore the pain without complaint. Stepping into her still-damp but fresh-smelling clothes afterwards, she felt like another being. To be clean and bug-free for the first time in over a year was glorious. She felt lighter, peaceful. *Human.* 'Simon?'

Now sitting at the table, himself looking like a stranger – a neat and presentable one, at that – black hair now shiny and knot-free, shirt and jacket, though ragged still, laundered and newly ironed, he'd fixed her with a wide-eyed stare. Frowning, she said his name again and he blinked. 'Bugger me. Pip, is that thee?' he asked quietly.

She raised a self-conscious hand to hair Tabby had finished brushing the tangles from. Silken strands met her palm and she drew a lock through her fingers to examine it.

'By. Laddo here is right. Look for yourself.' The scullery maid held up a silver tureen and Pip gazed at the reflection staring back from the shiny surface. Curls the colour of beaten butter hugged a white face. Above cheeks speckled with freckles sat two bright pools of the deepest green, almond shaped like those of a cat, framed by dark lashes and brows. The sight of this long-forgotten person was startling; she shook her head in denial.

'Such beauty hidden under the muck – unbelievable!'

Pip blushed to the roots of her hair at Tabby's compliment. Murmuring a thank you, she sidled over to slip into a chair beside Simon.

'Cook? You giving me a hand, or what?'

It seemed a long time before the woman heard the young domestic speak. Her attention was on Pip. She was looking at her with the queerest expression, and Pip coloured again under the intense scrutiny. Cook closed her eyes for the briefest moment then cleared her throat. 'Aye. Aye, lass. Let's sort this last 'un out.'

'You all right?'

Now busy at the tub, she nodded to Tabby over her shoulder. Her tone was quiet, flat. 'Aye. Tired, is all.'

'And me. By, my back won't like me the morrow, I'll be bound.'

Watching them humping out and lugging in yet more fresh water, gratitude and not a little admiration filled Pip. It was clear they were exhausted after their busy workday, had likely been up from their beds before dawn, but still they were taking the time for them. And for what? Was what Simon suspected true? Were they to stay on here? It seemed too fantastical a notion to believe. Yet what, otherwise? Why else were they doing this? She hadn't an answer. Someone, surely Cook, would explain soon?

'Now then.' Smiling, the woman beckoned to Mack. The lad trotted to her willingly enough – as much as his painful feet would allow – and raking her eyes over him, she shook her head and sighed. 'Rotten bloody shame, it is. Eeh, I don't know. Come on, lovey, off with 'em.' She helped him peel his jacket and shirt away but when she stooped and attempted to untie his laces, he backed off.

'Nay. It hurts.'

'Now come along and don't be a babby. How am I meant to see you cleaned up all bonny, like, if you don't take off your ruddy boots?'

As she removed, with some difficulty, his left one, he whimpered pitifully but at her soothings, bore it. At her first tug on the next, however, he let out such a scream that everyone almost jumped from their skins.

'Now then, now then,' murmured Cook, eyes creased in sadness. 'Aye, this is worse than I thought – nay, stop out of the way a minute, I'll mend him, don't fret,' she added to Pip and Simon, who had risen from their seats, worry etched on both their faces.

'Bloomin' heck, he'll rouse the whole house with that carry-on.' Tabby, glancing upwards then to the doors, bit her lip.

The woman quashed her concerns. 'This household is well used to such things in the night, as well you know. Poor lass,' she added in a whisper, almost to herself, her own eyes straying to the ceiling, and Pip and Simon shared a frown.

'Why's that, then? What poor lass?'

'Never you mind.' Cook's stern look silenced Simon. 'Now, here's what we're to do,' she continued in a softer tone to Mack. 'You're to get in the bath, boot an' all. The water, here, will loosen it enough for me to remove and shall soothe your skin while it's about it. All right?'

'It'll not. It's stuck. It hurts!' Despite his protests, he allowed the cook to lower him into the tub. His cladded foot made contact with the water and he gritted his teeth. 'It stings!'

'All right, all right. Now we'll leave that hoof to soak

69

awhile. Meantime, let's get the rest of you scrubbed and cleaned.'

This she did, washing every inch of his scrawny frame and light, shoulder-length hair with gusto, while Tabby treated his clothing. Then came the moment they were all dreading.

'We can't put it off any longer, lad. That thing has to come off.'

After a long hesitation, he heaved a deep breath and nodded bravely.

'Good boy. Now, let's see what the damage is. Prepare yourself.'

Mack gripped the bath's edge until his knuckles turned white as slowly, with gentle twists and tugs, Cook eased the boot away. The pungent smell of infection burst forth, stagnating the air.

'God in heaven . . .'

Following Cook's gaze, Pip caught a glimpse inside the boot before the woman could hide it away – clumps of Mack's flesh had gone with it, stuck to the leather inside. She slapped a hand to her mouth. Oh, the poor lad . . . No wonder he'd been complaining about the pain as he had for so long. Blighted with such injury, the sorry mite must have suffered agony. It would be a miracle, she reckoned, if he ever walked normally again.

Fat, silent tears were coursing down his face. He clung to Cook and she patted his head.

'Now, now. Don't take on so. That's the hard part behind thee.' She looked to Pip and Simon with anger in her eyes – directed not at them but the world in general. 'Who's responsible for this child?' she asked. 'For all of you, for that matter. How have you found yourselfs this way?'

'Me,' muttered Simon after some moments. 'I'm

responsible for him.' The latter part of Cook's enquiry, however, he ignored.

The woman looked to him, sighed, then resumed her inspection of the foot, holding it aloft in the lamplight.

Like his other before its introduction to the soap, this foot was covered in a grey film – layer upon layer of dirt. Yet that's where the similarities ended. Clusters of bubbles – weeping blisters, some as large as penny pieces – covered the toes and sides of the foot. But it was the heel that had Cook shaking her head in concern, and Tabby, Pip and Simon looking away, cringing. Here there were two open wounds, as if the flesh had been eaten away, oozing blood and pus.

From what Pip had just seen inside the boot, it was clear what had happened, what she had suspected ailed him. Given that Mack – indeed all three of them – never took their boots off, the sores, when they began to heal, had done so around the broken leather, almost fusing together. Bare feet constantly in soggy and damp ill-fitting boots was the culprit. It was a wonder she and Simon hadn't suffered the same fate before now.

Amidst the youngster's whimpers and with tender strokes, Cook cleansed the foot as best as she was able. She then turned to Tabby. 'Fetch us a tin dish from the cupboard, there. Ta, lass. Now, if this don't work, I don't know what will – swore by her potions, did my granny. Aye, lad,' she added to Mack, nodding, 'we'll have you mended in no time, you'll see.' Throwing orders at Tabby to fetch her this, that and the next, she crossed to the table and the girl scuttled about bringing her what was required without question. Cook poured and mixed and ground a whole host of ingredients. Finally satisfied with the look and consistency, she crouched again by the side of the bath and held Mack's injured foot aloft.

He pulled an expectant pained face as she began applying the paste-like ointment but it soon slipped from him and he gazed up in surprise. 'It don't hurt, that, missis. 'Ere, I'd say it feels nice.'

Cook smiled. 'Soothing it, is it?'

'Aye!'

After coating the heel liberally, she fetched a cloth from a drawer, ripped half of it in two lengthwise and wrapped the remainder around the foot, tying the torn ends together, thus securing the bandage in place. She then lifted him up and out of the tub, dried him from top to toe and helped him on with his clean clothes. Fists on hips, she stood looking from him to Pip and Simon with a satisfied nod. 'Would you look at them, now? Did you ever see a more striking transformation or finer kiddies than these?'

Tabby smiled agreement then smothered a yawn with the back of her hand, and Cook motioned to the door that led upstairs. 'Go on, lass, get yourself off to your bed – and take my thanks for your help the night along with you.' She gave her a gentle shove, and without protest the exhausted scullery maid did as she was told.

Cook turned her attention to the children, now sitting close together at the table. 'Same goes for the three of youse. But first . . .'

The plates of floury crusts and ham, and cups of milky tea, were empty in no time. Again, the woman gave a satisfied nod. As Tabby had done, she too gave a yawn, though made no attempt to stifle hers. She wiped her tired eyes then jerked her head and without a word, her three charges too made for the door.

'I'll follow in a minute, just need to bank down the fire and extinguish the lights. 'Ere and mind yourselfs when you reach the landing. No loitering; we don't want that Hardman piece catching sight of youse. I haven't the energy for any palaver. There'll be time enough to put her in the picture the morrow. Aye, and the rest of them, an' all.'

Too tired to dwell on just what the housemaid's reaction upon discovering them beneath this roof would be – not to mention what the master and his family would make of it – they dragged their weary selves upstairs.

True to her word, Cook slipped into her bedroom shortly afterwards. She clicked her tongue to find them huddled on the rug like before. 'What's this? Why, lying there youse favour the master's dogs. Up. Come on now, into that bed, the three of you. I'll take the chair, here. No arguments,' she murmured when they made to protest. 'It's a sound kip you're short of and that's what you're getting. Go on, go on. Oh aye,' she added as an afterthought, 'the pot's beneath said bed should you need to go during the night.'

Shuffling under the blankets, they released blissful sighs in unison. Cook smiled, tucked the coverings around them, then, taking another blanket from the bottom drawer of the chest, eased into the chair by the window.

Heavy eyed with contentment, Pip snuggled closer to Mack and Simon, their breathing already steady with sleep. Glancing to the cook's bulk through the darkness, a smile stroked her lips and tears pricked her eyes. Eeh, but how would they ever thank the woman here enough for this? Tabby, too, aye, for she was nice, as well. She'd promised to keep her silence, hadn't she? But all this, really, was the doing of but one person. Aye, this angel here. *I love you*, she thought. 'Thank you,' she said.

'You're a good lass,' Cook whispered back. Moments later, she too was snoring softly.

Some time later, whether Pip had dropped off then awakened to the sounds, or whether she was dreaming, she couldn't be certain. A slight frown touched her brow at what appeared to be faint sobs drifting from another part of the house. She hadn't time to ponder as deep sleep claimed her once more.

Chapter 5

'PIP? LOOK, PIP.'

She opened her eyes. Squinting in the weak sunlight, she followed Mack's finger. 'Ah.' She smiled sleepily.

'What is it?'

'That there's a robin redbreast. Bonny, eh?'

The boy, wide eyes on the small bird hopping along the window ledge outside, grinned. It was then Pip realised how lovely she felt. She wasn't cold or cramped or damp with dew, nor was her stomach sick with emptiness. She was toasty warm, cosy, content. In her half-conscious state, she'd forgotten where she was, about last night and everything that had transpired. Slowly, she raised herself on one elbow and looked about.

The chair in which Cook had spent the night was empty, the blanket returned to the drawer. She swivelled her gaze to her right. Simon lay on his front beside her, head resting on his arms, his breathing rhythmic with sleep. She sighed peacefully but a prickle of sadness soon chased away her soft smile. Where would they be this time tomorrow? What did today hold?

As she recalled just what day this was, happiness quickly returned. Slipping out of bed, she dropped to her knees on the bare boards and clasped her hands on the coverlet. She'd forgotten to say her prayers last night, she remembered with a guilty bite of her lip. She'd been so exhausted, it had slipped her mind entirely – she'd make up for it now, give double thanks. Thrice, even; today of all days. 'Dear sweet Jesus, son of God . . .' she murmured piously to the ceiling.

'You and your ruddy prayers.'

Pip opened one eye at the quiet words, thick with tiredness, spoken above her head. Simon was watching her, he too through one eye. She gave a quick smile. 'Does no harm.'

'Aye, and no good, neither. Yet still, you never miss a day, d'you?'

'Well, I did yesterday so must make up for it, now. Quieten down a minute, eh, while I do. Besides, look at the fortune bestowed on us yesterday. Proof of God's goodness, this is. Aye, he delivers, lad. The least we can do in return is give thanks.'

Simon looked as if he would say more, but instead shrugged and turned back over in the bed. Closing her eyes again, Pip resumed her prayers. She'd just finished and, having risen, stood grinning watching Mack, tongue poking from the side of his mouth as he inched closer to the window to get a closer look at the bird still hopping beyond the pane, when the door opened.

Tabby entered, an earthenware dish covered with a muslin cloth in her hands. Even at this early hour, she appeared dead on her feet; Pip's heart contracted for her. She and Cook had gone above and beyond for them last night, must have snatched barely a few hours' sleep between then and now. By, but they were lovely, and selfless too, aye, the pair. She smiled warmly. 'Good morning, Tabby, and a very merry Christmas to thee.'

The girl shoved the door shut with her hip. 'The same to you, an' all, Pip,' she said, smiling. 'Here you are. Cook sends this with instructions to rest yourselfs and she'll be up to see youse shortly.' She placed the dish on the bedside chest and wiped an arm across her brow. 'By, it's bloomin' chaos in the kitchen down there. The poulterer's boy were late this morning delivering the turkey, which had Cook flapping around like one herself, squawking curses. And I've been watching the ruddy Christmas pudding while it's steaming since dawn – and there's a few hours yet to go, too – to ensure it don't boil dry, for woe betide if it should. Cook wouldn't think twice about the rotten delivery boy and his late bird, then; she'd stuff and roast me instead, I reckon.

'And Miss Lucy's for making the workload twice as hard, her careering in and out every two minutes. A reet ball of excitement, she is, this morning. 'Ere, and Hardman, the housemaid, she's got the divil's own temper on her, has had to dust and polish and sweep the kitchen and passageways and rooms with extra care, it being a special day, like. And all that besides lighting the fires, making beds and the hundred and one other chores required – not to mention seeing to the master's wants.

'It's more staff we need, that's what. Ay, we'll be crawling to our beds by the day's end, you'll see. Anyroad . . .' She jerked her head. 'Eat up, then, afore it grows cowd. And if you've room after that lot, and the family leave owt – they've only partook of a light breakfast today, mind: lamb chops, mashed potato and griddle cakes; oh and baked apples with sweet cream . . .'

The children gazed at each other then back to Tabby in amazement. That was a *light* breakfast? By!

'But, well,' the girl continued, 'if there's any leftovers, which there usually is, I'll keep them warming for youse by the fire. Meantime, I'll fetch thee up some coffee and . . .' Lifting the pitcher out of its matching bowl on her way to the door, she continued over her shoulder, 'I'll fill this with hot water while I'm about it. You can see to your ablutions after your breakfast.' In the next moment, she was gone again.

'What is it, Pip?' Having rapidly lost interest in the robin at the mention of food, Mack came to stand beside her, eyes fixed on the dish.

She lifted the cloth and licked her lips. 'Eeh, look now!'

With a yawn and a stretch, Simon was sitting up in bed as she spoke. He too peered at the fare and his stomach let out a loud growl, making them giggle. He rubbed his hands together. 'Let's have it, then. You and Bread sit down on the bed, here, and we'll have ourselfs a feast. By, it smells gradely.'

Helping themselves to the kidneys and bacon and bread, they ate in silence; only now, they didn't wolf the food down as they had the previous night and beyond. That all-consuming hunger they were so used to wasn't here this morning, thanks to Cook's generosity yesterday. Moments later, Tabby returned with the promised coffee, the mugs clinking softly in her hands, and the filled pitcher lodged in the crook of her arm.

'Ta, thanks,' they each said, relieving her of the steaming drinks and blowing at them before sipping tentatively.

'Grub all right for you, was it?' At their nods, she lifted the empty dish and again wiped an arm across her glistening brow. 'Right, back to the fray.' She pulled a face, grinned, then was gone once more.

Filling the washbowl midway with clean water, Pip and the lads washed their hands and faces as instructed then sat back on the bed, unsure what to do. When the doleful peal of St Silas's bell from adjoining Ashton Old Road mingled with the toll of Ardwick Green's St Thomas's, they rose and crossed to the window. All along the street, residents, their servants in tow, were answering obediently the call to join as one to give thanks and celebrate Christ's birth. Then *their* front door opened and there emerged the man they now knew to be Mr Philip, with a lady, her hand resting lightly on his arm – Miss Lucy's mother Mrs Goldthorpe, they surmised.

Another lady followed close behind. *Miss Josephine?* Pip asked herself, wondering why in heaven Cook had spoken of her so; she didn't look very poor, not in any sense of the word. Then there appeared bonny Miss Lucy with the sour-faced nursemaid, Finch. Lastly, Hardman and Tabby took up the rear. She knew that later, as was customary, the domestics would enter the house the same way as they had left: through the main door with the family, it being a special occasion.

Within seconds, they had merged with the high-spirited throng strolling leisurely through the crisp morning air.

Some minutes later, footfalls, heavier than the scullery maid's before, sounded on the stairs. The door opened and Cook appeared, face cherry red from the heat of the kitchen.

'By, them rotten stairs shall be the death of me . . . Morning, lass, lads. Family are away at church; I'd have been up to youse sooner, only I had the master to see to, like.'

'Morning, Cook, and a merry Christmas to thee,' offered Pip, as she had to Tabby. The response she received now, however, was tinged with laughter.

'Oh aye, for some, lass.' Then her eyes flicked to the

79

picture propped behind the mirror and her smile faded. She repeated, on a whisper this time, 'For some.'

Pip followed her gaze. Despite her curiosity as to the pretty girl frozen in time, whom she and the lads had wondered about last night, she knew better than to be bold enough to ask questions. 'You look tired,' she murmured instead. 'We kept you from your bed last night, Tabby, an' all . . . Sorry. And ta, ever so.'

Cook's face softened. She crossed the space and tapped Pip's head. 'Now don't take on so. No thanks from you, for none are needed. I did only what anyone would with a beating heart in their breast.'

Simon let out a snort. 'Then the people of Manchester must be living miracles, passing their days with a hollow space where theirs should be, for we sure as hell don't see much from most.'

'There's many a desperate soul beyond these walls, lad. Folk can't give what they've not got.'

'Aye, and I'll tell you summat.' Fixing the woman with a solemn stare, he nodded. 'It's them what has nowt or barely nowt theirselfs what give the most. Truly, aye. And that says a whole lot about the way of things and the world, its workings. Oh, it does.' He breathed slowly then asked, 'What's the deal then, missis? Put us straight, eh? Why we still here?'

Cook lowered her bulk into the chair opposite. 'Well,' she said, looking at them in turn, 'I'm for offering youse a home if you want it.'

A hot rush of something, as if a fiery river had burst its banks, flowed through Pip and she gasped. She became aware of Mack gripping her hand and she squeezed back. Simon's face, however, showed none of the emotion they were feeling at this incredible offer; though there was definite shakiness in his next word:

'Why?'

'Why, you ask?'

'That's right. And how; how are we meant to stay hidden? Surely it'd only be a matter of time—?'

Cook cut off his questions with a chuckle. 'Course it would, aye. You'd be sniffed out straight away. That's why I intend on telling the master this evening.'

'But . . .?' Pip shook her head. 'Happen you get the boot?'

'Me? Huh! Never.'

She didn't know what to make of that statement – Cook had delivered it with such sureness. 'He'll not mind? He'll not, really?'

Pulling her aching body from the chair with a groan, Cook turned for the door. 'Don't youse fret about a thing. Now, sit tight a while longer. Best for now that you stop out of the road and from under my feet. There's work enough still for ten down in that kitchen and unless I shift myself back to it and lively, I'll be terrible behind and there'll be merry hell to pay upon the family's return. They'll be wanting their grub after that long sermon – a simple luncheon it is today, mind, thank the Lord. Aye, oyster patties and cold beef, bread and cheeses, mince pies and the like. 'Ere, and my spiced punch . . .'

Again, the children shared a disbelieving stare. It was a wonder these rich hadn't split their bellies before now.

'By, puts heat right through your innards, that does,' Cook was saying now, 'and a good thing, too, on a winter's day like this 'un. I'll be sure to save youse a half-glass each for later. How's that hoof of yourn bearing up, little one?' she asked, motioning to Mack.

'Only a bit sore today, missis.'

She nodded. 'I'll apply another dose to it when I've a

81

minute to catch my breath. Now, youse good kiddies rest easy, get back in the bed awhile and give your bodies some kip. You'll see me again soon, God willing. I just pray them bleedin' soufflés rise . . .' she grumbled to herself, hurrying from the room.

Alone again, the children sat staring at each other, neither moving nor speaking, for a good minute. For all that was swirling around each of their brains, Pip knew, was the magical, unbelievable, *glorious* words that mammoth-hearted woman had uttered. A home? For them? *Here?*

'Oh, lads . . . lads . . .'

Pip's words came on a shuddering breath. At Mack's watery grin and Simon's wink, she dropped her face into her hands and sobbed her soaring heart out.

*

The ringing of the church bells, announcing the end of service, carried to the children some time later but now, none stirred. They had taken Cook's advice. Snuggled up to Mack beneath the blankets, Simon beside them, Pip blinked lazily then closed her eyes once more.

It felt queer doing nothing. Not having to worry where the next morsel was coming from, tramping the cobblestones looking for shelter for the night or fretting how they would keep warm. But nice, aye. Wonderful nice.

'Right, luncheon's finished,' Cook's voice sounded, making them start. They sat up rubbing their eyes and she jerked her head. 'Come on down to the kitchen while we've got five minutes. We'll not be disturbed. The household have took to their rooms for a nap afore dinner.'

'Oh, Tabby will be glad of that,' said Pip. 'She looked fit to drop earlier.'

Amusement rumbled up from Cook's stomach and burst from her mouth in a hearty guffaw. 'Not the servants, lass. By, could you imagine the like – God alive! Nay, it's the family I speak of. By!' she said again, shaking her head.

Pip didn't think that was fair; after all, the domestics were the ones who had done all the hard work, with more to come. All the family had done was visit church and eat themselves silly. Dirty work was done by unseen hands; the middle class wouldn't dream of sullying theirs . . . However, hers wasn't to reason the rights and wrongs of matters, so she didn't. She slipped from the bed and she and the lads trotted behind Cook down to the kitchen.

Through the entrance leading to the scullery they saw Tabby standing with her back to them washing up a mound of pots in scalding water, her mottled hands and forearms redder still from the heat. Yet she was bearing it well, must be used to it after all. The housemaid, to Pip's relief, wasn't present.

'Hardman's clearing the dining room,' offered Cook, as though seeing her thoughts. 'Now, when she enters, you let me do the talking. Best she's told first. We'll deal with the master and his family later, after dinner.'

Mack, young as he was, appeared unfazed at this, didn't really understand the enormity of the situation. Simon, however, was biting his lip; seeing this, nerves twisted Pip's stomach. If the older lad was apprehensive, then she too had cause to be. Simon always knew best.

Besides the table, piled with vegetables ready for peeling, the room had been scrubbed and tidied and amber light from the fire's glow gave the space a comforting feel. Delicious smells of sage and onion and cranberries mingled with that of the roasting bird and despite their good breakfast, Pip's stomach rumbled. She was certain Cook could read minds when, again, she seemed to hear her musings:

'My spiced punch and some gingerbread for youse in a minute, my lovies. First things first . . . Prop your hoof on t' chair beside you, young 'un.'

As promised, the woman tended Mack's foot and applied a fresh bandage. Then she ladled from a huge silver bowl a dark and delicious-smelling drink into three glasses and passed them across, followed by a plate of still-warm biscuits. Their eyes continually flicked to the green baize door as they ate and drank, knowing Hardman's return was imminent yet willing her not to appear. Lord above, when she discovered them sat here . . . She was a vicious piece and no mistake. She'd run to spill their guilt to the master in a heartbeat, surely. Then where would they be? Back on the streets, scratching by as ever, all this lot snatched from under their noses. Tears thickened Pip's throat, making it impossible to swallow another morsel. She returned the gingerbread to the plate and folded her hands in her lap, eyes downcast.

From a small wooden barrel in the corner of the kitchen the cook had filled a glass of beer for herself; sipping this, she watched them as they ate. Now, she addressed them quietly. 'There's things need speaking of if you're to stop on beneath this roof. Now I'm not one for shoving my nose into other folks' affairs, but well . . . If I'm to fill the master in on the situation, make him see this is for the good of youse, I'll need to know a few things.'

Simon's eyes narrowed. 'Like what?'

'Like just who youse are. Where you've sprung from. How in God's name you've ended up in this sorry position. Now I ain't blind to the needy – by, there's many a poor soul what calls those streets out there home. It's a sad state the world's in, it is. But youse . . . three siblings adrift, with no one to offer a kind hand? No family, at all? How's that come to be?'

Pip spoke first: 'We ain't siblings, Cook. In fact, we ain't related at all, not none of us.'

The woman's eyebrows stretched to meet her hair-line. 'Then how did youse . . .?'

'He don't really recall.' Simon nodded to Mack. 'I stumbled upon him living in a ginnel up Deansgate some year and a bit since, in a state of collapse from the hunger.' The older lad shrugged. 'I took pity on him, took him along with me.'

'You've looked after him ever since?'

Simon nodded.

'Providing for yourself must have been struggle enough?'

Again, he shrugged. 'I sometimes sold newspapers when I were able, or shined shoes when I'd the tools. Otherwise . . . You allus find a means to an end when you're that needing of a crust. I did what I could to get us by.'

'You're a good boy, and you yourself no more than a babby—'

'Bread might be a babby yet, can't be more than four year old I reckon, but I ain't, missis. I'm twelve – or thereabouts.'

Pip was surprised. She'd thought Simon older. They were in fact the same age.

Cook cast him a soft, sad smile. 'Aye. Aye, lad. And the lass, here?'

'She met Bread and me coming up a year ago, now.'

Pip looked over the boys with gentle eyes. 'They let

85

me go along with them and I were more than a bit grateful of it.' She cocked her head to Cook. 'Safety in numbers, you know?'

'Aye. Eeh. I don't know what to say to this. A crying shame, it is, and no mistake. Another thing while we're about it: why do you, Simon, address the mite here so?'

'Bread were all he whined for night and morning in t' beginning – fair drove him mad, had the hunger. Me an' all, aye, his crying. It sort of stuck.' The older lad threw a thumb towards Pip. 'She don't like it, mind, gave him his new name. I don't reckon he even recalls, now, what name he were given at birth. Be it Bread or Mack, suppose any's better than none, eh?'

Another sad smile touched Cook's mouth. 'And thee? When did you find yourself destitute? I must know the ins and outs, lad, you understand?' she added when Simon hesitated.

He flicked his gaze to the fire. 'Father wed again barely a month after Mam died and the piece he chose . . . I've called the streets my home for half my life, now, and never regretted forra second bolting from that house. She were the divil's own spawn, made my life hell. She never wanted me, see, only Father. He couldn't see it, believed it were me being difficult. In t' end, he wanted nowt to do with me, neither. She saw to that, turned his thinking. I couldn't bear it, nay, had to get away, for her cruelty . . .' He paused, cleared his throat. 'I'd have finished up in a box afore much longer, else.'

The room was silent. Sorrow filled everyone's eyes, none more so than Pip's. She'd never heard Simon speak of his past before; and no wonder, she realised now, watching him fiercely trying to bite back tears. Oh, but she was sorry for him. What must he have suffered;

not to mention afterwards, too, since making his escape. *Six*. Half his life! The poor, poor lad . . .

'Then I'd say you're well shot of them, love, the pair.' The woman patted his hand twice then turned to Mack. 'You, young 'un. Where's your mam and father, your family? Come on, now, you can tell Cook.'

He screwed his eyes, as though trying to remember. Then his face cleared and his bottom lip trembled. 'Granny,' he whispered.

'You lived with your granny, lad?'

'Aye.'

'And where's she now?'

He lifted his small shoulders in a shrug. 'She went. The house got shut and I couldn't get in.'

Cook's brow furrowed. 'Your granny shut you out of the house?'

'Nay. The man.'

'The man . . .? The landlord? Is that who you mean?'

Mack nodded. Cook shared a look with Pip and Simon. 'She had it away on her toes without him, and the landlord took the house back, leaving the lad destitute?'

They didn't have an answer.

'Is that what occurred, young 'un?' Cook pressed Mack gently.

He blinked a few times in confusion, not understanding. Then: 'Granny coughed and then she went.'

The three of them nodded slowly as realisation dawned. The youngster hadn't been abandoned at all – at least, not intentionally. His granny had grown sick and passed away. Clearly, there had been no one else, or perhaps nobody willing, to take the boy in. He didn't seem to remember his parents; had they died much earlier and his granny had taken him on? It made sense, explained the situation he found himself in once she

87

was no longer here. He'd simply fallen to a life on the streets, just like that, alone and forgotten. Eeh, the poor babby.

'Well.' Cook's eyes were suspiciously bright. 'How about this: you can look upon me as a new granny, if you'd like. What says you to that? That do thee?'

Slowly, Mack's face spread in a smile. 'Aye, missis. Ta, missis.'

Nodding, Cook cleared her throat a few times. 'Same goes for the two of youse, an' all,' she told Pip and Simon, who cast her shy looks, smiling, their pleasure evident. 'Now, we've heard the lads' woeful tales ... What's your story, lass?'

Panicked tears immediately sprang to Pip's eyes. Sensing her reluctance – speaking of her mam hurt too much – the woman nodded understandingly.

'I know, lass, I know; memories can be both a blessing and a curse, it's true. But just maybe, you'll feel the better for putting words to it. Unburden that mind of yourn, you'll see.'

Nay, nay, you don't understand ... what she did ... How can I utter it? Pip agonised, almost tasting the shame of it. She took a shuddering breath. Then her lips parted – and in the same instant, the green baize door opened too and the housemaid appeared.

Chapter 6

JESS HARDMAN STOPPED dead in her tracks.

After scanning the three faces at the table with bemusement, she turned her gaze to Cook. 'What's this, then?'

'Sit down a minute, Hardman.'

The housemaid looked as if she'd ask more of the older woman; then silently, she crossed to a chair.

She didn't recognise who they were; their introduction to soap and water had clearly had a bigger impact on their appearance than they believed, Pip realised, then terror-filled dread returned to her, pushing out all else. Under the table, she felt for Simon's wrist and squeezed.

'You cleared the dining room?' asked Cook.

'Aye.'

'Proper, like?'

'I said, didn't I?' Hardman retorted but her words were tinged with distraction rather than irritation. Eyes creasing thoughtfully as they settled on the orphans once more, she folded her arms. 'I'm sure I . . .' Suddenly, recognition finally dawned – her head snapped back on her shoulders. Mouth settling in a thin line, furious disbelief blazed from her eyes. 'I don't . . . What are *these* doing in here?'

Cook's voice was even. 'I'm for letting them dwell here. You gorra problem with that?'

The loud squeak, as the housemaid scraped back her chair, rent the air. She jumped to her feet. 'Too bleedin' right I've a problem! That, that . . .' She thrust a finger towards Simon's face. 'That gutter rat, there, shamed me in front of Mr Philip and the others yesterday. Fortunate it is for thee, an' all, that they were witness to your performance, for I'd have cuffed your head from your neck if they hadn't been there!'

'You swindled me.'

At Simon's quiet response, she made to lunge across the table. The slap that Cook delivered to her face before she could reach him brought her up short. Holding her glowing cheek, she gazed at the older woman open-mouthed.

'Sit that arse of yourn back down.' Cook spoke as calmly as before.

'But—!'

'Do it!'

After a hesitation, the housemaid dropped back into her seat, expression sullen.

'Now.' Folding her arms over her huge bust, the cook addressed her quietly but firmly. 'I've decided that these here kiddies are to stay. Whatever feud exists betwixt you and the lad here, ends now, you hear? And the same goes for thee,' she added to Simon grimly. 'If we're to live beneath this roof together, we must do so peacefully, else it'll be the worst for us all. Right?'

'Mr Philip'll not be best pleased about this—'

'And what of it? The master shall have the say, not his son.'

'You think you can just do as you please in this house, don't you? Well, I'm not standing for it, I tell you—!'

'You'll do as you're bloody well instructed, missy! Nigh on forty year I've toiled for Albert Goldthorpe,' she said, jerking her thumb in the general direction of the master's room beyond the ceiling, 'and his dear wife, God rest her soul. I were here when Mr Philip entered this world, and Miss Josephine afore him, too. So aye, I've a tie with this family – a strong one at that – which goes beyond owt you'd understand. And that which binds us, on my part at least, is love; aye, I'm not ashamed to admit it. My feelings for this family . . . well, most of them, anyroad . . . go beyond mere sense of duty.

'Now, the master knows me and my ways of old. I like to offer the hand of kindness when I'm able, to any soul what needs it.' Her gaze moved over the children. 'These poor mites haven't a single body beneath God's blue sky to care for them. Norra one. Through your actions – aye, yours, missy, you and your nastiness brought them to me –' she pointed out, nodding, when Hardman made to protest, 'they've found theirselfs at Bracken House, and I for one'll not cast them away. And the master, I'm certain, will agree with me. So, it's like this: you put up or ship out, got it?'

For half a minute, the housemaid glared at Simon, Pip and Mack in turn. Then she burst out, 'The workhouse is where they ought to be! That's what them places are meant for, after all: down-and-outs and the like. I'll happily take them along myself in the morning, it's no hardship—'

Tabby's furious gasp cut her off. The scullery maid had been standing silently by the door; now, she stalked towards her. Throwing the cloth she held on to the table, she bunched her hands into fists. 'You talk of the workhouse like you know of it, aye? You know *nowt*, Jess

91

Hardman. I were cast into Fletcher Street Workhouse in yon Bolton town. Ay, didn't know that, did you? That's right; I'm one of these down-and-outs you speak of. And I'll tell you for nothing, I'd not wish the divil hisself in such a place. These kiddies committed no crime deserving of such punishment as the poorhouse bar losing their mams, same as me.'

Cook's tone was soft. 'All right, lass, settle down.'

'Well, she gets on my wick, she does.'

'You could come along in t' morning an' all, then, I reckon – aye, back where you belong!' the housemaid hissed, thrusting her face close to Tabby's.

'Why you spiteful, black-hearted—!'

Cutting off Tabby's tirade and making them all jump, Cook brought her palm down on the tabletop. The room fell silent. Nostrils flared, she turned her stare on Hardman. 'Cease that vicious tongue of yourn, bold piece. Whatever you like to believe, you've not a shred of standing in this house, and you'd do well to remember it. You forget sometimes, I think, your place here. It's the mistress of this establishment you fancy you are, I'm certain, with your selfish manner and false grandeur ways.'

Hardman's face was scarlet with indignation. 'I've more standing than that one!' She thrust her chin towards Tabby.

'That mebbe so, but I'm above the lot of youse put together, missy,' Cook shot back, proving there was no such thing as equality even in the servants' quarters. 'Shall I tell you summat else? D'you know how many domestics I've seen come and go in my time? More than I can count, let me tell thee. Housemaids are ten a penny. You'd do well to remember that, an' all.' She paused with narrowed eyes, as though daring the young woman to make further response. Receiving none, she nodded, indicating that was the end of the matter. 'Now, we've got work to do so we'd best shake ourselfs. You, Tabby, back to the scullery and them dishes. Hardman, get some water on the boil to take up to the family for freshening up when they waken.

''Ere and another thing,' she added to the housemaid as she flounced towards the fire, 'norra word to the rest about these children when you are summoned. It's the master should be informed first, and that I'm for doing myself when the dinner's over and finished with. D'you hear me?'

'Aye.'

'Aye what?'

The audible sound of gritting of teeth was followed by, 'Aye, Cook.'

Again, the woman nodded, satisfied. 'As for youse,' she told a subdued Pip, Simon and Mack, 'go on up back to my room so as not to get under our feet. I'll be along to collect you later to see the master. Be good and rest up. Go on, now.'

Without a word, they did as they were told – rising as one, they crossed to the door. It was clear Cook had spoken the truth, Pip saw, glancing over her shoulder before leaving the room: servants were indeed not afforded the same luxury of resting as were their employers. The pace had instantly picked up. The rush for Christmas dinner was on.

This crew of women saw to the running of the house like a tight ship with Cook at the helm. Nonetheless, thoughts of lounging idly upstairs as they created the family's elaborate fare brought to Pip a stirring of restlessness. If only they had been allowed to stay, she and the lads could have helped out, lessened the harassed servants' workload. She could peel veg well enough, and Simon and even Mack could surely be set to some task or other . . .? Then she caught Hardman's eyes and the hatred spewing from them, and whipping around Pip scurried upstairs after the boys to the safety of the eaves.

*

'Oh, the day has been glorious, *glorious*, from beginning to end – and there is even more fun to come! But anyway, as I was saying, after breakfasting, Mama permitted me to enter the drawing room. The candles, which Papa had carefully placed on the tree's branches, had been lit and they shone like a hundred diamonds. Then the gifts, all wrapped in coloured paper, were given out. There were embroidered pieces for each of us from Aunt Josephine – handkerchiefs and suchlike – and a crystal inkwell for Papa from Mama, and a jewel-studded fan for her from him, as well as earrings *and* a brooch – oh, he does like to spoil Mama so . . .'

Pip sat enraptured as Lucy regaled them all with the wonderful Christmas she'd had. The family had finished dinner shortly before and while the adults had retired to the drawing room, the girl had taken the opportunity to slip to the kitchen for a brief visit.

In the centre of the table stood the now near-stripped turkey. Cook had brought the children down to the kitchen as the dinner was almost through and when Hardman, summoned to the dining room at the meal's end, had carried back the family's leftovers, Pip's mouth had dropped open. It seemed hardly a thing had been touched. *And all that hard work Cook had gone to as well!* she'd thought with sadness and not a little anger. By, it could have fed her, Simon and Mack for two, three days even; and how glad they would have been of it too but a day ago, literally starving to death on those mean streets out there.

That folk behind these fancy walls and clean painted doors lived such extravagant lives, she wouldn't have believed had she not witnessed it herself since entering this house. The privileged lot seemed not to give a single thought to, or care about, the thousands upon thousands clawing for survival a mere few streets away in the slums; that they were forced to do anything – beg on their knees, steal, assault, sell their very flesh for a few coppers – for a few morsels just to stay alive. By, they really hadn't a clue how the real world was – the one they were either blind to or chose not to see, to think on.

'Aye, prime Norfolk bird; only the best for this house,' Cook had announced earlier, carving the remainder to go with the small chicken, vegetables and potatoes for her own, the two servants' and the children's dinners. She'd explained that, as was commonplace, the legs were not removed by the higher classes – only the best part, the breast carved by Mr Philip, had been eaten by the family. The legs and whatever remained went back to the kitchen for the staff. In recognition of rank, Cook and Hardman had got a leg each, whilst Tabby was given the wings – one of which the thoughtful maid had given to Simon, him being the biggest of the three waifs.

Despite the dizzying, heavenly taste, each mouthful more wonderful than the last, Pip had been forced to swallow down something altogether more bitter with the delicious meal: guilt. So many a poor soul back in Ancoats and beyond wouldn't be feasting as they were this day. Some wouldn't have anything at all. It just didn't seem right. No, it didn't.

Yet despite the sting of injustice Pip felt, despite her

feelings of confusion and anger at the cavernous in-equality between a few with everything and the plenty without a thing, she harboured no ill feeling towards the girl sitting before her now. An angel she looked in her stunning burgundy frock, cuffs trimmed with fur, the bodice's tiny buttons winking silver-white in the firelight. And that smile of hers, perfect poppy lips stretched across sparkly teeth. Miss Lucy was lovely, and good-minded to match. Pip felt she could look at her, listen to her, for ever.

'And there was a silver snuffbox for poor sick Grandy and also a silver letter opener – oh, Papa received one of those, too – and a silk-lined sewing basket for Aunt Josephine, and . . .'

When the girl, pink-cheeked with pleasure, eventu-ally came up for air, Pip asked, 'What of you, Miss Lucy? Weren't there owt under yon tree for thee?'

Lucy laughed. 'Well, of course, silly! I was keeping the best part for last. I received three clockwork toys – mice, they are, with long, thin tails – and books, and plum-coloured ribbons for my hair, and a new hairbrush . . . Ooh, and a pincushion in the style of a strawberry; it's quite adorable! And some exquisite mittens, and *two* dolls, not just one as I'd expected, and . . .'

Several times, out of the corner of her eye, Pip spied Simon shaking his head, but ignored him. And when Cook said, 'Now now, Miss Lucy. I'm sure the lass don't want her ears bashing with all this – remember, some folk ain't so fortunate as thee, and it ain't nice to brag,' Pip got in first:

'Nay, oh nay, Cook, I want to hear. By, it's a lovely story.' Clasping her hands together beneath her chin, she sighed dreamily. 'Eeh, you are lucky, Miss Lucy.'

But the young miss had gone a dull red colour.

Dropping her gaze, she bit the inside of her cheek. 'Please forgive me, Pip, boys. I . . . did not think . . . Mama always says that my tongue has a nasty habit of galloping away with itself before my brain has given it permission; I fear she's right.' She patted Pip's hand, smile soft. 'I'll bring my dolls in to show you tomorrow. You may keep them the whole day, if you'd like? I must go now, or Papa will send Finch to look for me and that shan't be a good thing for either of you three.'

Cook nodded. 'That's right. And remember, Miss Lucy, no mention of the children yourself, neither, till I've had words with your grandfather.'

'I shan't utter a thing, Cook, certainly not. Oh, I do hope Grandy gives his consent. He will, won't he?' she asked, gazing up with her beautiful big eyes at the large woman.

Cook threw her a wink. 'You hop along now, Miss Lucy, and enjoy the rest of your night.'

'Thank you, Cook. Oh, I shall! I'm to recite some poetry, and there will be songs to sing, and Mama will play the pianoforte, then we shall play blind man's buff . . .' The girl broke off with a sheepish grin. 'Sorry. I'm doing it again, aren't I? Oh! Oh, Cook!' Clicking her tongue suddenly, she tapped her forehead. 'I almost forgot. Here, for you. And there is one for both Hardman and Newby. Go on, take them.'

Hearing their names mentioned, the two younger servants abandoned their chores to sidle to Cook's side. The older woman, after taking the flat parcel from Miss Lucy, pulled back the paper. Squares of snowy material stared back – Cook gasped. Fingering the shaky pink lettering in the corner of one handkerchief, her eyes were bright.

'Eeh, now . . . Bless your young heart.'

'That says *M.M.*, for you. And those, *J.H.* and *T.N.* – they are yours,' she told the others.

Tabby blinked back at her, amazed; even Hardman managed to crack a smile of pleasure. 'Ta, thanks, Miss Lucy,' they said in unison, stroking the gifts.

'Aunt Josephine has been teaching me embroidery.'

'That'll be good for her.' Cook's voice dropped. 'How's she been the day?'

Lucy adopted the same solemn countenance as the servant. 'Well enough. And Papa insists she'll feel better still, later, in the company of their guests.' The girl looked doubtful at this – then her mouth stretched in a wicked smile. 'You know Aunt Josephine got the ring in the Christmas pudding?'

Earlier, Cook had amazed Pip, Simon and Mack, who had breathed a collective 'Ahh' at the sight of the glistening brown cannonball, its surface dazzling with blue flame, on its way to the dining room. Beforehand, as she'd adorned it with a sprig of holly and soaked it in brandy to set alight, Cook had told how secreted amongst the fat raisins inside were several small tokens: a coin, ring and silver thimble, which represented different meanings to the finders.

Now, Lucy's smile grew into a grin. 'That means she shall be married within a year; oh, Cook, her face was a picture! Secretly, I rather hoped she'd get the thimble, which meant she'd have remained a spinster for at least another year. Huh – that would have shown Mr Sutton-Shaw! Grandy found the coin and shall enjoy good wealth. Papa is funny – I rather think he'd hoped for it, for he didn't look too pleased!'

Cook's lips twitched as she hid a smile. 'Aye, I'll bet he didn't. Anyroad . . .' She motioned to her gift. 'Tha did reet good. I shall treasure it.'

'Thank you. Though I'm afraid I have a way to go . . .' The girl pulled a sorry face at her attempts. It fell further when she glanced to Pip, Simon and Mack looking on. 'I would have made one for the three of you had I known . . . I shall make extra special gifts for you all next year,' she promised with a nod.

Pip's face spread in a smile. 'Ta ever so, Miss Lucy.'

'You're quite welcome. Now I really must be getting back or else—'

'Child? Child, where have you got to?'

The girl in question poked her tongue at the door and Finch calling for her beyond. 'That woman is truly the worst thing to happen to me!' she stated in her tinkling voice, sounding every inch a woman full grown rather than a mere child. 'Oh, Pip. Nursemaids are such a trial, aren't they?'

Though Pip was at a loss how to answer this – what on earth did she know about such things? – she felt happy Miss Lucy had asked. It was as though she forgot sometimes that Pip wasn't of her class. And didn't that, surely, bode well for the future? Pip didn't care a fig, and if Miss Lucy didn't either . . . They were going to be firm friends, she just knew it. 'Oh, um . . .' she responded after a moment, 'Aye, I'm sure they must be.'

'Well, bye for now!' With a flick of her wrist, Miss Lucy gave them a wave and on a flash of puffy white petticoats and bouncing black curls, skipped from the kitchen.

Without having to be told, Hardman and Tabby disappeared to resume their duties – though a smile hovered about their mouths, the pleasure at their gifts seeming to have distracted them from their exhaustion. Cook refilled her glass from the beer barrel and lifted down a heavy, age-faded book from a shelf set in an alcove by the fire. Returning to the table, she leafed through the pages with a soft frown.

'Surely to God in heaven they ain't wanting yet more grub the day?' asked Simon, indicating the recipe book with his thumb.

Cook gave him a bland smile. 'A light supper will do them. They've their guests arriving later once Miss Lucy's away to her bed.'

He shook his head, but Pip didn't catch his next words nor Cook's response – her attention was still on the door.

I wonder what it's like in there? she thought. She envisioned the family sitting around a roaring fire, lights from candles adorning the lavishly decorated tree twinkling merrily on their smiling faces. She pictured Miss Lucy and her mama and papa. What must it be like to experience such wonderment, to share a Christmas such as they had with each other? Family. A proper one, with a mother and father and an aunt and grandfather. And more food than you could eat in a month. And gifts; dolls with china faces and hair ribbons and books. And love. Aye, and togetherness. By, there was nothing greater, surely? The time of their lives was what they were having right now, she'd bet. She sighed longingly.

'All right, there, my lass?'

Pip blinked up into Cook's kind face. A lump had formed in her throat and she was unable to speak. She nodded.

'Good. For I think it's time I introduced you to the master. Don't youse?' Three pairs of eyes stared back at her solemnly. 'He retired to his room after dinner so it's in private we're for speaking with him. We'll not be disturbed.' She rose, straightened her cap then smoothed down her voluminous apron. 'Follow me, then.'

The baize door swished noiselessly at Cook's push and again at their backs, shutting out the kitchen and safety, and Pip and the boys glanced behind them, wishing they could scuttle back to the warm room, their hideaway, free from the danger of possible dismissal. But Cook was striding along the short passageway ahead and they had no choice but to follow. They climbed three wide steps, turned a corner and emerged into a long hall. For a brief moment, all three halted and stared about them in awe.

The brightly polished boards beneath their feet shone like black crystal, reflecting their shoddy boots. Their eyes travelled up and around the dark-red wall-papered walls, huge portraits of stern-looking men and women in thick gilded frames glaring down on them accusingly, as though even they knew these trespassers shouldn't be here beneath this magnificent roof. Small kidney-shaped tables supported by spindly legs dotted the walls here and there, adorned with china pots holding all manner of plants – some large and thick-leafed, some draping across the table's shiny surface, some standing erect like lofty people with their noses in the air . . . Every which way they turned screamed opulence and importance. The children hurried on.

Immediately they turned another bend, the sound of laughter and voices reached their ears and Pip felt her heartbeat quicken. Fixing her eyes on the doors up ahead, she tried to picture the drawing room beyond and the family within. She could hear Miss Lucy, clear sweet voice raised in merriment as she regaled the adults with some tale or other. As though they had acquired a mind of their own, upon coming level, Pip's feet made to halt. Shaking herself, she quickened her pace.

Holding on to the banister, they climbed a set of thick carpeted stairs. Up, up to a broad landing with several doors leading off into the softly lit distance. For the first time since leaving the haven downstairs, Cook swivelled her head to look at them. Then she was off again. She halted at a set of double doors to their left. The master bedroom. Again, she turned and this time, assessed properly the children standing uncertainly before her. After tidying down the lads' hair, tugging at their tattered waistcoats and straightening their jackets, she gave Pip the same attention, shaking out her too-short skirts and running through her hands the two long plaits Tabby had created, to smooth out the unruly curled pieces that had escaped confinement.

She scrutinised the three of them again, then shook her head. 'Might evoke more sympathy were you looking a little more wanting,' she muttered to herself, ruffling the lads' hair then Pip's. Stepping back, she eyed them once more, her narrowed gaze thoughtful. 'Mind, youse looking sloppy might garner the wrong impression, like . . .' she told herself on reflection and again she began tidying their hair. A deep but tired-sounding voice floated through the doors, halting her hand:

'Who goes out there?'

The woman turned a hopeful look to the children. 'Well, here goes nowt. Best foot forward, loves.' Putting back her shoulders, she grasped the brass knobs and pushed open the doors.

Chapter 7

A GOOD FIRE crackled in the grate. Opposite, in the glow of its dancing flames, the master of Bracken House shifted in the large bed to turn his smiling face towards the doorway.

Albert Goldthorpe opened his mouth to utter a greeting. Then his gaze moved from the cook, standing straight-backed, hands clasped in front of her, to Pip and the boys by her side. His lips drew together and his bushy grey eyebrows followed suit. Finally, he brought his quizzical stare back to the servant. 'Mabel?'

That he'd addressed the cook by her Christian name surprised Pip – Simon, too; glancing at him, she saw that his frown matched her own. What happened next, however, shocked her to the core.

Cook shut the doors – and this seemed to signal that she was safe to be herself; away from the rest of the household's prying eyes and ears, she visibly relaxed. Releasing a long sigh, she crossed to the bed. 'Budge yourself, lad. My bleedin' pins are fair done in.' Nudging aside the master's legs beneath the coverlet with her bottom, she sat none too gently on the edge of the bed. 'Eeh, aye. That's better.'

Lying close together on a chaise longue to the side of the window, two large dogs peeped up sleepily – the animals she'd seen last night on the Green with Tabby, Pip realised. Then her head snapped back to the bed as the master repeated, 'Mabel—?'

'Aye, I'm getting to it,' Cook cut in quietly, eyes flicking to the children. 'You see, Albert, it's like this: the bitter cold drove these poor young wretches to yon house last night. It's safe to say they've norra soul betwixt them, neither. What were I meant to do, I ask you? Cast them out of a Christmas Eve? Now you know me, I couldn't do that.'

The master's gaze travelled across the room. He studied them in turn. Then: 'Come here, children.'

Automatically, Pip and Mack looked to Simon for confirmation. He made towards the bed and they followed close behind.

'Your name, young man?'

He dragged his cap from his head and clutched it in both hands. 'Simon, sir. This here . . .' He drew the younger boy forward. 'This is Br— Mack.'

'And you, lass?'

Looking at him fully, Pip felt herself shrink under his deep-grey stare. Even in his current position, pale and invalided in his bed, he cut a striking figure. His silver-specked black hair and drooping moustache of the same colour framed a strong but open face. Becoming aware that she'd been staring at him too long, she swallowed and dipped her knee. 'Sir . . . Pip, sir.'

'They're a well-mannered lot, as you can see,' Cook said; not in a wheedling tone, merely stating a fact. That she hadn't need to beg or harangue this man was clear to them all. Master and servant existed not between them. They appeared almost as equals.

'You're orphans?' At their nods, Albert scrutinised them more closely. 'I must say, you appear surprisingly neat and clean for destitute children. How is that so?'

'Missis Cook washed us, in the tub afore the fire.' Mack nodded, smiling. 'And Tabby helped, and my feet ain't half better, sir.'

Surveying the chirpy mite's innocent face, the corner of Albert's mouth lifted. 'Is that so? And what, pray, was the matter with your feet, lad?'

'They hurt; bad, like. Missis put an ointment on and they went better. Are your trotters playing silly beggars with you, an' all, sir? Is that why you're abed when it's not even late?'

Pip shot Mack a horrified look, sure that his boldness would invoke the adults' wrath, but instead, Cook and Albert chuckled.

'Actually, yes, in a manner of speaking. I injured my ankle some weeks past falling from my horse—' He broke off on a rasping cough and when Cook had helped him take sips from a crystal tumbler on the bedside table, added, 'I've felt rather unwell since, seem to have developed a nasty chest illness into the bargain, as you can see.'

'Ask the missis, here, to rub some of her medicine on your body. It'll make thee better, sir, it will—'

'That's quite enough of that sort of talk, young 'un.' Cook's face had turned several shades redder. 'Rub . . . *indeed*! Did you ever hear the like!' Amusement creased the master's eyes; throwing him a stern look, she cleared her throat loudly. 'Now, as I were saying, these mites, they've no one, Albert. And nowt, whilst we've aplenty. And they'd work their keep, I'd see to that. They'd be no drain upon thee or yon house, nor would you or the family know their presence, for they'd be out of the way in my kitchen.'

All laughter had left the man's face; he steepled his hands on the bedclothes, eyes half closed in contemplation. 'How can you be certain they really do have no

105

one at all, no guardians out there somewhere who at this very moment are worrying themselves sick over their whereabouts and welfare?'

Cook cast them a pitying look. Then briefly, she filled the master in on Simon and Mack's circumstances.

'So you, lad, cannot actually claim orphan status. You have no way of knowing whether your father still indeed lives.'

Thrusting his hands deep into his pockets, Simon stared down at his boots. 'I'm as good as, sir, and that's the truth.'

'And a damn sight better off for it, too, by all accounts,' muttered Cook, the anger when relating his past to the master still evident in her voice. When Albert inclined his head in quiet agreement, she next turned her attention to Pip. Slowly, her brow creased – she nodded in remembrance. 'Tha didn't get the chance earlier when pasts were being aired. What *is* your story, then, lass?'

Everyone was watching, waiting; Pip clasped her hands together in front of her to stop them from shaking. She'd known the questions would arise again some time and now they had. And she'd have to tell, she'd have to, though the thought of uttering the words made her guts twist with pain and that crippling shame . . .

'Young miss? You've gone as pale as a pound of tripe. Are you quite well?'

The master's concern brought a lump to her throat and hot tears to her eyes. She swallowed desperately. 'I . . . I . . .'

'Lass?' Cook was speaking now. 'Remember what I said, that the telling shall lift the weight from your mind and you'll be the better for it? D'you recall that?'

Pip nodded. 'Aye. I . . . I do, Cook.'

'It's all right.'

The murmured reassurance from the taller lad by her side brought upon Pip a warm sense of calm. She turned to look at him. The scowl he always wore was there, oddly comforting in its familiarity. The eyes that locked with hers were slightly creased and though he said nothing more, she felt the pressure from his arm touching hers increase as he leaned closer.

Bringing her gaze back to the master, she wetted her lips. 'I have no parents, sir, for my father died afore I were born. And my mam ... My mam took her own life.'

In the deafening silence, a lump of coal shifted in the grate, sending crimson sparks fizzing and popping up the chimney. One of the dogs lifted an ear and an eyelid, sighed drowsily then went back to sleep. No other sound was heard until, from somewhere deep in her gut, a jagged sob rose and tore from Pip's throat. That was the first time she'd spoken those words aloud. Tears, hot and salty, burst forth to cascade down her cheeks and she could do nothing but stand gasping, struggling desperately to wrench out air through the black pain clogging her chest.

Cook was on her feet. Her arms, like fleshy warm wings, enveloped her. She buried Pip's cheek in her mountainous bosom and with a hand stroking the top of her head, murmured soothingly, 'Now that's all right, that's all right. Now you let out that hurt and Mabel May shall hug it all away. That's right, lass. Aye, I'm here.'

'All right, Mabel.'

The woman glanced around at Albert's words. 'You mean ...?'

'The children can stay. Must, in fact. I insist.'

'Ay, lad. It's a pure gold soul you possess and no

107

mistake. You'll not regret it. And I'll make sure you ain't troubled in any way, neither. You'll not even know they're here. Ta, ta.'

Pip couldn't breathe, couldn't think, couldn't *believe* . . . God above, was it really true? Had her ears heard right or was she dreaming? Oh. Oh!

'I rather think it's you who should be thanked, Mabel, not I,' Albert said on a smile – to which three voices immediately responded:

'Ta! Ta, Cook! Ta, master! Oh, ta!'

'It's a heaven-sent stroke of luck you've had bestowed upon you, crossing paths with this woman, here. I trust you realise that.' The master's face was suddenly serious. 'She has a heart bigger than anyone I've ever known. Don't give me, but more importantly Mabel, cause to regret my decision tonight.'

'We'll not, nay never. Oh sir, Cook!' Pip's tears were falling once more, only now for a completely different reason. She still couldn't quite believe this. *Please, Lord,* she prayed inwardly. *Please don't let me be asleep. And if I am, don't let me waken just yet. Let me enjoy the magic of this moment a while longer.* They were staying! They had a home!

Forgetting his poorly foot, Mack performed an on-the-spot jig, winced, then laughing took up the act again, face alive with utter joy, making them all smile. Snatching Pip and Simon's hands, he pulled them in a stumbling dance: 'Diddle-dee, diddle-dee. A dwelling place for me, thee, thee!'

Following Cook's lead, Albert threw back his head and laughed heartily. In that moment, the doors were thrust wide and in barged Philip Goldthorpe.

Pip and Mack had held back in the street when Simon confronted this gentleman over Hardman's

108

wrongdoing – now, from the safety of Cook's shadow, Pip took in his appearance properly. Tall, well dressed, beetle-browed and dark-eyed, he possessed a formidable air. Collar-length hair as black as his father's, but free of silver, brushed the stiff white material as he swivelled his head around the room. He surveyed the scene, expression serious.

'May I ask what on earth is going on?' Though Philip spoke quietly, there was a hard edge to his tone. 'Father? What is the meaning of this? Who are these . . . people?'

Cook answered for him. 'I planned on informing you and Mrs Goldthorpe on our way back to the kitchen. Though seeing as you're here, now, Mr Philip . . . The master's kindly given permission for these poor little 'uns to dwell at Bracken House. As I promised him, so I'll tell you the same: their presence shall have no bearing on thee, nor the rest of the family for that matter. They'll work for their keep and will be under my watchful eye in yon kitchen below. The arrangement will prove no trouble to any one of you, for none shall arise. I'll see to that.'

Before the master's astonished-looking son could respond, Mack piped up, 'We'll not pilfer no chickens like that moggy did and get ourselfs booted out. We'll not, sir, 'onest.'

'Hush, child,' Cook murmured. She turned back to Philip. 'I'll leave you and the master in peace. I've my duties to be getting back to.'

Planting his feet apart and blocking her exit, he swung his head around towards his father. 'Is this true? You have given your permission for this?'

'That's right.' Albert nodded curtly as though re-instating the decision. 'As Mabel said—'

'Father, please. I do wish you'd address the servants

109

accordingly.' He moved to close the door, adding over his shoulder, 'You know Caroline's feelings on such matters.'

'Your wife would do well to remember whose house this is. Mabel has been with this family over half a lifetime. I'll address her as I see fit. Besides,' he added, raising an eyebrow, 'there was a time when you wouldn't have had such qualms yourself, lad.'

The air crackled with tension. It was evident that father and son had a stormy relationship; they seemed almost strangers as they stared at one another. Mind, thought Pip, you wouldn't be blamed for thinking it – they barely seemed like they were related at all. Apart from sharing the same colouring, the two men were nothing alike. Even their speech was different. Mr Philip spoke with the same articulateness as Miss Lucy. His father, on the other hand, sounded as if he had started life lower down the social scale, delivering certain words with an unmistakable Lancashire tongue. His use of 'lad' and 'lass', the flat vowels that had a habit of sneaking in amongst the refined tone . . . She frowned curiously then braved a swift look at Philip.

His face had taken on an angry hue; he straightened his shoulders with a lift of his chin. 'Never mind all that. Just what these urchins are doing here is a far more pressing matter, I think.'

'Their names are Simon, Mack and Pip. They are destitute orphans lucky to have survived their harsh life as long as they have. They recently happened across our door in a desperate state. Mabel has taken them under her wing. I for one do not see the harm in it.'

'Don't see . . .! But Father, neither of us know a single thing about them. The housemaid suffered a confrontation with them only yesterday, insists they are no good.' He ignored Cook's slow shake of the head, the anger at disobedient Hardman's loose tongue flashing from her eyes. 'She's threatening to walk unless these waifs are cast out tonight. As you insist on employing the absolute minimum to serve beneath this roof, it's a risk we cannot afford to take—'

'Others, and you along with them, deem the number of servants one possesses a sign of prestige and position. I myself am not concerned with such trivialities – I prefer to keep my circle small. If the housemaid chooses to terminate her employment with us, so be it.'

His son breathed deeply – and Pip did likewise. *Oh, master . . .! Please please, God, let Hardman leave,* she prayed silently. Then Mr Philip was speaking again and she peeped up at him.

'Father.' He spoke slowly, as though trying hard to contain his wrath. 'We are already severely understaffed—'

'We manage perfectly well.'

'*You* may. What about the rest of us? A workforce of this size is utterly inadequate now that my family and I are residing here, too—'

'And whose fault is that?'

Mr Philip's eyes widened then slowly narrowed. But he didn't speak. He stared back at the older man coldly.

'You alone are to blame for your downfall. Your actions are the reason you and your family have been forced to reside beneath my roof at Bracken House. *Your actions.* Remember that.'

'How could I not, when you kindly continue to remind me of the fact,' his son muttered.

'Besides,' continued Albert, unperturbed, 'there are three young people standing right in front of you who shall, Mabel insists, prove advantageous to the household.'

111

'But—'

'But what? You just said yourself we are in need of more staff. There they are!'

'And pray, what use will these ... these *vagabonds* prove to be?'

'Simon?' Albert's voice was purposeful. 'You know your way around a garden, I trust?'

He blinked, surprised. 'Sir?'

'There, that's settled,' Albert stated. 'We could use a hand outside, clearing and tidying and such.'

Simon nodded. 'Aye. Ta, sir. I'll do my best.'

'Of course you will. And you, lass.'

'Me, sir?' Pip's head shot up. She swallowed nervously.

'I dare say you'll make a fine kitchen maid, will prove most helpful to Cook, here.'

'Oh, sir! Sir, I . . . thank you, sir!'

Albert smiled and next trained his gaze on Mack. 'You, young lad, will make yourself useful, I'm certain. Grooming the dogs, here ... Yes, yes, and cleaning boots and suchlike. How does that sound?'

Mack grinned. 'Gradely, sir, aye!'

'Right, well. That's settled.' With a lift of his eyebrow, Albert finally turned back to his son.

'So *now* you change your mind about employing more hands? Because *she* suggests it?' Mr Philip thrust a finger towards Cook.

''Ere, less of the she. I've a name and will be happy if you'd remember it,' the woman growled quietly, hands on hips.

Yet again, Mr Philip ignored her. 'Well, Father? That's how matters stand, is it?'

'You're acting in a most puerile manner. I trust Mabel's judgement implicitly. If it's valets, ladies' maids and the like you've been imagining, my boy, you're sadly mistaken. I will not entertain such frivolity. We need to curtail our outgoings somehow.' The master's voice dropped to a hard murmur. 'Wouldn't you agree?'

Again, that narrowed gaze settled on his father. 'And Hardman?'

'As I said, whether she remains or decides to leave, the choice is hers.'

'But . . . these urchins could be thieves, criminals! You're really willing to take the gamble?'

'And you know all about gambles, isn't that so?' Albert shot back. The air crackled with tension. He leaned back against the pillows. 'Now, return to the festivities with your wife and child. I should like to rest.'

Gazing upon the older man who had now closed his eyes, signalling the conversation had come to an end, Philip breathed slowly. He flicked furious eyes to Cook, who stared back calmly. Then he turned and left the room. When his footsteps had faded, she jerked her head and Pip, the lads close behind, followed her back downstairs.

The hall was empty, the drawing room door fastened closed. Now, no laughter or merry voices travelled through – Mr Philip's return had clearly soured the mood inside. Biting her lip, sorry for Miss Lucy, Pip hurried on.

Cook uttered not a word until they were in the kitchen, where she strode straight to where Hardman sat at the table. Hauling the guilty-eyed maid to her feet, she shook her hard. 'You nasty-minded piece, yer! Running to the master's son the minute my back's turned, is it? By, I've a mind to slat you from this house right here and now!'

'But . . . but . . .' She gazed at Pip and the lads in astonishment. 'Mr Philip assured me . . .'

'And the master put him straight. *He's* decided these little 'uns can stay, as I knew he would, for he's kind hearted, unlike some. So whatever his son assured you . . .' Slowly, Cook's eyebrows drew together. 'Though why he'd go out of his way to defend you so . . .' Her eyes widened. Then she laughed mirthlessly. 'Why, you brainless young . . . I know what you're about, missis. Oh, I know your game, all right.'

Despite the crimson stain now covering the maid's face, she lifted her chin. 'Tha knows nowt!'

'Is that so? Well, let me tell you, Hardman. You ain't the first – by *God* you ain't! – nor shall you be the last, I'll be bound, what's caught Mr Philip's fancy over the years—' She broke off suddenly to glance at Pip and her face hardened in a protective look.

Pip stared back in puzzlement – which grew when she caught Simon staring at her with the same expression as Cook. Then he and the older woman shared a look and as though reassured by whatever silent message passed from him to her, the cook's face relaxed a fraction. Still, Pip didn't understand, but she hadn't time to ponder as Hardman's voice sliced through the silence:

'So then?' A worried note lurked behind the words, belying her defiant stance. 'What's to happen? Does the master want me gone from here?'

'He's for leaving the decision at your door.'

A little of the anger left her face. 'Well . . . I'll have to think on it.'

'Why, you ungrateful young . . .' Cook shook her head. 'You'd do well to think on summat else, an' all, while you're about it.' Stretching to her full height, she stepped closer. 'You . . . and him . . . It ends. Now. You hear me? Else it'll be the worst for you, missis. That's the truth.'

After a moment, Hardman lowered her gaze. Then she resumed her seat without another word.

The room and its occupants passed the next hour in near silence. An uncomfortable undertone held them in its grasp, yet despite this Pip couldn't help her feelings of happiness. Seated quietly at the table, she and the lads shared regular secret smiles as the servants went about their duties. She just wished all beneath this roof could be pleased they were here to stay, but perhaps that would change in time? Surely once Mr Philip and the housemaid saw that they were trustworthy and hard-working to boot, they would realise the error of their snap judgement and things would settle down? At least she prayed it would be so, continually.

At any rate, the master had given his consent. That, when all was said and done, was the most important thing. He made the rules around here. And they had Cook on their side; a formidable supporter who possessed perhaps more standing here than she should, but who would defend and protect them from bad tongues and vicious minds, Pip was certain. Nonetheless, it would be all the better for them were the rest of the household to accept them.

Hardman was summoned to the drawing room, where she was informed Miss Lucy had been put to bed and that the adults' guests were soon to arrive – the signal for Cook to begin preparing drinks and supper. It was to be a standing buffet, which the guests would help themselves from rather than be waited on by a servant. As the older woman dragged herself reluctantly from her chair, Pip rose and sidled across to her. 'Cook? Can I help?' she asked shyly.

She thought for a moment then nodded. 'Aye, all right. Anyroad, it's better you learn now than later.' She

115

pointed across the room. 'Go in the cupboard, there, and fetch me the large mixing dish with the pansies painted around the rim, good lass.'

Smiling in delight – Pip felt a rush of pleasure to be assisting the overworked servant – she did as she was bid. She was just helping Cook measure flour into it when Tabby emerged from the scullery, where she'd been busy.

'What's this, then?'

The cook glanced over her shoulder. 'Young Pip, here, has begun her duties as the new member of our workforce.'

'Eeh, I'm that happy,' Pip told the other girl, puffing out her chest. 'I'll make the master proud, aye, will prove to him what a good kitchen maid I can be – with Cook's help, here, of course.' She smiled up at the woman but when she turned back to Tabby, it slipped from her face. The scullery maid was gazing back open-mouthed, eyes wide with incredulousness. 'Tabby? What is it?'

'*I* should be next in line as kitchen maid! Years, I've been here – how is it Pip's given a position higher than my own the minute she walks through yon door?' she added to Cook, folding her arms. ''Taint right, this. A soddin' scullery maid I'm to remain till the end of time, is that it?'

Cook had the grace to look shamefaced. 'D'you know, I didn't think, lass. It weren't intentional on the master's part – nay, nay, you can be sure of that. Eeh, now, what's to be done?' Gnawing at her lip, she looked from one girl to the other.

'I'll be scullery maid instead, Tabby, if you'd like?' offered Pip without hesitation. She cared not a jot what position she held so long as she could remain here and was earning her keep. 'As you said, you've been here longer than me. It's only right and fair.'

Now, Tabby wore the abashed expression. 'Ah, Pip, you're kindness itself. I shouldn't have snapped at you, nor acted like a babby. It's just ... well, I'd always assumed ... you know?'

'I know.' Pip crossed the space to give an affectionate squeeze to Tabby's arm. 'It's only right you want to climb higher in the ranks; you've earned it. I've seen how hard you work. Please, you be kitchen maid. I'm sure the master won't mither so long as the work's done by someone.'

'Shall I tell you summat, Pip?' Tabby put her arm around her shoulders and hugged her close. 'I reckon me and thee are going to get along just fine. Whatever Hardman or anyone else for that matter reckons about youse stopping on here matters not. You've a friend in me, aye, and allus shall.'

Pip was overcome with emotion. She smiled tearfully from Tabby to Cook, who grinned back, eyes just as bright. And inside her breast, a stirring of belonging, of love, was born. And it felt like she'd come home.

Chapter 8

TABBY'S GRAND NEW position as kitchen maid lasted all of half an hour.

She was used to assisting Cook in the odd chore when she was run ragged: chopping and peeling and helping to dish out or garnish the meals, that sort of thing. Creating the food itself, however, was another matter.

How anyone could muck up meringues as many times as the girl had, Cook exclaimed, she didn't know. First, Tabby had added yolks to a bowl instead of the whites – the latter she'd discarded, and so a fresh batch had to be prepared. Second time around, she got the eggs right, only to add a tablespoon of salt to the mixture instead of sugar. Once more, she'd tried again. So intent was she the third time on getting this attempt right, she'd taken her eye off the mock turtle soup warming on the fire, which boiled over, wasting a fair amount and almost ruining the pan in the process. Cook, not known for her patience at the best of times, was not amused.

'You're all thumbs, missis! God alive, clumsy ain't in it! A dozen eggs, I ask you, to make simple meringues! Wasteful! Wasteful!'

Simon and Mack had struggled to contain their laughter, just as Cook tried to suppress her building crossness. Pip, on the other hand, had watched on with a sorry feeling inside her for the girl. It was clear her enthusiasm at climbing the ladder was rapidly waning – not only was Tabby bad at her new position, she seemed to be thoroughly disliking the whole experience.

After dropping a soufflé which, despite Cook's earlier fears, had indeed risen beautifully – for all the good it did! – Tabby threw her hands in the air in defeat. Before Cook could, she pointed out the obvious: 'I ain't cut out for this malarkey. Pip, please, accept your place back. This here cooking business is foreign to me, and ruddy boring to boot. The scullery's where I should have stayed, where I'd *rather* be, thank you very much!'

Cook had looked relieved but Pip had felt it only right to at least attempt to change Tabby's mind. 'But you've hardly given yourself a chance. Happen you'll start to like it once you've got better at it.'

However, Tabby was adamant. 'Nay, not me. Besides, it's cleaning I'm good at – it's the best I am, aye, I'd go as far as saying. Anyroad, I wish you luck, Pip, for you'll be in need of it!'

As it turned out, Pip wasn't. To her own surprised pleasure, she took to it as though she'd been running her own kitchen for years. Cook was amazed.

'Would you look at that, now! By, you've done grand, lass.'

Gazing proudly at the fare on the table ready to be carried through to the dining room, Pip smiled. Lobster salad, beef and tongue sandwiches, meat rolls and dishes of fowls as well as jellies, blancmanges, tartlets and fresh fruits winked back from their silver beds. 'I only helped prepare them, Cook. It's you what did the real work.'

'You cooked the lobsters, didn't yer? And a treat they

look, an' all. See the lovely colour on them; you mastered the timing just right. You certain you've never toiled in a kitchen afore?'

Pip nodded. 'Well, I helped out Mam where I could. She ... got sick sometimes, and the running of the home fell to me. Not that I minded, like,' she hastened to add lest they thought bad of her mother. 'And nothing like this today. A pauper's feast were what we sat down to each night but we managed.' *We did, aye. And we were happy, the two of us. On good days, anyroad,* she added to herself. A vision of Mam, healthy and happy, swam in her mind. Her throat thickened. Oh, but she missed her. And she hated her, too, at times. For she'd left her, alone, had seen no other way out of the hellish illness that plagued her. But still, more than any other emotion, Pip loved her. Nothing could outweigh that, not ever.

The jollifications were well under way by the sound of it when Hardman re-entered the kitchen some time later, hands piled with empty platters. Before the door swung shut, refined speech and laughter floated through from along the hall beyond. Helping herself to another slice of cake at the table with Simon and Mack, Pip smiled.

She'd detected Mr Philip's voice amongst the rest, now raised in merriment rather than the anger of before in the master's bedroom, and she was glad of it. However unwelcoming he'd been, the displeasure that had spewed from his eyes and mouth regarding them staying and the hurt and embarrassment he'd evoked in her, she wouldn't have wanted the night ruined for him entirely. It was Christmas, after all, and didn't everyone deserve happiness today? She just hoped Miss Lucy had enjoyed it as much.

'Birdy looks to be flagging in the drawing room,' announced Hardman to Cook, emerging from the scullery after depositing her load on to Tabby. 'She has that pasty grey look about her.'

Before rising from her seat, Cook said sternly, 'I've told you afore now, Hardman, don't use that term when referring to Miss Josephine. Remember your place and have some respect.'

The housemaid shrugged. 'I mean nowt by it; she just reminds me of one, is all. Aye, a frickened bird – all wide eyes and perched on the seat's edge, as though she'll take flight and flee any second.'

'Aye, well.' Glancing to the green baize door, Cook pulled at her bottom lip distractedly. 'She can't help it, can she, poor love? It's her blood, that's what. It's bad. It's not flowing as it should, and she's suffering for it. Doctor Lawley reckons as much hisself.'

Again, Hardman raised then dropped her shoulders lazily. 'She could will herself well again, I reckon, if she wanted. If you ask me, it's a matter of choice.'

'Well, no one *is* asking you, are they, so just you still your tongue,' the cook shot back. Then she craned her neck to call, 'Tabby, love? Is Miss Josephine's favourite cup and saucer washed up yet?'

'Aye,' came back the reply. 'I'm just for returning the crockery to the dresser, only I've been busy, like . . .'

Despite the obvious worry that Hardman's earlier statement had evoked, Cook smiled wryly at this. 'Bloody slacking more likely,' she said quietly, adding loud enough for Tabby's ears, 'Well, fetch them through, will thee? The lass is for needing them shortly by the sounds of it. Out last night visiting that Sutton-Shaw one, then again today traipsing to church . . . and now the bother of entertaining the guests in there . . . That's what's done it, aye. She's took on too much and it's burnt her out. Set her back days, this will, you mark my words. It's Mr Philip's doing, that's what.'

'Mebbe it's what she needs, to get out a bit more.'

'You know as well as I, Tabitha Newby, it does her more harm than good.'

Pip and Simon exchanged a puzzled look. Just what was wrong with the master's daughter, at all? They had overheard several references, now, as to her well-being and none good. Bad blood? What did that mean? And Hardman had hinted that it was all in Miss Josephine's mind, that she could, if she chose, make herself well on her own.

Glancing to Cook, now pouring tea into the china vessel Tabby had fetched her, Pip's curiosity got the better of her: 'Please, Cook, what ails her? Miss Josephine, I mean.'

'Aye.' Simon folded his arms. 'I reckon we've a right to know now we're for dwelling here. Happen it's catching – I'm not for getting sick if I can dodge it.'

The woman looked at them in turn. Then she sighed and nodded. 'All right. All right. You see, it's like this—' Whatever she'd been about to reveal was cut short as the door suddenly burst inwards and the ladies of the house stumbled into the kitchen, making them all gasp.

The shorter of the two held the other by the arm and tried unsuccessfully to draw her back out. 'Josephine, this is quite improper! Come along to your room and I shall summon Cook myself—'

'No, no, I ... can't ... Oh! Mabel, thank ... goodness!'

Cook was at Josephine's side in seconds. Murmuring softly, she took the pale and violently shaking woman's elbow and guided her around. 'Breathe, now, miss.

122

Deep ones, like the doctor showed you, that's it. Come along to your room and I'll make you comfortable. Tabby,' she added in a bark over her shoulder, 'the tea.' The scullery maid, like everyone else completely unperturbed by the event taking place – a sign they were well used to such things – did as she was bid. On a cloud of faint perfume and Miss Josephine's gentle sobbing, the sound of which Pip recognised as that she'd heard during the night, they disappeared, leaving the other lady to regain her composure in the doorway.

Caroline Goldthorpe – Miss Lucy's mam, Pip realised, thoughts of Miss Josephine melting as she eyed this finely dressed lady. By, but she was dour looking, and stern mouthed to match. How she and her husband had created someone as wonderful as their daughter was astonishing. Brown hair in a plain chignon, long faced and sharp chinned, she peered around the room coldly.

'So. You must be the strays that my husband has been telling me about.' Her clipped voice seemed to ping off the walls. 'Well?' she added when Pip and the lads remained silent. 'Do you not possess a tongue between you? Speak!'

'Aye, Mrs Goldthorpe, that's right.' Simon spoke quietly, though defiant anger lurked behind his eyes. 'We've the master's say-so to be here. And we'll do our best to see he don't regret giving it – Cook, an' all, to boot.'

Jewels winking at Caroline's throat threw off splinters of light as she cocked her head. 'Is that so?'

'Please, Mrs Goldthorpe, we just want us all to get along.' The words escaped Pip's mouth before she could halt them. She gazed back fearfully. 'I, I mean ... Forgive me, I—!'

'Like . . . *friends*, you mean?'

Trying hard but failing to gauge the woman's feelings on this from her stony face, Pip bobbed her head. 'Aye, yes,' she whispered.

Hardman had been standing by the fire. At this, she turned and walked away with a soft snort.

'Why you . . .' Nostrils flaring, the lady walked towards them; instinctively, Pip's arm went around Mack protectively and she pressed closer to Simon at her side. She thought the lady would strike her but instead, she spoke on in her icy tone: 'How dare you! You deem yourself on a par with this family, with me? *Friends?*'

'Just you leave Pip alone.' Eyes boring into Caroline's, Simon half rose from his seat. 'She meant nowt by it, was being nice is all. It's just her way.'

The room fell quiet. Though his boldness must surely have surprised her, Mrs Goldthorpe's features altered not an inch. She smiled. 'I'll see to it that you're gone from this house by the end of the week. Mark my words.' Arching a shapely eyebrow, her smile grew and her tone dropped. 'Cook isn't the only one who can wrap that old man upstairs around her finger.'

A moment later, she was gone. The door breezed shut and the children looked to each other in silence.

'You'd do well to keep one eye at your back.'

Pip swivelled her head. Hardman, leaning against the wall by the window, nodded. If not exactly friendly, she continued evenly:

'Sour bitch, she is. And snidy as they come when she's a mind for it. Aye. Watch her.'

'Thought you hated us, wanted us gone from here?'

The housemaid folded her arms. Rather than focusing her stare on Simon when answering his questions, her eyes bore into the door Caroline had just exited through. 'I do.'

'Why the warning, then?'

'Because my feelings, on both counts you mentioned, run deeper for that one just now than the three of thee.'

Hardman dislikes and wants rid of Caroline even more than she does us? Pip frowned. Then remembering the housemaid and cook's heated discussion in this very room earlier, her cheeks grew hot. She stole a glance at her. Jess was rather bonny looking in her own way, she admitted. By, but she couldn't imagine her and Mr Philip together! Was his wife aware? She doubted it – from what she'd just seen of her, surely Hardman would be from this house in a heartbeat? It was a rum do, all right. Messing with the maids – and him a gentleman, too. Mind you, Pip reminded herself, that status meant not a thing, did it? Look at the filthy piece who tried to lure Mack away that day. He'd been a gentleman as well, hadn't he? Rank and wealth meant nothing really in some respects. You were either good or you were not, regardless of class. It was that simple.

Her thoughts switched back to Mrs Goldthorpe. What did she have planned for them? Would she make good on her threat? Surely the master wouldn't let her convince him to make them leave? He didn't appear to hold his daughter-in-law in much regard if his tone was anything to go by when he'd told his son she'd do well to remember whose house this was. *Oh, but why* couldn't *they all just get along?* Pip asked herself again. Was it really hoping for too much? Would the few who for whatever reason had taken an instant dislike to her and the lads one day change their opinion? She prayed so. It was all she could do.

When Tabby re-entered the kitchen, Pip rushed to

her side. 'What on earth happened? Is Miss Josephine all right, now?'

'Aye. Least she will be. Cook's with her, promised her she'd stay at her side till she falls asleep. Don't fret, the lady shall be fine.' Before Pip could ask more, the scullery maid glanced to Hardman. 'You may as well retire for the night. The guests should be leaving shortly but if the family need owt in between, I'll see to them. Same goes for you, little 'un,' she added to Mack, who was nodding off by the fire.

'Aye, go on, lad. Me and Simon shall join you soon,' Pip told him, and on her reassurance he took himself off to bed.

Likewise, Hardman needed no second telling – shrugging, she escaped to her room.

'Silly sow.' Tabby jerked her head after the housemaid. 'Fancy her getting herself mixed up with the son. And him what's had a piece of nigh on every servant to ever grace his father's doorstep.'

Pip slipped into a chair at the table beside the older girl. 'Aye?'

'Cook liked to think he'd curb his roving-hands ways upon his marriage to Mrs Goldthorpe – clearly not.' She lowered her tone. 'You noticed that likeness in her room upstairs?'

'Cook's room?'

'Aye, the one of the young girl wedged behind the mirror?'

Simon nodded. 'We were wondering over that.'

'Well.' Tabby leaned closer. 'That there's Cook's daughter.'

'Where is she now?' asked Pip.

'The master springs from Bolton town some ten miles from here. His parents were farming folk but it were never their son's calling. Upon their deaths, he sold the land and went into the mill business. He knew what he were about, all right; cotton were quickly becoming king and he struck at the right time. Quickly made a fortune, he did. You've noticed he don't quite speak as the nobs do, though he's striven most of his life to better hisself, to *prove* he were just as good as the rest of the rich?'

At Pip and Simon's nods, she shrugged. 'He's none the worse for it. His roots shaped him into the kindly being he is the day. You are who you are – no getting away from the fact for most, nay.' Leaning back, Tabby folded her arms. 'Anyroad, Cook went to work for the master and his wife shortly after their marriage. In time, she fell for and wed their groom, the master gave them a little cottage to dwell in on the grounds, and they had their one and only child some years later – Lydia, behind the mirror.

'Now, as you've seen for yourselfs, the master don't stand on ceremony. Though he ensured Miss Josephine and Mr Philip were raised proper, summat I reckon he'd have liked for hisself, old habits die hard; Lydia were allowed to mix with the young lady and gentle-man. They grew together, were inseparable, became as though they were each from the same womb. But course, this couldn't last and the passing years drew them in directions more becoming of their stations. Miss Joseph-ine's time were swallowed by lessons with her mother: pianoforte and embroidery, social engagements and suchlike – skills she'd need to find herself a suitable husband – whilst her brother were sent away to school. Lydia followed Cook into servitude as housemaid.'

'How d'you know all this? You'd not have been employed here in them days. You're little older than Pip and me,' Simon pointed out.

'Aye, you're right. The master plucked me from the workhouse and brought me to work in his household shortly afore he moved the family here to Manchester.' The scullery maid motioned to the beer barrel across the room. 'It were Cook what regaled me with the history, had five too many one night and grew maudlin over Lydia, as she's wont to do at times.'

Fascinated by the glimpse into these people's pasts, feeling she'd gained a better understanding of them already, Pip was keen to steer the conversation back. 'So what occurred, Tabby?' she pressed before Simon could enquire about anything else. 'Where's Lydia now?'

'No one knows. Not even her own mam. And it's Mr Philip to thank for it.'

Pip exchanged a look with Simon. It was he who asked quietly, 'Why's that then? What did he do?'

'Cook said he changed at school, wasn't the selfsame lad whenever he returned for the holidays. In his place developed a spoilt and selfish piece. Whether down to his rich new student friends or the professors what taught them, she couldn't rightly say. He began addressing her as Cook rather than Mabel as the family had allus done. He'd often retreat to this very table to seek out her hugs and sage advice whenever he were troubled as a lad; now, he steered clear of the servants' domain, no longer spoke to her unless to bark an order. This hurt – she'd been more like a second mam to him than a mere domestic. He began throwing scorn on the master and what he deemed his lowly beginnings, which upset both his father and mam, and criticised Miss Josephine for her over-familiar ways with the servants. He'd changed for good, for the worst. The house was allus glad to see the back of him.

'All but Lydia, that is. Though he snubbed her as he

did Cook and the rest, she saw only the childhood friend she loved. Pity for her, he saw her now as the gentry are often wont to with their maids: a plaything to be used and discarded. He had his way with her, got her with child, then denied all wrongdoing. She, having been convinced he'd wed her upon discovering her condition, grew mad in the head. Cook wanted to tear *his* head from his body for him, but Lydia pleaded with her. She loved him still. And the pain and shame that she were unmarried and carrying a child as well as the truth that he'd turned his back on her, didn't return her love as she'd believed, drove her from the house.'

Pity and disbelief held Pip's tongue; she didn't know what to say. She nodded when Simon muttered something about Mr Philip being a swine, then managed to whisper, 'Oh, poor Lydia. Cook, an' all.'

'Aye, on all counts. Despite the best efforts of Cook and the master, who were beside hisself as much as her over the loss and his son's behaviour, they never did find her. She seemed to have vanished from God's earth. Cook prayed daily her daughter would return one day, when she were ready, awaited it with all her heart. When the master sold his Bolton mill and purchased the bigger one he owns now, and the family upped sticks here to Manchester so he could be closer to his premises a few years back, Cook fretted herself ill with thoughts of Lydia returning and not finding them at their old residence. Aye, that much I were witness to. She put the word out to neighbouring servants and their employers alike to direct her here should she ever reappear, who promised they would. Poor wench is still convinced her daughter will appear on the step one day. Me, I'm not so sure.

'As for Mr Philip . . .' Tabby took a swig of her tea

before continuing. 'A swine, aye, he certainly is. And that wife of his is no better, found a sound match in her, he has. Mind, 'taint love what binds them, oh no, least not on his part. It's the dowry she fetched upon their marriage, no doubt, what snared him. His filthy ways with countless maids since is proof.' She lifted an eyebrow knowingly. 'Servants talk, you see, and word soon spreads amongst us. The master don't know the half of it. Cook's hushed up much of the goings-on to save him the heartache and shame.'

Simon nodded slowly. 'And now Hardman.'

'Aye. Seems she's the latest. It'll end in nowt but tears – hers, that is, you mark my words. Mind, there's little point in warning her. Hard faced as she is, she'd only say we were spouting falsehoods to spite her.' Tabby tossed her head. 'He'd think twice were he to put his mucky hands on me.'

'Or you.' Simon was looking at Pip with the expression he had earlier with Cook – his eyes burned with protectiveness and she flushed, realising now the meaning.

'I'd break his face for him, I would,' finished Tabby.

'Miss Lucy's nice, mind,' Pip had to say after a silence. Despite her parents' rottenness, she'd turned out differently, only good. Pip felt compelled to point this out, defend her.

Tabby and even Simon nodded agreement.

'Mind,' Pip continued, 'one thing I can't fathom: why didn't Cook leave? How could she bear to stay under the same roof with someone what had treated her daughter so?'

'The master,' Tabby answered simply. 'She loves him – Miss Josephine, too – as though they were her own kin. Albert Goldthorpe begged her to remain with the family and she agreed. Mind, as is to be expected, she can't stand the sight of Mr Philip no more. But for his father and sister, she'd be gone from his life like a shot. All she can do is avoid his presence as much as she's able. Not such an easy task, that though, now he's back beneath the master's roof with his tail betwixt his legs.'

'Aye, I've been wondering on that, an' all. The master upstairs made mention earlier how Mr Philip's at fault entirely for his situation.'

At this from Simon, a mirthless smile touched Tabby's lips. 'Then good on the master! I wish I could have been there to see his face – that son of his needs telling, all right.'

'He were purple with anger.'

The girl laughed, but again no amusement showed in her face. 'I'll bet. You see, he's a weakness for the gambling. Frittered all his and his wife's brass besides a fair chunk from the mill. There were blue air in this house when the master discovered his son's antics, I can tell you. Stealing like that from your own father, I ask you. It's a good thing the master found out the way of things when he did. He could have been facing ruin, else. When Mr Philip's home were seized by creditors, the master had no option but to let him and his family move in here. Worst luck. Hope they're for buggering off out of it again soon. Put a black cloud over this house, they have, and it's showing. Bar Miss Lucy, of course,' she added with a quick grin and roll of her eyes when Pip made to open her mouth in defence of the girl again.

Pip returned the smile, then her brow wrinkled and she sighed. 'Mrs Goldthorpe had a few choice words for us earlier.'

'Threatened to be rid of us,' added Simon.

However, Tabby wasn't concerned at this: 'Ah, ignore her. She's no say on much here. The master'll not be bent by that one.'

Warm reassurance touched Pip. Hadn't she suspected as much? She smiled again.

'It's bitter she'll be 'cause you've come to work here and youse ain't of her choosing. Had to leave most of her servants behind, she did, for the master refused to fork out for their wages. Who can blame him, with the debts he's forced to pay off what his son's racked up? Aye, scattered to the four winds when they moved here – all but Finch, that is. The master relented on that one for Miss Lucy's sake.'

'But Miss Lucy hates her.'

'Aye! Eeh. They're a rum lot these money-folk, eh?'

'You've got that right.' Simon pulled a face at them in turn. The three of them chuckled quietly.

When later Pip and Simon lay close either side of Mack, the moon's silver stroking the peaceful room through the crack in the curtains, she said, 'I reckon we've not to repeat owt we've been told the night, lad. Tabby could get into bother, else. Cook mightn't be best pleased we've been tongue-wagging about her and the family.'

Simon agreed. 'Is the owd 'un for stopping out the night through d'you think?'

Turning her eyes to the empty chair in which Cook should have been slumbering by now, Pip frowned. 'Happen Miss Josephine's still bad, like. What d'you think it is what ails her, lad?' She felt him shrug. 'Cook were about to tell us till the ladies interrupted. I should have asked Tabby again but the matter left my mind what with everything else we've learned the night.' She'd try again tomorrow, she determined. Whatever it was, this bad blood business didn't sound good and she felt wholly sorry for the master's daughter, who from what she'd seen and heard of her didn't seem a bad sort. By, but this was a troubled household and no mistake.

Soon, Simon's breathing steadied and, following suit, Pip pushed her thoughts aside and settled deeper in the bed.

When they awoke early next morning, Cook still hadn't returned to the room.

Chapter 9

THE SECOND DAY of Christmastide meant more to some at Bracken House than others.

British tradition stipulated that, since the wealthy needed to be waited on on Christmas Day, the servants were permitted the following day off to visit their own families. Gratuities given by the master for good service rendered to him throughout the year was common practice; a Christmas box was presented to all who served his home, from his live-in domestics to the weekly washerwoman and even the shops' delivery boys. A direct acknowledgement was becoming at this time of year – a belief that Albert Goldthorpe rigorously observed and always had.

For Cook and Tabby, its arrival was greeted with little more than a passing glance. Without kith or kin, for the girl it was a day like all the rest. Cook did have a married sister dwelling in Manchester but the woman had sent word not to visit, as her husband had a mighty cold and Cook might carry germs back and contaminate the whole of Bracken House, which would never do. And so, the two servants did as they normally would: whiled away the hours in the kitchen. Though work was considerably lighter at least; they spent much of the time sitting around the fire indulging in well-earned rest.

Hardman and the nursemaid Finch, however, had donned their hats and, with unaccustomed smiles, left to visit their respective families for a few hours. Clutched in their hands were their boxes, each containing a small gift: a new looking glass and matching comb set, as well as a monetary bonus and paper-wrapped package of leftover food from the previous day's fare. Their relatives would be doubly pleased to see them.

Insisting the newcomers were not to be excluded, the master had presented Pip and the boys with a shiny florin apiece, much to their shocked delight. They had thought it a mistake when Cook informed them they were to accompany her and the other servants into the study, where the gifts were always presented. Only Albert was present – Pip had breathed a sigh of relief on observing this. As Finch was away, Mr Philip and his wife had taken Miss Lucy out for the day. Those two, boring holes into their heads with their disapproving glares, would have spoilt the moment. And a special one it was, for it spelled acceptance, that they were now fully acknowledged as part of this house.

One by one, they had approached the master's large mahogany desk. His ankle and chest still weak, he hadn't risen, had greeted them smilingly from his plush leather chair. Seasonal good wishes were given and returned, hands were shaken, boxes presented and murmured thank yous followed, which Albert received with nods and further smiles. When it was the orphans' turn to approach, he'd leaned forward as though pleased to see them again.

'So, young ones. And how are you faring at Bracken House thus far?'

'We're faring well, sir, aye. Very good, ta,' Pip had responded for them all, desperate to show gratitude, her eyes flicking about his face shyly. 'By, it's in heaven we are here.' It was true. Despite those who were determined to put a damper on their presence.

'Well, I'm happy to hear it. You're adapting to your new role as kitchen maid, lass?'

At this, she'd stolen a glance at Tabby, who had pulled a wry face, and definite merriment lurked behind her response: 'Aye, master. I loves it.'

'So I can tell.' Ever so slightly, his smile slipped; cocking his head, he'd scrutinised her thoughtfully with what seemed the same look Cook had when she'd taken stock of Pip following her transformation from the bath. 'Hm, extraordinary . . . '

'Sir?' Pip had tilted her own head in puzzlement.

'Yes? Oh. Where was I?' Blinking back to the present, Albert had cleared his throat. 'A merry Christmas to you, Pip. May the remainder of this year and the one ahead treat you kindly and bring you health and contentment.'

'Aye, sir. Thank you, sir. And all the same to thee.'

After he'd enquired about the lads' well-being and wished them the same good fortune as the rest, they'd returned to the kitchen, and Pip had been thankful for it. Clearly, he was due his rest, hadn't seemed himself for a moment there, had likely over-exerted himself. She hoped he'd soon feel well. Oh, but he was kind. To them all, aye. A more fair and honest master such as he you'd be hard pressed to find, she'd bet.

Now, beyond the window, violet-black smudges were rapidly switching the winter-white sky to night. Eyes heavy from the flames' heat and hearty dinner, Pip sighed contentedly. She glanced to Simon and Mack, sitting to her left on the rag rug before the kitchen range, and they smiled. After returning their smiles, she swivelled her eyes to the woman and girl.

136

Tabby, curled in a ball in a fireside chair, was dozing peacefully. In the seat opposite, head half turned away, Cook looked to be asleep too. On closer inspection, Pip saw she was staring into the fire's hypnotic glow, as though in a world of her own. The expression of such soft sorrow touching her doughy features brought a lump to Pip's throat. Lydia's absence must sting sharper still on days such as this.

She couldn't pretend to know what a mother's loss felt like. She likened it instead to a child's loss of a parent – it was all she could do – which she was only too familiar with. The raw anguish was heart destroying; Pip wouldn't wish it on her worst enemy. Particularly not this lovely, selfless woman here. And how much smarter the pain must be for her. For as far as they knew, Lydia wasn't dead. For whatever reason, she was gone from her mother's life by choice. Not knowing how she fared, whether she lived or breathed . . . In a way, that was worse. Aye, it was. That must surely hurt far more.

As though sensing she was being watched, the cook turned her head. She brought a half-smile to her lips. 'All right, lass?'

Pip nodded. On impulse, she reached for the woman's podgy hand, which rested on the chair's arm, and pressed it to her cheek. For a long moment, she was quiet, then: 'I'm glad to have found you, Cook. I . . . I love thee, I do.'

Silence greeted the declaration. Peering up, she was about to apologise, believing her over-familiarity had made the woman uncomfortable, but the words never made it. Tears were dripping down Cook's cheeks; instant ones sprang to Pip. They gave each other a watery smile.

137

'And me! I love thee, Missis Cook, an' all.' Mack clambered across, grasped her other hand and flashed his gappy grin.

'Aye, suppose you're all right.' Simon winked and she chuckled.

'D'you know summat? Youse ain't too shoddy yourselfs.' Though emotion shook Cook's words, she looked a little happier, and Pip's heart lightened. 'Now,' she added brightly, quickly scrubbing at her face with her sleeve and rising to her feet, 'hows about youse help me prepare the master's tray? He slept through his meal, shall be famished by now, poor love. 'Ere, there'll be some cake in it for thee?'

Laughing, they nodded, with Simon adding, 'Famished my backside! They do nowt but guzzle beneath this roof. Aye, and we're for going the same road, an' all – mind, you'll not ever hear me complain over that!'

Pip was suddenly struck by the change in the older lad before her. As had Mack and no doubt she herself, he'd lost that drawn, wolfish look; his features shone pink with health. Animation now danced behind eyes that once held only desperation; or worse, emptiness. He had hope again. They all did. With an inward sigh of bliss, she joined them in their task.

They had just returned to the rug, and Cook was heading for the green baize door with the laden tray, when the back door opened and Hardman entered the kitchen. The tip of her nose was red and her lips blue from the cold; instinctively, the children shuffled sideways to allow her access to the fire. However, she hurried towards Cook and in a swift movement, relieved her of her load.

''Ere, what are you about? That there's for the master—'

'Never mind that. It's upstairs to his daughter's room you need to be.'

The surprised anger immediately left Cook's face. 'Why? What's to do with Miss Josephine?'

Pip raised her head in interest. No further incidents had occurred following yesterday's queer disturbance and she hadn't as yet managed to find the right time to ask anyone about the woman's illness. Cook and even Tabby, her coming from the workhouse, had seemed to feel the absence of their own relations that little bit more today. Besides, they had used the hours to rest up; given they had earned the relaxation thrice over, she'd been loath to disturb them. And anyway, she was still new here. It would feel like she was sticking her nose into the family's business, where it didn't belong. Now, though, her curiosity had returned and it mounted at Hardman's next words:

'She's hanging out of her window again. I saw it upon my return just now. I tell you, she's going to fall out of it one day soon the way she carries on. Then this bad blood of hers shall be the least of her concerns, for it's a cracked skull she'll have – and that's if she's lucky.'

Cook closed her eyes for a second. Glancing to Tabby and seeing she was still asleep, she motioned to the dresser with, 'Pip, lass, fill that china cup there with tea from the pot and follow me. Lads, youse sit good, like, till we return. You,' she continued to the housemaid, jerking her head, 'go on and take the master his tray. And hear this: not a word to him about the miss up there. I'll not have him fretting. You hear?'

Hardman nodded and after quickly donning her apron and cap, disappeared through the baize door. Cook wasn't far behind.

Pip hadn't time to ask questions. Fulfilling the order, she rushed from the room to catch the older woman up.

*

'Now then, Miss—'

'Mabel? Oh, you're here! I shouted but you didn't . . . didn't hear, and I . . . I, I cannot . . . breathe, I . . .'

'Now then,' Cook repeated, hurrying to her side. 'Come on away from there and into the chair.'

'No, I . . . need air, you see.' She struggled to get the words out. 'I . . . cannot . . .'

'Deep breaths, now. That's it, come along. Eeh, you're frozen to the marrow.' Supporting the tall slim woman with an arm across her shoulders, Cook brought her other hand around to chafe Miss Josephine's bare arm.

'I'm sorry.'

'Nay, now. None of that, none of that.'

'So sorry, Mabel . . .'

'Ay, lass. My poor love. Just you sit still and fill them lungs of yourn. Nice and steady, that's it.'

It began as a hot rush that started from Pip's toes and travelled up, up, filling her face with colour. Then it drained from her at speed, leaving her ice cold, making her stumble from the spot she stood rooted to in the doorway. Eyes wide, mouth half open, she continued to gaze at the terrified looking lady who was trying desperately to regain her composure. Memories flitted and disappeared dizzyingly in Pip's mind. A feeling of fullness wrapped around her throat, as if invisible hands were choking her. The cup rattled in the saucer she was gripping as she began to shake. Alerted by the sound, Miss Josephine looked her way for the first time.

'Who are you?' She turned red-rimmed eyes to the cook questioningly. 'Mabel?'

But the older woman was too busy surveying Pip in surprise to answer. She stepped towards her. 'Lass? There's no need to be afraid. Miss Josephine will be sound again shortly.'

Bad blood . . . Rubbish, rubbish! her brain yelled. Doctors and their mad guesswork when faced with something they didn't understand. Nor did they want to try to; no, no. Easier for them to explain it away as something else entirely. That or dismiss it altogether. *Mam, Mam . . .*

'I . . . am not fit to, to see anyone, Mabel. Please, I . . .'

Pip's mind pleaded with her, insisted she couldn't be witness to this, not again, that she'd endured enough of it in the past to last a hundred lifetimes. Her heart, however, spoke louder and though she tried, it wouldn't be silenced. She placed the tea on the dressing table to her left. Then with tears blurring her path, she crossed to the lady's chair.

Josephine's ragged breaths shortened further as she watched Pip's approach – her shame and fear were tangible. She rose and sat back down, body restless with desperation. Then she clutched at her neck, eyes huge with sheer panic. 'My God . . . It's closing up, Mabel! My throat . . . It is! I . . . I'm going to die! Please, go away, go away!' she added with a choked rasp to Pip, swiping an arm through the air between them.

Face wreathed in helplessness, Cook made to go to the lady's aid but Pip stopped her with a hand on her arm.

'This is it! Lord, help me! I knew . . . knew it would come, *knew* I was dying. It's here. Oh, I'm going to die—!'

'You'll not, Miss Josephine.'

'I am, I am!'

'You'll not,' Pip repeated quietly, soothingly. Calmness, from instinct alone, filled her. She dropped to her knees at Josephine's feet. By now, the lady's face had turned a deathly shade of grey and her head bobbed sharply on her shoulders from her violent shaking. Terror-ravaged eyes locked with Pip's. She met them with her steady stare. Without another word, she reached for the lady's hand and brought it to her chest. The heat of the clammy palm seeped through Pip's thin bodice. The hand jerked, as though Josephine would remove it, but keeping her hold on top, Pip pressed it more closely to her.

'What are you . . .?'

'Sshhh. Relax, now, Miss Josephine.'

'But I . . . cannot . . .'

'Can you feel my heartbeat beneath your touch?' murmured Pip.

After a long moment, the lady nodded.

'Good. Now, I want you to concentrate on each beat. Count them in your mind. Can you do that?'

Miss Josephine didn't confirm this. However, neither did she disagree. She simply stared back, a slight frown creasing her sweat-slicked brow.

'Now, try and bring your own heart rate down. Try and get it to match mine.' Pip brought Josephine's free hand to the lady's breast. 'You feel the difference?'

'I . . . Yes. Oh, mine is thumping at thrice the speed . . .!'

'Patience, Miss Josephine. Both of ours will be beating in harmony in no time. Long slow breaths, one after the other.' Pip demonstrated. 'Slower. That's it.' She nodded, smiling gently, when the lady did as she told her.

Like this they remained for several minutes, neither speaking, just staring at one another. Gradually, the fear began to leave the woman's eyes. Her trembling body stilled, her breathing became noiseless.

'Our hearts. They're beating in perfect rhythm,' Miss Josephine whispered.

Smiling, Pip took the woman's soft slim hands and rested them both in Josephine's lap. Then she rose and walked behind the lady's chair. Here, with the heels of her hands, she massaged her stiff shoulders. 'Is that gentle enough, Miss Josephine? I'm not hurting thee?'

The woman shook her head. 'No,' she uttered, trance-like. 'It's relieving.'

'It's the tensing, you see,' Pip explained quietly to the back of her head. 'It tightens the muscles into steel-hard knots. You'll feel lighter in a minute once they've loosened.'

Again, they lapsed into silence. The shoulders grew less firm and Pip then worked her fingers into the creamy-skinned nape. When eventually she lowered her arms and returned to stand in front of her, Josephine greeted her with a serene expression.

'Better, Miss Josephine?'

Tired but peaceful eyes creased. 'Yes,' she whispered.

After fetching the abandoned cup and saucer, Pip placed them by the woman's elbow. 'Drink your tea then have a lie-down. Your body needs rest to recover.' She gave a last soft smile. Then she stepped back, clasped her hands in front of her and lowered her gaze as indication that her work here was done.

Throughout, Cook had intervened in neither speech nor movement. She'd simply watched on in complete amazement. Now, eyes like saucers, she craned her neck towards the young lady. 'Tha really all right, now, lass?' At Josephine's equally surprised nod, she turned to Pip. 'You knew exactly what to . . . How did you . . .?'

Before Pip could answer, Josephine, her voice gentle and refined and free from excitement, spoke. 'Who are you?' she asked in wonderment, as though addressing a saintly being sent down from heaven.

'Pip, Miss Josephine. The new kitchen maid.'

'Pip . . . It suits you. A lovely name for a lovely girl.'

She smiled shyly. 'Ta, thanks. Yours is a bonny 'un, an' all.' With reluctance – she could have remained in this nice lady's presence all night – she turned to the older woman. 'Have I permission to return to the kitchen, now, Cook? Mack shall fret, else, if I'm gone too long.'

Josephine answered for her. 'You go,' she murmured. 'I'd like a word with Mabel, here, before I rest. And Pip,' she added, voice thickening, 'thank you.'

She nodded, smiled, then slipped from the room. She managed to hold her emotions in check for most of the journey. Reaching the short passage that led directly to the kitchen, her racing mind and aching heart drew her to a shuddering halt. In the seclusion of the dim light, she leaned her back against the wall and screwed her eyes shut.

'Oh, Mam . . .' The words slipped from her on a broken sob. Dropping her face into her hands, she let the bitter tears flow.

*

When Cook returned to the kitchen after her talk with Miss Josephine, she made straight to where Pip sat staring into the fire, just as she herself had earlier with the absent Lydia on her mind.

'I need a word in your ear, lass.'

Pip nodded, and after observing that Hardman was busy with her duties in another part of the house, Cook set Tabby and the lads the task of stoning plums at the table as a distraction. Satisfied they wouldn't be overheard, she sat down facing Pip. 'Well? Out with it. What

I've just witnessed up there ... God alive, I've never afore seen anyone able to calm the poor love down as you did. *How* did you know to do that?'

'One thing you all should know first, Cook: it ain't no such ailment as bad blood.'

'Nay?'

Pip shook her head. 'Nor is what Miss Josephine's dealing with summat she can control, as Hardman reckons. Least I don't believe it.' Her eyes creased as she fumbled around in her head for the right words to explain the condition she knew only too well. 'What she's suffering with ... It's like a fear that grips them for no reason. Summat tells them, in their head, like, that summat bad is occurring and they become over-whelmed with doom.'

Cook stared back blankly. 'What bad things?'

'I don't know. Nor do them what's feeling it. For the truth is, there *ain't* nowt bad going on.'

'Eh?'

'It's all in their mind.'

Cook's voice was little more than a whisper. 'Are you saying Miss Josephine's insane?'

'Nay, nay ...' Or was she? Pip bit her lip in contem-plation. Whatever it was, it wasn't normal, was it? Something *was* wrong with those afflicted. If it didn't begin as a madness, it was sure as hell bad enough to turn into that after a time for the poor, confused suffer-ers. 'Oh, it's hard to explain,' she continued eventually. 'Imagine occasions when you've been fearful for what-ever reason. That feeling you get, you know, when your hands grow clammy, you begin to shake and your heart's galloping like a crazed horse has been set loose in your chest?' At Cook's nod, she spread her arms wide. 'That's what they feel but for reasons they can't explain. It can

145

strike them at all times of the day or night – even in their sleep – and it's nigh on impossible to shake it. It does ease off, mind, after a time. Some bouts last minutes, others hours; you never can tell from one instance to the next.'

'It must frighten you sick. Not knowing when . . . just waiting for it.'

'Aye. Course, that makes them all the worse, even more anxious, like. It's with them, always.'

The woman covered her mouth with her hand. 'Eeh, that poor broken love up there!'

Tears clogged Pip's throat, making it difficult to speak. 'Can you only imagine what it must be like? Afraid to leave your rooms or be in company in case it hits? Folk staring, worrying, judging . . .? The shame of it, the confusion, wondering if you're going mad? And worse: the crippling terror that you're about to die? For it feels that way, Cook, to them. Aye, the fear's only too real. They grow dizzy, sick, believe their heart's about to pack in, for it's beating that hard. Their throat feels like it's closing so they can't catch one breath to the next, and so they panic more . . . And they don't know *why*. They don't, Cook – have no control over it. Oh, it's hell on earth, it is!'

As Cook watched her trying desperately to regain her composure, understanding slowly softened her eyes. She reached for Pip's hand and gripped it. 'Your mam. You've seen this with her, ain't you?'

'I miss her.'

'Oh, my lass . . .'

'It ruined her, mind and soul. The melancholy, it darkened her mind like a poisoned fog. Laudanum would remedy her for a time but all too soon it were back, worse than afore. She tried . . . she did . . . She couldn't fight it no more. Thoughts of being that way, for the rest of her days . . . It were too much for her. It were just too much.'

Cook drew her up from her seat and into her voluptuous lap. Resting her head on the woman's shoulder, Pip let the tears run down her face, and Cook, rocking her as though she was an infant, was comforting. 'Tell me about her, your mam.'

'She were called Annie.' Pip smiled wistfully. 'Oh, she were bonny, Cook, reet so. She were gentle, and kindness itself. We had only each other but it were enough, you know?'

'I do,' Cook murmured.

'Home were a cellar in Ancoats – Garrick Street, you know of it? Aye well,' she continued when Cook shook her head. 'It were rotten and cramped, but Mam made it nice as she could. Slaved in a mill for fourteen hours a day, she did, and every penny she earned went on me in some way or other. Whether the rent to keep a roof over my head or food to fill my belly. And she'd scour the second-hand stalls at the market in all weathers, to make sure I were clothed well. She'd have sooner died than see me destitute, or hungry, or barefoot—' She broke off on a soft sob and Cook patted her back. 'That's how I know, what she did . . . She didn't want to, were desperate, is all. She'd never have left me, else, never. She weren't in her right mind at the end, that's what. And it were the illness's fault. Never hers, nay. I *miss* her.'

'Miss Josephine wants to make you her companion.'

Cook's sudden announcement brought Pip's head up. A frown knitted her brow.

'I may as well tell you, for you had to hear it some time. Mind, after what you've told me here . . . You've not to fret about upsetting the miss, for I shall be the one to tell her nay. You've seen and are heartsore still enough with this, you going through it with your poor mam. You'll suffer it no more, lass. You have my word.'

Pip's thoughts raced, tripping over each other in her mind, repeating themselves, giving way to another then another, each more confusing than the last. Companion? Or nurse?

Her heart gave a sudden ache for the lady suffering alone upstairs. She was desperate. And who wouldn't be? Pip understood this. Miss Josephine had likely encountered in her today the first person to ever truly realise her torture. It was understandable she'd want to cling to it and not let it go. She wanted to feel safe, reassured, protected. The fact she saw no other place to get this but from a stranger – a child, at that – surely cut deep; it must have taken a lot of courage for her to even make such a suggestion. But as Cook had pointed out, Pip had seen enough of this with Mam to last her a lifetime. As sorry as she was for Miss Josephine's plight, she couldn't go through it a second time, she couldn't. The pressure, the strain on her own strength of mind . . . 'Ta. I, I just couldn't, Cook.'

'No need for sorrys. It's a burden too weighty for a lass of your age, anyroad, and I shall tell her so. She'll understand.'

Rather than feel relief, it was guilt that filled Pip and had her gnawing at her lips. But what would the lady do? Then another notion hit. She winced as pain struck like a fist inside her breast. A vision flitted behind her eyes, her mam slumped across the bed they had shared, lifeless eyes finally at peace, the empty laudanum bottles strewn around her cold body . . . What if Miss Josephine, left alone with her demons . . .? What if she too was to . . .?

Her mouth moved of its own accord. 'Cook?'

'Aye?'

'I . . . I'll do it,' she heard herself whisper. The agreement was out – there was no taking it back. Yet oddly, hearing it spoken aloud, she realised she didn't want to. A queer sense of calm overcame her. 'What's more,' she added in a voice steady with determination, 'I'm going to see her banish this.'

She'd failed with her mam; would she succeed this time? Pip asked herself afterwards in bed, staring into the darkness.

Time would soon tell.

Chapter 10

'NOT BAD. NOT bad at all.'

The dark grey woollen dress, long-sleeved, buttoned down the middle and finishing just above her ankles, sat snug against Pip's small hips – she ran her hands over them with a smile.

'Fits you like a glove, it does,' continued Tabby with a nod of approval. 'Tha did well, Cook.'

'I've a keen eye, lass.' Cook preened. 'Got the sizes spot on, I did, aye.'

Like Simon and Mack's new clothing, the material was plain and serviceable but better than anything any of them had worn before, ever. The same could be said for their sturdy boots. By, but they felt like the gentry themselves in these rig-outs.

Petticoats, too! Amazement filled Pip again, with thoughts of her snowy undergarments. And the lads had new caps, properly fitting ones, in the same shade as her dress. Sudden tears pricked her eyes. 'The master's the kindest man God ever created, I'm certain,' she whispered, smoothing down her new apron over her skirt.

Albert had given Cook instructions that morning to see that new clothing, everything that was required from head to toe, was to be purchased for the children, insisting that as they were part of his workforce it was only right he provided them with adequate attire. She'd headed into Manchester to fulfil his request before the children stirred from her bed. Their surprised delight upon wakening and being presented with the new things had been worth the pain to her corns caused by the walk, she'd told them.

Watching on from her seat at the table now, Cook smiled. 'I'm happy to agree with you there, lass. Only it weren't the master's brass what paid for your things; Miss Josephine insisted she buy them for you. The hand-kerchiefs, too. And this.' She reached into the wicker basket by her feet and pulled out another brown-paper-wrapped parcel. 'Go on, open it.'

Pip gasped at what was revealed: a beautiful shawl in emerald green adorned with black tassels. When, finally, she brought her gaze back to Cook, tears glistened on her lashes. 'It's the bonniest thing I ever did see.'

'Befitting for a bonny lass, I'd say.'

'But Miss Josephine didn't have to ... I mean, I agreed to what she asked because I want to help, not for what I could get.'

'Nay, now don't be daft. She knows that, as do I. This 'ere, it's just her way, a show of gratitude, like, for agree-ing to her proposal. Anyroad, the master were for fitting you out in new like the lads, weren't he, regardless? Don't matter much as to who finished up paying for what.'

Her new uniform, for her new position ... Pip's shoulders straightened involuntarily. The quietly firm resolution she'd awakened with filled her again. She breathed deeply. Today marked a new chapter in her life. Would her determination to succeed at it be enough? a small voice in her head asked, but she pushed it away. She'd do her very best to see that she did – time would soon tell, she told herself again, as she had last night.

Throughout the discourse, the housemaid had looked on in silence, arms folded. Now, glancing to the lads sitting with proud faces as they admired again the cut of each other's new waistcoats and jackets, her mouth tightened further. Then her eyes flicked towards Pip, running the length of her, and she slapped the tabletop. 'This ain't right, you know! Three days, they've been here. Three rotten days and she's gone from smelly, gutter-dwelling orphan to bleedin' lady's maid?' fumed Hardman, nostrils flaring. 'She's bagged herself a better standing in this house than me, what's slaved here nigh on three *years*. Nay! Nay! I'm not having it, I'm not!'

Cook simply rolled her eyes, indicating that Pip should ignore the tirade, but she felt compelled to apologise anyway: 'I'm sorry, Hardman, I am. This ain't my doing; I never meant to upset anyone, truly. It's more a companion I'll be, really. Miss Josephine asked, you see, and—'

'It's all right, Pip. She'll get over it.' Tabby, kind as ever, and this time without a shred of bitterness towards the newcomer who had indeed 'leapt straight to the top of the tree' in less than a week, patted her shoulder. 'It aggrieves folk like Jess, is all, to see someone furthering theirselfs. Ignore her and anyone else what wags you a vicious tongue. I, for one, wish you nowt but luck.'

''Ear 'ear!' chimed in Cook, raising her mug of tea.

After shooting them all a fury-filled look, Hardman swung from her chair and out of the kitchen.

Cook rolled her eyes once again. Then she too rose from the table. 'Right, love. Best foot forward. Miss Josephine's awaiting thee.'

A host of emotions had become Pip's companions

since the cook voiced the proposition last night: excitement, anticipation, uncertainty and, if she was honest with herself, more than a little dread. Now, a new feeling struck: a sense of loss. She gazed upon the lads almost in panic. She'd been absent from their company for barely any length of time since they found one another on those unforgiving streets out there; the thought of doing so now made her want to cry like a baby.

Miss Josephine would want her by her side as much as possible. She'd even had a bed made up for her on the dressing-room floor should she require her during the night. When would she find time to visit the kitchen? She wouldn't miss the housemaid, that much was true, but this room . . . How often would she get to see it after today? And its occupants, who spent the majority of their waking lives here? Only Hardman's position gave her free run of the house – the other servants, Simon and Mack now included, had neither cause nor permission to stray beyond that baize door. Aye, Cook and Tabby, she'd miss them sorely. But these lads of hers . . . She'd come to rely on them, their company. She'd grieve their presence on a whole other level entirely.

'Tha leaving us, now, Pip?'

Taking Mack's hands and lowering her burning eyes, she nodded.

'But why must the lady have you? *We* want you, an' all.'

'Oh, lad. I'll slip down to see youse whenever I'm able . . .' She broke off when his bottom lip wobbled and her own followed suit.

Simon didn't say anything as she followed Cook to the door, peering back over her shoulder several times, but his eyes wished her luck and his slight nod told her to be brave and that she could bear this, that he believed in her. She gave them both a last, lingering look. Then she dragged her head back to the front and walked from the room and people she'd come to regard as home and family.

'Pip! Oh, thank goodness.' Miss Josephine's words came out on a gentle breath. Her face was wreathed in smiles. However, her eyes failed to match. Even when pleased, the young woman carried a sad expression. Also, she looked tired, likely found sleep difficult due to the worry. Glancing around for evidence of relaxants, Pip spotted two bottles on the mantel: the plainer one containing laudanum, the other a decorative vinaigrette of smelling salts. 'Please, dear girl,' the lady added, 'come in, come in.'

'Ta, thanks, Miss Josephine.' After bidding a whispered goodbye to Cook, who delivered her at the door and returned to her duties, Pip crossed the blush-coloured carpet. Then she raised her head, and for the first time scrutinised the lady seated in the fireside chair before her properly.

She'd been so focused yesterday on making her better, she'd barely taken in Josephine's appearance at all. Dressed in a simple day dress in duck-egg blue, small slippered feet peeping out from under her domed skirt, she cut a beautifully girl-like figure. She wore a delicate lace and ribbon frill on the back of her head, beneath which shiny hair the colour of marmalade and parted down the middle sat softly over her ears, secured in a thick roll at her nape. No finer features had the sun ever shone on, Pip was sure. And yet from what she'd witnessed, inside she appeared just as lovely. Like her father, she addressed the cook by her Christian name, seemed to have inherited, and held on to, his goodness and respect for all people, whatever their station. Unlike her brother.

'You look much better, Pip, I must say. They fit all right, the clothes?'

'Aye, Miss Josephine. Ta ever so.'

Smiling, she inclined her head. 'Please, do sit down.'

Pip perched on the edge of the chair facing her new mistress and folded her hands in her lap. An abandoned tray on a table beside her showed Josephine had barely touched her food. Plagued with digestive issues and a nervous bowel, Mam too had often had no appetite. Also, if this lady's tiny waist was anything to go by, her corsets were likely laced too tightly, which wouldn't help matters.

She felt the difference in temperature in here keenly. The room was chilly – a glance at the fire showed it hadn't yet been lit. After the heat of the kitchen, she had to fight the urge to shiver. She turned her head to the empty grate. 'Did Hardman forget your room today, Miss Josephine? Have I to see to the fire for you instead?'

'You're cold, Pip?' Josephine removed the fine wool shawl draped loosely around her shoulders. 'Here. Wear this.'

'Nay, nay, I couldn't.' She shook her head, aghast. 'I'm all right, Miss Josephine, 'onest. I were thinking of you, is all.'

'If you're sure . . .?' At Pip's nod, she laid the creamy material over the arm of her chair. She picked it back up, plucked at it for a moment, then placed it down again. She was as restless and fidgety as an infant. 'I can't bear the heat. I feel hot almost all the time. It makes breathing even more difficult and—' She broke off, cheeks pinkening.

'That'll be the blood pumping extra fast inside you, like, when your illness starts and sets your heart all of a gallop. It's the same when you exert yourself too much, you know? It's just like that. Nowt to fret over, Miss Josephine.'

Silence filled the air between them, then: 'Pip?' Josephine's voice had dropped to a whisper. 'What's wrong with me?'

Pity churned in her guts at the quiet desperation in the eyes, a soft brown specked with gold, gazing back at her. 'I don't rightly know,' she responded frankly. 'Mind, this I'm sure of.' Hesitantly, head dipping in shyness, she held out her hands to the woman, who gripped them. 'You're not in peril, Miss Josephine, though it likely feels that way oftentimes. And I . . . I . . .' She knew that once the next words were given life, she'd have to honour them. There would be no going back on it. She took a deep breath. 'I vow to thee, I shall try my hardest from this day to see you get better. For I believe it's possible, aye; surely it *has* to be? Surely this . . . condition can be cured?' *Just . . . you mustn't let it into your mind, you must try, for it'll blacken it beyond return like it did with my mam,* she added to herself with a pain in her heart. *But you'll not, I know it. And I'm going to help thee, Miss Josephine, for I've learned, learned from her.*

Pip had spoken gently, soothingly; nonetheless, Josephine's breathing had begun to quicken. Her long fingers tightened around Pip's shorter ones. 'You really believe I can be well again? Doctor Lawley is not so certain. He believes my blood has stagnated and is poisoning my heart. His attempts at letting it regularly and leech therapy hasn't worked—'

'Nor will it, Miss Josephine, I don't reckon, for your blood's just fine and well,' Pip cut in quietly. 'From what I've witnessed . . .' She sighed thoughtfully, trying hard to find the right words. 'It's like . . . summat in here, inside,' she continued, tapping her forehead, 'has . . .

156

fell out of balance. Summat's telling thee you're at risk when you ain't, that summat bad's about to occur when it's not. The fear breeds panic. That warning, that sense, is working when it shouldn't. You see? It's gone skew-whiff. We just need to find a way to straighten it out all nice again, like.'

'You seem so certain . . . How do you know all this, young as you are?' The woman's brow creased in curios-ity. 'Who are you? Whence have you sprung? I mean to say, Cook did fill me in on your circumstances during our discussion last night, but . . .' Her frown deepened. 'This knowledge you possess . . . How do you *know*?'

'My mam, Miss Josephine, suffered as you yourself are.'

'She did?' A glimmer of hope touched the woman's features. 'I often feel I'm the only soul in the world with this – this thing. And your mother? She escaped this dreadful curse? She knew peace again?'

'Aye. Aye, Miss Josephine.' It wasn't a mistruth. Through death, Mam had. Pip swallowed down the lump that rose to her throat.

'I'm so very pleased – relieved, too – to hear you say that. Although how utterly dreadful that she later passed away; and her deserving of enjoying that free-dom of mind, having beaten her illness. I'm so very sorry, for both of you. What was it . . .?'

'A sickness took her,' Pip was now forced to lie after a long moment. How in heaven could she speak the truth, that the very demon she'd promised to banish from Miss Josephine had brought about the melancholy dark-ness that had claimed her dear mam? It would set the fraught woman into a frenzy of terror – no, she couldn't know. Not yet, at least. Happen one day, when she was better, stronger, the lady's nerves would be able to bear the telling.

157

'You must miss her. I miss my own dearly.' Josephine rose suddenly and crossed to a small desk. From one of its drawers, she brought out a sheet of paper. She resumed her seat, smiled and handed it to Pip.

It was a likeness of a lady in her middle years. But for the dark hair, it could have been a depiction of the self-same one facing her.

'My brother possesses quite a talent, does he not?'

'Mr Philip drew this?'

The woman nodded. 'It's a hobby he's enjoyed since being a small boy.'

'Your mam was reet bonny, Miss Josephine. You're her image.' A sudden thought struck Pip; she frowned. 'Cook has a picture up in her room, drawn in what looks like the same style as this—'

'Lydia.' Sadness coated the word, and Pip regretted mentioning it. Of course, she must miss her old friend. 'You're quite right. Philip drew that, yes. He presented it to Mabel as a birthday gift when we were young.'

Before any ill feeling . . .? Knowing Cook's dislike for the artist, it perhaps stuck in her craw that he'd drawn it. However, clearly her need to see her beloved child's face every day outweighed her animosity.

Josephine's eyes took on a far-off look. 'We, my brother and Lydia and I, were quite, quite close as children.' She cleared her throat.

'Sorry, Miss Josephine. Is tha all right? I didn't mean to upset thee—'

'You didn't. I'm fine, really. All that you've spoken, particularly about your mother . . . Pip, hearing you talk of her, of her struggles and success . . .' She leaned forward in her seat and the softest, most beautiful smile appeared to caress her lips. 'She's bred within me a tiny seed of something I feared never to feel again: hope.

Belief, also. That I may be the woman I was again. For I want to be *me*, oh I do.' A sudden laugh, sweet and girlish, escaped her. She blushed gently. 'My good friend, Mr Sutton-Shaw, he … He's so very understanding towards me, and kind and … I believe he may marry me, you know,' she whispered.

Despite Miss Lucy's remarks and her opinion of him, Pip said: 'He sounds a very nice gentleman, Miss Josephine.'

'He is. If only I were well again, I'm certain he'd …' She broke off to sigh. 'My brother does his best to encourage me to leave this room more, to meet with people, with Mr Sutton-Shaw – he does so want to see a union between his friend and me. However, this affliction draws me into making shameful spectacles of myself. Christmas evening, fleeing from the drawing room and jollifications as I did …' She closed her eyes and shook her head, her chin drooping to her chest. 'It frustrates and angers Philip. Caroline also. I'm afraid that Alexander – Mr Sutton-Shaw – will soon lose patience with me altogether, too.'

'Then we must make this – *you* – right, eh, Miss Josephine? Work to fix it, together. Time's what it'll take, how much I can't say, but we'll not weaken, will we?'

'To heap half the burden such as this on to the shoulders of one so young … Forgive me, I'm sorry, it's just there's no one else at all who understands as you seem to.' The lady bit her lip, nodded, bit her lip again. Then she straightened her shoulders and took a deep breath. 'Together.'

The next moment, they turned their heads simultaneously as the door swung open and in breezed Miss Lucy. The girl gasped to see Pip and clapped her hands in delight. 'Oh, hello! Papa said that Grandy had given his permission for you and the boys to stay! Papa's a dreadful grump; he was not best pleased,' she added with a lift of her eyebrow, 'but I am, Pip. Indeed, very much so! Oh, but I did so want to visit the kitchen to see you all. Alas, Finch refuses to take her beady eyes off me for a moment. Humph! I shall get my own back on her, you see if I don't! Anyway, how are you?'

Pip couldn't contain her pleasure. She grinned shyly. 'Very well, ta, Miss Lucy. By, but it's gradely to see thee.'

'Why are you up here? Oh!' she continued without taking a breath before Pip could explain, 'I'll fetch my dolls, as I promised, for you to play with. Pip is my friend – we met in the kitchen on Christmas Eve,' she added to her aunt, before swinging her grin back to Pip. 'What do you say? Though you must be very careful not to break their delicate china faces, for Mama would be terribly upset with me. Should I, Pip? Shall I get them? Would you like that?'

'And pray what about our appointed embroidery lesson?' Miss Josephine's question held a note of amusement. 'Finch, and indeed your mama, have entrusted you to me in good faith. What if either of them should happen into here and—?'

'They shan't, Aunt Jo. Finch was already dozing by the nursery fire when I left, and Mama shan't summon me to visit her and Papa in the drawing room for hours yet.'

Summon . . .? *Visit?* The young miss needed permission to see her own parents? Pip thought, hiding a sad frown. There was an allotted hour during the day when she could spend time with them, when they could spare the measly minutes? By, but these nobs were a queer bunch, all right. No warmth, most of them. Unfeeling, aye. She felt sorry for this girl here, she did. Brass

160

aplenty or no, she'd rather not have had Lucy's life. She and *her* mam had spent every spare second they could together. Pip wouldn't have wanted it any other way, nay, wouldn't have traded places with this poor lass for a gold watch.

Now, Miss Lucy adopted her most persuasive pout. 'Pip's my new friend. And I promise to concentrate extra hard at tomorrow's lesson. Please, Aunt Jo?'

'All right, child, you win.' Smiling, the woman flapped a hand to the door.

However much Pip's excitement at the thought of spending some time playing make-believe with Lucy, she remembered the main reason she was here. Unlike the young miss, she was an employee beneath this roof, not a resident or guest. She wouldn't want her mistress thinking she was taking advantage, so she had to ask: 'Miss Josephine, are you sure?'

'I am, Pip. Besides, how can I say no to that pretty face?'

Pip understood this; she couldn't imagine ever being able to deny lovely Lucy anything.

Her niece skittered, laughing, from the room – and slowly, Josephine's smile melted. She twiddled her fingers together in her lap in an anxious motion.

Pip moved to her side. 'Cook said as how the embroidery is good for you; mebbe the lesson *should* go ahead.'

'Cook speaks truth. The lessons occupy my mind, thus calming my frayed nerves. However, you are children. And children should, I believe, find fun where they can. I shall busy myself with my needlework regardless. I know you're here should I need you.'

The lady's last words had been tinged with embarrassment; also guilt – it was more an apology than an observation. Pip smiled softly in understanding. That this full-grown adult was forced to depend on a mere girl to feel safe, reassured, must be a difficult truth to swallow. Then another thought struck. Now, it was she who wore the uneasy expression. 'Miss Josephine?'

'Yes?'

'Mrs Goldthorpe, Miss Lucy's mam . . . I don't believe she likes us much, me and the lads downstairs. Happen she'd be angry were she to discover me in her daughter's company?'

The woman shook her head in reassurance. 'Oh, I'm sure—' She broke off at the sound of approaching footsteps and smiled. 'Too late to speculate on such matters, now. Here's Lucy back.'

Yet it wasn't the young miss who appeared in the doorway but the very woman herself. Caroline paused at the threshold. To say she looked surprised was putting it mildly. 'What on *earth* is she doing up here?' Josephine's brief explanation brought an angry hue to her cheeks. She cast Pip a waspish look before turning a withering stare on to her sister-in-law. 'For goodness sake, Josephine. Scraping to this . . . girl – of the lower class at that – for guidance? Have you no shame at all?'

Josephine blushed to the roots of her hair. Her embarrassment was tangible. She opened her mouth but Caroline continued scathingly before she could speak:

'Besides which, I'm astonished at your naivety. She's playing you, is likely laughing up her sleeve that she's managed to worm her way up here. Doctor Lawley has explained quite clearly on numerous occasions what ails you. It's your blood, which you know only too well he's striving to cleanse. I think you ought to be grateful, not cast aspersions on his medical capabilities.'

'I have much respect for Doctor Lawley. But Caroline,

162

his efforts thus far have been in vain. The bloodletting, cold baths, castor oil and goodness knows what else.' Her sister-in-law glanced away, and Josephine nodded empathetically. 'See, you agree. I'm right, am I not? His intentions are good but his methods are proving useless—'

'You must give it time, that's all. Doctor Lawley knows what he's doing.'

'No, he doesn't. I shan't be requiring his assistance any longer.'

'What?'

'My blood is just as it should be. Pip says—'

'Pip? *Pip?* This one?' Caroline thrust out an arm to point a finger at Pip, who shrank back at the sudden movement, believing she was about to strike her. 'She's preying on your desperation to be well.'

'Caroline, please. You're scaring the young mite—'

'And *you're* enabling yourself to be hoodwinked. She's using you for her own ends.'

'She's going to help me restore my health.' Josephine spoke quietly, calmly, though her tone carried sadness. 'I have made my decision and would be grateful if you will respect it.'

Caroline looked as if she'd say more. Instead, she breathed deeply. A definite smirk appeared to play at her thin mouth. 'My, my,' she murmured. 'She's got you right where she wants you, hasn't she? No doubt you have Cook's backing on this? Your father's?' She gave a mirthless snort when Josephine's eyes affirmed it. 'You'll regret your foolhardiness, you mark my words. This waif is a trickster and a fraud. Your ailment will worsen, oh it will, and you shall have no one to blame but yourself.' She straightened and looked down her nose. 'Heed my advice or ignore it. The choice is yours to make. I have said all I wish to on the matter. Your brother, however, shall have plenty to add, you can be certain of that. As a matter of fact, speaking of Philip . . .' Her eyes held a sly glint. 'The reason for my being here is that he sent me to inform you that Mr Sutton-Shaw requests the pleasure of your company this evening. However, I'll be sure to tell him that you'll be otherwise engaged with your . . . friend, here.'

'No, no. Please. I should like to see Alexander very much.'

Caroline was silent, then: 'Hm. I dare say Alexander shares your sentiments. Whether he'll be of the same mind when he discovers you've cast aside the doctor and risk putting your mental well-being in jeopardy remains to be seen. I grant you, he's a fair and decent man. He's weathered your illness with neither action nor word of complaint. But remember, one's patience can only be tested so far, Josephine.'

The pale face creased. With a shaky hand, Josephine dabbed her nose with her handkerchief, and Pip sidled to her chair hoping her presence would offer comfort and wishing she had an ounce of Simon or Cook's gumption to tell this nasty woman to leave her mistress be. But she was afraid, both of Caroline and of making matters worse; she could only stare at her feet and pray she'd leave. A moment later, her heart sank to her boots.

'Mama!'

As Caroline glanced from her daughter, who had appeared at her side clutching her dolls, then to Pip, Josephine half rose from her seat. 'Forgive me, I gave consent . . . Lucy said they had already made one another's acquaintance. They're just children, sister-in-law.' Her voice was soft. 'What harm can it do?'

'Quite.'

'You're in agreement?' Josephine's eyes expressed the surprise that had filled Pip.

'Thank you, Mama!' squealed Lucy. 'Oh, Pip,' she added, hopping from one foot to the other, 'we're going to have such fun!'

However, confusion had struck Pip into silence. Caroline was giving consent to this, after everything she'd just spewed out, the clear hatred of her that she harboured? Deep suspicion was turning her cold and when Caroline turned slowly to look at her, a trickle of dread touched her spine. The lady wore the queerest expression. One of almost . . . was that excitement? But why? What . . .?

'Half an hour, Lucy. Then you must return to the nursery and Finch, who will take you for your walk in the Green. Remember, fresh air is good for your constitution. Agreed?'

'Yes, Mama.'

With neither another look nor a word to anyone, Caroline nodded once, turned and left the room.

'Well.' Plucking at her lip, Josephine stared at the closed door. Then she caught Pip watching her and brought a small smile to her face. 'Take a seat on the chaise longue with Lucy. Go ahead, Pip. Enjoy yourself awhile.'

'You're all right, Miss Josephine?'

'Yes, yes. A little breathless, perhaps . . . My embroidery will calm my nerves.' She reached for the sewing basket atop the table to her right. However, her slight frown remained and again she uttered, this time to herself, 'Well.'

Aye, well indeed. Pip too shot a last look at the door. Then Lucy was beckoning her across and despite her unease, she couldn't help but feel happy. Pushing her concerns and the memory of Caroline's sly eyes from her thoughts, she allowed herself to be a youngster for once.

Oh, but Lucy's company, her laughter and sunny smiles were a tonic; Pip failed to recall the last time she'd known such pleasure. Throughout, she'd half expected the door to burst open and Mr Philip to storm in upon them, demanding an explanation from his sister regarding her recent decision concerning her health, but it never came. Eventually, she'd allowed herself to relax. Yet all too soon, Josephine was calling time on their games apologetically, and the reluctant children parted company.

Minutes later, when passing the window, Pip caught a glimpse of the young miss strolling by the lakelet beyond the park gate, Finch looking on from a bench. She sighed softly. She wished she could run down there and continue the fun with the girl. Of course, that wasn't possible for numerous reasons. However much she and Lucy got along, how she liked to pretend they were not so dissimilar when they were together, the truth was a very different matter. They were oceans apart, none more so in their social positions. Lucy was a somebody. Pip was, in the grand scheme of things, a no one. They themselves, and children to boot, worried not about such a triviality. Adults could learn a lot from them if only they cared to, she thought.

A little later, her despondency was quelled when, returning her embroidery to its basket, Josephine announced that she must change for lunch and that Pip might take herself to the kitchen as she would have her meal in the dining room today with the family. Cook had revealed yesterday that more often than not, Josephine ate here in her room where she felt most comfortable for fear of bringing on one of her episodes, and so Pip was delighted with this announcement. Not only did it mean she could spend time with the kitchen's occupants but it seemed a good sign that Josephine was pushing herself towards if not overcoming, at least managing, her ailment.

Did the need to impress a certain gentleman have anything to do with this? She was sure it must. Mind, whatever it was that drove her to want to be well mattered not so long as it worked, did it? Josephine was testing the waters with lunch; if she got through it well enough, she'd feel able to receive Mr Sutton-Shaw this evening, that was likely her thinking. Oh, but Pip hoped she would. This gentleman seemed good for her.

She paused at the door and turned to face the lady. That ever sad and slightly worried look was on her face, and Pip felt an odd sense of pride in her. 'It's good, Miss Josephine, that you're for taking your meal downstairs the day. If you don't mind me saying so . . . I'm reet proud of thee.'

'Oh, Pip.' Blinking rapidly, the woman seemed to light up from the inside. 'That's the nicest thing anyone has ever . . .' She smiled through tears that had sprung to her eyes. 'I feel . . . it's difficult to explain . . . somewhat stronger now I've found you. Does that sound silly?'

'Nay, not a bit. It's just . . .'

'Just what?'

'It's a shame you've been unable to see that you had this strength in you, long afore I came, allus have had it. *I* see it in you, Miss Josephine. You'll pull yourself from this dark time, and you'll wed that Sutton-Shaw one of yourn, and you'll live a happy life. I just know it.'

Happen you'd have come through this sooner, too, if you'd

had a body to tell you this before now, Pip added in her mind, thinking of what she'd seen and heard, of the way in which Miss Josephine's brother and his wife were wont to treat her. Support and a kind word here and there went a long way.

She surely missed her mother so, but Albert was here still and Pip would bet his daughter had his affection, him being the good man he was. And she had Cook. Still, they didn't really understand her troubles, did they? She appeared so very lonely; it hurt Pip to see. *Mind, she's got me, now, too,* her inner voice added, and she was surprised to realise she felt protective of this lady almost as much as she had her mam.

'Oh, Pip,' repeated Josephine in a broken whisper. She smiled and Pip returned it then slipped from the room.

'Lads are away outside taking stock of the garden,' Cook hastened to mention the moment Pip entered the kitchen, eyes widening in worry to see them absent. She swallowed her relief. The fear of abandonment was with her always. 'They'll not get far with it, mind,' the cook continued, 'for the ground's frozen solid. Anyroad, it'll do them good to get from this room awhile. They're growing restless, I reckon, and that's never a good thing for young boys. Better they find summat to occupy them.'

Pip understood this. When you were used to being on the go constantly as they were, trawling the streets seeking a safe place to lay your head the night or finding a scrap to eat, it was strange not having to worry about a thing now. It must be especially so for Simon, who had been the one to look after them. He'd never seemed to stop when they were destitute, was always trying to come up with ways to see they survived another day, hour. He'd worked hard to protect them, his quick

168

mind always busy, thinking up the next scheme. She just hoped he'd soon adapt to this easier life of theirs without too much bother.

'Tabby? Hardman?'

'Hard-faced one's busy with her duties in the house somewhere. Tabby— oh, here she is.'

Pip smiled at the girl emerging from the scullery, who flashed one back then took a seat between them at the table.

'How's it going, lovey?' Cook placed a cup of tea in front of Pip and poured another for Tabby. 'You settling down to it, like?'

'Good, aye. Miss Josephine's decided to eat her lunch in the dining room.' She nodded, pleasure running through her, when Cook raised her eyebrows.

'Well! A genuine miracle-performer you've proven yourself to be. She well then now, like?'

Pip blinked in astonishment. Earlier she'd ruminated on how, despite some folks' good minds and intentions, they really didn't have the foggiest idea what this ailment was like, did they? She shook her head slowly. 'Nay, Cook. This . . . it can't be mended in a day. It mightn't ever be, and that's the truth. I can but try, is all. Mind, she looks to be determined and that's half the battle won already, for you must want to help yourself to get better, you know?'

'Oh. Aye.' Cook appeared a little disappointed, then her face creased in a smile. 'Anyroad, you'll see her through all right. If anyone can, it's thee, for I don't mind saying no one else has the answers nor the knowledge that you seem to have.' Her smile grew. 'Aye, yes. Will do the poor love good to dine with the rest for once. There's fresh flowers on t' table, an' all; they'll cheer her mood no end.'

169

Pip nodded agreement, but her own mood had dipped somewhat. She just prayed Mr Philip and that wife of his didn't upset her. Knowing them, they would be on her the minute she entered, demanding she rethink her decision, and what would that do for her?

I don't lie. I do know what I'm about with this illness, have endured it all before, she said to herself, wishing she could speak it out loud to the naysayers who seemed to hate her, that she could make them believe. She'd never think of conning anyone, she wouldn't, let alone Miss Josephine. She just wanted to help. Why couldn't their vicious minds allow them to see that?

Should she tell Cook her concerns, tell her what had transpired? After a moment's deliberation, she shook her head. The woman had standing in this household and she knew it – whether upstairs or down, she didn't seem to care who you were. Outspoken as she was, she'd likely give Caroline a tongue-lashing as she had with Hardman, or complain about her behaviour to the master, and that would surely make matters worse for Pip. No, better she rode this out as long as she could.

Happen the waspish lady would come around, she tried to tell herself hopefully. She'd raised no objections to her and Lucy sharing company, had she? Just maybe . . .? But deep down, Pip knew it was unlikely. She'd probably only agreed to the play time to please her daughter, was perhaps already busy concocting something to ensure the opportunity never arose again. Sadness brought an ache to Pip's chest. Why, just as things were looking up, must something or someone always have to come along and spoil it? It just wasn't fair, it wasn't.

A sudden deafening crash behind her chased all thoughts from her mind and she jumped several inches from her seat. She whirled around – and her mouth ran dry to see Mr Philip storming through the door and making straight towards her, face as dark as thunder. *Dear God! What in the world—?*

'You! You callous young gutter-monkey!'

''Ere, now! What's all this, what's all this?' Cook was on her feet in a flash but he pointed a quivering finger in her face.

'Oh no. No, you don't. Not this time shall you call the shots, not with this. My father is furious with this scheming chancer, too. You shan't twirl him around your finger this time.' He turned blazing eyes back to Pip, who shrank away, terrified and confused in equal measure. What was wrong with the gentleman – his *father*, too? What had she done?

'Sir, please! I don't know what—'

'Save your lies. Now, up. Move yourself!' he bellowed, sending Tabby skittering back to the scullery in fear and Cook shouting out in anger. He ignored them both. Lips twisting, he took a firm grip of Pip's shoulder.

She whimpered as he hauled her to her feet. Philip made to manhandle her to the door and she scrambled for the woman's arm, crying, 'Cook! Help me, please! I've done nowt, nowt!'

Belying her bulky frame, the servant rushed forward and blocked his path before he knew what she was about. Fists on hips, breathing heavily, she thrust out her chin. 'Now I'm for asking you again, lad, and this time, you'll give me an answer. What's all this? You taken leave of your senses altogether? What's the young love here meant to have done?'

'This has nothing to do with you, nothing at all. I'll thank you to remember your place and mind your own—'

'Mind my eye! She and the lads along with her are under my watch. I've every right. Yon master will attest to that, an' all.'

'Is that so?'

'Aye!'

Philip leaned in close to the cook, eyes spitting steel. 'Yon master, as you call him,' he ground out mockingly, 'wants this devilish piece from this house as much as I – forthwith.'

Heavy silence filled the air between them. Finally, Cook shook her head. 'You lie.'

'What have I done?' Pip twisted her body, still held vice-like in Philip's grip, to stare up at him. Her voice was thick with terror and tears. 'Please, sir, tell me, for I know not what! Oh,' she blurted suddenly as a possible reason occurred to her. 'Is it about Miss Josephine's decision to stop the doctor's visits, 'cause sir, that were her choice entirely and—!'

'What? What's this?' he cut in angrily; her heart and stomach dropped.

That wasn't it . . .? Then what? her jumbled mind screamed. *What?*

He threw her a contemptuous look then turned it on Cook. 'I'll tell you what she's done, shall I? Earlier, against her better judgement and out of the goodness of her heart, my wife allowed this one, here,' he shook Pip like a dog with a rat between its teeth, 'to play with Lucy. And how did she repay Caroline's kindness? She assaulted my daughter. Pulled her hair, nipped her young skin and struck her on the arm, while Josephine had her back turned, with threats of further violence to come should Lucy tell.'

A whooshing noise had filled Pip's ears. Mouth gaping, she could only gaze in sheer horror at this man spouting these incredible words. This wasn't real. She was dreaming. She had to be!

Cook swivelled her eyes towards her slowly. Her fleshy face was a sickly shade of grey. 'Lass?' Her voice was a rasp. 'What says you to this?'

'It's lies. Lies! I'd never harm Miss Lucy, never never ever! Ask her, the young miss herself. She'll tell you I'm innocent of this. I love her, I do, would *never* . . . ' With a cry, Pip burst into noisy tears; she couldn't contain them, for she hadn't a single clue why this was happening. She felt sick with horror. That they could think this!

Caroline. She was behind this vicious witch hunt. Hadn't she sworn to be rid of them by the week's end? Hadn't she said that Cook wasn't the only one who could wrap the master around her finger? This was her doing. Her allowing them to play together earlier . . . Caroline had planned this! Oh, but what was she to do? And the master believed his daughter-in-law's lies, wanted her gone from here. She couldn't bear this, she couldn't bear this!

'Come with me.'

He pulled her to the door; craning her neck, she gazed desperately to the back one. 'Simon! Simon!' she cried, but of course he couldn't hear her and the next moment, she was half dragged up the staircase in a tip-toed trot.

Philip threw open the door to the master's room and pushed her inside ahead of him. She stumbled to a halt in the centre with a whimper. Then Cook, huffing and puffing, was at her side. Philip swung the door shut, sending the noise rattling through the house.

Pip lifted her head. The first person she saw was Caroline, stiff-faced by the window, Finch hovering nearby. Her heart thumped painfully. *You've done this, you!* she wanted to scream to the lady. She glanced to the bed and the stern expression on the old man's face brought fresh tears to her eyes and pain to her guts. Burying the fingertips of both hands in her mouth, she bit down on them, shaking uncontrollably. He was looking at her in deep disappointment, maybe slight disgust. *It's all lies, sir!* she implored him silently. Then someone else caught her attention, seated at the foot of the bed, and her breath caught noisily in her throat. Slowly her arms fell to her sides. 'Oh, Miss Lucy . . .'

The girl, her back to her, dipped her dark head further to her chest with a muffled sob. Her upset was tangible and despite her own devastation and fear, Pip longed to comfort her. Lucy must surely be as confused as she, for both knew Pip hadn't done any of the nasty things they were saying she had, wouldn't dream of it. 'Miss Lucy . . . I don't understand—'

'Silence.' Despite his obvious anger, Albert cut her off quietly. 'Now, Pip. I trust you know why you're here?'

'Sir, I—'

'What has been brought to my attention . . .' His voice dropped. 'How dare you.'

'Nay, sir, please—!'

'I put my trust in you and you've stamped it into the dirt beneath your heel. What you have done today to my dear granddaughter seated there is wicked beyond words.' He shook his head almost sadly. 'I provided a roof, food, clothing . . . I put my trust in you. You've let me down. More so, you've let Mabel, here, down.'

'All right, lass.' Cook held Pip back from further protest with a hand on her shoulder. She stepped forward. 'From what tongue has this accusation sprung, Albert?'

'Now, Mabel. I know you've grown fond of the girl—'

'Aye, the lads also.'

'But the fact remains you've been poor in your judgement. That girl has molested my granddaughter and is fortunate I'm not bringing an assault charge upon her head. She leaves, today.'

Cook delivered her response calmly. 'I asked who's said these things.'

Pip's eyes immediately swivelled to Caroline. However, the name that fell from Albert's lips brought shock so acute, she staggered. Had she really heard right? She shook her head slowly.

'That's right. It was Lucy herself,' he repeated. 'I for one know that my granddaughter would not invent such lies. Every person here present knows it, too. Including you, Mabel. Am I right?'

Cook stood rigid, face bone-white. Then: 'Miss Lucy?' She addressed the back of the girl's head. 'Is this true? Pip did these things to thee?'

'Yes.'

The answer swirled like smoke on the air to clog Pip's lungs; she couldn't breathe. 'Nay. Why, Miss Lucy? *Why!*'

'This has gone on long enough.' Philip strode forward and took hold of her arm. 'Come along with you. Out.'

'Sir, please listen to me.' Where Pip found her courage, she didn't know; yanking herself free, she dropped to her knees by Albert's bedside and clasped her hands to her chest. 'I love Miss Lucy as a sister. As God is my witness, I'd never harm a hair on her head, not for nowt on this earth. You must believe me. *Please.*'

'The child has just confirmed your crime from her own lips!'

'And I've norra single clue why, honest I ain't, for I'm innocent!' Swinging her head, Pip beseeched the girl's back. 'Please, Miss Lucy. Tell them I'm guilty of no wrongdoing. We played nice, is all. We had fun, and we laughed and enjoyed ourselfs. I did nowt, never would. I'd *never* harm thee! Please!' Lucy's only response was muffled weeping. Pip turned desperate eyes to the servant, still standing statue-like in shock beside her. 'Cook, you believe me. Don't you?'

'I . . .' Her doubt was clear to all.

Pip experienced a pain deep in her breast the like of which she'd never known before. She gasped as though winded. 'Nay, not thee . . .'

'Miss Lucy, she said herself . . .' Cook's creased eyes were bright. '*Why* did you hurt the young angel so?'

Pip rose on jerky limbs. Then she flew across the room and out of the door.

Tears blinded her as she careered down the stairs and through the hall. Her mind was numb, heart frozen. When a hand touched her shoulder, she barely registered it.

'I warned thee. Didn't I say she were a vicious bitch?'

Pip turned blank eyes to Hardman. She nodded.

'She's the one put Miss Lucy up to this, I'll be bound.' The truth left her cold. Again, Pip nodded.

'Caroline Goldthorpe needs getting rid of. For good and proper.'

Of its own accord, her head moved in agreement once more.

'Then you'd be free to return. We'd *all* be free.' The housemaid's tone dropped to a hard murmur. 'You want that, aye?'

'Aye.'

Hardman's mouth curved in a mirthless smile. 'Meet

176

me the morrow. Three o'clock by London Road Station.' She turned and walked away.

Empty of thought and reason, Pip did likewise, disappearing from Bracken House through the front door and running full pelt down the street.

Chapter 11

HOW LONG SHE'D been curled up in the privy, Pip couldn't say. Its familiarity was oddly comforting. Tightening into a ball, she buried her head in her arms.

Her dazed mind had been incapable of rational thought and on instinct alone, her feet had carried her to the only place she knew: the slums of Ancoats. She couldn't even recall the journey, yet here she was. Back in the darkness and fear and suffocating hopelessness of the place. Back where she'd begun. She'd never felt so utterly miserable.

Night-time noises drifted from the street beyond the broken door: slurred shouts and singing, laughter and curses of drinkers homeward bound, swirling with the dizzying thoughts filling her head until her brain was exhausted. Worst was the pain in her heart and her guts, which had increased steadily with the hours. *Simon, Mack.* She'd left them behind.

So lost had she been in the numbing grief, she hadn't thought to seek them out, explain the situation. Without a moment's pause or thought she'd sprinted from the house, from the agonising truth that all believed her a demon capable of such wickedness and wanted her gone. And however much she regretted it, she also knew a tinge of gladness. For the lads just might be permitted to stay on at Bracken House – after all, she was the monster in the household's eyes, wasn't she? The boys were guilty of no wrongdoing. And they deserved to remain, to continue the new life they had found, to be healthy, clean, safe. If she'd pelted to the garden and poured out the incident to them, they would have been at her side in a heartbeat and she'd have hated herself for it afterwards, because they didn't deserve to be cast out.

But neither did I, her inner voice said, and she squeezed her eyes shut to block out the images returning to play behind them, mocking her with their cruelty. She saw again Caroline's stony face and glinting eyes as she watched the proceedings. Oh, but she hated her, *hated* her! And Philip's anger, the words he'd spewed, the names he'd called her. Was he in on the act or had his wife hoodwinked him, too, into believing the horrid tale? she wondered. She shrugged. It mattered not, now, did it? One thing was clear – Philip did take after his father in at least one respect: he harboured for his off-spring a deep and fierce love. How she wished she had her father to care for and protect her, as Lucy did. But he was gone from this world.

Speaking of Miss Lucy . . . Hunched over as though in physical pain, her distress, her voice as she'd uttered the one word that had torn Pip's heart in two: 'Yes.' And her own mother was behind the act, had forced her child to speak it, to be rid of Pip, to ruin her life. Why, why? Just what had she done to deserve such vitriol?

The master's anger and disappointment flitted back and cut just as deep this time around. Yet it was the memory of Cook's expression, the uncertainty that had taken root in her grey eyes at Lucy's admission, that seared far more. For Pip had begun to look upon the

179

large and formidable being almost as a mother figure. She felt betrayed, let down, heartbroken that the saviour she'd come to love had turned on her. *For nothing. I've done nothing!*

And Miss Josephine. Oh, but she must be beside herself. How would she cope? Would she hate Pip for deserting her in her time of need? And she'd promised to aid the lady, too. She'd vowed to see her through her illness, to help her combat it. And now, Josephine would grow more agitated at the prospect of fighting this alone again, would get worse and all would be lost with Mr Sutton-Shaw, and her future would be ruined. *Oh why, why?* Pip asked herself of Caroline again, tears burning.

But Simon and young Mack, the thought of never seeing them again . . . the pain of that overrode all else and now her anguish burst forth. The crying awakened her pain-shocked brain. Great gushing sobs tore from her, making her splutter for breath. *Lads, lads. I miss thee, need thee* . . .

'Nay, mister. Please, mister!'

The small scared voice sounded mere feet away from Pip's hiding place; gulping down her emotion, she listened harder. After some moments, the child – for that's clearly what it was – spoke again:

'Nay. Nay, please. I don't want to!'

Frowning, Pip shuffled towards the door and squinted through one of the numerous holes. At first, the dark street appeared deserted. Then a tall figure flitted in the pool of murky gaslight close by and she held her breath. The silhouette shifted into view but though it was facing her and but a short distance away, the dim light failed to pick out its facial features clearly; though it was quite obvious it was a man – a *gentle*man at that.

His tall hat and the trim cut of his cloth proved this, as did the shiny cane he carried under his arm, its tip winking gold in the lamp's glow. He glanced up and down the street and, satisfied no one was approaching, returned his attention to whatever business he'd been about.

'Mister, I don't like it.'

Pip's heartbeat quickened at the fright in the young-ster's voice – the youngster in this gentleman's company, she realised, peering through the gap between his legs and spotting two small boots that stood facing his own. He seemed to have the child wedged against a wall, in a nook between two warehouses.

'Come, now. Dry your tears. Don't you want the shil-lings I promised you?'

The banging in her chest sped to a gallop. She recog-nised that smooth, refined voice only too well. *The man who had attempted to lure away Mack a short time ago.*

God above, but he was trying it with another! And from the sound of this one's distress, he was doing what Simon had said he would: he was hurting the poor mite, or soon would. She couldn't sit here and allow it to hap-pen, she couldn't, despite her fear. And afraid she was, for this man was dangerous and violent to boot, had proven it with his cane that day across Simon's back. She must intervene, no matter the outcome. She'd never forgive herself otherwise.

Slowly, slowly, she eased open the door and edged outside. Keeping to the shadows, she stole closer.

'Oh, nay. What are you . . .? Oh, you mustn't, mister!'

Sounds of a struggle could be heard, then: 'Cease this nonsense!' the gentleman snarled, his patience gone. 'You, boy, will do my bidding or feel my wrath. Do you understand? Quiet!' he added when the child

181

began to weep softly, the sound muffled as though the man had a hand over his mouth. 'Or so help me, you'll regret it.'

Pip bit down on her lip until she tasted blood, her every nerve urging her to spring on them, stop this monster from harming the boy further. Yet still, fear held her back and she cursed her cowardice. The gentleman's breathing had quickened and it seemed his victim had given up resisting; he uttered no sound, now. Suddenly, Mack's bonny grin and laughing blue eyes crashed through Pip's mind and hot fury flooded her veins. Of their own accord, her hands balled into tight fists. She stepped into view. ''Ere, stop!'

With a gasp, the gentleman whipped around.

'You'll harm the mite no further, d'you hear?' she announced boldly, though the quaver behind the words gave her terror away and she cursed inwardly. She cleared her throat to banish the shakiness. 'You leave him be.'

'I don't believe ... *You* again?' In one swift movement, the gentleman lunged, catching her off guard. She lost her footing and his face twisted in a grim smile as she hurtled backwards. Her buttocks hit the hard flags first, the impact stealing the breath from her, and she rolled into the gutter, hitting her head on the journey, to lie in the filth in a crumpled heap. Through bleary eyes, she peered up, a hand out in front of her to ward off his inevitable advance. 'Nay, leave me ... Someone help me!' she cried hoarsely, trying to haul herself up.

Clogged steps struck the cobbles as the little boy made his escape up Great Ancoats Street; swearing under his breath, the man threw Pip a furious look. 'You interfering gutter-dog. I'll snuff you out this time, you see if I don't! It's not as though anyone shall miss or mourn a parasite such as you, is it?' He closed in on her, fingers, like bony talons, outstretched, and a scream ripped from her. To her relief, her act had the desired effect: he paused, worry flitting across his long face, and glanced left and right.

Taking advantage of the moment's distraction, she skittered to her feet. Her head felt weightless, her vision fuzzy. When she reached up to the tender spot that had made contact with the ground, something hot and sticky met her touch. *Blood.* Her hair was wet with it and she knew a moment's panic as dizziness swooped again, stronger than before.

Please don't let me faint, for I'll be at this devil's mercy completely and Lord knows what he's capable of, she willed herself as she swayed slightly on the spot. She had to get away. She must, but how? His looming form would be on her before she could take a few steps. *Help me, Lord, please!*

Assistance came not from God, but from two figures turning the corner.

The gentleman, peering towards the newcomers with a mixture of scorn and unease, drew in a furious breath. Pip took her chance. Surely he wouldn't seize her or give chase with witnesses up ahead? Twisting on her heel, she bolted in a somewhat drunken sprint in the opposite direction. Her own were the only pounding feet to be heard. The gentleman hadn't set off after her in pursuit; relieved tears sprang to her eyes. Gasping, she continued down the street, trying desperately to regain her balance. Her injured head had begun to thump and nausea was rising.

Before hurtling around the corner into the inky blackness of Mather Street, she thought she heard someone call her name. Certain it was her muddled senses playing games, she didn't stop. Nor did she look back. Ignoring her burning lungs, she picked up her feet and ran faster.

A few turnings later – how many, she couldn't say, couldn't be sure of anything, now – kaleidoscopic colours popped and burst behind her eyes, merging with the pewter of the cobblestones. She was aware of juddering to a halt in the centre of the road. Then weight left her body and she folded to the floor in a dead faint.

*

'Ay, you're for wakening finally. All right, lass?'

'Mm?'

'Drink this.'

Fiery liquid trickled down her throat and she gagged and spluttered. Though surprisingly, after some seconds, it seemed to help. The pain she felt in numerous places numbed to a dull ache and the muggy feeling inside her head slowly subsided.

''Tis brandy, is all. For the shock, like.'

Pip squinted through the gloomy light of a single candle. A squat man in his middle years sat on a low stool beside her, stroking his long dirty beard, eyes holding relief. She raised herself on an elbow. 'Where am I?'

'Nan Nuttall's place.'

'Who?'

'Nan Nuttall. She runs the common lodging house you're sitting in.' He rose and crossed to a small deal table propped against one wall. A fire burning low in the grate lent some of its meagre light to his features. He was painfully thin, she saw; his sunken cheekbones and hungry stare, as he tore with his hands a heel of loaf in two, were testament to a strife-worn life. Returning to her, he held out a piece.

Having grown accustomed to Bracken House's regular meals, which were of substantial proportions, her stomach seemed no longer the shrunken thing it had been. Used to being filled now, and not having eaten since lunchtime, the hunger she'd been fortunate not to know for a while had crept upon her like a stealthy foe. That familiar instinct of survival told her to snatch the crust and feed, but she had to ask: 'Mister, is tha sure?'

'Aye. Go on, take it.'

'Ta, thanks.'

'Nowt left to drink, mind,' he told her through a mouthful of stale crumbs. 'Sorry.'

'It's all right,' she lied, quite desperate for a sup of milky tea.

'Folks calls me Peter.'

'I'm Pip.'

'Pip?' His brows, like fat slugs, bunched together. 'Like what you find in fruit?'

She shrugged. 'S'pose so.'

'Aye, well. Takes all sorts to make a world.'

She nodded and they lapsed into silence as they ate their spartan meal. Afterwards, she felt much better. She fingered the back of her head. Though it was tender to the touch, the blood flow had at least ceased.

'Took a tumble, did thee?' Peter motioned to her injury.

'Aye.'

'That'll be what had you passing out, no doubt, as you did. I spotted thee in the road, thought you were a dead dog forra minute. Gave me a shock, you did, when I saw you were a lass.'

'You carried me in here?'

'That's right.'

'Ta. Ta, Peter.'

It seemed to take an effort to bring a small smile to his lips, as though he wasn't used to it. Mind, given his obvious circumstances, it was little wonder. A body on the dire side of life had little reason to smile.

'There's many a bad 'un lurking round these 'ere streets when the sun's high – the night hours are worser still. And well, when I spied you by chance through the window . . . I couldn't very well leave thee alone out there, could I?'

The truth in his words she understood only too well. She shuddered. 'Ta,' she repeated.

'You destitute, like?' he asked, as though sensing her experiences of the past.

She hesitated in giving an affirmative answer. But why? She was, wasn't she? A lump formed in her throat. That she was back on these mean streets again! The horror, fear, uncertainty – and this time all alone. Lord, how would she bear it?

'Thought as much. Mind, to look at thee . . .' He nodded to her dress.

She clapped a hand to her mouth. 'Oh! Oh nay, I . . .' Shame coloured her cheeks. In her haste earlier, she'd forgotten all about her clothing, should have given everything back straight away. What must the household think of her? A thief as well as a brute . . . 'I stole it,' she whispered.

'Aye, well. We does what we must, eh?'

'Nay, you don't under— I've never once stolen owt in my life afore.'

'Don't fret much over it. All will seem brighter the morrow, it allus does. You're welcome of my bed. The floor don't mither me; it's not like I ain't passed a night on t' ground afore now. And these here boards look a sight comfier than the flagstones out yonder. I'm just blessed of the dry roof over me. And the warmth. Aye, I'll be reet in front of yon fire.'

Relief washed through Pip. Thoughts of returning outside, where that devilish gentleman and others of his ilk roamed, had her shaking with dread. 'Won't Nan Nuttall mind?'

It was his turn to shrug. 'Whether she will or no, it'll be too late, won't it, by morning? She'll not venture down here no more the night.'

'But happen she sends thee packing? What will you do the morrow night?'

He released a gruff chuckle. 'I haven't the brass for the morrow's bed and ain't likely to find it, so there's no worry on that score. In any case, I'm for moving on come daybreak.' He made for the table again and lifted the stub of candle. 'Come on, I'll show you to next door. 'Tis sleep you need; to heal, like. You'll feel better come morning.'

It was now that Pip realised they were in some mode of communal kitchen-cum-sitting area. Light from the candle Peter now held up showed a small, grubby-looking cooking range with a few sagging chairs crushed around it. Besides the table she'd already seen, several stools and empty wooden crates completed the furnishings. It wasn't grand like Bracken House, by any stretch of the imagination. Yet as Peter had pointed out, it was at least dry. And preferable to the streets in that it was safe, if nothing else.

They entered a long room crammed with iron bed-steads; in here, filth and poverty stagnated the air like a noxious gas. Trying not to openly grimace, she followed the man to an empty bed squeezed between two others, the walking space leading to it barely passable, so narrow was it. This Nan Nuttall knew how to make brass, all right, Pip thought, reckoning there should be half the number of beds in here. But, beggars couldn't be choosers, could they? And that's what she was, now, once again. At least she would have to be tomorrow if she wanted to eat, survive. And the day after that, and the next day . . . *God above, she was going to cry again.*

'You'll receive no trouble from any person here present,' he said loud enough for the seemingly slumbering room to hear. He added in a clear and grim warning, 'Mind, if you've need of me, just yell.'

'Ta, ever so,' she whispered, hoping his veiled threat to the others would be sufficient to steer them away from trying anything with her and that she wouldn't be in want of his assistance. She knew what folk who frequented these establishments were capable of. The dregs of society, all ages and every manner of criminal and sinner passed through the doors of lodging houses such as these, which choked every pocket of this city. She, Simon and Mack had passed a night here and there in such places when they could spare the pennies.

Peter left to return to the room next door and she glanced at the dark lumps of humanity all around her, huddled from the biting cold beneath every manner of coverings: threadbare blankets and sheets, and ragged scraps of material that had once been God only knew what; even newspaper. Anything that could be used to chase the chill from your bones, was.

Thoughts of Cook's clean and comfortable bed, the boys' warm bodies snuggled close either side of her, the heady sense of sheer contentment she'd known and wouldn't again brought back the agonising ache inside.

She clenched her teeth together tightly to quash her emotion. She couldn't let it escape, she couldn't, for she'd never be able to stem it. She felt torn to bits inside, worse than she'd ever known or thought possible. Broken, utterly. Alone. And she wouldn't ever be mended. She couldn't make this better. No one could.

Thoughts consumed with loss, she unlaced and removed her new boots through instinct alone and placed them under her lumpy, and rather smelly, pillow. Experience had taught her that desperate people carried out desperate deeds – any possessions that could be spirited away from the sleeping would be, and it would be a miracle indeed if you ever saw them or the perpetrators again. Then she laid her head down, dragged the scant covers around her and pulled her body into a tight ball.

My lads, my lads. The silent cry repeated like a mantra in her tortured mind. Just before a restless sleep claimed her, words from another whispered alongside them, and Pip frowned softly.

'She's the one put Miss Lucy up to this, I'll be bound.'

The memory of Hardman's speech, and the truth of it, left Pip as cold as it had last time.

'Caroline Goldthorpe needs getting rid of . . .'

Before exhaustion claimed her, Pip's head moved of its own accord in a nod.

For good and proper.

Chapter 12

WHEN PIP AWOKE, Peter was gone.

It was shortly after sunrise and most of the beds'
occupants were still snoring when she'd jolted from a
bad dream. After slipping on her boots, she'd padded
to the communal room only to find it empty. A feeling
of sadness had overcome her and it remained with her
still as she exited the lodging house and made off aim-
lessly down the frost-stroked street.

She would have liked the opportunity to thank the
man who had come to her rescue last night. Plucking
her from the cobbles and carrying her to safety, he'd
saved her from God alone knew what fate – as he'd
pointed out, the slums were a danger to man, beast,
and all in between once the sun retired for the night.
He'd shared what little food he'd had with her, not to
mention the last of his brandy; all that kept his chill
body warm most nights, no doubt. His bed, that he'd
likely had to beg the brass to pay for, he'd given up for
her. More importantly, he'd been kind, understanding.
And he hadn't expected nor wanted a single thing in
return. Some folk – aye, there were still some around
despite it feeling to the contrary at times – really were
golden hearted.

Pip said a prayer for him. Then she wrapped her

arms around herself as a shield from the cold and trudged on to London Road, where she knew it would be busiest.

Cotton mill and factory workers had long since begun their shifts, and mostly she encountered a multitude of street traders, hawkers, dead-eyed men scouring the city in search of a day's work and swarms of barefoot children. Women were in short supply; those not in employment would be occupied tending to home and hearth.

She attempted to beg from one or two people but found the words wouldn't come and, mumbling apologies, she'd scuttle off, face ablaze. She couldn't do this alone. Realisation had panic gripping her chest like a physical thing. She didn't want to – shouldn't *have* to. She was guilty of nothing, nothing! Injustice stung afresh. She needed the lads, *needed* Bracken House. Lord, how would she survive? The sudden thought that if this was life from now on then she'd rather cease to be, entered her mind and instantly she was sorry. Folk desperate to live died by the second from all manner of causes the world over: disease, old age, even murder – who was she to warrant such a notion, young and healthy as she was? But oh, she was desperately lonely, afraid, hadn't the slightest idea what she was to do.

On she roamed, with little thought or reason, and by midday, the gnawing hunger she'd felt upon awakening had developed, like a growling monster dwelling within her. Her throat was parched and her new boots had rubbed her heels to ribbons. The pain in her heart, however, outweighed all.

As the minutes and then hours crawled along, she found herself thinking more and more of Jess Hardman and her whisper to meet her today. What could she want? She detested her and the lads at the best of times; why choose to go out of her way to meet with Pip? Mind, the housemaid had said before, hadn't she, that her hatred for Caroline Goldthorpe burned brighter. Did she have some plan or other to be rid of the lady, which she'd admitted she wanted to do, and needed her help to achieve it? Well, Hardman could go and whistle. As much as she disliked Lucy's mother too, Pip wanted no part in whatever scheme the housemaid had up her sleeve.

Or do I? her mind whispered. *Wouldn't life be much easier all round if Caroline was gone? I might just be able to return to Bracken House if she was and . . .* Common sense returned, scattering the tempting possibility from her mind. Despite everything, she didn't want to seek revenge. She wasn't that kind of a person. Caroline and others like her were the wicked ones, not she. Bitterness had no part in her life, never had, for it was a fruitless emotion sure to bring but misery to the one who harboured it. Her sins would catch up with the woman eventually, God always made sure of it. At least Pip's conscience was clear and would remain so. The truth would out some day, it usually did.

No. Whatever Hardman was concocting, she wanted no part in it.

Nevertheless, Pip found herself walking in the direction of the station as the appointed hour approached. Glancing up and down the street, she awaited the maid's familiar figure impatiently. She wanted to see her, aye, to find out how the lads were. Had they been allowed to stay on at Bracken House? Oh, she hoped so. After all, they hadn't been accused of anything, had they? There was no reason – or at least Caroline surely hadn't invented one just yet – for them to be cast out. Despite her feelings of betrayal, abandonment, she must also know that Cook was well. Tabby, she missed her too. And Lucy.

Oh Miss, why didn't you speak out, tell them I was innocent, that it was all lies? I thought we were friends. She swallowed down tears. She couldn't be angry with her. The blame lay not with her, not a bit. She was but a child, one who had been manipulated by her own mother. She'd forced her daughter to lie, caused her untold grief and upset, it had been clear. What parent would do such a thing? She couldn't fathom the actions at all.

Ten minutes passed, then twenty. Still Pip stood, eyes trained to the corner of the street. Another score crawled by, and still there was no sign of her. After an hour, it was clear Hardman wouldn't show and Pip had to swallow disappointed tears. What had kept the house-maid from coming? she wondered, turning reluctantly and walking away. Had something else occurred at Bracken House? Or had it just been a spiteful ploy to hurt Pip further? Was Hardman, at this moment, laughing to herself with thoughts of Pip standing here in the cold; had she never had any intention of meeting her? *Oh, to hell with them all!*

Dashing away her spilling tears with the back of her hand, cursing the day she'd ever set eyes on Bracken House, Pip picked up her skirts and ran.

What took her down Garrick Street's narrow road, she didn't know. Her feet seemed to have taken on a life of their own. Or perhaps she wanted to feel close to her mam? Either way, she wished she hadn't; the sight of the sad-coloured, tightly packed terraced houses had her shivering with grief. Misty eyes sought out their cellar of old, and for an age she simply stared at it, thinking, feeling. It appeared more run-down than she remembered.

Or had love cast it in a pleasant sheen when she'd lived here with her poor mother? She couldn't say. Her gaze strayed down the steep steps to settle on the battered door. Again, she pictured in her mind it swinging open and her mother emerging, matted shawl draped across her shoulders, brown curls bouncing and lips parted in smile. The sting of her tears grew unbearable; she closed her eyes.

'Pip?'

The word tapped on the edges of the fog filling her head. Breath catching in her throat, her eyelids parted slowly. Half expecting that she'd conjured the past back to life, she blinked at the door below. But no – still it stood closed. No mam filling the doorway. No one, nothing. Her lips trembled in disappointment. Hunger was toying with her, had her senses confused, that's what. Shaking her head, she squeezed her eyes shut once more.

'Oh, lass.'

There was no mistaking it this time; someone *was* speaking. But . . . who . . .? Pip opened her eyes again, turning this time, and her brow creased in a deep frown. The woman standing behind her wore her shawl wrapped tightly, not lying loose. Nor was her hair rich chestnut and unbound, but iron grey collected at her nape in a knot. It wasn't Mam, but Cook. And Simon was by her side! How, why . . .? What were they doing here?

'Cook? Eeh, Simon!'

'God alive.' Cook gazed back in amazed relief. 'Thank the heavens above! Ay, lovey, where's tha been?'

Before Pip could answer, the lad caught her in a crushing embrace. Then, pulling back, he shook her none too gently by the shoulders. 'Where the hell have you been? Me and Cook, here, have been scouring these streets in search of thee for most of the night. You've had us worried summat sick!'

Tears welled up at his harshness. She tried to hug him again but he sidestepped her, eyebrows knotted, face dark. 'Lad—'

'Why didn't you settle down in the privy, as we normally used to of a night? I'd have found you right away if you had. Daft, that's what you are!'

'I, I did! But that fella, you remember the gentleman what tried hurting Mack, he were at it across the way from me with another and—'

'You went after him?' Simon's tone was incredulous.

'What's this, now?' Cook looked horrified. 'What gentleman?'

'Some filthy bleeder we've crossed paths with afore,' Simon ground out, 'who's a taste for young flesh – and this 'un, here, went *after* him!'

'I had to. The poor little mite were crying . . . but he escaped and I managed to, an' all. A kindly man offered me shelter in a lodging house for the night, so all's well.'

'All's . . . all's *well*? After the night we've had? We thought we spotted thee at one point, called out your name, but nay.'

Simon broke off to give an angry shake of his head and Pip sighed inwardly. She'd believed, had she not, that she heard her name called last night when fleeing from that varmint? Yet injury and numbing terror had affected her logic. Oh, if only she'd turned!

'Owt could have occurred,' added Simon.

'I just . . . didn't think. You weren't there!' she burst out on a sob.

'Aye, for you abandoned me and Bread, that's why! Norra goodbye, nowt!' He dragged a hand across his mouth. 'What were you playing at, fleeing from Bracken House like that without a by-your-leave?'

'You talk as though it were of my own choosing.' Anger was filling Pip, now; he had no right to talk to her so, as if she was in the wrong. 'I were slat out in case you'd not heard.'

Slowly, the animosity faded from his face. He heaved a sigh. 'Aye. I know. All this . . . none of it's your fault. I were just so bloody . . . nearly out of my mind with . . .' He ran a hand through his hair. 'It matters not, now, anyroad. You're well, so no harm done.'

He'd been afraid for her safety and not a little hurt that she'd run out on him. That was the reason for his anger. Although, being Simon, he wouldn't say it, it was written all over his face. Pip's eyes softened. Tentatively, she reached for his hand and curled her fingers around his. 'Sorry, lad. I were fair mad with upset, weren't thinking straight.' She tightened her hold and he reciprocated. 'By, I ain't half missed you,' she murmured. 'Mack, an' all. The lad's all right?'

'Aye.' It was Cook who spoke. Her expression was one of deep guilt. 'Oh, love. That I disbelieved you for even a second . . .'

'You mean . . .?' Pip looked from one to the other. 'Cook, you know I were speaking the truth? You see it, now?'

'I do. The master and his son along with me. Miss Lucy, she broke down shortly after you scarpered, told how she'd been forced to speak them wicked untruths. Eeh, the poor lass, she's in pieces. Me and Albert, that we could be hoodwinked like that . . . It's a good lass you are, we should have known. Oh, we're that sorry, aye.' Her eyes were watery. 'I'd a feeling it would be worth checking this here street, recall you saying this is where you once dwelled and figured your memories of your poor mam would draw you here.' She put her hand on Pip's shoulder in a tender touch. 'Come back, lass. Will thee?'

The sweet feeling of justice! She could have wept with relief. They believed her, *finally*. They thought ill of her no longer, wanted her *home*! 'And her what put the young miss up to it?' she forced herself to ask, for how would she ever know peace again there amidst Caroline's evil doings?

'Huh! That one's gone.'

'She . . . has?'

With a satisfied sniff, Cook nodded. 'Aye and for good and proper, an' all.'

Shock and confusion filled Pip but before she could probe further this extraordinary news, the woman spoke again:

'Anyroad. There'll be time aplenty for the telling of all that once we're home.' She flashed a hopeful smile. 'That's if you'll have Bracken House, and us, back?'

Pip laughed tearfully. 'But the master; he really wants me to return, an' all?'

'He does. So? What says thee?'

As if she even had to *think* about it! 'Aye. Oh ta. Ta, Cook.'

As they turned for Ardwick Green, a host of thoughts swirled through her mind. Caroline was gone! But where? And what of Mr Philip? Cook had said that along with his father, he now knew the truth – what had his reaction been? More importantly, what reception would she receive from him upon her return? The guilty party was, after all, his wife . . . Just what had gone on?

Oh, but she ached to see Lucy, to reassure her she

blamed her for naught, that they were still friends. Mack, Tabby also, she'd missed something awful. As for her mistress . . . 'Oh, Miss Josephine!' Pip stopped in her tracks to turn concerned eyes to the woman by her side. 'She's all right, ain't she, Cook?'

'Well as can be, you know? She'll be fair pleased to see thee, mind.'

'And me her. Eeh, I'm going home,' Pip added in an excited whisper. Yet when they reached the corner, she hesitated.

Glancing over her shoulder, she cast a soft smile in the general direction of Nan Nuttall's decrepit abode. In her mind, she thanked Peter for his kindness and promised she'd not forget him.

Then she linked her arms through her companions' and the three continued on their way.

Chapter 13

PIP WAS AWARDED a grand return. The moment she stepped over Bracken House's threshold, Bink and Lunar, the master's Labradors, hurtled across the kitchen to greet her with wet tongues and wagging tails. Mack, a grooming brush in his hand, wasn't far behind. With a grin as bright as a summer sun, he threw himself into her arms and clung to her, as though afraid she'd vanish again if he let go.

'Eeh, lad.' Closing her eyes, Pip pressed her cheek against his. 'Now, then. I'm back, I'm back, don't fret.'

'Why did you leave us, me and Simon? Did you stop loving us for a bit, Pip, is that it?' the youngster asked brokenly.

''Ere, what? Never! You two are what my heart beats for, allus shall.' She glanced to Simon over Mack's shoulder with a tender smile. The one he returned to her was, uncharacteristically, just as soft.

'Right, now. Let Pip here up for air, my lad. The lass needs a sound feeding, I'll be bound, poor love.' Cook shepherded her to a chair at the table beside Tabby, who hugged her close and told her she was glad she was home, then bustled around the fire with purpose. Pip's stomach growled in anticipation – if there was one thing the woman could be relied upon to do, it was to stuff your guts close to bursting. Oh, she was *back*!

In no time at all, the hot beef and onions and large helping of potatoes, not to mention thick floury bread, and all washed down with two cups of tea, had vanished and she felt much better. Cook had just placed a generous helping of ginger cake and fresh cream before her when the baize door opened and Hardman appeared. Catching her eye, Pip gave her a knowing look.

It was obvious to her now why the housemaid hadn't shown for their arranged meeting: Caroline was gone so whatever she'd been plotting, there was no need for it now. Although Hardman didn't look exactly brimming with joy at the development, Pip noticed. She'd had a sneaking suspicion why Hardman yearned for Caroline to be out of the way – Philip. With his wife gone, she'd surely assumed she would have the master's son to herself. Then why was her mouth downcast and obvious displeasure lurking behind her eyes? It didn't make sense but Pip pushed the questions from her mind with a shrug. None of that mattered, now. She was back, and neither wanted nor needed to concern herself with it.

Plonking Albert's empty lunch tray on to the table, Hardman flicked her gaze to Pip. Discreetly, she gave her an almost disappointed shake of the head, and Pip's puzzlement returned. What was wrong with her?

'Master were asking just now whether you'd returned and if you'd had any joy locating this one,' the housemaid told Cook. 'He said when so, you were to inform him right away.'

The cook nodded. 'I'll take Pip up shortly. Poor thing's famished and needs to finish her meal.'

'Could I call in to Miss Josephine first, please, Cook?'

asked Pip, pushing her empty bowl away. 'I'd like her to know I'm back, that I'm here for her again. Been worried about her summat awful, I have, since yesterday.'

'Best you visit the master first, lovey. He'll not keep thee long, then you can see Miss Josephine—'

'Nay, she can't.' Hardman shook her head. 'Doctor's in with her and gave strict instructions they're not to be disturbed.'

'Oh no. Were the poor miss taken ill in my absence?'

Hardman nodded. 'Mr Philip couldn't calm her so sent for the doctor. Mind, he's been up there a while, now.'

Pip's stomach dropped. Miss Josephine had been forced to rely on him again because she hadn't been here? But he didn't understand her ailment, wasn't making matters better with his daft diagnoses of rotten blood and suchlike. Oh but she felt guilty, she did, for she felt she'd let Miss Josephine down. Had she had another attack? She must have been so afraid. And she'd promised the lady she wasn't going anywhere, that she would do her utmost to help her conquer it. She must see her, check she was well.

'Can we see the master, now, Cook?' she asked, scraping back her chair. The sooner she'd fulfilled Albert's request, the quicker she could go and see her mistress. After all, the doctor should have left by then; Hardman had just said herself that he'd been here some time.

Miss Josephine was still on her mind when Cook showed her into the master's room minutes later. Though all thoughts melted and she shuddered to a halt to see Lucy sitting cross-legged on the bed playing cards with her grandfather. The girl looked around at their entrance. Instantly, her eyes widened and filled with tears, and Pip's did likewise. Though Pip knew her own gaze shone with only reassurance, Lucy's eyes were filled with raw guilt. She rose slowly and came to stand in front of her.

'Pip . . .'

'It's all right, Miss Lucy,' she murmured with a soft smile.

The blue eyes creased further. 'You're not angry? Oh, but I don't deserve your forgiveness, I'm sure. What I said . . . that wicked lie against your good character . . . I'm sorry! Oh, I am, Pip, really! I never meant . . . never wanted to . . .'

'I know, Miss Lucy, I know. You're not at fault, nay never. You're my friend, allus shall be.' Pip barely got the words out before the girl flung herself at her and caught her in a crushing hug. Smiling, she returned the embrace. Eeh, but she did love this innocent lamb, had missed her as much. She was so very happy things were well again between them.

'Where did you go to, Pip? Were you quite safe? We have been worried so, Grandy and I.'

The thought of polluting her pure mind with the reality of life beyond these walls, the slums and all they contained, filled her with horror. She forced another smile. 'I were all right, honest. Don't matter none now, for I'm returned – and oh, sir,' she added with feeling, turning to Albert, 'I'm that thankful. Ta ever so for having me back at Bracken House.'

He and Cook had looked on quietly with sad smiles as she and Lucy made their peace; now, Albert released a heavy sigh. He indicated for her to come closer. She did and to her great surprise, he reached for her hand and held it between his. His kindness brought tears to her eyes. Not for the first time, she marvelled at the grand good fortune that had first brought her to this door.

'We have indeed been worried. Dear Pip . . . we have treated you with great dishonour. I can only apologise with unreserved sincerity. Rest assured, the perpetrator has left this house and shan't set a toe inside again. Why she did it . . .' He shook his greying head. 'I don't know, nor do I understand, what she wished to gain from such an act. Again, I'm sorry I doubted your word. We all are.'

'She really ain't coming back, sir?' Pip was agog with astonishment. This, from Albert's own lips! And yet neither he nor his granddaughter appeared upset at the loss, not a bit. This really was rather surprising; Caroline was, after all, Lucy's mother. Not a very good one, it was true, given the distress she'd put her child through but still . . . And Mr Philip? Where was he? How did he feel about all this? Just where *had* Caroline gone?

'Certainly not. She packed her effects and vacated this house yesterday evening.'

'And halloo to that!' Lucy added, covering her mouth with a giggle when Albert wagged a finger at her in mock sternness. 'Oh, Pip, imagine it! She's left at long last.'

'You're not . . . upset, Miss Lucy? Even a little?'

The girl gazed at her as though she were mad. 'Why of course not!'

'And Mr Philip?' Her surprise mounting, Pip murmured the question to the master.

'I shouldn't think so,' he replied with an easy lift of his shoulder.

'Oh. Well. Well, I . . .' She didn't know what to say. She'd known Caroline was a devilsome piece, but by! This lot, her own kin . . .?

'Ah! You've returned, I see.'

The voice, followed by the approaching footsteps behind her, made the hairs on the back of Pip's neck stand to attention like well-trained soldiers. Her head swivelled around and she could do nothing but stare in confused horror at Caroline standing in front of her. *No. No . . . But what . . . how . . .?*

'Pip, isn't it?' A disarming smile stroked her lips, though Pip was certain she detected an altogether different emotion lurking behind the ice-blue eyes. 'On behalf of myself and my husband, please do accept our regret for the recent wrongdoing towards you. Given it was a member of our personal staff who committed the act, our consternation is stronger still, as you can imagine. However, as I'm sure my father-in-law has assured you, Finch has gone and for good.'

Finch? *Oh my . . . of all the slippery, double-dealing . . .* Pip swallowed hard. Obvious, at least to herself, smugness now glistened in the lady's gaze and Pip felt bile rise in her throat. She'd wormed her way out of it. She'd placed the blame at her employee's door and the family had fallen for it. No wonder they hadn't appeared overly concerned at the loss of the guilty party, in particular Lucy – they had been referring to Finch all along! Whilst all the time, she'd believed, had *hoped* it was the real villain who had been shown the door. For despite what she'd discovered, she just knew that the nursemaid hadn't been the one with a hand in this whole sorry mess. Caroline had.

Given her position, she'd successfully shifted the blame to cover her own back. And what did this mean for her, for the lads? Surely her vendetta against them wouldn't stop here? No, this wasn't over. *But God above, what have I done to deserve this?* she silently beseeched the Almighty, biting down on her lip to curb the tears threatening to escape.

'Of course,' Caroline was saying now, though Pip

barely registered the words through the sad fog clogging her mind, 'I shall ensure that the next nursemaid we take on is of a more agreeable nature. The recent incident shall not be repeated, I assure you.'

Silence hung between them, then: 'Pip, say thank you to Mrs Goldthorpe,' murmured Cook, giving her a small nudge. 'She's the one what insisted that Finch piece be got rid of and pronto.'

I'll bet she did. 'Ta, thanks, Mrs Goldthorpe,' she forced out on a painful breath.

Caroline flashed a too-nice smile, nodded to the others, and was gone as swiftly as she'd appeared.

'Oh, but Grandy, I don't want another nursemaid!' whined Lucy, snuggling close to him, her rosebud mouth puckered in a pout. 'I shan't have one, no! I shall tell Papa; he will persuade Mama that I'm not in need of one. Won't he, Grandy?'

As a means of placating the child, Albert patted her head. But his attention was on Pip. The lines on his brow deepened as he frowned. 'Are you quite well, lass? Indeed, you look fit to drop. Mabel,' he added, glancing to Pip's side, 'put the child to bed right away. She has been through the mill, poor mite, and shall require some time to recover from her ordeal. I insist,' he continued to Pip firmly when she made to protest. 'Rest is what you need and that is what you shall have. Now, go on. Mabel will see you right.'

'I will that. You can ease up in my bed the night, lass.'

Too sore of heart to argue, Pip, after returning Lucy's sweet goodbyes, allowed herself to be led from the room. Outside, however, she drew back as they headed for the stairs. 'Cook, I'm all right, really, honest.' She inclined her head to Miss Josephine's door. 'Let me see the lady? Oh do, please?'

'But Albert said—'

'I'll rest soon, honest I will, when I've seen that Miss Josephine's well. Can I, Cook?'

Surveying Pip properly, her face took on the expression that the master had worn a moment ago. She cocked her head. 'Summat's troubling thee still. What is it?'

The temptation to spill her guts and cry out all that was going on – Caroline's deception, the real truth – was crippling. But something, perhaps fear of Cook releasing her wrath on to the lady and creating a whole other level of trouble for her, made her hold back.

'If there's owt the matter, owt at all . . . You know, don't yer, that you can depend on me?'

'Aye, like last time?' The words were out before Pip could bite them back. She blushed crimson. 'Cook, I . . . didn't mean that. I'm sorry, I am, honest—'

'Tha talks truth, though,' Cook interjected, averting her gaze. When she spoke again, her voice shook with stark regret. 'I let thee down. I was wrong, aye, I say I was wrong. But know this: never shall I doubt you again.' She brought her stare back and it took Pip's breath away to see it shining with something she'd hungered for without realising it, that she hadn't seen in another adult, another woman, for such a long time: love.

She felt her chin wobble but was powerless to stop it, and the next moment she was enveloped in Cook's arms and weeping softly into her snowy apron. 'It were awful, Cook, awful. I don't ever want to leave here, leave you, again.'

'Nor shall a soul try and make thee, neither. Not again. Not on my watch. Wicked bugger, that Finch; I never did take to her. You know, she gave no reason as to why she made it all up. Miss Lucy told how she'd cornered her in the Green after playing with you, said as how she must seek out Mr Philip upon her return to the house and spew the untruth exactly as she'd told her, else it'd be the worst for her. Frickened the dear angel out of her wits, she did. You know the lass wouldn't have bad-mouthed about you otherwise, don't you? She's taken to you, lovey, and it's nice to see. You'll try and forget all this, now, eh? Put it behind you, like?'

So that's how Caroline had done it. Of course, she should have guessed. She hadn't persuaded her daughter to tell such lies; she'd have known she'd have been in hot water and unable to wriggle out of it had Lucy slipped up. No. She'd ordered the nursemaid to do her dirty work instead, had had no qualms about Finch threatening her child to do the deed. She was horrid, horrid. And quite clearly capable of anything. Just how did this bode for her? Dread snaked down her spine.

With effort, she forced out the lie: 'Aye Cook. I'll dwell on it no more.'

'There's a good, bonny lass. Now, I'd best get back to my duties.' Cook gave her a last squeeze. She sniffed twice, three times, then nudged Pip towards the door up ahead. 'Go on with you, then, else you'll have me bawling into the family's soup and that'll not go down reet well, will it? 'Ere and if the doctor's still with her – though he really should have taken his leave by now – you show him your powers. Happen he could learn a thing or two from thee.'

Pip grinned at Cook's cheeky wink and when the woman had disappeared, hurried to Miss Josephine's room. Pressing her ear to the door, she listened for signs of the doctor's presence. After a moment, a strange grunting reached her, followed by what sounded like a strangled cry. *Miss Josephine.*

Worry gripped Pip's chest. With no thought in mind but her mistress's well-being, she twisted the gold doorknob.

Whatever she'd expected couldn't have prepared her, in a thousand lifetimes, for what she was presented with.

A feeling she'd never experienced before tied her guts into fiery knots. She wasn't even completely sure what she was witnessing, but she knew without question it was wrong. That the man shouldn't be doing that to her.

Miss Josephine lay propped up in the bed against a mound of pillows. Her head was turned to the side, eyes closed. But though her cheeks blazed with obvious embarrassment, even shame, her expression wasn't of horror or fear, nor dislike – quite the reverse. As the wispy squeaks of satisfaction proved, she appeared lost only in enjoyment.

What pleasure she found in the act – cream nightgown pushed above her widely parted knees, Doctor Lawley, with a somewhat bored countenance, standing at the foot of the bed, one hand moving busily at the secret place between her legs – Pip couldn't say. She knew little of medical practices, it was true, but he shouldn't be *behaving* in this manner, surely? Forcing her he mightn't be, but still . . . So engrossed was he in his task, it was only Pip's gasp that brought his head around. Their eyes locked and for some seconds, they simply stared at each other in shock.

No words were spoken and Miss Josephine still hadn't noticed her presence as, shaking her head slowly, Pip backed away. When she found herself on the landing, she turned tail and ran down the stairs, dizzy with confusing emotions. She reached the broad hall and as she drew level with the study, the door suddenly opened and she almost careered into Mr Philip leaving the room. His surprise turned to anger, which then slipped from his face and he surveyed her in mild interest.

'I was informed you had returned.'

She hardly heard her response over the thumping of her heart: 'Aye, Mr Philip, sir.'

'Finch was the instigator in that vicious tale, so I'm told?'

Nay, you're wrong there. It was your own wife, though you'd not believe me in a week of Wednesdays and proving it is nigh on impossible, she said in her mind. 'Aye,' she murmured.

'Then I . . . Well, perhaps my treatment of you . . . However, Lucy named you from her own lips, so naturally . . .'

Aware this was as near to an apology as she was likely to receive, Pip nodded. 'I understand, Mr Philip. You took your daughter's word as truth, as would any sound father.'

There was the slightest softening of his eyes. Then he cleared his throat and frowned. 'It seems *my* father has made up his mind about you and those friends of yours staying, so here's some advice you'd do well to heed: stay out of my way. One wrong move from any of you and, whatever my father's views, I shall personally evict you from this house with my own two hands. Do you understand?' he added, sterner still when she didn't answer – her gaze had strayed once more towards the stairs.

'Aye, yes . . . Course. Sorry, Mr Philip.'

He followed her stare and his eyes narrowed. 'What is it?'

'Nowt, sir—'

'Don't tell me nothing. You're shaking.'

Should she spill all about what she'd seen concerning his sister? He'd be furious; happen he'd give the doctor a sound thrashing and he'd deserve nothing less, but then again, what if he grew angry with Miss Josephine, too? She didn't want to get her into trouble, for Pip was certain none of this was of her doing. The old quack up there had surely turned her mind somehow, and yet . . . Would keeping her silence mean these sorts of goings-on continued? If she revealed what she'd seen, Mr Philip would put a stop to it right away. Surely that would be better for Miss Josephine . . .?

'Speak, girl. That is an order.'

Her stuttered recollections, made all the more diffi-cult to spit out by her burning embarrassment, barely made sense; or so it seemed to her. Nevertheless, the man before her seemed to grasp her explanation with-out trouble – he cut her off with a sharp intake of breath.

'*Caroline.*'

His harsh murmur brought Pip's head up sharply. He believed his wife was at the root of this? But how? Oh, was there no low to which that ghastly woman would not sink! 'Sir?'

Anger had flooded his face once more but again, albeit with clearly more effort this time, he replaced it; now with forced control. He glanced left and right, then up the staircase. 'Take yourself to the kitchen and remain there until you're sent for,' he told her through gritted teeth. 'Breathe not a word of this to a soul. Do you hear me?'

She nodded timidly. She didn't know what it was when he stared at her intently like this. It made her feel queer inside. He frightened her something awful when his temper was up, that's what.

'If my father was to discover . . .' He ran a hand across his smooth, chiselled chin. 'By God, you had better make sure he doesn't! You just keep your mouth *shut*. Now go. *Go*,' he growled, sending her on her way with a shove. Moments later, he'd returned to his study. The door slammed shut and she headed for the kitchen with a heavy hammer of dread in her breast.

Just what would happen? Had she done the right thing?

Chapter 14

'MISS JOSEPHINE'S DISCOVERED you're back and is asking for thee,' announced Hardman not half an hour later. She'd been summoned to carry tea up to the lady and though Pip would have willingly taken on the task, Mr Philip's instructions for her to remain here until sent for had deterred her from offering.

Clearly, the doctor had finally taken his leave. Had Mr Philip confronted him about what she'd told him? she wondered, biting her lip. Was Miss Josephine even aware of what had occurred, what Pip had seen? Scraping back her chair, she took a deep breath. She was about to find out.

She yearned to see the fragile woman. She felt the strongest urge to protect her and, Pip told herself resolutely, that's what she was going to do, whether certain folk beneath this roof liked it or otherwise. First things first, she had to try her hardest to get rid of that doctor for good and proper. Hopefully, now she was back, Miss Josephine would uphold her decision that his visits were no longer required. She was determined to get to the bottom of this. He was up to no good, she was sure. And from the name Mr Philip had let slip, his low-bellied wife was once again at the root of the problem.

Now, pausing outside her mistress's door, she drew in

air again to steady her nerves, unsure what the outcome of this summons would be. After smoothing down her apron, she knocked twice and entered.

'My dear, dear girl.'

'Eeh, Miss Josephine, I have missed thee.' Crossing to the chaise longue, Pip took the slender hands held out to her.

Sad and anxious eyes relaxed a little and some colour appeared in her pale cheeks as Pip sat beside her. She smiled with a sigh. 'Oh, I cannot tell you how pleased I am that you're back. When I heard what had happened – what they *claimed* happened – I just knew right away it was pure fabrication. If nothing else, I watched you with my niece and it's clear to see you're most fond of the girl. What possessed Finch to commit such a deed, I suppose we shall never know; but oh,' she continued in the same breath, closing her eyes in relief, 'none of that matters, not now, for you're here with me again. I . . . had a terrible attack of the nerves earlier today.'

Pip felt colour stain her cheeks. 'Aye. Hardman said.'

'Philip, he insisted Doctor Lawley be sent for.' Now, it was the woman's turn to blush to the roots of her hair. She dabbed at her mouth with a lace handkerchief. 'Oh, thank the Lord you're back,' she whispered again with feeling.

What did he do to thee? Why? she wanted to ask but knew she couldn't. The woman's embarrassment was tangible. How could Pip reveal she'd witnessed the sinful act? She couldn't, she couldn't; the shame of it really would be more than the delicate nerves could bear.

'I'm that sorry I weren't here. But I shan't be leaving again. And Miss Josephine?' Pip stared earnestly into her eyes. 'You'll not need that man again, nay never.'

Something, perhaps in Pip's passionate tone, made worrying suspicion crinkle the lady's brow. 'You . . . didn't speak with the doctor today, did you, dear girl?'

'Nay, Miss Josephine.' It wasn't an untruth. Not a word had passed between them. Nevertheless, her colour mounted.

Josephine's face relaxed. Averting her gaze, she lifted her china cup and sipped. Noticing her hands shaking slightly, Pip sought for words of a lighter nature to divert her attention before her growing anxiety could bring about another attack.

'How's Mr Sutton-Shaw, Miss Josephine? Well, I pray?'

To her relief, this seemed to work; the woman lit up. She glanced up coyly from beneath her lashes. 'Indeed, quite so. He's calling in at Bracken House this evening. Hopefully, I'll be well enough to see him for a short while.'

'Oh, you shall!' Pip nodded emphatically. 'Oh, you must, Miss Josephine, for I see he makes you happy.'

The woman's enthusiasm grew. 'He does, Pip. But what if I should, should begin to feel . . . you know, unwell again, and make a fool of myself—'

'You must tell yourself you'll not. And believe it. Go on, Miss Josephine, you can do it.'

With a curt flick of her head, she took a determined breath and said, 'I will not become unwell.'

'Aye. Aye!'

'I *will not* become unwell!'

'Eeh, that's right, that's it!'

'*I'm* in charge of myself, not this wretched affliction!'

Pip clapped her hands, grinning.

'I *shall* meet Mr Sutton-Shaw, and I *shall* enjoy myself!'

'Ay, Miss Josephine.' Pip felt breathless with pride.

'Oh, but what if . . .?' she murmured suddenly, gnawing her lip. 'What if it *does* return and—'

'Nay, nay, don't say it, for it gives it power over thee. *Believe.* You *must*.'

'*I* decide what I do, when I do it, and with whom!' Josephine burst out, the fire returning to her eyes. 'It's not the master of me!'

'Nay, it ain't.' Pip's choked words hung in the air. They smiled at one another tearfully. 'Mebbe soon, when your strength's grown, the two of you could take walks in the Green. The fresh air would do you good. It's close by home so would give thee reassurance should you feel unwell.'

'One step at a time, hm?' The lady laughed. Taking her by the hand, she drew her across the room. 'Come, Pip. Help me decide which evening dress I will wear. Shoes, too. And a necklace and earrings,' she added on a giggle, as carefree as a woman half her age.

Chest fluttery with happiness, Pip followed gladly.

After a pleasant hour and much jollity, they had decided on a low-necked gown in sage-green silk that swished about the lady's slim figure with each step like liquid. Matching slippers of a slightly lighter hue peeped from beneath the large crinoline skirt. Josephine had just sat down at her dressing table, a rosewood box opened out in front of her, jewels and pearls winking from the fire's glow in the room's fading light, when a knock sounded and the door opened.

'Oh.' Philip paused in the entrance. His surprised gaze took in his sister's appearance. Though a frown accompanied it, he returned the smile she gave him over her shoulder then crossed the floor. 'You're well?'

Josephine nodded. 'Has Alexander arrived yet?'

'Alex . . .? Josephine, are you sure—?'

'Quite.' She swivelled around and laid a hand lightly on her brother's arm. 'Please, I would so like to see him. I'm feeling much better, Philip.'

His black brows drew together. 'So you seem.' He released air slowly. 'Would that be due to the doctor's visit?' he forced out. 'It is his . . . intervention that has brought about this notable recovery—?'

'No.' Josephine's neck and face blazed. 'No,' she repeated a little more calmly, though her breathing had quickened. 'Pip. Here.' She pointed to her. 'This girl is the one who has, yet again, brought my fraught mind under control. She is the one, the *only* one, I need to help me through this. I do not wish to see that man ever again.'

Philip's stare flicked to Pip. With her eyes, she begged with him to let the matter drop; for now at least. Miss Josephine was feeling the best she had in a long while, it was clear to see. *Please, sir, don't ruin her hard work by upsetting her with memories of that tyrant's touch. She needn't know I saw what I did, for it'll bring more harm to her than good. Please, please . . .*

As though he'd read her plea, he inclined his head a fraction. Returning his attention to Josephine, he stared at her for some seconds. 'Alexander should be arriving any moment. If you're certain you're up to it, I'll see you downstairs in ten minutes.' He'd spoken almost softly; he finished his speech with a somewhat awkward pat of his sister's shoulder.

'Philip?'

Having made to leave hastily, as though embarrassed by his show of kindness, he now paused by the door. 'Yes?' he asked without turning.

'Thank you. I shan't let you down.'

He lowered his head. Then he left the room, closing the door quietly behind him.

'How you fettling, Miss Josephine?' asked Pip minutes later when, having helped put the final touches to her appearance, she stood looking up at her at the door.

'All right, I think.' The woman fiddled with the string of emeralds around her throat. 'I will *not* become unwell.' The mantra from earlier fell from her lips. She flashed a shaky smile. 'Here goes. Wish me luck, Pip.'

'I shan't if you don't mind, Miss Josephine, for luck's not in it. It's in you. It's your strength, that's what. I know you can do it.'

'Oh, dear girl . . .' Josephine's gloved fingers brushed Pip's cheek in a brief caress. 'You will be close by, however, should I need you?'

'I'll be here in this very room, Miss Josephine. I'm going nowhere, don't fret. Now, off you go and enjoy your evening.'

After some seconds and several deep breaths, the lady opened the door. Another lungful of air later, she was gone.

As a protective mother might when her child is let loose without her, Pip distracted herself with tidying the large room, hanging up dresses discarded during the choosing period and putting back shoes. She was returning pairs of sparkling earrings to the jewellery box when the clop of hooves and crunch of iron-rimmed wheels carried through the partially opened window. She crossed to it and peeped around the curtain. A private carriage was just drawing away and midway up the steps to the front door was a tall, slim gentleman. *Miss Josephine's Alexander Sutton-Shaw.* It had to be.

From her vantage point, Pip caught only a glimpse of the round black crown of his tall hat and shiny shoes of the same colour. Moments later, he'd disappeared inside the house and, letting the curtain fall, she returned to her duties with a smile. It was obvious he was keen on the master's daughter; kind and patient, too. And from the little she'd just seen of him, handsome to boot. Oh, but she hoped the evening would go well for Miss Josephine, for the pair of them. The couple had a promising future ahead, she just knew it. He seemed not only the one the lady wanted but what she needed. Perhaps he'd be the making of her.

An hour or more had passed without incident when the door suddenly swung wide and Hardman entered the room, mouth pursed. She plonked a cup of tea down on a side table with a disgusted sniff.

'Is that for me?'

'Miss Josephine summoned me, instructed me to bring you up a sup. Fetching and carrying for the likes of you, I ask yer!'

'Sorry. Ta, thanks.'

'Aye well. Just don't get used to it.'

'I'll not.' Pip's tone dropped. 'Hardman?'

'What?'

'How's she doing, like, Miss Josephine?'

The housemaid shrugged. 'All right, I s'pose.'

'Oh, that is good.'

Shrugging again, the woman turned to leave.

'Hardman, wait.' She did – Pip went to stand in front of her. 'Yesterday, when I were banished from this house—'

She cut her off with a mirthless snort. 'Finch's doing, my left eye.'

Pip nodded. The queer realisation that this woman – who had never attempted to disguise her dislike of her, indeed resented her and the lads' very presence beneath this roof – was her sole confidante in all this didn't go unnoticed by her. Jess seemed to be the only one besides herself who knew how devious Caroline really was. 'But afore I left, when we spoke . . .'

Her eyes moved to Pip, then away. 'If you were left

waiting long outside the station, it can't be helped. There weren't no point keeping the meeting, was there, given that devilish bitch wriggled herself out from the finger of blame?'

'Aye, I figured that's why you never showed.'

'Then what? Why you going on about it?'

'What you said, about getting shot of Caroline—' The last word rattled in Pip's throat as the housemaid took her arm and pulled her away from the door.

She drew her to a halt in the centre of the room with a rough shake, hissing, 'Christ sake, keep your voice down.'

'I'm sorry, I—'

'Just you forget I said owt, right? You're all fine and dandy, now, ain't you, with yon feet back by Birdy's hearth.'

'Course I ain't fine and dandy.' Anger was rising in Pip; she disentangled herself from the housemaid's hold. 'Mrs Goldthorpe loathes the very sight of me, so it seems. Why, I don't know, but she does. Aye, yes. She ain't finished with me, you can be sure of that, won't be happy till I'm gone from Bracken House for good.'

'You mean . . .?' Hardman's hard stare intensified. 'You still want to help me get shot of her?'

'What? Nay, nay. I never did in the first place, was just upset when you first spoke on it, didn't know what I were thinking.'

The woman's face turned puce. 'You guttersnipe time-waster, yer! Get out of my way.' She made to barge past and from the room but Pip hurried to block her path.

'Wait, please. It needed airing, that's all. I didn't mean to give you false hope, I just . . .' She scraped a hand through her hair. 'Truth be told, Hardman, I hate that woman too for the hurt she's caused me but . . .'

'But what?'

'When all's said and done, she's a Goldthorpe. This is her home. She's a right to be here, whether we like it or no. Besides . . .' She hesitated but curiosity got the better of her and she added, 'How were you planning on getting rid, anyroad? Whatever you'd a mind to think up, the family wouldn't take your word over hers. Surely you'd be found out and what would the consequence be? You'd be out on your ear without a character reference.'

'Words? A tall tale or some such against her? You think *that's* my plans for her?' Laughing quietly, Hardman shook her head. 'My God, you are young after all. Oh no, when I do summat, I do it right. What I want is her gone from here *for good and proper*. Remember, like I said? No coming back, never to return.'

She'd spoken in such a chilling tone, the hairs on Pip's arms sprang to attention. She licked her lips. 'You mean . . .?'

'Just you keep your snotty nose out of my business, you hear? Forget words have even passed betwixt us, for should you speak of this to anyone, that vicious bitch downstairs won't be the only one to make an enemy of me. The lads would follow, and I'm sure you don't want that? Am I right?'

The threat to her and the boys' safety was clear – Pip shrank under the housemaid's glare. She didn't think it an idle warning neither, not if her plans for Caroline were anything to go by. The housemaid was no different from the woman she wished to destroy, Pip knew with rising dread. Not really, no, for both were hell bent on getting what they wanted and woe betide anyone who got in their way. They were as bad as each other and just as dangerous. Was this really where she and the lads should be? Living amongst such vindictiveness, looking over their shoulders all the while, afraid for their safety? She'd thought this a haven but it seemed those streets out there posed less of a threat than Bracken House. *Dear God, dear God . . .*

'Remember, keep your trap shut, or else.'

Pip was shaking as she watched Hardman walk away. Yet before she could stop herself, her tongue took over, forcing her to ask timidly, 'Is he really worth it, Mr Philip?'

Hardman ground to a halt. 'Shut your mouth unless you want the feel of my hand across it. You know nowt.'

'Nowt can come of it; he's wed. He's messed around with countless others afore thee—'

'You what?' Hardman spun around, face full of murder. 'Liar!'

'It's true, Hardman, honest! Cook's daughter, Lydia she were called, she fled after he got her with child and abandoned her. Her, the others, they didn't deserve it. *You* don't deserve to be treated this way, not by him nor anyone else. Please, don't do owt daft concerning Mrs Goldthorpe, for you'll suffer the consequences and it'll be for nothing—'

'Why, you poisonous young *bitch*. He wouldn't . . . wouldn't do that—'

'He did! I'm sorry, I don't want to hurt you, Hardman, but it's the truth.' Pip held out her hands in an open gesture towards the housemaid, who had stalked back and was now bearing down on her, eyes spitting steel. 'Tabby heard it from Cook's own lips.'

'Well, Cook's a damn liar as well!' To Pip's surprise, tears sprang to Hardman's eyes. 'He wouldn't do that,' she repeated on a whisper.

Despite everything, Pip's heart contracted for her; she

reached out a hand in comfort but it never reached Hardman's arm. A dull creak from beyond the partially opened door stilled her progress; she and Hardman stared at each other wide-eyed then whipped their heads towards the source of the noise. Someone was out there, on the landing – that had clearly been a floorboard they had heard. *Lord above, what they had been discussing . . .* Surely not! As one, they scurried to the door.

The broad landing was deserted. Not a soul was about; they released a simultaneous sigh. Then what had caused the sound? Pip bit her thumbnail as Hardman inched towards the top of the stairs and peeped down them. Her frown, when clearly she'd seen that again there was no sign of anyone, brought another relieved sigh to Pip. Without a word, they returned to the bedroom, closing the door behind them. They stood staring at each other for a long moment.

'You reckon . . .?'

'Can't have been. They couldn't of scarpered from view that quick.'

'But the noise . . . someone must have been out there—'

'Just shut up about it, will you? It was no one, no one.' Yet Hardman's voice lacked conviction and her face had paled. 'I must go.' She jabbed a quivering finger at Pip's nose. 'Think on, you hear? You just keep that trap shut!' She turned and hurried from the room.

Pip stood rooted, gazing at the door for an age. She felt light-headed with dread and her legs were shaking. *Had* someone been eavesdropping out there? For how long? Just how much had they heard?

Another, more horrifying prospect crashed through her, making her gasp. What if it had been Caroline? But surely she'd have stormed the room, demanding answers,

222

would have flung them both out in an instant? Or maybe she was biding her time, awaiting just the right moment to pounce with her new-found knowledge; maybe had something else planned for them . . .?

Stop it, stop it! Pip told herself, squeezing her eyes shut before her paranoia sent her raving mad with terror.

God in heaven, why did problem follow problem beneath this roof? Oh, she didn't know how much more worry she could bear. Covering her face, she dropped into a chair and let her tears flow.

*

'Pip? Oh, dear girl, wake up!'

Blinking in confusion, she shook the drowsiness from her head.

'What a thoroughly perfect evening it's been. And oh, you'll never believe it! Guess. Guess what has happened!'

By now, the sleep haze was fading – and realising she lay sprawled on the mistress's chaise longue as though she were some fine lady herself, Pip sprang up, cheeks reddening and apologies falling from her lips. 'I'm so sorry, Miss Josephine! Oh, I don't know what came over me, forgive me, please, I—'

'My my, don't take on so. No harm done, no harm done. Rest on, dear girl.'

Pip was struck by the woman's lightness of tone. Not a trace of the nervousness she'd grown accustomed to lingered. It was then that she took in properly the glowing cheeks and eyes shimmering with joy. The sight made her young soul sing. 'All went well, you say, Miss Josephine?'

'The evening passed without incident, Pip. I can barely believe it.' The lady clasped her hands together and sighed, smiling. 'Your advice worked wonders. I believed I would be well and I was. That is to say, I did begin to feel somewhat light-headed at one point; however, I chanted to myself to remain calm and told myself that the feeling would pass, and the faintness gradually eased off without much trouble. You, young lady, are an angel sent to me from the heavens.'

Pip laughed but Miss Josephine didn't follow suit. The lady had been speaking earnestly, she realised. She truly believed her to be a saint or some such. Pip shook her head, saying softly, 'I've said it afore, Miss Josephine, and I meant it: it's been inside yourself all along. You hold the means to be well again, not me. I just helped guide your thinking in t' right direction.'

'Oh no. You've done so much more than that. You made me *believe* that I could, you know? I'm almost too afraid to say this out loud, but . . .' The woman's smile broke through the biting of her lip. 'I think . . . I really think I may be cured, Pip! Oh, can you imagine it, after so long . . .? I'm back. I'm *me* again.'

Pity stirred in her breast. However much she wanted to agree, despite how far Josephine seemed to have come, she was sceptical. Surely a miraculous recovery, and so soon, was wishful thinking? Though not for anything would she dash this woman's hopes, she felt she had to err on the side of caution. 'Aye, mebbe, Miss Josephine. Small steps, eh? You're on your way, mind, there's no doubt of that,' she said with feeling. But Josephine didn't appear to be listening. She was staring off into the distance with dancing eyes and Pip smiled curiously. 'By, Miss Josephine, but you look fit to burst with excitement. Summat occurred the night, did you say?'

The woman's gaze swivelled around to meet hers, then as though she couldn't contain it any longer, bubbling laughter left her. She hugged herself tight. 'It's Mr

Sutton-Shaw. He asked to speak with my father earlier . . . and I knew, I just knew . . . '

'Oh, oh!' Springing to the edge of her seat, Pip held her breath.

'Father gave his blessing – Alexander and I are to be married!'

'Oh, Miss Josephine!' On impulse, she threw her arms around the lady. 'Congratulations, congratulations! Eeh, I'm that pleased for thee.'

'Thank you, dear girl,' she said, voice cracking, returning Pip's hug. 'We're to announce it properly on Tuesday, the first day of the new year, with a grand dinner here at Bracken House. I cannot express how happy I am. I'd begun to think it wouldn't happen for me and yet it has. And oh, I do love him so. More importantly, my feelings are reciprocated. I'm so very fortunate, Pip.'

'He's the lucky 'un, Miss Josephine, bagging someone as lovely as thee for a wife.'

'Oh, Pip. What would I do without you?' They held each other again. 'You will of course come with us to the new place?'

A frown touched her brow. She drew back slowly. 'New place?'

'But of course. Once we're married, we shall have to have a home of our own. Hopefully, it shan't be too far away from here but that will be for Alexander to decide. Wherever it may be, I'd like to take you with me, as my personal maid.'

The thought hadn't crossed her mind that Miss Josephine would leave Bracken House but of course, once wed, she would. On the one hand, she felt honoured that the lady thought enough of her to ask. And she so wanted to stay with her. But leave here – Cook, Tabby,

225

Miss Lucy? *The boys.* She swallowed hard. Never, never. She couldn't – wouldn't – leave Simon and Mack behind.

'I'd fair love to, only . . . '

The woman's face fell. 'What is it?'

'The lads, Miss Josephine. They're like brothers to me. I'm sorry, I can't be parted from them.'

'Then bring them along.'

Pip's heartbeat quickened. 'You mean it?'

'Of course. I'm sure Alexander won't mind. We shall need to acquire staff for our new home in any case and he shan't want the bother of all that. Yes, I'm sure we could find them something to do.'

'Oh, oh, *thank* you. Much as I'll carry gratitude in my heart for the master till my dying day for giving us a home at Bracken House, I'd hate to be parted from thee, will follow thee gladly.' She laughed brokenly. 'You'll not regret this, Miss Josephine.'

'I'm sure I shan't, Pip.'

'Eeh, wait till I tell the lads!'

'Go on.'

Pip leapt to her feet. 'Aye? You sure you don't need owt, you'll be all right a while?'

'Yes, yes. You go.'

'Ta, thanks, Miss Josephine. I'll not be long gone.' Flashing a grin, she hurried from the room.

Outside, she paused for a moment and closed her eyes. *A fresh beginning.* The thought flitted through her. Smiling softly, she nodded. Pray God, she and the lads would be welcome, by all, at the new house. Free from the open looks of dislike and resentment of their presence – Caroline, Hardman, the scheming and vicious games and all that went with them. They would feel wanted, safe. Calm. Aye, and it would be wonderful, that sense of security which here they had never really felt. Folk beneath this roof wanted them gone and were not afraid to show it. Hopefully, the next place really would feel like home. A proper one, where they belonged completely.

She glanced around the beautiful space wistfully. She'd miss this place. It had been kind to her. It had provided her with happiness, hope for life again. Her gaze rested on the master's doors. Despite feeling a painful pang, again she smiled. God love him. He was a true gentleman, as good as they came. She hoped Alexander Sutton-Shaw would prove likewise.

A sudden thought occurred to her; she tapped her lips agitatedly. The creaking she and Hardman had heard outside the door ... Miss Josephine said he'd been up here earlier to see the master. Was Alexander lurking on the landing? But surely he'd have mentioned it to the others. What reason would *he* have for keeping silent? Nodding, she told herself she was wrong. As the housemaid said, it had been nothing. And the more she thought about it, the more convinced she became. This house was aged after all; the odd creak was to be expected, wasn't it? With a lighter heart, she made her way downstairs.

'Don't try to deny it, Caroline. The orphan girl saw everything.'

Pip caught the harsh voices coming from the study midway across the hall and, head down, planned to hurry past in case the occupants should emerge; now, hearing herself being referred to, she paused. Never would she dream of eavesdropping but surely, if she was the topic of conversation, she had a right to know what was being said? She glanced left and right then inched closer to the door.

'This isn't funny,' Philip continued through what

sounded like gritted teeth when his wife laughed. 'What a thing for a child to witness – not to mention what this could do to Josephine's already fractured nerves. It could traumatise her, turn her frigid, ruin her marriage before it begins. Anyway, I thought Lawley believed that hysteria is caused by the disturbances of a wandering womb? That it can roam around the body, obstructing passages, which stagnates the blood as it cannot circulate?'

'Indeed. But alas, the use of leeches and even bloodletting in the area has not imparted strength to her body, nor lessened her unmanageable emotional excesses. Along with others, Doctor Lawley now suspects women are oftentimes affected by female semen. Stored in the body due to a lack of marital intimacy, it turns to poison and causes high-strung behaviour. He considers his method today to be the cure. It isn't immoral, Philip. Penetration never occurs, thus ensuring the patient remains undamaged—'

'Stop. I cannot listen to any more.'

'We'd exhausted all else. It was the only option left open. Of course, the last resort would be to send her to an asylum. After all, it may be the workings of demonic possession . . .'

'Surely not?' He sounded horrified. 'Some women are prone to nervous maladies. It's simply the vapours affecting the mind. That man doesn't know what he's talking about, I'm sure. When you informed me of this course of action he'd suggested weeks ago, I specifically ordered you not to give consent, did I not?'

'Well yes, but—'

'Then why give him leave to do just that?' he cut in over Caroline, followed by what sounded like him thumping the desk in anger. 'What were you *thinking*?'

228

'What I was thinking was to make that pathetic wretch upstairs well enough not to scare Alexander away altogether,' Caroline burst out. 'Despite your misgivings, it seems Lawley's method – unconventional, I grant you – has worked. Did you *see* her this evening? She was like a new woman.' Again, she released a knowing laugh. 'Who knew, hm? Pent-up frustration caused her ill health. A man's touch in the right place was all she'd been short of—'

'Don't talk that way. It's immoral, Caroline, however you try to dress it up. Thoughts of that old rogue violating her like that . . . It turns my stomach.'

'You speak as though you actually care. This, her and Alexander's union . . . It was your idea, if you recall?'

There followed a charged silence – Pip, her hand pressed tightly to her mouth, could do nothing even had she wanted to. What on earth was going on here? Mr Philip had had some knowledge of what the doctor was about . . .? A new treatment? The depraved act she'd witnessed was intended as a cure for Josephine's illness? She shook her head in confusion. The planned wedding – it was a ruse set up by the man beyond this door? But how? Just what was his game? Why did he want his sister married off? More to the point, was Alexander aware or was he just as much a pawn as his intended in this twisted plot?

'Don't let's dwell on what has brought Josephine to her senses at last but that it has happened.' Caroline's words now carried a wheedling note. 'What is done is done—'

'No more, do you hear me? Doctor Lawley has paid his last visit to this house.'

'Of course. Unless, that is, your sister should require his . . . services again—'

'I said no more, damn it!'

Again, there came a silence, then: 'Whatever it takes to see them married, Philip; we agreed, remember? After all, who in their right mind would intentionally shackle themselves to a lunatic? He could change his mind. Alexander had to see that Josephine was getting well – after tonight, it appears he's in no doubt. The idea worked. They're to be married, and bless your lucky stars for it. If anything, you should be thanking the doctor and me.'

'My sister insists it's the intervention of the child – Pip, I believe her name is – that aids her recovery.'

'Utter poppycock!' The fury dripping from the furious words brought ice to Pip's veins; she shivered uncontrollably. 'That meddling vagabond has turned her weak head.'

'Be that as it may . . . Doctor Lawley and his depraved treatment are banished from this house.'

Caroline released a long breath. When she spoke again, her voice was heavy with scorn.

'You're well aware that Josephine's condition worsening and the subsequent possibility of Alexander calling the whole thing off would be the ruin of us. The risk is one we can ill afford to take, and yet . . . Fine. On your head be it. But I warn you of this: I shan't hang around to witness your downfall. I'll be gone from Bracken House before I know the shame of that, and I'll take Lucy with me.' Philip's gasp at this brought a smug edge to her tone. 'That's right, you hear me correctly. My parents would be only too willing to take their daughter and granddaughter in.'

'But—!'

'All of this, the position we are in—'

'Don't say it. My father is to blame, remember, not I.'

'How could I forget? I despise him for what he's reduced us to.' Caroline's hiss sliced through his interjection. 'Alexander and Josephine *must* marry. That is all there is to it.'

Footsteps from inside suddenly approached the door – snapping out of her dazed state, Pip bolted for cover behind a huge potted plant nearby. She thought her heart would smash through her chest, so fiercely was it beating. Holding her breath, she peeped through the glossy green leaves to see Caroline emerge from the study.

The woman seemed to be struggling to regain her composure. Slowly, her eyes swivelled up the stairs and a look of pure loathing gripped her features. 'Orphan *wretch*. Damn you to *hell*.' The next moment, she had marched away.

Emerging from her hiding place, Pip willed her shock-weakened legs to work. What she'd just heard . . . What devilment were those two about and why? Just what did Philip and his wife hope to get out of the marriage? The oddness of it made her head sore.

Furthermore, yet again, she'd managed to strengthen Caroline's animosity towards her without meaning to. That the lady resented her for letting slip her knowledge of the doctor's activities was clear. Last time she'd got on the wrong side of her, when mentioning that perhaps they could be friends, Caroline had concocted the terrible tale about her abusing little Lucy and almost ruined her. What revenge would the woman take this time? Pip didn't dare imagine.

As if in a trance, sick with worry, she headed for the kitchen. Then, reaching the baize door, she turned and retraced her steps upstairs to Josephine's room. She was in no fit mood now to announce to the lads the news she'd been so excited about shortly before. Nor could she bear to face those she loved, for surely they would notice her distress and want to know the reason. Then she'd have to come clean about the happenings in this house – some of which she herself wasn't sure of. Cook and Simon would be furious to learn about Caroline's treatment of her and she knew once the words were given life, she'd be unable to contain them and the whole sorry truth would pour out. And she couldn't risk that, could she? It would cause ructions beyond her control.

They held her in high regard, she knew, loved her even, and would be furious that she'd been suffering so, alone, at Caroline's hand. And the master would hear what had gone on, and what would the outcome be then? As she'd warned Hardman earlier, Caroline was a Goldthorpe; whatever the accusation, her word would be taken as truth by those who wielded authority here. As proven once already, *her* word mattered not when it came down to it, did it? No. She couldn't risk folk knowing, Pip told herself once again. Not yet, in any case.

'Lads are away on an errand for Cook,' she lied as explanation to her mistress, who had greeted her speedy return with raised eyebrows. She busied herself with resuming her duties from earlier, tidying the rest of the jewellery away and replacing lids on face creams and straightening bottles of toilet water.

'Come, Pip.' Josephine inclined her head to the chair opposite her own, a short while later. The winter sun had long dipped behind the clouds and the soft lamp-light cast the opulent room in a rose-gold glow. 'Buttered toast and hot chocolate time, I think; what do you say?' she asked with a smile.

Pip's buttocks had barely touched the seat when she

was back on her feet. 'Aye, Miss Josephine. I'll fetch them right away.'

'No, no, child. I meant the refreshments for both of us. You stay where you are.'

Recalling Hardman's resentment at having to fetch and carry for her with the tea, she hesitated. 'It's no bother, honest—'

'Give the bell pull a tug, would you?'

With some reluctance, Pip closed her hand around the thick tassel hanging by the fireside to summon the maid downstairs. Within moments, Hardman's soft tapping came at the door and at Josephine's command, she entered the room – retreating seconds later with a face like thunder. Pip's heart dipped. There was another who hated the sight of her as it was, angered further still without her intention. She felt close to tears. Just how much more of this bad feeling could she bear? She was heartily fed up with it.

'Are you all right, Pip? You seem a little subdued.'

Sorry tears immediately clogged her throat. She nodded. 'Aye, Miss Josephine. You?'

'Oh, I feel wonderful, just wonderful.' The lady breathed a contented sigh. 'Do you know, this evening has proved a turning point, I believe. That I managed successfully to alleviate my symptoms before they had a chance to manifest . . . I'm proud of myself. I haven't felt as easy of mind in such a very long time. I just cannot believe I'm cured, dear girl.'

Again, Pip wasn't entirely convinced and responded carefully. 'Aye, tha should be proud, an' all. Reet well, you're doing, Miss Josephine.'

'It's down to Alexander, you know,' the woman murmured, staring off into the distance with soft eyes. 'His love feeds my veins with strength.'

Oh, Miss, Miss . . . All was not well with all this, she felt it in her guts. Mrs Goldthorpe – and Mr Philip, also, it seemed – were up to something where this young couple's union was concerned, but what? *Please, Lord. Don't have them ruin it for this kind lady, here, and her intended,* she prayed silently. Was there anything she could do? she wondered suddenly. True, she couldn't very well reveal what she'd overheard earlier to Miss Josephine, but maybe . . . Maybe if she knew what they were about and why, she just might be able to help make sure in some way that the couple caught up in this plot didn't get hurt?

'Miss Josephine?' she forced herself to ask. 'Have you known Mr Sutton-Shaw long? How did you meet, if you don't mind me asking, like?'

'We made each other's acquaintance during the spring, shortly after my brother and his family began residing at Bracken House. Philip introduced us. They were away at school together as boys. To be honest, I was struck by him on our very first meeting.'

'Him and Mr Philip are good friends, then, aye?'

'Oh, quite. Alexander moved into the vicinity last year; Philip was most pleased to have his old friend back in his life. They were rather close at school, I believe.' She laughed. 'They've been thick as thieves again since.'

If Mr Philip held his friend in such high regard, why was he conspiring behind his back to do him wrong? And considering the men were so close, how hadn't Alexander picked up an inkling of suspicion? Unless . . . ?

A deep frown creased her brow. Was Alexander *in* on this, whatever it was? No, surely not – from what she'd heard of him, he was a sound and decent gentleman. Besides, what would be his motive for marrying her if not for love? And yet . . . for reasons unknown to her, she couldn't shake the worm of mistrust. There was much more to all this than met the eye, she just knew it.

Pip barely noticed the housemaid's return with the tray, so lost was she in her puzzling thoughts. After nibbling at a slice of toast and forcing down a half-cup of chocolate, she asked permission to retire to her bed. She must be by herself with her musings, to try to make sense of what she'd learned and was yet to find out, and how. Not only didn't she want to see Miss Josephine get hurt but, having been asked to join the new couple's future staff, her and the lads' futures were at stake, now, too. She must discover what was afoot.

Curling up in her makeshift bed on the dressing-room floor, she pulled the blankets to her chin. Despite the need to be alone, she ached for the comforting feel of Simon and Mack's bodies against her own. She'd do anything for a hug right now, to pour out her worries. Thoughts of the upcoming marriage and the scheming by some to see it gone through with swirled around her tired brain for an age. Yet the twilight hours' deathly silence, broken now and again by owls' hoots beyond the Green outside, brought no answers and fear of the unknown intensified her need for the lads' company. What the time was, she didn't know, when she finally pushed aside the covers and padded out.

Sounds of Josephine retiring for the night had long since filtered through to her. Now, the lady's gentle snores eased Pip's guilt somewhat as she continued to the door. She sounded at ease; surely she wouldn't be missed for a few minutes?

'I'll be gone but a short while, Miss Josephine. I just need to see the lads, be with them a while, that's all,' she whispered through the gloom in the direction of the four-poster bed.

Collecting a spill from a vase on the mantel, she made for the far wall and the single lamp still burning dully – Miss Josephine insisted she couldn't sleep in full darkness – and after lifting the glass dome, touched the spill to the violet flame. From this, she lit a candle and, shielding the guttering light with her hand so as not to disturb the woman's sleep, slipped from the room.

She encountered not a soul nor sound on her journey; slowly, slowly, so as not to aggravate the old knob, she opened the door to Cook's room. Her eyes went immediately to the chair by the window – to her surprise, it was empty. Then her gaze settled on the bed and her heart skipped a beat before starting up a series of gallops that pained her chest. Cook wasn't in the chair because she was in the bed instead. Her ample bulk beneath the coverings was unmistakable. Pip's head flicked around wildly. The lads were nowhere to be seen.

'What in the name of all that's holy . . .?' Cook jolted awake with a gasp when, in her mindless panic, Pip rushed across and shook her shoulder frantically. 'Lass? Saints preserve us, what—?'

'Simon, Mack – why ain't they here? Where are they, where are they!'

''Ere, now, calm yourself. Lord, child, they're but across the way. Master gave his permission earlier for me to assign them the spare room – they couldn't very well share this 'un with me for ever more. Besides, it made sense, that there one doing nowt but standing empty, like.'

'I thought summat had happened, that they'd left me.' Pip sagged, relief washing over her.

'Now don't talk daft. Them lads wouldn't leave you, not for a gold watch. 'Ere, hang about, missy,' she added, squinting at the pitch sky through the gap in the curtains, 'what the divil you doing wandering about this part of the house and at this hour, anyroad?'

'I missed them, Cook, is all,' she murmured, feeling a little silly admitting it. 'Eeh, but I'm that sorry for disturbing thee, I am. I'll go, now, let you catch your sleep.'

Sighing, the woman patted Pip's head and her tone was soft with understanding as she said, 'Aye, it's time you need to adjust, youse being in one another's pockets, so to speak, as you allus were. Go on, now, lovey. Away to your bed afore you catch your death of cold. You mind how you go, go on.'

Pip rose, nodding, and after a last apology to this work-worn woman who barely got half the sleep she needed each night at the best of times, left the room. She cast her eyes along the landing to the boys' door and her mouth lifted at the corners. Their own room! By, they must be beyond pleased, the pair. More importantly, they were together. Oh, if only she was sharing with them, too . . . Pushing the thought away, she mentally shook herself. She had a bed of her own and responsibilities along with it. She was working, now, wasn't she, like an older girl, and it was about time she started acting like one instead of a clingy babby. Her position must come first. Miss Josephine needed her. As Cook said, she'd get used to the changes. She must. Nodding, she turned to leave.

'Pip?' Head thrust forward, Simon stood squinting in his doorway. 'That you?'

'Aye,' she whispered. 'Did I disturb thee?'

'You did.'

'Sorry, lad. I wanted to check you and the little 'un were sound, is all.'

'Aye, well. You may as well come in a minute.' Leaving

the door ajar, he turned back into the room. By the time she entered, he'd returned to the bed he shared with Mack, who was slumbering peacefully nearest the wall, and jerked his head. She hurried across and slipped beneath the blanket beside him.

Neither spoke for some time, then: 'All right?' he asked.

She nodded against his shoulder.

'Sure?'

'Aye.' She snuggled closer into his thin chest and in an uncharacteristic show of affection, he rested his chin on top of her head.

'Your Miss Josephine's well?'

Again, she nodded. 'She's to be wed, you know.'

'Aye. The servants were speaking on it earlier.'

'She wants to take me with her after the event, to her and Mr Sutton-Shaw's new dwelling, as her personal maid. You and Mack, an' all.' Simon was silent; she bit her lip. 'Will tha come?'

'Suppose so.'

'Eeh, lad. Ta, thanks. I'd not of consented without.'

Again, they lapsed into companionable silence. The urge to spill her concerns about all she'd discovered about this house struck Pip anew but once more, she told herself to hold her tongue, at least until she could be sure just what was going on, or tensions became too unbearable to keep them to herself. He'd only fret, and what was the use in both of them worrying?

'Mr Philip, the dirty dog, makes late-night visits next door.'

The warm bed and the boys' comforting presence, enveloping her like a blanket of calm, had begun lulling Pip to sleep; now, she opened her eyes and raised herself on her elbow to look at him through the darkness.

Simon nodded. 'I heard Hardman sneaking him in her room earlier. Hushed voices and . . . sounds . . .' He broke off before continuing with a definite note of embarrassment in his tone, 'For at least an hour, they carried through yon wall. She'll end up with a full belly if she ain't careful.'

'God help her, an' all, for like Cook's Lydia afore her, he'll not see her right, you can bet,' Pip murmured.

'Oh aye. It's slung out on to the cobbles to fare alone, she'll be, and that'll be that. 'Ere and it can't come soon enough for me. She gets on my wick with the vicious looks and sly remarks she's fond of throwing my way.'

'Happen we'll be out of it at the new house by then, if it should occur, anyroad,' she answered hopefully. For unlike Simon, she wasn't convinced that matters would pan out as cleanly as he predicted. Hardman didn't seem one to take rejection on the chin and disappear, as Philip's other 'problem' had. She'd kick up merry hell, turn the household on its head, so long as she got what she wanted. And what was she expecting from the master's son? He was married already, wasn't he? Sudden clarity had her nodding slowly with grim realisation. *If he was widowed, however . . .*

Dear God, was that her plan? *Was* she truly capable of going so far as to get shot of his wife to have him for herself? And yet, despite the terrible notion, it was the housemaid's safety that overrode Pip's thoughts more than that of Mrs Goldthorpe. For from what she'd proven, Pip believed at least, the fine lady was capable of worse evil-doing than the besotted servant, should she so choose. Just how would she react if she discovered her husband had been messing with another woman – a lowly breed of class to boot, which she seemed to hold in utter contempt – right under her

239

nose? She daren't imagine. As she'd said to Simon, she just hoped she and the lads were out of it should such a thing occur.

A little later, Pip climbed reluctantly from the bed and whispering Simon goodnight, headed back to her own at the opposite end of the house. As much as she'd have liked to stay, her duties beckoned. Josephine might waken and need her; understandably, the woman wouldn't be best pleased to find her absent.

Upon reaching her own dark and deserted landing, Pip was certain she caught a faint whiff of Caroline's perfume. The atmosphere seemed to thicken; the hairs on her arms stood to attention. Glancing about, she bit her lip with a frightened frown.

Suddenly, at the far end of the space, illuminated in the moonlight from the high window by the stairs, she thought she saw a shadow shift. The very air stood still.

Whirring around, heart thumping, she hurried for the sanctuary of Josephine's room.

Chapter 15

'*DEAD?* GOODNESS! BUT how?'

'Heaven alone knows, love. Seems she took a tumble on the stairs around dawn. Mr Philip discovered her an hour or two since.'

'Oh my, how dreadful,' cried Josephine then turned sharply as Pip, who had been enjoying the last few minutes in bed before the day's work began and, overhearing snippets of the speech in the adjoining room, careered inside, wild-eyed with horror. 'Oh, Pip . . . I'm afraid Mabel here has dreadful news—'

'I, I heard, Miss Josephine.' Pip had to grip her hands together behind her back to control their violent shaking. How could this be? Dear God . . . *She'd gone and done it, now. Oh, Hardman, why, why; it's the gallows, now, for certain. Terrible, terrible . . . !*

'You all right, lass?' Cook laid a hand on Pip's shoulder. 'Eeh, such a thing to take in for one so young . . . Now, you mustn't fret, for I'm here. That's it, now,' she added, cooing softly, as Pip flung herself into her comforting embrace.

'Oh, Cook . . . this is awful!' A memory from last night, the smell of expensive scent and a shifting figure on the landing out there . . . Just what had Caroline been doing loitering around in the dark at that hour, anyway? When had Hardman stolen upon her and how? Had they crossed words and the housemaid lost her temper, saw it as the perfect opportunity, while the unsuspecting household were abed, to put her heinous plan into action?

Oh, she couldn't think on it, she couldn't. And oh – oh, poor Miss Lucy! She was now motherless, just like herself. For all of Caroline's faults, the child didn't deserve the anguish her loss must have brought to her . . . And Pip could have made sure this was avoided had she confided her concerns to someone. She'd known what Hardman was planning and she'd done nothing. This was too much, too much!

'I want to see the lads,' she choked on a whimper. 'Please, I . . . need to be with them.'

'Course you do, aye. Come, I'll see thee down to the kitchen. Don't fret,' she added quickly, seeing the pain that had appeared in Pip's eyes, 'you'll not be met with no ungodly sight on the way – the body ain't present. It were removed a short while since. Come on, now. I've got thee.' Supporting her, she walked her to the door.

'Why did no one waken me sooner?' asked Josephine when they were outside. Eyes turning to the stairs, she shuddered.

'Your father thought it best to spare thee the strain to your nerves, least till she'd been taken away, like.'

Pip agreed this had been a wise move on her master's part. Her mistress was wringing her hands furiously and her eyes looked huge in her ashen face. Had she witnessed the full horror, the lady would have been beside herself.

'I still don't understand how this could have happened, what—?'

'Don't take on so, lovey,' the cook cut in gently. 'As I

242

stated, Albert sent me to fetch you, so you hurry along, now. Happen he can answer thee better. An inspector fella's just left him. Surely he'd have had summat to tell your father. Go on, go on. I'll be with youse once I've seen the lass here downstairs.'

Despite her own distress, Pip sought to calm Josephine, sensing an attack of panic wasn't far away. 'Listen to Cook, Miss Josephine. Deep breaths. Just send for me should you need me and I'll be there right away.'

'Yes . . . Thank you, dear girl.' Gulping in air, the lady nodded, turned and hurried for the master's room.

Dragging in steadying breaths herself, Pip followed Cook across the landing. Unsure what she expected to find, when they reached the top of the stairs she had to force her stare downwards. To her relief, there didn't appear to be any visible trace of death; no blood that she could see, no horror. All looked as it should. Cook or Tabby must have cleaned the area; the realisation brought a small frown to her brow. Did the police usually collect all the evidence they needed from a crime scene – because that's what this was – so quickly? Well, they must, she told herself. What did she know about such matters, anyway?

Entering the kitchen, she saw the scullery maid and Simon seated at the table, hands wrapped around cups of tea, expressions subdued. Beside them, Mack was nibbling on a slice of bacon. He left his chair to sidle up to Pip.

'I'll be back shortly,' promised Cook, exiting the room again.

'All right, lad?' Pip asked the youngster, pulling him close.

He nodded solemnly. 'Policeman came, Pip.'

'Aye.' She looked to Simon, who motioned to a chair,

and guided Mack back across. Sitting opposite the others, she rested her head in her hand and heaved a sigh. 'I can barely believe it,' she whispered.

Tabby and Simon nodded, the former saying in a hushed tone, 'Police might want to talk to you, later, when they return.'

The moisture left Pip's mouth. She had to swallow several times before she could utter, '*Me?*'

'And Miss Josephine, of course. Youse are the only two they ain't spoke to yet. Us lot have already told them what we know – not that there was owt, mind, us being asleep and snoring in our beds when it occurred. Don't worry, it's just what they must do, they said. Everyone present in the household has to be accounted for at the time of the death, is all. They're only doing their job. They'll not be expecting you to tell them owt they don't know already, nay. Waste of time, lass, I know, but there you go.'

God above, she couldn't breathe . . . Should she tell them what she knew, what Hardman had been plan-ning, or keep her silence? The housemaid would swing and she might just as well have put the noose around her neck with her own two hands . . . But what then if she withheld the truth and they saw through her lies, assumed she was in on it, sent her to the gallows along with the guilty party? Lord, she couldn't bear this . . .

On jerky legs, she rose from her seat, crossed to the back door and flung it open. A sharp wind greeted her and she sucked it in gratefully.

'Aye, you catch a few lungfuls, lass,' Tabby told her. 'It's a shock, all this, I know. I scarcely believed it when I heard. Now I know she were a divil at times, but still . . . well, it's a fair terrible way to leave this earth, aye.'

244

Oh truly, truly . . . 'How's Miss Lucy bearing up?' she managed to ask, without turning, after some moments.

'Miss Lucy?' This from Simon. 'We ain't seen her the day. Happen she ain't aware as yet.'

'And . . . Mr Philip?'

'It's mebbe affected him, aye. Mind, he ain't likely to show it, is he?' offered Tabby. 'You all right, lass?' she added, frowning, at Pip's disbelieving shake of her head. 'You're a shocking colour. No offence, like, but I didn't think there'd be much love lost betwixt youse. You and Hardman were hardly the best of friends, were you, if truth be told?'

'What? Hardman? *Hardman's* . . . dead?'

The scullery maid and Simon exchanged a look. 'Come and sit down,' he said, as Tabby reached for the teapot and filled a cup for Pip. 'Seems the shock's gone to your head.'

She plopped back into her chair, stupefied. She'd believed, simply assumed . . . and all the time . . . 'How can this be?' she whispered to no one in particular.

'Seems she tripped somehow at the start of her duties this morning, on her way to light the family's fires afore they wakened. Her box of blacklead and brushes were found strewn around her at the foot of the stairs. She injured her head in the fall – police reckon she'd not have suffered. It were just a terrible accident, lass.'

Nay, it wasn't! Pip's mind screamed. Again, the vision of what she just knew had been Caroline lurking around at the ungodly hour last night crashed through her thoughts. Why else unless with devilment in mind? Had she discovered her husband's tryst with the maid? Happen she'd followed or gone in search of him, maybe heard the same as Simon had? Or maybe she *had* been the one who had disturbed the squeaky floorboard

245

yesterday outside Josephine's room? Caroline had heard everything – Hardman's plans to be shot of her. She'd struck first before the maid had a chance . . .

If that's the case, will she come after me next? After all, I know too much, don't I? Pip asked herself, weak at the prospect. *I were privy to Hardman's scheme, am involved in this whether I want to be or otherwise.* Icy fear ran the length of her spine. What was she to do? Was she merely over-thinking this whole horrible mess?

The answer came immediately with sickly truth. She knew that woman was behind this. Hardman just happening to take a tumble on the stairs she trod scores of times every single day? No. It was too incredible a co-incidence to be true. She'd lain in wait for her while the house was slumbering, must have, and pushed her down the stairs. And she'd got away with it, by all accounts, given what the police were surmising.

She must speak to someone about this. She couldn't keep it all to herself any longer. Her gaze swivelled immediately to Simon. He was the only one she could turn to, could trust unquestioningly to see her side of things.

'Come with me, get some fresh air. It'll do you good.' Simon spoke before Pip had the chance to. She sighed in relief.

'Aye.'

'Bread— Mack, I mean,' he added, rolling his eyes and muttering how he'd never get used to the name change, 'you stop here with Tabby. We'll not be long.'

Wrapping her new shawl around herself and knotting the ends together tightly against the winter cold, Pip shadowed the older boy. They were silent until they reached the metal gate to the Green, where Simon produced a key from his pocket, unlocked it and slipped

246

through. Pip followed. They halted by the poplar tree where they had spent part of their first night here.

'Me and Cook have been talking on it . . . We reckon it's better you bend the truth to the police.'

Her breath caught in her throat. Had he guessed? 'Bend the truth about what?'

'About you visiting mine and Mack's room last night. Now we know, and you know, there's nowt in it. But well, happen the police would up their questioning, believing you might know summat about the murder, were they to hear you'd been skulking about the house just a short while afore it occurred, like. We just reckon it's the best thing all round not to say owt—'

'Oh!'

He blinked at her in confusion. 'What?'

'You said . . . murder. You know? You know it weren't an accident?'

His lips tightened. 'I'm convinced it weren't. Mind, I didn't voice it to the police – what would be the point? They'd not consider for a second my word over one of *their* kind, would they? I'd gain nowt but eviction from the house for my troubles, and what good would that do me, any of us?'

A wave of relief coursed through her; she had an ally, at last. Someone else who knew, who she could confide in. For carrying this crippling burden alone was threatening to crush her. 'Oh, lad. I knew too, *knew* she was behind this the moment I realised—'

'She?'

It was Pip's turn to blink. 'Aye. Mrs Goldthorpe.'

'*Mrs* Goldthorpe? Mr, don't you mean.'

'Simon, I don't . . . You believe Mr Philip is behind Hardman's death?'

'Well, of course he is. That bastard is as slippery

as they come; he's gotten shot of her, all right. Happen she were threatening to blow the truth about their goings-on? I don't know. But I'm certain it were him, aye yes.'

Despite his conviction – and if she was honest, the possibility of there being good enough cause for it – Pip knew instantly he was mistaken. 'Lad, it's his wife what's guilty of this crime, not he, I'm sure of it,' she murmured after glancing about. 'Oh, the things I've not told thee, told anyone . . . You wouldn't believe.'

'What, what?'

In hushed tones, she revealed everything: Caroline's hatred and nastiness towards her from the off; her involvement in the vicious rumour that she'd assaulted her daughter, and her implicating Finch to cover her own back; giving the doctor consent to violate Josephine with his newfangled 'healing technique', and her disregard for the lady and Pip's feelings on the matter; the queer scheme she and her husband had concocted and how they were hell-bent on the upcoming marriage going ahead; the whole nasty business with Hardman, how the maid wanted shot of her rival, that they might have been overheard discussing her wish to be rid of Caroline for good, that the eavesdropper might have been the intended victim herself . . . She left out nothing. With each sordid confession, the weight lifted from her like a physical thing.

'God above . . . You've carried all this alone, all this time? Why didn't you come to me?'

Her love for him strengthened. *He believed her, without question!* She could have cried. 'I didn't want to worry thee. You see, lad? She's poison through and through and capable of worse, I'm sure. I just know she's played a hand in this. I don't know what to do.'

248

He was silent for a long moment, then: 'Nowt. You do nowt. For now, at least.'

'Aye?'

'If she suspected you were planning on exposing her . . .'

'Lord knows what she might do next – and to who,' she finished for him.

Nodding, he swore beneath his breath. His anger was tangible. 'Funny, but them filth-riddled streets we once called our bed don't seem so bloody bad no more. Pray to Christ the marriage goes ahead and we get out of this madhouse, and soon. For all our sakes.' Suddenly, he took her shoulders and his voice dropped to a soft growl. 'Promise me. If owt else occurs, if that bitch so much as *looks* at thee wrong, you seek me out and let me know. *Promise*, Pip.'

'I promise. Eeh, I don't know what I'd do without thee,' she choked, blinded by tears.

'That's summat you shan't have cause to find out. I'm going nowhere, never.'

She clung to him. Though he didn't return the embrace – that's not how he was and she wasn't offended – he did lean into her, his way of allowing himself closeness.

'Come on,' he said eventually, pulling away. 'Police said they'd be back after lunch. We'd best get on, discuss what answers you're to put to their questions.'

*

By evening, it was as though Jess Hardman had never been at Bracken House.

True to their word, an inspector and his colleague had returned to take the customary statements from Miss Josephine and Pip – a half-dozen questions were put to them at the most. Had they heard anything unusual? What time had they wakened that morning? Had they stirred from the room, for whatever reason, during the night? Pip thought her heart would leap from her chest as she'd answered a shaky no – to her relief, and a little surprise, the man had barely glanced her way. Smothering a yawn with the back of his hand, he'd edged to the door, as though impatient to be done with what he clearly saw as a cut-and-dried case. An accident had occurred, as accidents were wont to do every second of every day the world over; he obviously saw no need to drag the matter out.

How cheap the life of a servant, a lower class. She'd have bet both eyes more would have been done had it been a significant member of the household that lost their life. The police had seemed more concerned for the Goldthorpes' reputation – their association with such an incident could tarnish their good name should word circulate too widely – than the untimely death of a young woman. They had seemed almost apologetic for disturbing the house again with their presence and Pip, resuming her duties as normal after they had been shown out, was sure they wouldn't see the officers again.

On instruction from the master, Tabby had journeyed to Hardman's family in nearby Salford to deliver a canvas bag containing the maid's effects and, Pip suspected, a generous purse from the dead girl's genuinely sorry employer as a token of goodwill for services rendered, to tide over the grieving relatives now a wage down. And that had been that. The housemaid was gone. Caroline Goldthorpe had literally got away with murder. The truth had brought a burning knot of self-reproach to Pip's gut that refused to leave her.

Bar Miss Josephine, of the family she'd seen nothing. Miss Lucy, to shield her from any unpleasantness, had been kept out of the way in her grandfather's room. What Mr Philip was feeling, thinking, whether he was suspicious of his wife's involvement, Pip didn't know; she had seen nothing of him so could gauge no clue. As for the woman herself . . .

Tabby – who until a replacement was acquired now found the housemaid's duties heaped atop her own already heavy workload – had been summoned by Caroline earlier and told to inform Cook that the lady was to take dinner in her room today and would require a tray. Until then, she was busy reading and was not to be disturbed.

Reading! How her blackened mind was able to settle on such frivolities, Pip was at a loss to understand. Hadn't she a single ounce of moral decency? Mind, did she even have to ask herself that? The woman had a touch of Lucifer himself in her, it was clear.

Having calmed Josephine who, shaken by the day's drama, had taken longer to settle than usual, Pip finally crawled into bed shortly after midnight. She lay staring at the ceiling for an age, mind too wrought with anxiety for sleep.

One thing above all else overrode: what was to be done about Caroline? Simon had said do nothing, not yet. When? Had he a solution to all this? But what?

As she normally did in times of trouble, Pip closed her eyes and envisioned her mother's smile and gentle gaze. Snippets of memory, which the passage of time hadn't yet spirited away, played in her mind and she sighed with a yearning of such intensity it hurt. They were all she had left, now, of that too-short piece of her lifetime. She cherished them, would for ever. And as she

251

drifted to sleep, her mother's voice, reciting one of her many comforting passages from the Bible, cradled her on her descent, bringing a feeling of ease to the heaviness in her heart and feeding her soul with hope:

'Fear thou not; for I am with thee: be not dismayed; for I am thy God: I will strengthen thee; yea, I will help thee . . . '

And she trusted that, somehow, all would be well.

Chapter 16

FOR THE BETTER part of the afternoon, Pip had whizzed through Bracken House like a bee with an itch. To and fro between Miss Josephine's quarters fetching this and the other for her mistress who, jittery with excitement, had struggled to decide between the vast array of dresses and shoes and matching jewels . . . up and down the stairs for numerous cups of fresh tea in her favourite china cup to calm her nerves . . . back and forth to the window to scan the street for Mr Sutton-Shaw's anticipated arrival . . . She was exhausted. But pleased, aye – glad, too – for the upcoming event had broken the stifling gloom that had held the household in its grasp for the past few days.

This morning had seen the birth of a brand new year, and Pip had welcomed it with open arms. She hoped 1861 would fetch more certainty and happiness than the last twelve months she'd gladly left behind. She'd been quietly delighted when Miss Josephine, unsure whether it would be right and proper to press ahead with the engagement dinner today owing to recent circumstances, had finally been persuaded by the master. Her mistress needed this; they all did. It had been something to look forward to, to lift their minds from the darkness for a few short hours. Also, if all went to plan, the chance to dream of the bright future awaiting them in the yet undecided new dwelling. And she prayed hourly it would be theirs for real, and soon. Leaving the badness of this place behind couldn't come fast enough.

Already, Hardman seemed but a distant memory. For varying reasons, no one mentioned her if they could help it, yet her aura lingered and a solemnity touched every corner and crevice, filling the air and those who breathed it still with quiet unease. However, the coming of this fresh dawn had, to everyone's private relief it seemed, shifted the mood for the better.

Still, Pip had seen nothing of the Goldthorpes. Her position kept her in this room for most of each day. When she had ventured beyond the door, with her mistress's permission, to snatch a moment with the others in the kitchen, she'd encountered not a soul on the outward or return journey. Neither had any of the family visited Josephine's room. Whether they had on the occasions she'd been downstairs, Pip couldn't say. But Miss Lucy aside, who she missed and worried over frequently, she was glad of it, particularly Caroline's absence. How she'd feel upon seeing the poisonous piece next, she didn't know. The thought filled her with angry shame and terror in equal measures.

She'd confided to Simon only yesterday that keeping her silence about what she was now convinced was murder was slowly eating away at her moral fibre. She had a constant taste of bitter sickness in her throat with the knowledge that she'd done nothing and uttered less, had allowed that murderess to get away with her wicked deed completely. Again, he'd told her to do and say nothing yet. Getting anyone to listen to her suspicions would be difficult enough, believing them more so, she knew, so Pip did as the lad requested, though it pained

254

her physically. Hardman deserved justice, she did, despite her faults. Caroline had to be punished.

According to Simon, Mr Philip looked to be punishing himself enough for the pair of them. The night following the housemaid's death, he'd heard the stumbling drunk master's son let himself into his dead lover's room. What Simon was certain were muffled sobs had carried through the wall for some minutes, then the gentleman had left as quickly as he'd come. Had he wanted to feel close to Hardman? Had he really felt something for this one, this time? Surprisingly, it appeared so.

'Well, Pip? Will I do?'

Snapped back to the present, she glanced across the room. A small gasp escaped her. 'Eeh, Miss Josephine . . .'

Finally, she'd decided upon a plain but striking outfit in soft rose. Her hair she'd dressed in unborn buds of the same flower. Bright-faced with anticipation, her cheeks held the same hue. She looked radiant.

'Do you think Alexander will approve?' the lady asked, a quaver of uncertainty in her tone. Her breathing was heavy, her eyes wide.

'He'd have to be daft, dumb and blind not to. Now then, deep breaths,' she murmured as Josephine's head began bobbing softly with her shaking. Despite her recent claim that she was almost well for good again, Pip knew she'd been wise not to encourage the assumption and thus raise her hopes too much. Time is what it would take. Patience, too. There was no fast fix.

'I, I'm trying, truly I am . . .'

'Sit down a moment.' Pip helped her to a chair. Frowning worriedly, she made her own steady breathing louder as a guide to encourage the woman to reach the same speed. Her nerves were getting the better of her, she was beginning to panic. If Pip couldn't help her regain control, Miss Josephine would get herself into a state and refuse to attend the dinner; that wouldn't do anyone any good, especially herself.

'What if the meal doesn't go to plan? Perhaps Mabel has forgotten something, or the table hasn't been set correctly? Or, or . . .?'

'Have I to slip down and check, Miss Josephine?' Pip offered, knowing the lady was fretting unnecessarily – large, elaborate meal or not, Cook was a master at her job – but willing to do anything if it curbed her anxiety.

'That would put my mind at ease. Would you?'

'Course, aye.'

'Thank you, dear girl.'

'You'll be all right till I return?'

Reaching for a handkerchief to dab away perspiration from her upper lip, Josephine nodded. Pip hurried from the room.

Her toes had barely touched the bottom stair when a knock came at the front door ahead of her. Leaning around the wide banister, she glanced along the hall. No sound or sign of movement. She took a few steps and stood, unsure what to do. The caller was surely Mr Sutton-Shaw – he was due any time now. Another rap sounded and when again no one appeared to answer it, she moved towards the door. She didn't know if she'd get into trouble for greeting visitors but surely it was better than leaving them perishing from the cold on the step? Tentatively, she turned the handle.

The wave of shock that struck her full force when gazing upon the man who was revealed almost choked her. To say he was surprised, too, was putting it mildly. They could only stare, wide-eyed, at one another for some seconds.

When her legs threatened to buckle, she made to

256

slam the door shut but he wedged his shoe in the opening and thrust his face into hers, hissing, 'What the *hell* are you, you young slum-mole, doing here at Bracken House?'

Pip opened her mouth but her scream never reached her lips – grabbing handfuls of her bodice, the man who regularly visited her nightmares pushed her before him in a tottering dance. When they reached the study, he released her with one hand to thrust the door open and hauled her, gasping with terror, into the room. Kicking the door shut, he shoved her from him towards the large desk by the window, which she hit her hip against, the shot of pain knocking the breath from her. Before she could make a dash for the door, he was looming over her once more.

She whimpered. 'Nay, please—!'

'Everywhere I turn lately you seem to be there.' Grasping her arm, he twisted it painfully up her back. 'What is your game? Who the devil are you?'

'Ah! I didn't hear you arrive, old boy . . .' Entering by sheer chance, Philip halted in the study doorway. His greeting dying, he frowned in confused surprise at the scene before him.

Pip went weak with relief. 'Oh! Mr Philip, please help me—!'

'What is this? Alexander?'

The name seemed to career from wall to wall before crashing through her brain. God above, no . . . What fresh hell was this? It wasn't – couldn't be – true!

With some reluctance, the man who had targeted Mack that day with depravity in mind, whom she'd helped another young innocent fend off only days ago, released her with a curl of his lip. He turned cold eyes to his friend. 'You mean to say you know this parasite?'

257

'Pip? Why, she's Josephine's new find.' Philip moved further into the room. Ever so slightly, his eyes softened at her distress. 'Is there something I should know? What has the child done?'

'Oh, Mr Philip, your friend is bad, he is, he—!'

'Silence!' Alexander Sutton-Shaw barked. 'You utter a word of any of this to upset your mistress and so help me, you'll rue the day you ever crossed my path. Now, get out.' He flicked his head to the door.

The fight left Pip on a drawn-out breath. A miserable tear escaped and splashed to her cheek. With a last look at Mr Philip who, still frowning, quickly glanced away, the last of her spirit sank. What was the point? Her voice meant nothing, nothing. It was finished, all of it. The future was as good as dead. Lord, *why*? She turned and walked slowly from the room.

Her tread took her in the direction of the kitchen but she'd taken no more than a few steps when a familiar voice called her name. As if in a trance, her soul heavy with devastation, she paused. 'Yes, Miss Josephine?' she murmured.

'Pip, dear, did you speak with Mabel? Is everything running smoothly?'

'Oh, I . . . Aye, all's well.'

The woman turned her around to peer at her. 'Alas, you don't seem to be. Whatever is wrong?'

The strength it took not to pour out the terrible, terrible truth, beg her mistress to believe her, to evict the man behind that door from the house, their lives, pained her physically. It would devastate Josephine. It would break her heart, her health along with it. She was besotted with the swine.

But surely, I can't stand back and do nothing, see her marry someone such as him? she agonised. And Josephine was expecting her and the lads to work for them afterwards, to *dwell* in the same house … Oh, why was danger and hatred at every turn? She was sick and tired of it! And she was weary with concealing the truth of wrongdoings.

Simon. She needed to speak with him. He'd know what to do.

She brought to her mouth what she reckoned was a convincing smile. 'Nowt's afoot, Miss Josephine. Don't fret. Mr Sutton-Shaw's just arrived.' The name tasted bitter on her tongue. She breathed deeply. 'You enjoy your evening. I'll be close by should you need me.'

A slow and blissful smile, which it hurt Pip to witness, caressed the woman's lips. She was calmer, now, than she'd been upstairs; it was clear she was determined that nothing would spoil this night. Pip would have been delighted at her strength any other time; now, her happiness felt tainted. She watched the woman she'd come to think a great deal of head for the drawing room with what she just knew were bright eyes and an excited smile. Heart breaking, she continued to the kitchen.

The room was a hive of activity. Cook and Tabby were flitting about like a pair of blind chickens as they put the finishing touches to a dinner befitting a small army. Pip didn't even recognise half the dishes – whatever their names, each looked magnificent. They had worked their fingers to the bone to make today as special as they could. Pip's heart sank yet again.

'Ah, lass!' Cook caught sight of her as she made to slope past towards Simon at the table. 'Eeh, you've arrived at the right time, aye.' She puffed at a tendril of damp hair stuck to her brow. 'I'm fagged, I am. According to Albert, we've a new housemaid joining us the morrow – it can't come quick enough! Until then, we

259

could use your help, here, the night if you're for lending it.' Without waiting for an answer, she turned to the scullery maid. 'Change your apron, tidy your hair and cap, then announce to that lot the grub's ready, lovey. Quick, now, afore it grows cowd.'

'What do you want me to do, Cook?' asked Pip when the girl had disappeared. The answer made her blood run cold:

'Help carry these dishes through to the hungry mob, will thee?'

Enter the dining room, where *he* was? Caroline, too? Oh, could this day get any worse . . .? But what choice had she? She couldn't very well refuse outright and her jumbled mind could think up no adequate excuse.

When Tabby returned, Pip swallowed hard. Taking the girl's lead, she picked up the platter that Cook indicated and, heart hammering, followed her from the room.

As well as Alexander and the Goldthorpes, some half a dozen others turned as one as they stepped inside the spacious, beautifully furnished room. The next moment, seeing they were no one of much significance, the guests resumed their conversations. Lowering her head quickly so as not to accidentally make eye contact with one of her betters, which was frowned upon for servants to do – and certainly not *wishing* to catch the stare of two in particular – Pip stuck close to the scullery maid.

They placed their loads on to the highly polished table, stunningly set with a china service, vases of fresh flowers and gold candelabra, bright silver cutlery winking in the flames' glow. Noiselessly, they disappeared to fetch in the next batch. This time when they returned, Pip caught Miss Josephine's eye, and her mistress gave a subtle smile. Appearing the picture of serenity, much to Pip's relief, she looked like an angel from heaven, beautiful in the soft light and rosy-cheeked from the effects of the rich-coloured wine she was sipping from a crystal glass.

Warmth flowed through her on seeing her mistress happy and at ease. Then she remembered what type of man had brought it about and her shoulders slumped. *Blast him.* Oh, she had to tell her, she had to . . . She glanced his way – and was startled to see him looking right back at her with an expression of such contempt that her hands began to shake. Quickly, she turned her attention to the dish, fearful she would drop it.

But her efforts were in vain. As she passed Caroline's chair, her foot caught on something and time seemed to stand still. She could only watch in complete horror as the platter flew from her hands, clattering across the wooden floor and sending food flying in all directions. She tumbled to the ground after it, landing heavily against the wall.

Dumb silence struck the room. Miss Josephine recovered first. Jumping from her seat, she hurried to Pip's side and, taking her elbow, helped her to her knees. 'Dear girl! Are you all right?'

'Aye, yes. So . . . so very sorry, I . . .' Cheeks aflame, she peeped around at the guests. Catching sight of Caroline and her sickeningly smug smile, furious tears sprang to her eyes.

She'd put her foot out. *She'd* tripped her. She'd done it on purpose, to humiliate her, and she was loving every second of it. Alexander's soft snort showed he approved wholeheartedly.

Pip's legs itched to run at them both and vent her emotion with her fists – a fact that both shocked and

261

incensed her even more. Never in her life had she known a temper such as this. She was gentle natured, could likely count on one hand the times she'd so much as raised her voice to another soul. Now, the struggle to dampen down her burning hatred of these two scared her. What had they done to her? She barely recognised herself. The yearning for revenge planted itself in her mind and she was powerless to shake it.

Tabby, who had been gazing across open-mouthed, now rushed over, put her arm across Pip's shoulders and shepherded her to the door. 'I've got her, Miss Josephine,' she told the lady, adding with a sweeping glance at the others, 'Sorry, very sorry. I'll clear that up right away.' With a gentle push, she sent Pip out, mouthing, 'Go on to the kitchen and recover yourself. I'll see to these lot.'

The door clicked shut in her face. Alone in the hall, she stood staring at the dark wood for a few seconds, breathing deeply. When she reached the kitchen and admitted to Cook what had taken place, the woman, recovering from her shock, brushed aside her apologies and motioned to the pot on the table. 'By, you're as pale as a pound of tripe. Sit thee down and take a sup. Eeh, did you ever hear the like; what a to-do! And my poor baked haddock – all that wasted effort, and for nowt. Ay well. It's my fault really, shouldn't have put you to waiting on, but were desperate, like. Don't fret, no one'll cast blame on thee. Put it from your mind. Accidents will happen.'

Pip gripped the mug's handle until her knuckles turned white. Gazing into the fire, she sipped at the hot brew without tasting it.

'So? What really occurred?'

Swivelling her eyes to Simon at his murmured

question, Pip felt the fire in her veins subside a little and a lump lodged in her throat. Tears threatened again and she averted her gaze. 'Meet me here, in the kitchen later on, when the house are abed,' she whispered flatly.

'Why, what—?'

Before he could finish, she rose and headed upstairs.

When later she heard Josephine enter the bedroom, Pip pulled the covers around her chin and feigned sleep. She couldn't bear to see her again tonight. One kind word from her and her resolve would crumble; she couldn't risk that, must discuss what was to be done with Simon, first. To her relief, her mistress didn't disturb her and a few minutes later, sounds of her retiring to her bed carried through, then silence fell once more. Pushing the covers away, Pip sat up and wrapped her arms around her knees.

How long she remained like this, she didn't know – long enough, she surmised, if her stiff back was anything to go by, for the last of the guests to have left and the family and staff to have gone to their beds. She rose and stole downstairs.

When she pushed open the kitchen door and saw faint light from within, she sighed in relief – he was already up and waiting for her. However, the tall figure she met when she stepped inside wasn't Simon. She froze to the spot.

Slouched in a chair, nursing a glass filled with amber liquid, was Mr Philip.

He didn't seem to have noticed her entrance. His dull gaze was on a sheaf of papers illuminated by the shivering flame of the candle on the table in front of him. Gone was the man she'd come to recognise. His stiff countenance was nowhere to be seen, his immaculate dress crumpled, the top two buttons on his shirt lying open and the sleeves rolled to the elbow. He looked in another world altogether, one all his own.

Pip licked her lips uncertainly. Could she retreat without drawing his attention? She put one foot out behind her and was about to move back towards the door when suddenly he lifted his head.

'Sorry, Mr Philip, sir, I . . . I'll be away to bed, now,' she mumbled, inching further away.

He scooped the sheets of paper into a leather folder and rested his arm on top, almost protectively. His speech was slightly slurred. 'What are you doing here?'

I could ask you the same thing, she thought, saying instead: 'I were wanting a sup, were thirsty, Mr Philip. I didn't think anyone would be awake. Sorry.'

Low laughter left him. He waved his glass towards her. 'Great minds, hm? Although the milk or whatever you were thinking of wasn't quite what *I* had in mind.'

'Sorry.'

'How is my sister?' he asked in a softer tone.

'Sleeping. I shouldn't have left her, should get back . . . Sorry.'

'Will you cease with that wretched word?'

At this, she almost apologised again – couldn't help it. He was a formidable character at the best of times; here, alone with him in the dead of night . . . She was more than a little nervous.

'Sorry means nothing, really, does it?' he added, almost to himself. 'It's a mere noise, without substance. Anyone can say it, can't they, but it eases nothing inside. In here.' He tapped his chest.

'It can if it's genuine.' The words hung in the air between them; she chewed her tongue, regretting having blurted a response. She should have remained silent, should just have made her excuses and gone . . .

'What if . . .?' His gruff voice was a murmur. 'What if an apology is heartfelt but the recipient is unable to hear? What then?'

She thought for a moment. 'I, I don't know, Mr Philip. Say it louder?'

He gave a snort of amusement. Then he bestowed upon her a small smile. 'Your innocence is something to be treasured. Don't lose that, will you?'

'Nay, Mr Philip.'

'You promise?'

She nodded. Feeling increasingly uncomfortable, she once more edged towards the door.

'I thought you needed a drink?'

Swallowing a sigh, she collected a glass and made for the covered pitcher of milk kept cool on the marble slab in the pantry. Then, changing her mind, she turned and filled it half full from Cook's barrel of ale. The fire had long since been banked down and the long room was chilly; the drink would warm her up and, she hoped, help her sleep. That was if she ever escaped this room . . .

Philip threw back his own glass, gulping half its contents. He screwed his face at the strong spirit then dipped his head into his hand.

Tabby had mentioned once that he'd escape to the kitchen as a youngster when troubled in his mind – was that what he was doing now? Pip wondered, eyeing him discreetly. Whatever demons were keeping him from his bed, she neither knew nor wanted to. Though she had a strong inkling, if she was honest with herself – Hardman. His clear sense of melancholy and attempt at escape at the bottom of a bottle . . . talk of apologies . . . His grief spoke volumes. Against her better judgement, she almost felt sorry for him.

265

Nonetheless, it wasn't for her to know nor be witnessing this. Her position, or more to the point his, went against it. He was drunk; what was her excuse? She must cut this meeting, leave him be, for his embarrassment tomorrow upon remembering their exchange might see him resenting her for it. The last thing she needed was another enemy.

Her gaze turned to the door. She was just about to slip away when the one leading to the servants' quarters opened.

Simon took in the scene. His eyes narrowed. He made to speak, pausing when she held a finger to her lips, then he swung around and disappeared. Pip hurried after him.

'Simon?' She reached out to him as he approached his and Mack's bed – but he snatched his arm back and she gasped. 'Lad, what's wrong?'

'Nowt, why would there be? Anyroad, go on back down. Don't let me keep you from enjoying yourself.'

She blinked, confused. 'That's the last thing I were doing, believe me. Mr Philip's that skennin', he don't know what day it is. I came to meet thee, remember, but found him slumped at yon table in your place.'

'And agreed to a nice cosy drink with him, eh?' He pointed to the glass she still held.

'Nay, I—'

'Well, on your head be it. Go on, get back to your fun and games. I want my bed.'

Her anger was rising; she grasped his shoulder and turned him around to face her. 'What are you talking about?'

'He'll snare you over my dead body!'

Slowly, realisation dawned. She blushed to the roots of her hair. 'Don't talk so daft—!'

'Aye? Daft, is it? He's an appetite that's never full when it comes to maids. Now Hardman's gone, he'll be on t' prowl for a replacement. Happen not you now, but in a few short years—' Suddenly, his whole countenance relaxed. He closed his eyes and released air slowly and the ghost of a smile appeared. 'By, I keep forgetting . . . Thank the heavens, we'll not be here by then, eh? He'll not get the chance, for we'll be away at the Sutton-Shaws'. Sorry, for snapping, like. It's just . . . I just, well, I don't want to see you go the same path as the rest and . . .' He frowned when she looked away sadly. 'What's wrong? What's happened?'

'Oh, lad. Oh, the day I've had . . .'

'Tell me.'

She raised her eyes slowly to his. 'It's ruined, lad, the lot. We can't go to work for Miss Josephine . . . and him.' She waited but when Simon merely continued frowning at her, added, 'Alexander Sutton-Shaw? He's the divilish piece what tried to lure our Mack away that day.'

'*What?*'

'It's true. Miss Josephine's in the dark about his wicked ways, that much is clear – likely him downstairs and that wife of his, an' all, I reckon. I ain't told Miss Josephine, it would break her heart. She loves him, deep like. I've said nowt to no one till now. What are we to do, lad? We can't dwell beneath the same roof, now, can't put ourselfs at risk, Mack especially. And well, the way matters have got with Mrs Goldthorpe, we can't remain at Bracken House, can we?' Her voice broke. 'Can you fathom it, at all? The rotten luck of it; why, why this bad fortune all the time, lad?'

Simon had joined his hands behind his head and was pacing the room. Finally, he halted by the window. His

267

back to her, he released a sigh that seemed to come from his soul.

'What will we do?' she repeated.

'We leave. The night.'

'Aye?'

'I'm fair fed up with the bloody lot of them. Leave them to it. We're done here.'

Deep in her heart of hearts, she'd been preparing herself for this, knew he was right. Still, the stab of pain at the prospect struck acutely all the same. 'Aye. Suppose we must.'

To leave their friends, though . . . Miss Josephine . . . Oh, how could she do it? But there was no option. There wasn't anything they could do, was there? Besides, they likely wouldn't be believed. Their short time here had come to an end. In some small way, she realised she was almost glad, was tired to the bones of it all. Things grew worse by the day and were certain only to get uglier. They must go.

'Go to your room and collect your belongings,' said Simon dully. 'I'll rouse the young 'un and we'll meet thee by the back door.'

She nodded, then, catching sight of her dress, told him, 'We must leave our new rig-outs behind. They're uniform. We ain't entitled to them no more. It's only right.'

Mack's feet were healing well; the thought of him returning to the old boots that had caused him so much misery tore at her. Nevertheless, they had no choice. The property didn't belong to them. She wouldn't give anyone the opportunity to brand them thieves on top of everything else.

'Aye. Now go on. Hurry.'

Swallowing tears, Pip turned and headed downstairs.

268

Entering the kitchen, she saw that Mr Philip and his leather paper carrier had gone. Bar his near-empty glass on the table, it was as though he'd never been there. She hurried out and up the main stairs.

Pip changed into her old garments quickly, trying her best not to feel sad and to ignore how different they felt to the new ones she'd been so proud of. Besides the Christmas box from the master containing her precious coin, she owned nothing in the world. Clutching it in her palm, she headed back. She told herself not to glance in her slumbering mistress's direction but, as she knew they would, her eyes betrayed her; she paused by the door and gazed at the lady for a long moment.

Terrible sorry, Miss Josephine. I love thee and wish thee well, but I must leave you. The silent words fell from her lips. Carrying a pain in her breast along with her, she left the room for the final time.

As he'd promised, Simon was waiting by the back door with a sleepy looking Mack. After stroking the youngster's hair and readjusting his cap, she shared a dull look with Simon. Neither spoke, for there was nothing more to discuss. She stole a last look around the homely room and followed the lads out.

The starless night barely had time to wrap its frosty arms around them when a demand that they get back inside hissed through their ears like splinters. Shocked confusion made them do as it bid. The door clapped shut behind them; whipping around, they found Caroline glaring at them in the kitchen's dim light.

'And where, pray, did you three imagine you were slithering off to?'

The woman's spite-filled eyes had Pip shrinking behind Simon. But he, after some seconds, lifted his chin and faced her head on.

'We're getting out of Bracken House, for good and proper, and from the divilment what dwells within it. We rue the day we ever set eyes on the rotten place!' He turned back to the doorknob. 'Let's go, Pip, Bread—'

'Oh no. Oh no, no, I'm afraid not.' Caroline's tone was chilling. A smile greeted their puzzled frowns. She glanced to Mack and flicked her head. 'You there. Back upstairs to your bed.'

He obeyed without resistance. 'Aye.'

'Wait.' Pointing to the ground at her feet as though summoning a dog, she ordered him back. 'Yes? Yes? Yes, what?'

Mack blinked up at her. Rubbing a bleary eye with his fist, he said, 'Aye, Mrs . . . Goldwart?'

'It's Goldthorpe, you imbecile. Gold*thorpe*.' With a curl of her lip, she pushed him from her, sending him staggering towards the servants' door. 'Get out of my sight.'

When he'd gone, Simon turned a steely glare on her. His hands were bunched at his sides, his nostrils flared. 'It's a good thing for you you're a wench, for so help me, you'd be nursing a bloody nose for that. Tripping Pip here earlier, now the lad . . . Don't you ever lay a hand on either again, you hear?'

Pip held her breath, yet a slow but steady stream of anger was rising in her, too. Lord, how she loathed this woman. She did, she did. She seemed to cause nothing but misery to all unfortunate enough to pass in her shadow.

In one swift movement, taking them both by surprise, Caroline threw out an arm and grabbed hold of Simon's ear. Eyes narrowed to slits, she twisted peevishly. 'Let's get one thing clear,' she spat over his gasp of pain, '*I* make the rules around here. One more word out of place from that infernal tongue of yours, and I'll . . .' Slowly, her face relaxed into a ghoulish smirk. 'Well, let's just say you'd be wise to pray you never come to find out.' As she had with Mack, she slung Simon away from her. 'Sit. And you.' Shooting Pip a look, she pointed to the table.

'We'll do no such thing, we're getting out of here—'

'Oh, you'll hear me all right, boy. Unless you want me to have someone summon the police here and now?'

Pip and Simon exchanged worried looks. The law was a thing to fear, particularly for folk like them, always had been. It was she who murmured, 'Police? But . . . we've done nowt.' *Unlike you!* her mind screamed, at the same time praying Simon wouldn't give life to the words. Lord, if she only knew what *they* knew . . .

'Nothing?' Caroline arched an eyebrow. 'Now that depends, doesn't it?'

'Depends on what?' asked Simon quietly.

'On who is doing the accusing. My word would carry infinitely more clout than the likes of yours, and you know it. Now, I shan't tell you again. Sit.'

Reluctantly, they did as she ordered. They watched with wary eyes as she approached them. Her stare was empty, stiff face unyielding. Why was she threatening them in this way? What was she up to?

'What is all this?' asked Simon in the next breath, as though reading Pip's thoughts. 'You've plotted to be rid of us since the day we got here; now you're telling us to stay? Why?'

'Josephine Goldthorpe must marry. I intend to ensure that nothing comes in the way of it. Therefore, you,' Caroline continued with a jerk of her chin to Pip, 'go nowhere. She seems to have got it into her mind that she needs you to help control her nerve disorder. If you

271

were to leave, her condition might deteriorate and the wedding could be put in jeopardy. I see that now. It is a risk I am not prepared to take.'

'Why would we do owt for thee?' Simon met her stare boldly. 'After all you've done, the trouble you tried to cause for Pip here . . .? We should have gone to the master then.'

'With what proof? Do you honestly believe I'd be so careless? Oh no. I'm most cautious in my planning. It's unfortunate that Finch had to go, I admit. However, I did what I needed to at the time.'

'Even at the price of your own daughter's happiness and well-being?' He was gratified when she glanced away. 'So, I'll ask thee again: why would we do owt for thee? For it is for thee, ain't it? You care not a fig for the lady upstairs, nor her happiness, I'll be bound. What game are you playing? What do you care whether she weds or not? What shall you get out of it?'

'Ask your fine master up there; all of this is his doing,' she ground out, almost to herself.

Pip frowned. Again, as when she'd overheard her with Philip in the study, the reference to Albert Goldthorpe being at fault. What did it all mean? However, she hadn't time to ponder; Caroline's eyes were again on them.

'There is no two ways about it – Josephine and Mr Sutton-Shaw must marry. That's all you need to know.'

'Mrs Goldthorpe?' Where Pip found her courage, she didn't know. It was, she suspected, love of Josephine and care for her well-being that had her lifting her chin in defiance. 'D'you know what make of man you're for shackling that fine lady to? He's a beast, aye. A filthy swine with a liking for ones much younger than his intended.' That had knocked the wind out of her sails – she nodded grimly at Caroline's stunned expression. 'It's the truth. We encountered him a while back on the streets.'

'You're lying—'

'Nay, she ain't,' Simon interjected. 'He's a feral demon in gentleman's clothing. You'd push your own kin on to someone like that, aye?'

'But . . . But they *must* wed.' Caroline swung angrily from the table to pace the floor. 'If they don't, it will spell ruin for us, *ruin*.' Abruptly she halted. 'I don't believe a word of it – and you're lucky I'm not hauling you before the courts on a slander charge. Attempting to drag the name of a gentleman such as Alexander Sutton-Shaw through the dirt; how dare the pair of you.'

'You know we speak the truth. It's written all over your phizog.'

'Silence!' Caroline took a deep breath before continuing with more composure, though her face remained void of colour: 'Josephine loves him. Her happiness is secured. Now, I suggest you retire to your respective beds and utter not a word of this to anyone.'

'And if we refuse?'

The lady glared at Pip, unblinking. She rested both palms on the table and a small smile appeared at her mouth. 'Then all three of you worthless waifs shall suffer for your folly. You and the boy upstairs will be incarcerated in the workhouse. As for him . . .' Her eyes swivelled to Simon. 'He'll dangle at the end of a rope with a noose around his neck.'

Pip lurched back in her chair. '*What?* I don't understand . . .'

'What is there not to?' Caroline's tone had dropped to a whisper. 'That's the punishment normally handed out to murderers, is it not? You, boy, had an axe to grind with the dead servant. Half the street heard you verbally attack her for swindling you out of money. The perfect motive, wouldn't you agree? I know the courts would.'

Simon shook his head slowly. 'Nay . . .'

'You were bitter, wanted revenge, and wormed your way into this house for that purpose only. You bided your time before gaining the perfect opportunity to get her alone while everyone slept. You confronted her – perhaps she said something you didn't like – your fury boiled over and you pushed the housemaid down the stairs. You killed her.'

'Nay, nay—'

'You witch!' Mindless of who she was speaking to now, Pip jumped to her feet. Sickened to the core, her breathing ragged, she pointed a quivering finger in the grinning woman's face. 'You can't do this!'

'Oh, I can and I shall.'

'They'll see through your lies, they will—!'

'That's a risk you can afford to take, is it? My husband and I, the scullery maid, even Josephine can attest to the confrontation outside. We all witnessed it, did we not?'

'And what about what I witnessed?' Pip was shaking with her emotions. She couldn't contain herself now. It had gone too far for that. 'You, lurking about the landing shortly afore Hardman met her end? I'll tell them *that*! I will! It's *you* what's the murderer!'

'Aha. Oh dear, oh dear.' Completely unfazed by the outburst, Caroline clicked her tongue. '*You* were absent from your bed, despite telling the police the contrary? Lying to an inspector of this city? And for what reason would that be? But of course – an obvious accomplice to murder. Your friend asked you to assist him in his heinous plot and you agreed. Seems you'll be spared the workhouse after all, for it shall be the noose for you, too—'

'Stop it, stop it!'

'The truth hurts, doesn't it?'

'It's not the truth, it's not! *You're* the guilty one, you—'

'The likes of you are worth not a jot, don't you understand?' Caroline threw the quiet words at them like hot knives. 'You think your word would carry an ounce of weight over that of your betters? Just you try me. You're nothing – less than that. Go against me and I'll crush you like cockroaches beneath my shoe. I'll crumble your lives to dust. That is a promise. As for your precious Josephine . . . She'll be committed to the asylum and the key tossed away. And it will be all your fault.'

'Once Miss Josephine's wed . . . we'll be free to leave?'

Pip had been shaking her head, eyes screwed shut. At this emotionless question from Simon, she gazed at him, incredulous. 'Lad, you're not for going along with it? Nay, we can't—'

'I haven't decided yet.' Caroline cut her off, again that smug smile of hers playing. 'What is it they say? Keep friends close, enemies closer still? You go when I say.'

'Simon, lad—!'

'We're powerless, Pip. Even if we run, they'll find us.' He lifted dull eyes to her face. 'We've no choice.'

To remain, they would be prisoners, regardless. And Mrs Goldthorpe was the guard. God above, that it had come to this . . . Just what did their future hold? Yet if they went against her, they wouldn't have one at all, their lives would be cut short on the gallows, she'd make sure of it. Pip didn't believe it was idle talk for a second. Simon had always done right by her and Mack. They could rely upon their worldly-wise leader to make the right decision. Now was no different. She trusted his judgement implicitly. Slowly, her head dipped in defeat. She nodded.

'I knew you'd see sense. Now, I suggest— Oh.' Caroline broke off as for the first time, her stare captured the glass sitting between them on the table. A slight frown creased her brow. 'So he *was* here. Then where . . .?' Her eyes hardened. She cleared her throat. 'This conversation is over. You two, get to your beds. And remember: keep your mouths shut.'

Her piercing glare bore into them for some moments then she was gone. Pip and Simon didn't follow suit. They sat for a long time, frozen with shock.

She'd come seeking out her husband. If only she'd entered seconds later, she wouldn't have caught sight of them leaving, Pip realised. Philip had managed to evade her acid, retreating not to bed but God alone knew where. Alas, they hadn't. Now, their lives were over. And there was nothing they could do.

Without looking her way, Simon held out an arm. Silently, she leaned across, wrapping both of hers around his neck.

With a simultaneous, hopeless sigh, they held each other tightly.

Chapter 17

DAYS ROLLED BY incident free. The children had awaited further trouble with quiet dread – they had begun to expect it, now – but it never came. If anything, the house had settled into an easy routine.

Caroline, if their paths should cross, acknowledged them in neither look nor speech. She acted as if they didn't exist, as was normal. It was as though the trouble in the kitchen that bitter New Year's Night had never taken place. It seemed forgotten, by her at least. Pip and Simon, on the other hand, were not afforded the same – even pretence at – peace.

How could they? They were being forced to remain here against their will. It was all they could think about. Worry for their uncertain futures was a dark companion during both their waking hours and otherwise. Regularly, Pip woke with a start from black and vivid dreams of Simon, or herself, sometimes the two of them, standing before the scaffold as Caroline waved them on with a demonic grin. And if the unfamiliar smudges of colour beneath the lad's eyes were anything to go by, the nights were not being kind to him, either.

Tabby had grown suspicious, Cook more so, particularly when their appetites began to wane with the fretting of it all. By some unspoken agreement, they remained tight-lipped, knowing instinctively that, should they mention a word, Caroline would see her threat through and their lives would be over. They were helpless. Hopeless. Nothing could make this right and it wasn't going away. They were at a loss what to do.

To Pip's relief, Josephine was too caught up in the forthcoming wedding to notice anything amiss. Yet her mistress's glowing happiness evoked only sorrow and regret and shame. Often, Pip was forced to invent some chore or other to escape her company for a short while and regain her composure. For the guilt was eating away at her; the fine lady she'd come to love was deserving of so much more. Better from Alexander, and from her sister-in-law. Better from her.

They barely saw anything of Philip these days. Whether as a distraction or because he had simply moved forward, he'd thrown himself into the overseeing of the mill. The cool, collected, level-headed gentleman was back. There were certainly no more late-night maudlin trips to the kitchen with only a whisky bottle for company, at any rate, as far as Pip knew.

The only beacon of light in the clogging darkness was Lucy. Always her sunny self, she brought life to every room and person she graced with her presence.

New staff had indeed been employed. Cally, the housemaid, was a somewhat lackadaisical young woman with a chirpy smile, the polar opposite of Hardman. The other new employee was a nursemaid in her middle years named Budd who, to everyone's surprise, the girl adored. If only the secrets plaguing Pip and Simon's fraught minds didn't exist, life at Bracken House would have been a pleasure.

The glimmer of a solution to their dilemma presented

itself one Wednesday morning, a fortnight to the day since the new domestics had joined the workforce. The Goldthorpes had just been served breakfast and the servants, enjoying a few precious minutes' respite, were seated in the kitchen eating bread and cold bacon washed down with tea. No one glanced up when Cally, returning from the dining room, entered. As she did normally, the woman sat in her chair and helped herself to food from the dishes in the centre of the table. However, this day differed in one aspect: the buxom housemaid's usually healthy appetite looked to have deserted her. She nibbled at a heel of bread then, sighing, returned it to her plate. Folding her arms, she chewed at her thumbnail, eyes flitting to them in turn.

'What's the matter with thee?' asked Cook through a mouthful of meat.

She plucked at her lip. 'Can I ask youse summat?' At their nods, she continued in a loud whisper, 'Do youse believe in . . . spirits, like?'

Tabby snorted, Mack giggled. Cook, however, didn't scoff in the slightest: 'Oh aye.'

Cally's eyes were like saucers. 'Do you? Really?'

'Aye. I've had an encounter or two through the years myself. Why d'you ask?'

'Oh 'eck . . . Oh!'

'What's up now, then?'

'I reckon the last housemaid here wants me gone. I can feel her, Cook, all around me. Her presence, and touching me, like.' She threw her apron over her face theatrically. 'Oh, what am I to do?'

The older woman rolled her eyes. 'Eeh, I don't know. You're a scatty mare, you are. Hardman's no more here than the bloody queen of England. I'd know it. I feel these things, me.'

Cally peeped over the top of the snowy material. 'You do?'

'Oh aye. Got passed down, it did, from my mam – famous for it were Annie May – to me. My sister, Jilly, has the sense too, though hers is aspying the future – reads the tea leaves, like, she does.'

'But . . . well, what about what I felt, then, out there?' Cally thrust a thumb towards the baize door. 'You telling me it were nowt but fanciful thinking?'

'And what did you feel?' Cook's brows suddenly knotted together. She leaned forward and, eyes widening, asked in a shaky whisper, 'You didn't feel ghostly fingers of death playing in your hair, did yer, lass?'

'Aye! Oh! How . . .?' The young woman's face had turned a shocking shade of white. 'See, see! I knew it, I did! Otherwise how did you know? Oh, I'm being haunted by the poor soul forced to wander this mortal realm for ever more—!'

'You've a ruddy great spider nestled in your cap.'

Cally's lamentations petered away. She blinked. 'Eh?'

'Them "ghostly fingers of death" you think you felt – it'll be them black hairy legs busy at making a web in yon locks.'

Swivelling her eyes upwards, the housemaid let out a screech and, dashing the cap to the floor, leapt up to crouch on her chair as though the ground was home to a hundred rats. 'Where is the dirty divil? Has it gone? Has it? Oh, Lord, it might still be on me, might have laid its eggs in my ears—!'

'Don't talk so bleedin' daft.' Cook could barely breathe for laughing. 'Eeh, I'm sorry, lass, I am. I couldn't resist. I were jesting, is all; nowt to fret over. Come on, drink your tea, now, calm your nerves.'

The scullery maid and Mack by this time had tears of mirth running down their faces. Even Pip had to cover her mouth with her hand to quell her giggles. Cally, on the other hand, was not amused.

'Rotten-minded swines, the lot! Could have given me a heart attack, you could. I hate them things – bleurgh! Mind, rather a spider than a dead servant tormenting my person . . .' Slowly, her lips twitched and swatting a hand at the grinning cook, she laughed along. 'All right, aye, you had me. I'll get you back for that, though, you see if I don't.'

'Aye well. For now, it's to work for you and the rest of us. Come along, no slacking. As my dear mam used to say: lose an hour in the morning and you'll be chasing it through the day.' She heaved herself up, the maids did likewise and, after draining her cup, Pip scraped back her chair.

Simon, who had been silent throughout the conversation, now laid a hand on her wrist, saying, 'Hang on a minute.'

'What is it?'

After looking to Mack and instructing him to collect the grooming brushes and go and see to the master's dogs, he returned his attention to Pip. His brow was creased, his dark grey eyes thoughtful. 'Sit back down. I think I've got an idea.'

She slid into the chair beside his that the youngster had vacated. 'About what?'

'How to get ourselves out of the mess we're in.'

A frown of her own appeared. 'What, with Mrs Goldthorpe?' she whispered, adding at his nod, 'Ay, tha does? But what, lad?'

'Miss Lucy drops into the kitchen most days after lunch, don't she?'

'Aye yes, I suppose she does. But what's that got to do—?'

'I'll explain proper soon. Go on up to your room, now, I'll see you later.'

Now, it was her turn to halt his attempt to vacate the table. 'Wait. What's the young miss got to do with your idea? I'll not use her, Simon, won't see her hurt for owt—'

'Nay, nay. Nowt like that.'

'You promise?'

'Course. Aye.'

Pip watched him leave through the back door to see to his duties in the garden. Still frowning, she headed upstairs.

That afternoon, as Tabby was washing up the lunch things and Cook was taking the weight off her feet by the fire with a glass of beer, the three children sat finishing their meal at the table. Cally was away somewhere, busy in the house. Swinging his legs and humming a tune, Mack was in his own innocent world. Pip and Simon, however, had but one thing on their minds. They glanced continually from each other to the door. Finally, as they were about to give up hope, Lucy skipped into the room bestowing on them all one of her smiles. Pip heard the older lad sigh in relief but had no time to wonder afresh at his plan; the young girl had rushed to her and now threw her arms around her neck.

'Good afternoon, Pip. I trust you're well?'

'Aye, Miss Lucy.' By, but it was lovely to see her, always. 'You're all right?'

'Of course.' She looked across to the fire. 'Hello, Cook. Have you ... been busy today?' she asked casually.

'Have I done any baking, you mean, young sneak,' the woman replied without turning, though amusement

282

bubbled beneath the words. She shook her head when Lucy giggled. 'Go on, get a cake from the stand over there, lovey.'

When the girl was seated again and occupied picking fat currants from the golden pastry, tongue poking out in concentration, Simon straightened in his seat as though preparing himself. He too now looked to Cook, and Pip bit her lip, wondering what he was about to do and whether it would work. Oh, but she hoped so, she did . . .

'Tell us about them spirits you've seen, Cook,' he called across, tone easy, as though their very futures were not relying on her unwitting cooperation, which of course they were. 'Remember, like you told Cally?'

She stifled a yawn with her arm. 'Nay, nay.'

'Ah, go on.'

'Another time, mebbe. I'm too fagged, lad, for tales.'

Desperation flashed in his eyes; he turned to Pip with a hopeless shake of his head, and thinking on her feet it was she who said in an overly loud whisper, 'It were nowt but daft talk, I reckon, lad. Lies, aye.'

As she'd anticipated, the cook's head snapped around. 'Lie, me? I ask you, bold piece! I'll have you know that my beloved husband, God rest his soul, has paid me many a visit since the Lord saw fit to take him back home. My mam, too, aye. So stick that in your pipe and smoke it!' She returned her attention to her beer with a haughty sniff.

'Aye, Cook. Sorry, Cook.'

Simon rewarded Pip's efforts with a soft wink. He glanced to Lucy who was sitting agog, clearly trying to process what she'd just heard. Then, loud enough for just the girls to hear, he said, ''Ere, I do hope Hardman ain't still lingering here at Bracken House. I mean, I'd not want to get Cook, there, into bother for revealing

283

that such things as spirits exist, but well . . . if they do . . .' He deliberately let his words trail off with a shiver. 'I've heard that the dead can become trapped, are unable to leave if they have unfinished business here. Like, say . . . if their lives were unexpectedly cut short, mebbe.'

The young miss was quiet for the remainder of the visit. Though Pip, filled with guilt and not a little anger that she'd allowed Simon to draw her into this bizarre scheme – the like of which she couldn't imagine solving their problems – and worrying Lucy as he obviously had, tried to distract her thoughts but to no avail.

'I have to go, now.' Lucy, her usual smile gone, eventually rose. 'Goodbye.'

'Just what's your game?' Pip whispered harshly when the girl left. 'How could you, lad? You promised—'

'Miss Lucy'll get over it, don't fret. I had to, had no choice.'

'Had to what? What was all that in aid of, anyroad?'

He glanced about, then leaned in. 'We can't say nowt concerning Mrs Goldthorpe's activities, right? And she won't come clean off her own bat, you can be certain of that. So . . .'

'Aye? So?'

'We frighten the truth from her. We'll scare her so bad, she'll be squealing her crimes like the sow that she is to anyone who'll listen.'

'How, lad? What will you do?'

'I'll make her believe she's being haunted by the housemaid's spirit. That her victim is out for revenge or some such.'

'Oh, lad . . .'

'You'll see. She'll be so frickened, she'll confess, she will.'

Pip's heart had sunk to her boots. She'd thought for a while there that he'd come up with a genuine course of action. God above, talk about the grasping at a solution by one who was past desperate . . . It was madness, a childish idea – because that's what they were: just kiddies, trying to make matters better the only way they could think how. She heaved a long sigh.

'Where would Miss Lucy have gone to after leaving the kitchen just now?' Simon answered his own question: 'To visit her mam for an hour.'

'Aye, and?'

'And, what d'you think will be the first thing out of the lass's mouth? You saw her; I reeled her in good and proper. She'll not be able to contain herself and, ta-dah, the seed will be sown. And I'll be the one to reap it. Oh, I will that.'

It wouldn't work. Pip knew this and yet what else did they have? She certainly hadn't a brighter idea. It was an impossible aim he was clinging to, for he had to feel he was at least trying something, she realised. She couldn't dash his hopes. Suppressing another sigh, she shrugged. 'Do as you see fit, then, lad. Just be careful, eh? Caroline Goldthorpe . . . Well, we both know what evil she's capable of. She'll show no mercy should she sniff this out.'

'She'll not.' Voice dropping, his eyes deepened in intensity. 'Pip?'

'Aye?'

'I can do this. I'll remedy this for us, I swear. You believe in me, don't you?'

He'd spoken with such sincerity, such conviction, that she actually almost did. Almost. She forced herself to nod. 'Course, lad. Course I do.'

His face relaxed a little and he gave a whisper of a smile. For a long moment, as he stared at her, it looked like he wanted to say more. Then for reasons she couldn't fathom, his cheeks pinkened and he rose quickly to his feet. 'Aye, well. I'd best get on.'

*

Josephine swished the square of silk over the stones, smiled, then repeated the action. 'Beautiful,' she murmured, a soft, faraway look in her eyes.

'Like thee.'

'Oh, Pip. You are a dear.'

She returned Josephine's smile then continued with the dusting of the mantel. Her mistress appeared so much calmer these days. Easy of mind, free of unnecessary worry. Her complexion was healthier, eyes brighter. Being in love suited her. Swallowing a sad sigh, Pip averted her gaze.

Josephine returned her attention to polishing the ring Alexander had presented her with to finalise their engagement, a thin band embedded with a cluster of amethyst and sapphire stones as pure and flawless as the bride-to-be herself and their future together, he'd told her. The gems themselves, he'd specifically chosen to represent his initials and thus his love for her. The sickening deception of it all, when her mistress had proudly informed her of this, turned Pip's stomach.

'Ah, dear girl. I didn't tell you, did I?'

Pulled from her thoughts, Pip shook her head. 'Tell me what, Miss Josephine?'

'Alexander and I were discussing our future home when he called yesterday evening. The subject of staff came up and I informed him I would like you and the boys to come and work for us.'

She was silent, then: 'Oh?'

'He was most pleased with the idea. Is he not the most agreeable man in the entire world, Pip?'

She'd believed he'd persuade her mistress to be rid of her. She'd also half wished he would. Now this . . . Forcing to her face what she hoped was more smile than grimace, she nodded.

'I believe he has a soft spot for the three of you, you know.'

This time, Pip didn't respond; she couldn't have got a word past the bile in her throat. *A soft spot.* The thought made her skin crawl.

'After all, as I told you recently, he too is an orphan of some years. He understands the pain that such a loss brings. Oh yes, yes; he shall treat you all with a tender hand, I just know it.'

Again, another false smile; quickly, she turned back to her cleaning.

'It's rather tragic that he hasn't any kith or kin to speak of. Now we're betrothed, we would have been making arrangements for our two families to meet. Ah, poor darling. Well, he does have a sister residing in France; rather a distance for me to travel, I fear, though maybe some day she will brave the crossing so we can make one another's acquaintance.'

Aye, and probably not, Miss Josephine, she said in her mind. *This sister of his likely hasn't a clue about you, nor the fact her brother's to be wed. The less folk that know of his scheme the better, was likely his thinking, I'll be bound.* In fact, he was probably lying about being parentless, too, for the same reason, she thought, gritting her teeth. To lie about such a thing, when others were forced to live the reality . . . He really was despicable. Who knew what further untruths he'd fed her lady to uphold this charade? And why? For what reason, *what*?

'Sister-in-law, hello.'

Lost in her musings, Pip hadn't heard the door open; at Josephine's greeting, her back stiffened. She didn't turn but carried on with her duties, head down.

'Alexander is downstairs and wishing to see you.'

'Oh, wonderful. Though I wasn't expecting him . . .' Josephine's hands fluttered to her hair then dropped to straighten her skirts.

'He decided to call in for a brief visit on the way to his gentlemen's club. Come along, then. He cannot spare much time.'

'Oh yes, of course. I, I just need to . . .'

Hearing the agitated note in her mistress's tone, Pip forced herself to turn. 'You look gradely, Miss Josephine, honest,' she murmured reassuringly.

'Really, Pip?'

'Aye. Go on, now. Deep breaths—'

'Come along, for goodness' sake,' snapped Caroline, flinging the door wide. 'He'll be gone before you've managed to leave this room.'

Pip shot Mrs Goldthorpe an angry look, but it quickly melted into a frown. She looked terrible – more so than usual. Her lips were pinched, her piercing eyes darker with barely suppressed feeling. Though twin spots of angry red stained her cheekbones, the rest of her was a pasty grey. For a fleeting moment, she wondered if Simon had put his plan into action already and the woman had discovered what he was up to, but quickly dismissed this. A child Simon might be. A fool he wasn't. Cunning from years of necessity, he wouldn't be stupid enough to give the game away, certainly not this early. Would he?

Barely able to wait a full minute after the two women had disappeared downstairs, Pip was following in their wake, though her feet took her not to the drawing room but on towards the kitchen.

Miss Josephine's voice, high with excitement, carried through the door as Pip passed: 'Oh, you have? The first week in May? Alexander, that's marvellous! An absolutely perfect time of year for a wedding.'

'Well, darling, I cannot advocate a drawn-out betrothal. It is merely precious time wasted, in my opinion.'

'Oh, indeed. Thank you, thank you . . .'

Pip closed her eyes, sighed, then hurried her step. After glancing around the kitchen and seeing that Simon was absent, she made for the garden at the back of the house. She found him on his knees, busy tending a sad-looking flower bed, a pile of dead weeds beside him. 'All right, lad?'

'Oh, better than.' A hint of laughter coated his response. He rubbed his hands together, brushed dirt from his trousers, then rose. 'Mrs Goldthorpe came to the kitchen earlier.' He nodded when Pip's eyes widened. 'The young miss did just as I knew she would.'

'What did Mrs Goldthorpe say?'

'Blasted Cook for filling Miss Lucy's head with nonsense. Cook gave her short shrift, mind – you know how she can be – and the lady went off with a flea in her ear. But Pip . . . I don't know . . .' He chewed his bottom lip thoughtfully. 'There were summat in her countenance, summat different. I reckon a worm of fear has taken root in her. I don't know, can't explain it, can't describe how she looked. Just *different*, you know?'

'I do, as it happens. I were for thinking the very same just now when she called on Miss Josephine,' Pip was forced to admit. 'Eeh, lad . . .'

Simon's smile grew. 'It might work. The bleedin' thing just *might*!'

'What will you do?'

'I've not thought that far ahead as yet. Careful planning is what's needed, here. For this to pan out like we want, it needs to be done right.'

'Well.' Pip cast him a sidelong glance as they made back to the kitchen. 'A date for the wedding's been set: the beginning of May. That gives us just a few short months to beat Mrs Goldthorpe at her own hellish game. Josephine can't marry that man, Simon. She can't.'

A flicker of uncertainty touched his eyes. But just as swiftly, it vanished, and the lad she knew and believed in implicitly was back. 'The month of May, you say? Aye, plenty of time, with some to spare. You'll see.'

Chapter 18

MUCH TO PIP'S secret astonishment, see she did.

Simon had set to work that very night, though the first she knew of it was when Caroline hauled her from her slumber with a rough shake. The woman, hair flowing freely around her shoulders, her long white nightgown standing out starkly in the darkness, leaned over her, hissing, 'What is the meaning of this? *Answer* me, you young wretch!'

'What, what . . .?' Brain sludgy with sleep, Pip could only blink in confusion.

'You know very well what. You, skulking . . . skulking around . . .' She paused, as though finally realising this was an impossibility – Pip had clearly been fast asleep just now. There was no escaping the fact. She'd been nowhere apart from her bed, and Caroline knew it.

'Mrs Goldthorpe, what is it? I were but dreaming; what have I done?'

It was a long moment before the woman's quiet response pierced the silence. 'It matters not. Get back to sleep.'

She sloped back to her own room, and Pip's small smile went with her.

'I thought it best to strike while Miss Lucy's words were still fresh in her mind,' Simon told her discreetly the following morning as they were eating their porridge. He flashed a shaky grin. 'By, I don't mind telling you: my heart weren't half thumping as I stole up the main stairs.'

'You could have warned me is all I'm saying. Frickened the liver out of me, it did, her looming over me like that in the dead of night.' Pip glanced about before adding, 'What did you do, then? Whatever it were, lad, it rattled her good and proper. She were fair wild for answers.'

'Listened at her room, didn't I, to make sure all were still within, then I opened the door – slow, you know, so's it creaked all eerie, like – before slamming it shut again. 'Ere, it were perfect. I almost scared my rotten self! The noise I heard her let out afore I scarpered . . . Honest to God, I wondered for a minute if she'd gone abed that night with a suckling piglet.'

'What are youse two giggling at, then?' Cook called across, smiling, as they smothered nervous laughter with their hands.

'Pip were just telling a joke,' Simon called back, thinking on his feet. 'You want to hear it, Cook?'

'Ay, lad, go on.' She came to rest her arms on the back of a chair facing them. 'Fond of a good belly tickler, I am.'

'How d'you stop a fish from smelling?'

She scratched her dimpled chin. ''Ere, I don't know. But I'd like to, aye.' Her profession winning through, she awaited the answer with genuine interest. 'How so?'

'Cut off its nose!' burst out Pip for him, recognising this as what an old drunkard used to tell them each and every night on his way home when they begged outside the taverns, before doubling up with laughter.

'Eh? Cut off . . .? Ay, you pair of daft swines, what're

you like!' With a shake of her head and a roll of her eyes, she returned to the bubbling cooking pot needing her attention.

The children, wiping tears of mirth from their eyes, smiled wistfully.

'Do you miss it, Simon? The slums, I mean.'

He answered just as quietly. 'Sometimes. Weren't all bad, were it?'

Pip shook her head. 'There were a few good souls hidden amongst the bad, aye.' A sudden vision of Peter, who had come to her rescue and given up his bed for her at Nan Nuttall's, appeared in her mind. Again, she smiled.

'I reckon often of late that we'd have mebbe fared better stopping put.'

She nodded. Owing to recent occurrences, she'd begun wondering the same.

'Come on.' He rose suddenly and motioned for her to follow. 'I've another idea.'

Once in the garden, she watched him go to stand by the trees bordering the perimeter. Peering up, he scanned them keenly, reaching to finger a bare, winter-hardened branch here and there then dismissing it with a shake of his head.

'What you thinking, lad?'

'Here, you search over there.' He motioned to the garden's opposite end.

'For what?'

'Sticks. They must be just right – long and thin, and the sturdier the better.'

'Will these do?' Pip asked minutes later, producing a handful, yet still with no idea what use he would find for them. She watched him bend them in different directions, checking their durability, his tongue peeping out in concentration. The majority he discarded but two seemed to pass his standards; along with one he himself had found, he hid them beneath a bush close by the back doorstep.

'How will sticks help? What's tha planning? Tell me, lad.'

'In a minute. First, help me find some strong twine.'

They located what he needed in the dresser drawer – fortunately, the servants were too occupied with their own affairs to notice. Simon stuffed the spool into his pocket. Then he took a deep breath and nodded, satisfied.

Pip raised an eyebrow. 'Well?'

He went to stand in a quiet nook of the kitchen, she followed, and they leaned with their shoulders against the wall, heads close together.

'I got thinking on summat Cook said to Cally. Remember, about ghostly fingers of death? I can't risk entering Mrs Goldthorpe's room while she's there, nay, but . . . Well, happen I don't need to. Them branches we've collected, I'm for tying them together to make one big long 'un. Then can you guess what I'm going to do with them?' A mixture of excitement and nervous anticipation sparked in his eyes. When she shook her head, he licked his lips then whispered, 'I'm going to pass it through the keyhole of her door and poke her with it – hard!'

Eyes like saucers, Pip's hand slowly travelled to cover her mouth.

'Last night, when I were up there, I got a view of yon bedroom upon opening the door – the Goldthorpes' bed stands nigh on facing the entrance and at no great distance from it. I reckon I can pull this off, I do. This will surely put the wind up her good and proper. Imagine it, woken from your slumber in the pitch-dark night by an unseen hand prodding at your person. The door's firmly secured and you know there ain't no one in the room with you that shouldn't be. By, she'll shit the sheets in fear, you see if she don't. I know I would!'

He'd succeeded in setting the wheels in motion with Miss Lucy, it was true. And, Pip had to admit, his antics last night had worked like a charm; Caroline had been visibly affected. But this new idea? She wasn't convinced. It was a bold move, even for the brave Simon. There was so much that could go awry. 'Lad, I don't know . . . '

'Thought you believed in me?'

'I do, honest, it's just . . . What if the twine comes loose, or the sticks snap? What are husband and wife going to think upon wakening to find a bunch of wood and string in the middle of their floor?'

'They'll not. I'll secure everything proper.'

'What if she springs up afore you've a chance to pull the contraption back out of the keyhole? She'll catch you red-handed.'

'Then I'll practise awhile pushing it in and out, build my speed up, like, afore going ahead. Besides, it'll be dark; she'll see nowt. And dumb with sleep as she'll be, I'll have had time to remove it and scarper afore she gathers her senses.'

Still, Pip wasn't reassured. And another, more worrying prospect occurred to her: 'What if you poke Mr Philip by mistake? After all, you can't be certain she sleeps on the side of the bed closest to the door.'

This time, the lad bit his lip. 'I never thought of that. Ay, well.' He shrugged. 'It's a risk I'll just have to take, ain't it?'

'Eeh, Simon . . .'

'Trust me. It'll *work*. It will.'

Knowing he wouldn't be swayed from this, she had

no option but to support him. Thoughts of what their torturer would do should she discover him set her chest tightening and her knees atremble. She brushed his hand with hers in an affectionate caress. 'Be watchful, eh, lad? Should summat occur, happen if the master's dogs hear you on the landing and bark, give the game away—'

'They'll not. They didn't last night.'

'But if they do this time, or if someone should spot you and demand to know what you're about in that part of the house, tell them . . . tell them Mack was crying for me. Aye yes, and you'd had no choice but to collect me afore he wakened the whole building. That's believable enough, eh?'

His eyes were soft at her concern. He nodded. Then drawing his hand away from hers, he patted his pocket. 'Right, I'd best get on.'

'Aye.'

'If your lady needs you with her and I don't see you again the day . . . Wish me luck.'

'Good luck, lad.'

Unsurprisingly, owing to the recent news, Josephine's anxiety struck severely that night. Now that a date had been finalised and the upcoming marriage was official, it had suddenly become to her terrifyingly real. She was unable to shake her overthinking, over-fretting about the minutiae that could possibly go wrong on the big day, and hours later she still showed no sign of clawing through the other side. Curled in a ball upon the chaise longue as the dizziness made it impossible for her to sit upright or stand, pale and drawn, her skin slicked with perspiration, she looked exhausted. Still, of its own free will, her body trembled violently and her heart rate outgalloped any thoroughbred.

Pip was at a loss what to do, had already tried every method she knew to bring an end to the bout but nothing had worked. The cruel truth that Josephine had been severely mistaken in thinking she had her condition under control, which the lady now realised, had served only to make her spirits and state of mind plummet, thus exacerbating things. So it continued on, relentlessly.

Eyes yet again drawn to the clock atop the mantel, her own heart gave a few hard thumps at the lateness of the hour. Simon would be putting his latest plan into action any time – pray be to God, he wouldn't be caught out. Gulping down her worry, she busied herself with instructing Josephine yet again to slow her breathing, though for different reasons – a much-needed distraction for them both.

'Am I dying, Pip?'

'Nay, Miss Josephine. It's just your mind fretting, is all, just like the other times. You'll come through it soon. Deep breaths, eh?'

'If mere thoughts of the wedding have brought me to my knees like this, then pray what will I be like on the actual day? I shan't be able to go through with it, will I? I'll ruin it just as I do everything else. I'm pathetic.'

'Nay, don't speak so. You're wonderful, you are.' *If only you yourself could see it.*

'Are you certain I'm not dying, Pip? Perhaps this time, it's a different ailment altogether that I've been struck with and—'

'It's one and the same, honest,' she murmured soothingly. 'You'll be well again shortly, you'll see.'

The lady fell quiet for a time, the only sound in the dimly lit room her ragged breathing. Again, Pip's eyes strayed to the clock. *Oh lad, lad . . .*

'My chest, it hurts so much from my heart's heavy beating. I, I feel nauseous, also.' Suddenly, Josephine smiled faintly. 'My mother would recite poetry to me whenever I was confined to my sickbed for whatever reason as a child. It never failed to make me feel better.'

'Do you recall them, the poems?'

'I'm . . . not sure. One or two, perhaps.'

Pip gently wiped her mistress's glistening brow. 'Then why not see if it'll work now? Close your eyes and say them in your mind. Say them nice and slow, think about the words; concentrate, like. Go on, Miss Josephine, give it a try.'

The lady did as she bid her. Minutes passed. Occupied once more with the timepiece across the room, it was a while before Pip noticed that the air had stilled – her mistress had fallen silent. She glanced down at her and released a long sigh. Josephine's expression was one of ease, the worry lines smoothed out. Her breathing was sedate, controlled.

'Better, Miss Josephine?' she whispered.

Slowly, she opened her eyes. Sleepiness thickened her words. 'Yes. Yes, I—' An almighty screech from next door sliced the response to ribbons.

Pip almost choked on a gasp. She rose slowly to her feet.

'My goodness! Oh, what in the world . . .?' Josephine scrambled up to stand beside her. Gazing at the door, neither moved for a few seconds. 'Oh, that's Caroline!' Josephine added as another shrill cry rent the air. She rushed for the door but before she could reach it, it burst open and the lady herself hurtled in, almost knocking her sister-in-law to the ground.

'You. *You!*'

Rooted to the spot, Pip could only stare in terror as

Caroline rushed towards her, teeth bared, claw-like hands outstretched as though she meant to tear the flesh from her face. 'I ain't, ain't done nowt, I . . .!'

'Liar. Liar!'

At the last second, Pip swerved from her path and ran, whimpering, to hide behind Josephine. Clinging to her nightdress as though her life depended on it – which, given Caroline's reputation, it very possibly did – she burst into noisy sobs.

Panting with pure fury, Caroline tried to rush at her again but Josephine held out a hand as a shield: 'Stop this! You're scaring the poor girl half to death. What on earth has got into you?'

'She's the one, she did it!'

'Did what? What is the meaning of all this— Oh, Philip, thank goodness,' Josephine continued on the next breath as her brother appeared in the doorway, face stiff with irritation.

'Hell's teeth, woman, come back to bed before you wake the whole house. It was merely a vivid dream, I told you—'

'That was no dream, Philip.' Caroline's eyes spat daggers at him. 'It was *real*. I felt it.'

'Enough of this nonsense! The door was secured from the inside – which you yourself insisted upon, remember, due to a similar incident you claim occurred last night—'

'That was different. This night, something, some*one*, touched me! It did!'

He looked decidedly embarrassed. 'You're making a spectacle of yourself. People cannot pass through locked doors, and you and I were the only two in that room, damn it.'

'That wretched little parasite, that one there, she did

it.' Ignoring her husband, she thrust a finger to where Pip was peeking out from behind her mistress. 'It was her, she—'

'Pip hasn't left my side all night. Not once, even for a second.' Josephine nodded. 'It's true, sister-in-law.'

'Miss Josephine speaks right. I ain't passed beyond yon door, honest, Mrs Goldthorpe.'

At Pip's timid words, Caroline's eyes narrowed into slits. 'Those pests you call friends; they're responsible, aren't they?'

'Oh nay, Mrs Goldthorpe, nay. They know their place. Never would they dare to stray beyond the kitchen.' To her sheer relief, Caroline looked as if she believed her. 'Cook would box their ears for them good and proper were they to even think it. She would, honest.'

'Lucy—'

'Is sleeping peacefully upstairs, Caroline,' snapped Philip.

'Then maybe . . . maybe Albert—'

He exploded. 'Don't be ridiculous! My father can barely stand without assistance. Now, enough of this. I've stated already, *no* one has power to pass through locked doors. It was a dream. Put it from your mind and come back to bed.'

Dropping her stare, she frowned. Her fingers plucked anxiously at her chin. She walked from the room without another word.

After shooting his sister an apologetic look, Philip followed Caroline out.

'Is all well down there?' The new maid Budd, leaning over the banister outside the nursery above, called down worriedly. 'Mrs Goldthorpe? You look as though you've seen a ghost.'

Innocent, unsuspecting, brilliant Budd! Of all the things

she could have said . . .! Thank you, thank you! Pip hid bubbling laughter when, with a squeak, Caroline dashed away to her room.

With calm restored, she and Josephine prepared for bed. Pip managed to contain her fizzing emotions until she was in the seclusion of the dressing room – here, they spilled forth and she was forced to clap a hand to her mouth so as not to alert her mistress. But it wasn't upset or worry or even fear that had her in its grip now, pumping her veins with excited energy that made it impossible to relax and led her to pace the small space. It was euphoria. Because Simon had been right all along. His completely ridiculous, utterly *genius* scheme, was working. Caroline was well and truly rattled. They were *besting* her! And things, if they put their minds to it, could surely only get better.

Fear and desperate need for redemption would drive the witch into confessing all eventually, she just knew it. Life would improve tremendously, for them all. Then it would be Alexander Sutton-Shaw's turn . . .

The thought brought a surprised smile to her lips. She nodded grimly. Seeing the results on Caroline had, it seemed, awakened in Pip something she hadn't known existed.

She and Simon would out those who had wronged them and others, if it was the last thing they did. There was no stopping them, now.

Chapter 19

OVER THE FOLLOWING weeks, Simon played his hand with expert precision. Blade-sharp instincts from a childhood spent every moment clawing for survival had served him well. It was as though he could read inside his victim's mind.

Some days, he seemed to sense that it wasn't safe to make a move. Perhaps Caroline would be lying in wait behind the bedroom door, in which case at the slightest disturbance she would be on him and the game would be up, he'd occasionally predict. Sure enough, the next morning the woman would be seen stomping around the house with eyes red-rimmed from lack of sleep and a face like thunder. The next night, knowing she was exhausted from her nocturnal failings, he'd revel in shattering her rest two, sometimes three, times at random intervals.

Mr Philip never witnessed a single act. His snores were all the signal Simon needed – the first he was aware of anything occurring was his wife screeching in his ear. That his tolerance at what he viewed as her wild imaginings was wearing thin was obvious. He now spent more time away from home than in it, seeking peace and normality at the mill or his club.

The effects of the terrorisation on the woman herself

and its unpredictability were staggering. Caroline had grown jittery, looking over her shoulder wherever she went. Her increasing confusion and paranoia saw her either withdraw into herself or explode into fits of rage at the slightest thing. She was convinced someone was out to harm her, yet was unable to discover who. She trusted no one. Pip and Simon knew it was only a matter of time, now – not if, but when – before she cracked.

Pip's initial lack of faith had left her. She believed in the lad completely and now aided him without question. Keeping lookout, providing in-house information on Caroline's movements; what she was able to provide, she did. And when a golden opportunity to up their antics to another level presented itself one Saturday afternoon, she seized it with both hands, unable to believe their luck.

Turning from the table with a silver tureen destined for the dining room, the new housemaid had caught her foot on a chair leg. Though she'd mercifully managed to catch her balance, she'd been unsuccessful in preventing hot soup sploshing down the front of her apron. Pip, on one of her short visits downstairs, had offered to fetch a clean one from Cally's room. She found what she was looking for in the chest of drawers and was making back for the door when she discovered it: there, on top of the wardrobe, hung a corner of white material.

What had made her glance up, she couldn't say. Then she stepped closer and the shaky pink initials J.H., laboriously sewn by Miss Lucy's hand at Christmas, winked back at her and she smiled.

Hardman. She'd meant for Pip to find it, she was certain. This, which Tabby had clearly missed when packing up the deceased's effects, was her contribution to the cause, her final act of revenge from beyond the grave on the woman she'd loathed as much as they did.

Slipping the handkerchief into her pocket, she'd hurried downstairs to show Simon.

Now, thanks to the general hubbub of the busy kitchen, the two of them were able to go over the final details of their plan unheard.

'You sure about this?' he asked again, though excited anticipation shone from his eyes. 'You know the risks . . .'

'Aye, I'm sure. It'll be easier for me to slip to her room unseen while they're away dining down here. I can be in and out and back to Miss Josephine's next door in seconds.'

'Be watchful, eh?'

She nodded. 'I will.'

'This find . . . it'll change everything. You see, she has her suspicions it's some unearthly being what's tormenting her so. But the handkerchief, emblazoned with Hardman's initials, suddenly appearing out of thin air . . . Mrs Goldthorpe'll be unable to deny it to herself any longer. This will seal the deal, Pip, you'll see. And the best part? She'll feel she can't reveal her incredible find to a soul.

'Think about it. If by some miracle someone decided to believe that the spirit of their dead housemaid were terrorising her as she claims, what explanation could she give for why she, of all people, was being targeted? What wrong had she done to the woman in life to bring on such a need for revenge as this in death?' He shook his head. 'Nay. The lady, she'd not risk it. She'd be forced to hold her tongue, and that'll eat at her state of mind further, it will. With no one to discuss or make sense of it with, alone with her decaying judgement . . . This'll break her. It will.'

Minutes later, her heart banging so fast she could hardly feel it, Pip was mounting the main staircase. It took her some moments to gather enough courage to reach for the Goldthorpes' doorknob; finally, closing her hand around it, she took some deep breaths. Then quickly, noiselessly, she opened the door and stole inside.

Making directly for the dressing table, she extracted the handkerchief from her pocket, smoothed the creases from it and slipped it inside Caroline's jewellery box. Here, there was less chance of Philip stumbling upon it by mistake. The next person to set eyes on the material would be the lady herself. Imagine her shock, confusion, horror – unable to explain let alone prove who had placed it there. Then the realisation when she spied the initials ... Pip's only regret now was that she wouldn't be present to witness it.

She escaped, closing the door again quietly behind her, and crossed the landing to her mistress's room, amazed at how smoothly it had gone.

In a few hours, Caroline would have to change for dinner. And no lady was suitably attired without her jewels ... Pip smiled. They didn't have long to wait.

Finding ways to distract herself was difficult; the slightest movement outside had her freezing to the spot, pulse quickening, palms clammy. Josephine couldn't fail to notice:

'Are you sure you're quite all right?' she asked again as time was approaching the appointed hour and Pip, her anticipation at fever pitch, fidgeted in her seat, unable to relax.

'Aye, Miss Josephine. It's just a headache, but like I said, it should shift itself soon enough,' she lied, biting

305

her lip in guilt. She didn't like being dishonest with the lady but what choice had she?

'You do look rather ghastly – no offence intended, dear girl. I insist you take yourself for a lie-down while I'm away at dinner. The rest and quiet will do you good. Don't argue,' she added firmly when Pip made to do just that.

Despite her turmoil, she couldn't help but smile. The worst bout by far of anxious sickness to have struck Josephine down seemed almost like a distant memory. Through poetry, she'd discovered a treatment that appeared to work more than anything they had attempted. Whenever an attack seemed imminent, Josephine now adopted the method that had guided her through that night's jet darkness, silently reciting her favourite poetry to become lost in their cathartic stanzas. Again and again, it miraculously garnered results.

Now, Pip was certain her mistress had turned a corner in dealing with her illness. Discovering something that alleviated her symptoms had instilled in Josephine quiet confidence. That she was coping with it effectively, which in turn made her less anxious, meant the attacks were becoming milder and less frequent. She was well on her way to recovery and Pip couldn't have been happier for her, nor prouder.

She'd always known Josephine was stronger than she appeared. Now, she herself had slowly realised it, too. Hopefully, this new-found knowledge would stand her in good stead in coping when secrets eventually emerged about her intended husband. For it would, somehow; it had to. Her discovering the truth was the lesser of two evils by far. She *couldn't* marry such a monster.

When finally Josephine rose to head downstairs, Pip took it as the perfect opportunity to find out how the plan was faring; damping down her eagerness, she crossed the room with her as if to see her out. So far, there had been no disturbance of any kind from next door. Perhaps Caroline was late in getting ready? Surely any moment now . . .? A scream, an incredulous shout . . .?

'Sister-in-law.'

Josephine's greeting, upon opening the door and seeing Caroline emerging from her room at the same time, brought Pip's head up sharply. *What? But why . . .?* Her gaze settled on Caroline's throat – and the string of rubies lying there. Her mind spun. *Then she must have opened . . . How had she not seen . . .? Or had she?*

'Shall we walk down together?'

Caroline nodded listlessly. As she slipped her hand into the crook of the proffered arm, her attention stayed on Josephine's face and she frowned, as though seeing her properly for the first time. 'You appear . . . different, somehow.'

As do you. However, unlike mine, your change is not one for the better, said Josephine's eyes. And yet there was no sign that she revelled in the fact. No withering look or cruel put-down. No desire to dominate one weaker than herself, as Caroline was wont to do with her. Because she possessed a kind soul. Ugliness didn't exist in Josephine. Instead she responded, 'Thank you, I feel it.' She flashed an easy smile. 'Come along, then, before the meal grows cold.'

Watching them cross the landing and descend the stairs, Pip couldn't fail to notice the striking switch in their demeanours. Josephine walked upright, her step assured. Caroline, on the other hand, allowed herself to be led, meek and passive as a lamb. The tables had turned full circle. And the realisation conjured up in Pip for the first time a stirring of guilt. For whatever

307

Caroline had done, she wouldn't wish what she feared the woman might be developing on her worst foe.

The anxious illness ruined lives – Pip was only too aware. Her very role in this house had been to help a tortured soul if not to conquer, then to deal with the crippling affliction. And now, was she contributing to creating it in another?

How was that right, or forgivable? She'd watched her own mam wither from it, lost her for good to its far-reaching effects. How could she deliberately inflict that on another? Miss Lucy, she too would be hurt by it in the long run – another little girl made to suffer a sick mother . . . *God above, God above.*

'Well? Did all go to plan? Did she swallow it?'

Pip barely registered Simon's eager probing the moment she joined him at the kitchen table. Chewing her nail, she shrugged, mind elsewhere.

'What's up? Pip? *Pip?*'

'Hm?'

The lad stared at her keenly. 'Summat's afoot. Tell me, what's occurred?'

'I just . . .'

'What?'

'Are we doing the right thing?'

He sat back heavily. 'You're jesting with me, here, right? Please tell me you're jesting with me.'

'Simon, Mrs Goldthorpe ain't looking too good.'

'Did she ever?'

'I'm being serious. What we're doing, doing to her mind . . .'

'That woman deserves it and more besides. She means to send me to the gallows, you along with me, would have no qualms should she so choose, neither. Or have you forgot that?'

'Nay, course not—'

'She set you up, got you booted from Bracken House, has hurt thee time and again. She's a rotten mother, a worse sister-in-law, stands on the backs of those she's meant to love without a thought so long as she gets what she wants. And she's a *murderess*. She's rancid through to the marrow.' His voice thickened. 'Don't fail me now, Pip, please.'

He was right. Of course he was. She opened her mouth but her reassurances never reached her lips as Miss Lucy's trilled greeting swept through the room. Bringing a smile to them instead, she asked, 'All right, lass? By, it's good to see thee.'

The girl rewarded them with her sweet laughter. 'And you, Pip, as ever!'

Hearing Simon's small gasp, Pip turned to him with a frown. He was staring intently at the young miss's bodice; following his gaze, her own eyes widened in terrible realisation . . .

'That's a pretty brooch you're wearing, there, Miss Lucy,' the lad said quietly, inclining his head.

It was all making sense. She and Budd took their dinner early in the nursery upstairs – she'd have had ample time to wander before her mother went to change . . .

The girl blinked in puzzlement. Then her hand strayed up and her mouth fell open in horror. 'Oh dear!'

'You been in your mam's jewels again, missy?' Cook, alerted by the raised voice and spying the beautiful diamond-encrusted piece adorning the dress, shook her head from across the room, where she was elbow deep in a large bowl of floury dough. 'Now you know you're not meant to mess about with them. She'll have your guts for garters. You'll not learn, will yer?'

'Oh, but they're so pretty, Cook. Look, see how the stones catch the light.' She twisted this way and that; then, seeing the elderly woman was unimpressed, dropped her gaze, abashed. 'I was only playing with them.'

'Such rich and precious pieces; playing, I ask you!'

'I must have forgotten to remove this one.' Lucy scrambled from her seat. 'I'll return it right away.'

'Hurry yourself, an' all. They'll be finishing up with their dinners in a minute. Go on, afore your mam knows owt about it.'

Casting Cook, her lifelong confidante, a grateful look, the girl ran for the door. Pip hurried after her.

'Wait, I'll come with thee. I've just remembered I've some tidying up to see to in Miss Josephine's room,' she lied. Catching Simon's eye, she nodded reassurance that she'd get to the bottom of things – his face was like thunder.

Quickly, she and the girl ascended the stairs. Pip waited at the door while Lucy rushed to return the brooch to the jewellery box. She emerged with a sigh of relief and Pip smiled. 'No harm done, lass.'

'Oh, that was a close one!'

'Aye. 'Ere, Miss Lucy . . .?' She paused, chose her words carefully. 'You sure you've returned everything, now? Happen, say . . . there were summat else you took and forgot about?'

'No, that's everything. Oh. There was a handkerchief in there, which I took up to my room earlier, but Mama shan't mind about that. She's probably already forgotten she put it in the box in the first place. It wasn't hers, you see – the initials were clearly marked J.H. It's the one I made for poor Hardman. Mama must have found it somewhere and believed it to be the one I made *her*.'

'You . . . took it up to your room, Miss Lucy?'

310

'That's right, to unpick the lettering.'

Pip's heart skipped a beat. With the owner's identity removed, the handkerchief was useless! 'Aye?' she managed to croak.

'I shall reuse the material to make a Sunday bonnet for my new doll. Aunt Josephine will show me how. And she has lots of trim and lace to add to it. It will be so pretty, Pip!'

You didn't know what you were doing, Miss Lucy, you ain't at fault. Oh, but now what? Simon insisted an item such as that would have been the crux in prompting Caroline to confess for sure . . .

'Aye, yes, I'm sure it will, will look lovely . . .' Mumbling something about having to go now as she had work to do, Pip escaped to Miss Josephine's room. Closing the door, she leaned against it and closed her eyes.

This was a great blow to their plan. What now? There were only so many times they could frighten Caroline by rattling door handles or some such. She'd grow used to it soon, or hatch a scheme to catch them out. No, it had to be something different, something completely unexpected, that she couldn't deny the significance of. Something directly linked with Hardman herself. But there was nothing else, nothing. *Oh, Miss Lucy. Why, why?*

She barely slept a wink that night and encountering Simon again the next morning, tired and disappointed tears burned her eyes. 'The handkerchief, lad, it's no more. Miss Lucy—'

'Don't matter about that. Not now.'

'Nay? How so?' She studied his bright face for a moment. 'Do you know summat?'

'Oh, do I.'

'What? Eeh, lad, I thought our plan were done for. Eeh, you are clever.'

His chest puffed proudly at the compliment. 'Well, I don't know about that . . . Anyroad, it's like this. Cook sends me to the study late last night, for she wanted her bed but Mr Philip's light still shone beneath the door. "Go and see if he's requiring owt more the night, lad," she says to me, so off I go.

'Well, I knocked and he permitted me to enter in a voice thick with drink. Sure enough, he were slumped at his desk with a bottle of summat – strong, aye, by the smell of him. And what did I happen to spy, spread out before him? Only a stack of papers; amongst them, a sketching of Hardman. Too late, he returned them to a leather paper-carrier and bundled them into a drawer, which he secured with a key. 'Ere, the likeness were impressive, mind. Some talent's gone into that, it has.'

The selfsame leather carrier she'd seen him with in the kitchen that night . . . Though she hadn't caught a glimpse of its contents, she'd sensed then his morose mood was to do with his lost lover.

'It'll be his art. Miss Josephine once mentioned he used to draw. He must have got the housemaid to sit for him. So, what were you thinking, like?' she whispered.

'I'm thinking we need to get our hands on it and plant it somewhere for Mrs Goldthorpe to find. I doubt she's aware her husband possesses such a thing – well, he's not reet likely to show her, is he! – so imagine her shock when she comes face to face so to speak with the one she thinks is out for her blood.'

'But how do we get it, the picture? If it's under lock as you say?'

'Aye, that's a problem. I had to retreat afore I could see where he kept the key.'

Pip's stomach turned over at the mere thought but she had to help. 'Happen I could search his effects; his room, pockets of his clothing and that? Meantime, when you get the chance, you give the study a going over. It'll surely not be that hard to find.'

'Be watchful, Pip. If you're caught . . .'

She nodded grimly. He didn't need to finish his warning. Both knew the consequences would be dire. 'And thee.'

When she returned upstairs to Miss Josephine's room, she halted in pleasant surprise to see her father sitting in the chair opposite hers by the fire. 'Morning, sir! By, it's good to see thee up and about.'

Though a little tired-looking, Albert's face held a healthy colour and his bright eyes matched his smile. 'Thank you, lass. It *feels* good, too.'

'Father's regaining his strength at last. Isn't it wonderful?'

'Oh, it is, Miss Josephine.' Pip answered with feeling, for the sight of him there had awakened in her a spark of happy hope. With the master back on his feet, their worries had lessened somewhat, surely? He was wise; and clever, aye. Confined to his room, he'd had the wool pulled over his eyes for too long, but not any more. He'd notice things were not as they should be beneath his roof, with his family, would sniff out the goings-on and put an end to them; he must, she told herself. His son and daughter-in-law's scheming concerning the wedding would be brought to light, and Alexander would be gone. *Please God.*

'So. Caroline's parents have refused outright to have her there, have they?' said Albert.

'Yes. Even for just a few days, as Philip suggested. He thought a change of scenery and spending time with her family would provide the tonic she needs but alas, it's not to be. He received their letter today. Apparently,

313

it wouldn't do her reputation any good to have her there as she is – their servants and friends may jump to the wrong conclusion and begin spreading rumours about her mental state.'

'A likely story. They fear the embarrassment and shame for themselves, more like.'

'Precisely. Can you believe it, Father? Their own flesh and blood? Philip is furious. The poor man is at his wits' end with her imaginings.'

Pip had crossed the room to busy herself with straightening the curtains when the adults had resumed their conversation; now, she struggled to retain her impassive stance. Thank the Lord Caroline's parents had refused her. With her gone from Bracken House, their plan would be ruined. And yet, even as the thought flitted by, an earlier feeling scratched at the outskirts of her conscience: guilt. She was sick, and growing more so, it seemed.

But she deserves it, remember . . .? Even the family appeared of a similar mind. That their concern was for Philip rather than the woman herself was clear to see. And who could blame them? Caroline wasn't someone you *could* easily feel empathy for.

Albert sighed. 'Where's Philip now?'

'He and Lucy have taken Caroline for a walk to get her some air. She had a bad night again.'

'I'll talk to the lad later. Something must be done. These claims of hers . . . she barely makes any sense these days. Perhaps Doctor Lawley could—'

'No.' Josephine spoke quietly but firmly. 'No, Father, there is no need to bother him with this. Let us see what Philip decides. As her husband, the decision is his to make, after all. Caroline will pick up, I'm sure. My reckoning is, she's sleep deprived. It can affect one in the queerest of ways. Rest is the surest balm for the mind.'

'I suppose you're right, lass. Well.' Soft grunts and shuffles signalled he was rising to take his leave. 'I shall see you at lunch. If you see your brother before I do, direct him to my room, would you?'

'I will. And Father?'

'Yes?'

'It's good to have you back on your feet and under mine.' Josephine blew him a kiss, Albert responded with a chuckle, then the door opened and closed and all was still.

'Pip?'

She sidled out from her hiding place. 'Aye, Miss Josephine?'

The woman had her nose buried in her sewing basket. 'Would you be a dear and fetch me some blue embroidery silk from next door?'

'Mr Philip and Mrs Goldthorpe's room?' If God Himself had smiled down on her from heaven, she couldn't have been more jubilant; free rein, to enter with full permission the very place she needed to, right now? And she'd thought she'd have to wait perhaps days for such an opportunity! The urge not to punch the air was overwhelming. She forced an easy nod. 'Course, Miss Josephine, aye.'

'You should find some in Caroline's red basket. By the bed, I believe she keeps it. Thank you, dear girl.'

And thank you. Telling herself not to run, Pip managed to leave the room at a normal pace. Once outside, however, she couldn't contain her impatience. Not having to sneak around or check if anyone was coming, for

315

she'd every right to be here, she entered the room without hesitation, closing the door behind her.

She found the silk where Josephine said she would and popped it into her apron pocket. Then she peered around.

A dark jacket, tossed carelessly over the arm of a finely carved chair by the far side of the bed, immediately caught her eye; this, she thought, would be as good a place as any to search first. She looked for a pocket, slipped a hand inside and felt about – and almost staggered when her fingers closed around something hard and cold. *A key!*

She gazed at the small metal object in awe, utterly amazed at the breakneck-speed find. How was this possible? The very first place she'd checked, there it was? It was as if it was meant to be.

For reasons she couldn't fathom, she knew without question this was the one they were seeking. But of course, there was only one way to be absolutely certain . . . With the precious object clasped safely in her bunched fist, she spun on her heel and headed out.

Josephine's door, she didn't even glance at; instead, she made in the opposite direction, skittering down the stairs as fast as her legs could take her. Before she knew what she was doing, she'd crossed the hall and was letting herself into the study.

Again, she closed the door behind her and looked about. She could have the drawing in her possession and the key returned to its owner's pocket in mere minutes, and no one would be any the wiser. Then, once Hardman's likeness had done its job on Caroline, she'd steal it and the key back and return both to their rightful places. Simple.

Imagine Simon's reaction when she next saw him,

how proud he'd be that she'd found what they needed, and all on her own. He'd be more than a little impressed. And she did so want to please him. She needed him to know he could rely on her, always, for that lad was the single most important thing in her life. Mack, too. Her excitement mounted. She hurried to the desk.

She opted for the bottom of the three drawers and again, her decision yielded immediate results. She could hardly believe it as she lifted the artwork out and placed it on the desktop. A quick glance to the door and a nod of satisfaction at the silence from beyond and she peeled back the leather.

The hard, sultry stare that locked with Pip's had her taking an involuntary step back. Simon hadn't exaggerated – God above, the *detail*. 'Eeh, Hardman,' she murmured, tracing a wispy touch along the house-maid's cheek. Then, with care, she rolled the sheet into a thin tube and slipped it up her sleeve.

She'd had every intention of returning the rest to the drawer without another thought. Yet the new face now staring back at her, which had lain beneath Hardman's, piqued her curiosity too greatly and she began leafing through them. Page after page of women were revealed, of varying types and beauty – and state of undress. Quickly, she moved on to the next.

And yet, there was one similarity: all were attired in domestic uniform. Realisation brought heat to her face. They were Mr Philip's conquests over the years, every one. As though as proof of prowess, he'd immortalised his immorality on paper for eternity. Did memories evoked by these long-gone faces bring him personal enjoyment? She squirmed with embarrassment at the thought.

The very last sheet was well worn. Age had curled its

corners and the drawing was more faded than the rest. Yet it had the power to rip the breath from her lungs and the life from her legs.

She crumpled to her knees, face contorted in a blinding shock that was absolute.

Gazing back at Pip from the yellowed page was her mother.

Chapter 20

'AH, THERE YOU are, I wondered where you'd—'

'This. *This!*'

Josephine blinked in surprise from Pip to the drawing she'd thrust out towards her. 'Where did you . . .?'

'Why would . . . why . . . why would . . .?' Her breaths came in jagged gasps. 'Please, I must *know.*'

'Dear girl—'

'Miss Josephine, d'you know who this is?'

The woman had risen from her chair, face wreathed in puzzlement. She nodded without hesitation. 'Of course.'

If the master's dogs had cartwheeled into the room, Pip couldn't have been more thunderstruck at what her mistress uttered next. She gawped at her, mouth hanging wide. '*What?*'

'I said that the woman in that picture is Lydia May.'

Pip shook her head. What was she talking about? Her name was Annie and she was her mother. Lydia May was Cook's daughter. Had the lady here lost her senses?

She turned the picture around and scanned it to check she hadn't snatched up a different one from the pile in the study by mistake. But no; again, her beautiful mother gazed back at her. Hot tears of frustration stung behind Pip's eyes.

'What is the meaning of all this?' Josephine spoke quietly, gently. 'Where on earth did you find that picture? More importantly, what has you in such a tizzy over it? Pip, speak to me. Dear girl, what is it?'

'Miss Josephine ... Miss Josephine ...' Breath-snatching clarity, the possibility, *truth* . . .

'Yes, yes? What's wrong?'

'Miss Josephine . . .' Pip scrabbled for the lady's hand and clung to it as though she was drowning. Which she was. A sea of chaos, pain, utter confusion, battered her mind. Wave followed wave, crashing the incredulous thoughts against one another.

She had to get out of here. She couldn't, *couldn't* . . .

'Pip, please, tell me what—'

'Air. I, I need . . .' She disentangled her fingers from her mistress's and walked from the room. Without thought or reason, for her legs were in charge now and she hadn't a say in it, she found herself in the study once more, where she placed the picture in the leather carrier along with the others and returned everything to the drawer. She locked it, turned, and retraced her steps. After dropping the key into the pocket where she'd found it, she again descended the stairs. Then she headed for the kitchen.

'All right, lass? Sup of tea? Lass, d'you hear?'

Pip, having ground to a halt, stared at the cook mutely. Emotion had deserted body and mind. She felt numb, nothing. She turned slowly, crossed to the back door and let herself out.

When she next became aware of herself, she was standing in the Green by the lakelet, gazing unseeing into its inky belly. Her senses were unaware of the surroundings; the birdsong, the smell of frost and winter foliage, the sting of the bitter breeze on her face, whipping her uncovered hair around her head like wild, golden snakes – nothing could touch her.

Mam never had mentioned a single member of her family. Dead, she'd said they were, long gone before her only child was born, and she didn't like to speak of them, for their loss hurt. Pip had believed it without question. Of course she had; why wouldn't she? Just the two of them. That's how it had always been. Only each other, in the whole world, is what they'd had.

Lies.

Speaking of the past wasn't something Mam indulged in; she would change the subject if Pip enquired about something. And it mattered not, not really, no, for they had needed no one else. And Mam made sure that the present was enough, and their future was the thing to look towards, nothing else. Just the two of them, for fathers and grandparents and siblings and aunts, great-aunts and uncles . . . they didn't exist. Not for her.

Lies. Lies.

'Don't ever flee from your problems, lass, for there's not a body alive can out-run what's in the mind. Face it, resolve it. Trust in God's protection and you'll not go far wrong.'

Those words had fallen from her mother's lips not long before she died. Her wisdom about things, about the world beyond their cellar door, had impressed Pip. She recalled thinking at the time that Mam had never run from anything for she knew instinctively it wasn't the way to beat your demons. Clever, she was. More than anyone else she knew, and she was proud of her.

Lies. Lies. *Lies.*

Something Cook had said recently, about the ability to sense spirits, now came back to Pip: 'Got passed down, it did, from my mam – famous for it were Annie May . . .' She squeezed her eyes shut. Everything

321

was slotting into place. Clearly, Mam had decided a new identity would be wiser, to fit with her fresh life. She'd adopted her grandmother's name. It must have been the first one that came to her when choosing – she must have thought a lot of her, been close to her. *Pity she'd deprived her child of the same opportunity with her own.*

How different life could have been. The anger inside her expanded further.

Mam had kept herself to herself, was civil with their neighbours but never allowed herself to get too friendly, too close, *reveal too much*, Pip realised now. She'd kept the world out and her secrets locked tightly within. She'd likely reasoned that in escaping to a larger town, there would be a higher chance of securing work. Blending in. Disappearing amongst the multitude of faces for ever. She'd ended up in Manchester, a suitable distance from her home in Bolton. Perhaps also, part of the decision may have been that her aunt, Cook's sister, lived here. Had Mam planned to throw herself on her mercy but for whatever reason decided against it, to go it alone instead, at the last minute? They would never know.

By some twist of fate, the very people she'd felt the need to cut free of had themselves relocated to the same city. And Cook, she'd fretted each day since, pined still for the daughter she was certain would return some day.

But she wouldn't. Because she was gone for good. Annie, *Lydia*, were one and the same. And both were dead.

How could this be? How could her mother have lied to her all those years? She'd been reared but a short distance from Bracken House, from kith and kin, for all that time with neither side having an idea how near to one another they dwelled. It was too incredible to accept, to bear. How had this, *any* of this, been allowed to happen? All those wasted years! So much loss, on both sides – with Pip stuck in the centre, missing out more than anyone, without a single clue it was occurring.

Again, numbness wrapped around her heart like a protective shield and she welcomed it, for the pain in her was like nothing she'd known before and never would again, she was certain. The one constant throughout her entire time on this earth, the person who had loved, protected, nurtured, was a stranger, a fake. Annie had never existed. Right now, Pip wished she herself didn't either.

Footsteps and familiar laughter floated towards her from beyond the railings. She blinked and moved behind a tree to steal a look at the trio passing down the wide street. *Father, mother, daughter.* A family. Perfect, right. As it should be. As everyone deserved . . .

Again, Miss Lucy's laughter – yet now, it brought none of the warmness to Pip's soul that it always had. For the first time, black envy of the innocent little girl she'd only ever loved, had felt instantly drawn to – *dear God, now she understood why* – who had the life she'd been cheated of, stirred. And Pip hated herself for it. She hated *him*.

The urge to scream at the top of her lungs to the world and everyone in it struck her with such force that pain stung her throat. Slowly, the corrosive fog clogging her breast began to clear. Bitterness towards her mother, which she'd never believed she could ever feel, was leaving her. It was replaced with an altogether stronger emotion – fury – towards another: Philip Goldthorpe.

Pip, she thought suddenly. Mam liked that name. A smile would stroke her lips whenever she uttered it. *Pip. Philip.* They sounded eerily similar, too much so to be coincidence. Had it been a secret reminder of him? Had bestowing it upon her daughter brought her a modicum of happiness, made her feel she was keeping his name and his memory alive? She'd never ceased loving him, had she?

A deadness settled within her. Neither her mother nor anyone else was to blame in all this. He was. He'd used her, cast her aside, *broken* her, left her feeling she had no option but to abandon all she'd ever known and loved. He'd ruined her life. In the process, he'd dashed any chance of a normal existence for the child he'd helped create. *For her.* And to all intents and purposes, he'd done so with an easy mind. He cared not a fig, wondered about it less. He'd ejected it from his mind as callously as he'd rejected the woman who adored him.

He deserved to pay.

He'd destroyed the lives of others. Now, it was his turn. She'd smash to dust all he held dear, as he'd done to her.

When she was finished with him, *he'd* be the one wishing he'd never been born.

Chapter 21

PIP RE-ENTERED THE house the way she had left. Immediately, Cook beckoned her across, firing enquiries about her health, believing it was the explanation for her queer behaviour minutes ago. Pip held up a hand.

'Aye, sorry for disappearing like that. I'm all right, now. I felt a bit sick, like, but it's passed.'

'Sick? Why? What's to do? You felt unwell long? You must say, for you'll hand it to the rest of us and that'll never do, nay.' Cook puffed out her chest and her head bobbed on her fleshy neck. 'Whatever it is, you've picked it up elsewhere, for I know well enough it ain't from my cooking. Oh no, that it bloomin' is not!'

'Nay, not that. By, your grub's finer than owt else around.'

'Aye, well.' Satisfied, Cook nodded.

'Honest, I'm well. Tired is all it is, I reckon.'

'You be sure to get a fair kip, then, the night, eh? You'll finish up making yourself ill for real. Now.' She motioned to the teapot. 'You wanting that brew?'

'Aye, ta. I'll just nip and show my face to Miss Josephine, let her know I'm all right, and I'll be back.'

'Go on, then, lovey. There's a good lass.'

Smiling, Pip crossed the room and exited through

the green baize door; then, when it swished shut again safely at her back, her act dissolved and she crumpled against the hallway wall. Closing her eyes, she crushed a fist to her mouth.

How she'd struggled to appear natural! How her gaze had yearned to stray about that woman's face just now! The fight not to had physically pained her. As for her even tone, the *smile* . . . Pushing all thoughts from her burning mind before they had the chance to overwhelm her completely, she headed upstairs.

Josephine raised her brows at her entrance; shaking her head apologetically, Pip fumbled in her pocket and brought out the embroidery silk. 'Terrible sorry about before, I—'

'Sit down, please, Pip.'

She did as she was bid. Expression contrite, she opened her mouth to spin her mistress the tale she'd concocted on the walk back from the Green, of how she'd come to be in possession of the picture, but the lady stopped her.

'It's all right. I understand.'

'You . . . do?'

'Of course. I was a girl once upon a time, too, you know.' Josephine flashed a small but wicked smile. 'Forever snooping in other people's private effects, I was – inquisitive, I liked to call it, though it would drive Mother mad.' She laughed softly at the memories. 'However, I feel I must say, you cannot take another's belongings when they are of so personal a nature. Philip must have gifted it to Mabel in days gone by. And you see, pictures . . . they are all poor Mabel has left of her daughter and she would be heartbroken should they get damaged. You understand that, surely? Now, I know you would never intentionally—'

'Cook?' Pip nodded slowly, relief washing through her. Her mistress's assumption was far more believable than the tall story she'd thought up. 'Aye, yes, Cook. I, I took it from her room. Only to show you, mind, for I were interested to know who it were, but was too shy to ask the owner herself. Besides, Cook would know I'd been rooting in her things, which I did but meant no harm, I just—'

'I know, I know. As I said, you were curious. I understand. But tell me, dear girl, why the insistence? You could barely get your words out when enquiring as to who the woman was.'

Feeling heat creep up her neck, Pip thought quickly. 'Oh, could I not?' She gave what she hoped was a nonchalant shrug. 'I'd been running . . . Happen that were the reason if I seemed a bit breathless, Miss Josephine? When I went to fetch the silk, I remembered the picture in my pocket and had to show you. Then, well, I rushed to put it back afore Cook should miss it.' She shook her head and sighed. 'I'm sorry. I act daft at times, I know. It'll not occur again.' She swallowed in relief when the lady chuckled. 'Am I forgiven, Miss Josephine?'

'Oh, Pip. There is nothing to forgive. All is well and no harm done. Now.' She lifted her sewing basket into her lap. 'I'm sure I can spare you for a while; go on downstairs and see your friends.'

'Ta, thanks.'

Outside, Pip again leaned against the wall and took some deep breaths. Thank goodness that was over and she'd got away with it. *Her aunt* . . . 'Mustn't think, mustn't think,' she muttered thickly, blinking back fresh tears. Another deep breath and she set off once more for the kitchen.

Averting her gaze from bustling Cook, she slipped

into a chair beside Simon. He turned to her quizzically –
and the pain in her intensified. She couldn't tell him,
couldn't tell anyone. He'd view her differently, she just
knew it. Or would he? Oh, she didn't know, didn't know
anything any more. Without a word, she felt up her sleeve
beneath the table and pulled out the rolled-up likeness
of Hardman. Then she felt for his hands resting in his
lap and placed it into them. His eyes widened but he too
didn't speak, shoving it from sight up the arm of his
jacket.

'How did tha—?'

'Don't matter.' She took a sip of her tea. 'Just promise
me one thing.'

'Aye, what?'

She looked him full in the face. Her response was
firm. 'Use it wisely. Make this your best attack yet. I want
his wife gone.'

That night, alone in her small bed, Pip silently cried
herself to exhaustion. Still, her battered mind refused
to release her to sleep. Dark and jumbled thoughts ran
amok, relentless. Throughout, Philip's face was at the
forefront. Staring, always staring . . .

When the faint rattle of a doorknob seeped through
the wall, followed by Caroline's fearful howl then her
husband's exasperated voice ordering her back to sleep,
Pip smiled.

A numb calmness settled in her once more. Pulling
the blanket around her chin, she dropped immediately
into a deep sleep.

*

Simon's tenacity in his build-up to what he'd termed
'the last rites' – the death of Caroline's lies – was nothing short of remarkable. He'd upped his tricks tenfold.

That way, he'd explained to Pip, when he did strike with the picture – whose absence, thankfully, Philip hadn't yet noticed – the effects on the murderess's tattered nerves would be explosive.

Now, his terrorisation wasn't limited to nocturnal hours. With Pip's help, he'd taken to braving her during the day, too, when and wherever opportunity arose. Knocking and scratching at doors, hissing through keyholes; he was relentless. Then, like a shadow melting away when the sun emerges from behind a cloud, he'd be gone. And his antics didn't end there.

Sneaking into the Goldthorpes' room and moving Caroline's belongings around was his new favourite thing. A well-thumbed book on her night table, he hid beneath the rug before the fire. The unmissable bulge was soon spotted and Caroline's confused ramblings carried through the bedroom wall to Pip and Josephine; the latter had shaken her head in consternation at the sound, much to Pip's inward pleasure. And yesterday, he'd even found the nerve to enter the drawing room; in broad daylight, too!

Asked by Cook to take along a message concerning that day's menu to the master, who was now well enough to spend short intervals in his study, Simon had spotted on the return journey Caroline exit the drawing room and head upstairs, leaving the door ajar. Having seen Mr Philip leave for the mill that morning and knowing there could be no one else present – after all, the housemaid had taken tea for only one through to the lady minutes before – he'd stolen across the hall. He was in and out and safely back in the kitchen in a flash.

Soon afterwards, the housemaid was once more summoned to fetch Caroline tea. The lady had noticed that her cup was empty, though for the life of her, she'd wittered to Cally, she couldn't recall taking more than a few sips . . .

'Not a full shilling, that one, I'm sure,' the harassed servant had muttered to Cook and Tabby, taking herself off once more to replenish the cup. Simon and Pip had struggled to hold in their grins.

Things were running brilliantly. The whole household had begun to view her differently, whispering behind her back. No one could fail to notice her erratic behaviour. Nor could Caroline be blind to what everyone was thinking. She and her husband argued constantly, and the rest of the family were growing increasingly concerned about her state of mind. Pip had witnessed the master and Josephine whispering together, faces grave, on more than one occasion.

As for the woman herself, she'd swallowed whole everything they had thrown her way, exactly as they wanted. It was better than either of them could have ever foreseen. Any day now . . . Her confession was teetering on the tip of her tongue, they were certain.

All of this was like balm to Pip's shattered soul. Without the distraction it offered, she'd have withered inside without a doubt. What she'd learned . . . She refused to dwell on it. Giving her thoughts free rein, even for a second, made her physically ill. Her young mind was unable to withstand the enormity of her discovery. Family. *Her* family. Every which way she turned . . .

Cook, her grandmother. Her body ached constantly to throw itself into the meaty arms, pour out her breaking heart. But for some reason – she wasn't sure what that was, just knew she couldn't utter the truth, not yet at least – she kept her silence. The master was her grandfather . . . It was like something from a mawkish story, it was, really. She'd have found it laughable were it not so tragic, not slowly killing her inside. An aunt, a half-sister ... God above, *Caroline*, her stepmother.

The notion sickened her. But not nearly as much as the thought of her father.

Father.

Pip still found that impossible to process. Philip Goldthorpe and her mother ... And who *was* she? Pip couldn't even answer that any more. Thinking of her as Lydia felt ridiculous. She was Annie. Always had been. Just Annie, her mam. *A stranger, now, with a new name, a whole new life she'd hidden from everyone, from her own daughter, her entire existence.*

How differently their lives could have played out had the one who was responsible done the decent thing. The poverty, pain, hardship ... Her mam might still be alive today.

She'd never accept it all, never. Nor would she ever forgive. And she'd not stop until she'd wreaked revenge on the man who had caused it all. He too would know the sear of loss.

Even as Pip made the promise, she was aware how ugly she sounded. What had happened to her? She barely recognised her own mind. She'd changed, hardened. She loathed who she was becoming, missed her old, calm and uncomplicated self. But for the life of her, she couldn't control it. She hurt inside, every inch, with each beat of her heart. And she was terrified at what would happen when she was no longer able to bear it.

Today was the final day of February and with its arrival, the weather had plummeted. Frost stroked every flagstone, cobble and plant with twinkling white – even the lake in the Green had succumbed to the icy touch, its liquid surface lost beneath a solid, cut-glass sheet. Inside the kitchen of Bracken House, however, the occupants were toasty warm. Cook had built the fire right up that morning and flames leapt merrily up the chimney back, casting the room in yellow-gold.

The air was heady with the aroma of cinnamon cakes and fresh bread. Mack, Tabby and Cally were engaged in making silly figures from a lump of floury, leftover dough: a two-headed sheep, a dog with six legs, a man complete with mutton-chop whiskers sporting a teapot for a hat; their laughter was enough to warm the coldest heart, while Cook glanced up at them now and then from the vegetables she was peeling with a smile.

It was the perfect picture of domestication and comfort, thought Pip, looking around, and she'd have happily basked in it but for the worry assaulting her guts. As it was, she was forced to feign a calmness she was far from feeling. For today, she and Simon were to play their final hand with Hardman's picture.

Nervousness flickering behind his eyes showed he shared her apprehension. What if the move failed?

Christ in heaven, should something go wrong . . . So much *could*. To call this a bold move was certainly an understatement. *Nay, don't think it,* she told herself. It had to work, *must*.

She watched him look to the small clock on the mantel then glance at the room's occupants in turn. He then gave Pip the briefest of nods. Her heart skipped a few beats. She rose shakily.

It had to be her. No one else was free to come and go through the house as she was. Simon might manage to sneak around in the dead of night when all were deep in sleep but could never get away with venturing inside Caroline's room in broad daylight. Also, it must be now. Earlier, they had overheard Cook mention that Caroline had taken a dose of laudanum to help her snatch some sleep. She'd be waking any time. Pip must move fast.

With the precious tool once more secreted securely up her sleeve, she murmured to everyone about heading back to Josephine's room and work, and left the kitchen. On the landing, she came to an abrupt halt. Her heart was galloping so badly she could hardly breathe and when she finally plucked up courage to continue and was standing before Caroline's door, she had to literally carry her right hand with her left towards the knob. Slowly, tentatively, she turned it and pushed.

Caroline lay on her back, the bedclothes a tousled mess around her. Though the drug had done its job and she was snoring quietly, still her features appeared ill at ease. Her brow was home to a small frown and her eyelids flickered restlessly. Skirting the bed, Pip made for the chair, slipped her hand inside the familiar pocket and took out the key. She dropped it safely into her own. After taking a moment to brace herself, she tiptoed towards her target.

She slipped out and unrolled the picture and smoothed it as best she could. Then, eyes wide with fear, tongue poking from her mouth in concentration, she carefully laid it on top of the woman's chest.

'I knew it . . . *Knew* it was you all along.'

Chapter 22

PIP HAD HALF turned away when Caroline's breathy voice rendered her immobile. A cry caught in her throat. Inch by inch, her gaze swivelled towards the bed.

However, Caroline's face was the same, eyes firmly closed. Confusion swiftly followed by sheer relief rushed through Pip – the woman had been talking in her sleep. Clearly, her dreams were just as haunted as her waking hours.

For a heart-stopping moment, there, she'd thought . . . But no, no, all was well. 'Thank you, Lord, thank you,' Pip mouthed with feeling.

Part one of the plan was complete. Grateful tears sprang to her eyes but she blinked them back and nodded. It wasn't over yet. Her stare never leaving Caroline's face, she lowered herself to the ground, lay flat on her stomach and shuffled beneath the bed.

Here, she allowed herself a moment's respite. Her cheek cushioned by the thick carpet, she closed her eyes and gulped in air. There was nothing for her to do now but wait.

Finally – how long later, she couldn't say; it felt like hours but in reality couldn't have been more than ten or fifteen minutes – Caroline stirred above her. Biting down on her thumb to stem a frightened whimper, Pip held her breath. She heard the woman draw herself up into a sitting position, heard the crinkle of paper as it was lifted. Then silence.

For an agonising moment, nothing happened. Blind to the proceedings above her, confused as to what was happening, the charged seconds seemed to last an eternity. Just as Pip's panic was about to spill over, Caroline let out a blood-curdling scream that bounced from wall to wall, ceiling to floor; Pip almost leapt from her skin. Then jump she did for real – into action.

Caroline had sprung from the bed and was rushing for Josephine's room; scrambling out from her hiding place, Pip snatched the picture from the floor where Caroline had tossed it in terror and ran to the door. She poked out her head and scanned the landing. Josephine's door was wide open and the high-pitched, manic tone intermingled with her mistress's soothing one spilled through. But the speakers were out of eye-shot, by the fire – quick as lightning, Pip darted past and down the stairs.

Her legs threatened to give way at each step but somehow she managed to make it to the hallway. Flinging open the study door, she raced inside. Her hands shook so much, she couldn't manipulate the lock and she nearly screamed in frustration when suddenly a soft click announced its surrender. Wrenching open the drawer, she drew aside the leather folds, returned the picture to the top of the pile, neatly fastened the carrier back in place and secured everything with the key. As quickly as she'd arrived, she was out again, clicking shut the door behind her and bolting back upstairs.

Midway, the voices reached her ears; by this time, Caroline's shouts had given way to teary babbling. Working now on instinct alone, Pip skittered next door and returned the key to Philip's jacket pocket. As she emerged from the room and turned for Josephine's, a door opened behind her and she whipped around to find the master peering blearily along the landing.

'What in God's name . . .?'

'I . . . don't know, sir, am just for returning to my duties,' she said over her shoulder as she hurried for Josephine's room, and Albert followed.

'Pip— Oh, Father, thank goodness!' said Josephine at the sight of them. Gesturing to Caroline, she shook her head helplessly. 'I cannot get any sense from her.'

The master strode forward. Taking his daughter-in-law's shoulders, he shook her, though not harshly. However, his voice held an impatient edge: 'What is the meaning of this nonsense that has torn me from my slumber? Caroline, answer me.'

'She's here. In there. I looked up . . . There she was!'

'Who do you speak of?'

Caroline opened her mouth, then closed it again. Her bloodshot eyes screamed contrition. 'Hardman,' she squeaked out.

The frown slipped slowly from Albert's face. He and his daughter shared a pitying glance.

'She's in there still. See for yourself.'

'Caroline, dear . . .' He took her elbow and turned her towards a chair.

'No, you must, you must. Why won't you go and, and see, and . . .?'

'Come, sit down—'

'No!' Pulling herself from the master's hold, Caroline swung back, a hand outstretched to them as though warding them off. 'You don't believe me, do you? *No one* believes me. She's there, you'd *see* it, if only you'd go and look!'

336

From her position by the wardrobe, Pip watched in fascinated horror. Caroline's eyes were wild and desperate and spittle had formed at the corners of her mouth. She appeared possessed, was barely recognisable as the woman who had taunted, threatened and bullied since the day the boys and herself had arrived here. A shell of her former self, eaten away with her own guilt, her own evil doing. She deserved nothing less.

'Stop this.'

'I saw her face, I tell you. I saw!'

'Caroline—'

'Fine! Fine! Wait here, you'll see.' She rushed from the room. Seconds later, she staggered back in. Gripping the hair at her temples, she swung her head from side to side in denial. 'It cannot be, it, it . . . It was there, it *was*, I—!'

'Enough. You neither saw, heard nor felt a thing,' Albert snapped, his patience burnt. 'Not today, not yesterday, nor any other! Do you understand? You must cease this madness at once.'

'Her there.' As though she'd just become aware of Pip's presence, Caroline struck the air with her finger. 'It's her doing, *all* of it, her and her gutter-dog friends. I know it!'

The unexpected turn of the woman's attention to her caught Pip off guard. She could only watch in disbelief as Caroline snatched up a pair of scissors from Josephine's sewing basket and, holding them above her head like a dagger, ran at her.

It took a moment for Pip to realise that the scream filling her ears was her own.

'Die!'

Her pleas were lost in Albert and Josephine's shouts. As Caroline loomed, Pip instinctively stuck out a hand to protect her face. A searing pain ripped through her palm. Blood gushed forth, spattering the nightdress of her attacker who, unperturbed, drew back her arm once more.

The room swayed drunkenly – Pip groped the air to ward off the onslaught. Mercifully, it never came. Albert caught Caroline around the waist in a bear grip and hauled her, kicking and shouting, to the floor. He prised the weapon from her fingers and passed it to a tearful Josephine hovering nearby, who rushed with the scissors from the room.

'Let me go!' Caroline's cries were beast-like. The intense hatred pouring from her eyes stole the breath from Pip. 'She must pay, she must!'

'Calm yourself at once! Mother of God, what is *wrong* with you?'

'Her! Her! She's what's wrong, her there, it's her doing!'

Suddenly, taking them all by surprise, Simon burst into the room. 'Pip! Oh, my God, what . . . You, you bitch, yer!' he roared and made to lunge at Caroline, but Cook's voice from the landing held him back.

'Shift aside, lad. I'll deal with this.' Face an angry puce, she marched into the room swiftly followed by Josephine. She flicked her eyes to Pip and her colour darkened. She stooped, gripped Caroline's arms and pulled her to her feet. 'Shurrup!' she yelled into her face when the woman began protesting loudly, shaking her none too gently. 'That's a-bloody-nuff of that! Just what d'you think you're about, maiming my lass, there? By, you don't get to touch none of them, none! Lady or no, I've a good mind to—!'

'What on God's earth is the meaning of this?'

All eyes turned, to see Philip standing aghast in the

doorway. He took in the scene slowly, incredulously. When his gaze settled on the bloodstained clothing and carpet, his face paled. 'What have you done, Caroline?' he whispered.

'Stabbed my lass, that's what—'

'All right, Mabel.' Albert's quiet command had the desired effect; folding her arms with a sniff, she fell silent. 'There has been an incident,' he continued grimly. 'Your wife attacked the child Pip with scissors. You must have that seen to, lass,' he added to her, his look deep with remorse. He turned back to his son. 'Take Caroline to your room. I'll instruct the housemaid to add laudanum to some tea and bring it up directly.' He glanced to his daughter-in-law, now standing limply, head and arms hanging loose, her energy spent. 'See me in the study once you have her settled. We need to talk.'

Before turning, Philip cast Pip a long look. She gazed back, eyes brimming with tears, couldn't have broken the stare had she tried. A host of emotions filled her chest; to her surprise and confusion, she had the strongest urge to run to him, cling to him. To call him . . . call him . . .

'I'm very sorry, Pip.'

A small sob escaped her. She watched as he guided his wife to the door. Caroline allowed him to lead her away without resistance. Then they were gone.

Philip. Father. *Father!*

'She'll recover sufficiently without the need of a doctor?' asked Albert moments later, motioning to Pip as Cook led her out.

The woman surveyed her injury. 'Aye, I reckon. I'll patch the love up. Appears nowt but a surface wound, glory be to God.' Meeting the master's eye, she gave him an *Eeh, I don't know – where will all this end?* look.

He responded with a sigh. 'If you're mistaken, inform me immediately and I shall send for Lawley right away.'

'Aye, lad.'

Josephine, pale faced, enveloped Pip in a hug. 'I'll leave you in Mabel's capable care, dear girl. Oh, that such a thing has happened . . .' She held a hand to her trembling lips.

'You'll be all right, Miss Josephine?' The shooting pains made her suck in air sharply but right now, her concern was for her mistress. She looked dreadful, ready to fall victim to one of her episodes at any minute.

'Please, don't fret over me! I'll be fine, just fine. Oh, Pip.' Again, her lips quivered with emotion. 'Go on, dear girl. Take as long as you need.'

Simon was waiting for her by the door. Though his face was stony, his eyes couldn't conceal his devastation. With her sound hand, she reached out and he gripped it.

Closely followed by Cook, they headed without a word to the kitchen.

Chapter 23

THEY HAD TAKEN matters too far.

Without voicing it, Pip and Simon knew it. They hadn't intended things to spiral into the chaos it had. Frighten Caroline, yes. Scare her so out of her wits that she'd confess everything and it would all be over, that had been the plan. Instead, their antics had managed to upset the whole household and left their victim a jab-bering, laudanum-soaked mess. And Pip or someone else could have quite easily been killed.

Enough was enough. Their attempts to best Caroline had failed. It was time to accept the fact and leave things they couldn't change as they were, for all their sakes.

Yet as they were soon to discover, life was never that simple. Unbeknown to them, matters were already out of their hands.

The Monday that would change the course of every-one's lives at Bracken House had started out as might any other. People rose, washed, ate and, depending on their station in life, began work or indulged in whatever activities they chose to pass the day. Though a subdued air still hung around them following the incident with the scissors, life ran on as it must and now, four days later, the whispers both upstairs and down had for the most part ceased. Topics of interest came and went, fresh news grew old, life moved on. And Pip was glad of it. As far as she was concerned, the sooner they put the unpleasantness behind them, the better.

She'd seen nothing of Caroline. The lady hadn't surfaced from her room, was recuperating, according to Josephine, and so Pip hadn't to fear a repeat performance of the recent occurrence. Though she'd brushed aside her mistress and the master's concerns about her resuming her post right next door to her attacker, she had secretly been worried. Caroline could very well have stormed the room again at any time, and maybe done real damage should she be so inclined. The following few nights, Pip had struggled to sleep but eventually, as hours then days remained incident-free, her anxiety eased. Clearly, the laudanum was doing its job; Caroline was getting the rest her body and mind needed.

Pip hoped her faculties would be returned to normal – well, whatever normal for her was – in due course. She just wanted to forget that the whole thing had ever happened. Being able to remove her bandage in another few days would help with that, she was sure. Thanks to Cook's nursing skills, her hand was almost healed. She was only too aware how fortunate she'd been. Had the instrument gone in just a little deeper, severed a tendon . . . But it hadn't and she'd thanked God in her prayers since. For all their sakes.

Rain blowing in on the wind from across the Medlock had fallen steadily since before dawn. Up in Josephine's room, despite the hour being not long past two, the lamps had been lit owing to the leaden sky beyond the window. The fire was crackling nicely, the rich aroma of fresh coffee clung to the air and Josephine's soft humming as she worked on her embroidery was soothing, safe. When a light knock came at the door, assuming it was the master, Pip didn't raise her head from where she stood by a side table arranging a vase of cream-coloured roses. Until the visitor spoke, that was, and she realised it wasn't Albert after all. Heat trickled to her cheeks. She fought to control her breathing.

Josephine returned the greeting. 'Brother, how are you?'

'Well enough, thank you.' Philip crossed the space. Halting by the fire, he rested his elbow on the mantel. 'I came to inform you that Alexander shall be dropping by later. I've informed Cook that she's to set an extra place at table should he wish to stay for dinner.'

'Wonderful. I shall look forward to it.'

Please go, please go, Pip willed him, her hands beginning to tremble. For he'd awakened in her feelings she could neither understand nor shake. The way he'd spoken to her, gentle, almost caring, when apologising for his wife's behaviour, the look in his eyes as they stared at one another, the burst of . . . something she'd experienced deep within her breast for him.

This man, who made up half of her. Whom she'd hated upon unearthing the fact, should hate still, yet didn't. Instead, she found herself wanting to be near him, thought about him constantly but didn't know why. Who had hurt and used and abandoned her mother. Who was her father. The person she'd never had but whom she realised now she'd always craved, always wondered over, dreamed about. Now she'd discovered him, the prospect of losing him again made her chest hurt.

He knew not a thing about it, wouldn't want to, wouldn't want her even if he did; she knew that. Nor did he deserve her. He didn't deserve the growing feelings she harboured for him, the time she now spent obsessing

343

about him. Still, he was in her head and in her heart and she couldn't evict him. Nor was she sure she wanted to. Her brain ached with it all. The struggle to keep her silence grew hourly. Could she really hold this secret for ever? Doubt brought her fear and yearning in equal measure.

'Are you sure you're all right, Philip?' Josephine murmured now, snapping Pip from her troubles.

He stared at his sister for a moment then looked away. 'Does he make you *very* happy?'

'Alexander?'

Philip nodded.

'Happier than I would have thought possible.' A small blush touched her cheeks. She smiled. 'And it's all thanks to you. After all, if he wasn't your friend, we never would have met, would we?'

'No.'

He'd sounded almost apologetic. Glancing his way, Pip frowned slightly. Could he possibly be regretting whatever scheme he and Caroline had concocted to ensure the marriage went ahead? Why now?

'You seem so much better lately. The change in you . . .' He blinked, shook his head. 'You ought to be proud of yourself.'

'Oh, Philip. To hear that from you . . . Thank you,' the lady finished with feeling.

His voice held just as much depth. 'I give you my promise: I'll make certain he looks after you.'

They shared a tender stare. Then Philip cleared his throat awkwardly. He inclined his head and left the room, but not before glancing at Pip. Her breath caught in her throat. Again, he moved his dark head – this time to her in brief acknowledgement – and was gone.

Father . . .

'Well, the clouds look to have shifted. See, the sun has emerged.' Josephine motioned to the window, smiling, her voice revealing her doubt that this day could get any better. She sighed contentedly. Glancing beyond the curtains again, she nodded. 'If the boys downstairs can be spared from their duties for a while, then the three of you must take yourselves to the Green. The brisk air will do you the world of good. You're cooped up in this house far too much; children of your age need the freedom to run and laugh and frolic whenever possible, I believe.'

Despite her inner troubles, the corners of Pip's mouth lifted. It was as though her mistress wanted to spread the happiness she herself felt – she possessed the kindest heart to ever beat on earth, Pip was certain. The offer sounded good. Aye, *really* good. To feel the sun's rays on her face and the wind through her hair was something she'd missed since leaving the streets. It made you feel alive, free. And, if she was honest, escaping Bracken House for a short while sounded lovely. Grateful as she was to be here, there was no denying the beautiful home could be stifling at times.

'I'm sure if you were to ask Mabel, she wouldn't mind packing you a small picnic. Inform her it was my suggestion, of course,' the lady added with a teasing wink.

'Oh ta, thanks. You'll be all right while I'm gone, Miss Josephine?' She asked this more through habit, now; the woman's ailment struck far less frequently these days.

'I will, Pip, yes. Run along and collect your shawl. You and your friends enjoy yourselves.'

Ten minutes later, Pip and Simon, with Mack skipping excitedly between, were making their way across the broad road to the Green. A small wicker basket hung over Pip's arm containing bread, cold beef, a large hunk of vegetable pie and dainty lemon cakes; the children's stomachs growled in anticipation of the feast.

Cook had been only too happy to oblige and had shared Josephine's sentiments entirely: 'An hour away from these here walls and the last few days of strife what's gone on within them; aye, youse need it,' she'd said. 'Be on your best behaviour, mind, don't be for bothering folk. And watch yourselves near the lake, no straying too close to the water's edge. You hear?'

They had nodded agreement readily and now, noses pointed to the brightened sky like sniffer dogs, drew in air gratefully. The crisp scent of evergreens and winter blooms that decorated the surrounding gardens, mingled with the musk of smoke from domestic chimneys, smelt glorious. The Green itself twinkled in the weak sunshine, as if the grass were sprinkled with crushed diamonds, and birdsong carried from high bare branches stretching towards the snowy clouds like black-boned fingers. An easy stillness enveloped them. By, it *did* feel good to be out.

They halted by the familiar tree and settled on the cold grass, backs against the knobbly trunk, not saying much, simply absorbing their surroundings. One or two others, taking advantage of the pleasing change in weather, strolled here and there, smiling and conversing quietly. Pip opened the basket and as she and Simon ate, they idly watched Mack, who had wandered off to explore.

Popping the last of her cake into her mouth, she turned to the lad beside her and smiled. However, he failed to return it and hers slipped. She frowned. 'All right?' But Simon didn't answer. His gaze travelled to her bandaged hand and she sighed. 'Lad, please. We've spoke on this a dozen times or more . . .'

'How is it?'

'Aye, healing. It ain't your fault,' she added in a whisper. Though how many times she must say this before he accepted it was another matter. 'We agreed to put it behind us, remember? All of it.'

'I can't.'

'Simon, you must—'

'I agreed to it, to you planting that rotten picture. I put you at risk.'

'Nay, I put myself forward, me.'

'She could have killed thee.'

They fell quiet. Pip leaned closer to him. He couldn't bear this. He'd protected her from harm, Mack too, since the day they met. He felt he'd failed her. He couldn't have been more wrong. He could never do that, never, in her eyes.

For some minutes, neither spoke, then: 'She didn't, though, did she? No real harm were done. Don't dwell on it no more, eh?'

'I'd never forgive myself had ... had summat worse ...'

'I know.' She rested her head on his shoulder. Again, they lapsed into silence.

'What's next, Pip? Just where do we go from here?'

With their plans dashed, the trackless future was a constant worry at the forefront of their minds. What would become of them? In less than nine weeks, Josephine would become Mrs Sutton-Shaw. Then what? Would they be forced to dwell beneath the same roof as that beast, at his mercy completely – especially sweet young Mack – with no Cook or anyone else to protect them? God above, surely not. Yet what choice had they? If Caroline stayed true to her word ...

Even were they to do a moonlight flit, she could spill

her lies to the police; they would be fugitives, forever looking over their shoulders. It was all such a mess. Their fates were not their own to decide. They were tethered here whether they liked it or not, could only wait and see how matters panned out. Badly, she'd be bound, if their luck was anything to go by.

'Here, over here! Hello, hello!'

Dragged from their thoughts, Pip and Simon glanced around to see Mack waving frantically across the expanse of green beyond the opposite bank, a huge grin on his face. They followed his gaze to where, in the distance at the furthermost edge of the park, two figures were out walking. The smaller shielded her eyes with her hand then, recognising them, picked up her skirts and skipped towards them. Pip's stomach dropped.

'Miss Lucy with her nursemaid, that, ain't it?' asked Simon, squinting ahead.

'Aye.'

He gave her a sidelong glance. 'Tha don't sound reet pleased about it, mind,' he stated in surprise. 'By, the two of youse are normally—'

'Aye, well. Things change.'

Frowning, Simon turned fully now to face Pip but hadn't time to question her further; laughing breathlessly, Lucy reached them, cheeks pink from the exertion, and flung her arms around them all. She didn't seem to notice Pip stiffen, and bestowed upon her the usual smile.

'Oh, how lovely to see you here! Budd's a darling and all but she isn't much fun, it must be said. It's her ageing bones, you see, so says she,' the girl added with a sad shrug and watched as the nursemaid closed the space between them, huffing and puffing like a pair of old bellows. 'Sorry for dashing off, Budd. Are you all right?'

'I will be, Miss Lucy.' The amiable woman smiled down at her charge then turned to Pip and the boys, saying, 'Hello.'

'Hello,' they chimed in unison.

'The weather picked up well, didn't it?'

'Aye, yes.'

'Well.' The woman eyed a bench across the way. 'I'll be over there, Miss Lucy, should you need me. Play nicely with your friends, all right?'

'Thank you, Budd. Come on,' Lucy added excitedly, pulling Pip by the arm and motioning to the boys to follow. 'Let us explore and have some fun.'

'I reckon we ought to be getting back, actually, Miss Lucy.'

The girl was crestfallen. 'Oh, but you can't!'

'We've been out no more than a handful of minutes, Pip,' protested Mack, his bottom lip beginning to tremble.

'We've time yet to spare.' Simon was surveying Pip with puzzled suspicion. He took Mack's arm. 'Come on, lad. Let's leave the lasses to their games – we'll head up this end and have ourselfs some proper enjoyment.'

Sensing something was amiss, he thought what was needed was to give her and Lucy some time alone to make up. *Nay, come back,* she cried silently, watching the lads walk away across the Green. She couldn't bear to be around the young miss, not now, not since discovering . . .

And yet she missed her. Every day, she hated herself more for her changed feelings, she did, but couldn't seem to shake off her resentment. The girl had everything she should have had, everything she'd been deprived of the whole of her life. Not that any of it was Lucy's fault, of course it wasn't, but nonetheless . . . Oh, it was all such a painful mess.

'Ooh, a fish! Pip, did you see? There, look, beneath the ice.'

Suppressing a sigh, she allowed the girl to drag her to the lake's edge. She followed her gaze to where she pointed. Sure enough, a largish shape hovered beneath the thin sheet that still covered the water's surface in places. Despite herself, surprise brought a small smile. She nodded.

'I'm finding a stick! You too, come on. If we pierce through, there, we shall be able to see it properly.'

'Careful, Miss Lucy,' called Budd from her seat a few yards away as, having found what they were looking for, she and Pip knelt by the dark waters.

'I shall,' the girl answered, tongue peeking from the side of her mouth in concentration. She and Pip had managed to create a small hole between the white veins of ice when Lucy exclaimed, 'Oh, bother. Oh, look now!'

''Ere, Miss Lucy!' Seeing the beautiful cloak, which had slithered from the youngster's shoulders, now floating on the lake's surface, Pip clapped a hand to her mouth. She bent further forward and with the aid of her stick, managed to hook the sopping garment. She and Lucy stared at it forlornly.

'Oh, child.' Tut-tutting, the nursemaid heaved herself from the bench. 'Come, we shall have to return to the house. You cannot remain outdoors without suitable attire in weather such as this. It's more than my position's worth should you catch a chill.'

'No! Oh no, please, let's stay, Budd. I'm quite warm, really, I am.'

'Now now, Miss Lucy—'

'It's all right, Budd.' Whatever Pip tried telling herself, she loved this girl, she did; she couldn't deny it, least of all to herself. Seeing the little heart-shaped face crumble, those big eyes fill with disappointed tears, her heart contracted and a rush of protectiveness, a need to make her happy, coursed through her. She should have been welcoming this excuse to escape her company. Instead, she wanted nothing more than to remain in it. The realisation brought a lump to her throat. 'Here, Miss Lucy, wear this.' She removed her shawl and secured it around the girl. 'She'll be warm reet enough, Budd, with that. It's my new one from Miss Josephine. It's a good 'un.'

'Oh, Pip.' Lucy planted a thank-you kiss on her cheek. 'But won't you be cold?'

Reaching up to stroke the spot that Lucy's lips had touched, Pip's voice was thick with emotion. 'Nay, I'll not, don't fret. Tough as owd leather, me.'

'What a thoughtful gesture, Pip.' The nursemaid smiled. 'All right, Miss Lucy, we'll stay a while longer. But please, do come back a little from the water's edge, would you? My nerves cannot take the thought of you falling in next.'

Grinning, Lucy shuffled back a few inches then picked up her stick to resume her game.

'Mine's broke, must have snapped on yon cloak.' Pip tossed hers into the water. 'Hang on, Miss Lucy. I'll find another.' She wandered towards a tree with low-hanging branches. Busy deciding which to select, what made her glance up she couldn't say. For a moment, she couldn't decide why the figure passing down the street in the distance seemed familiar. Then it drew closer and she laughed out loud in surprised delight. Abandoning her task, she ran to the railing. 'I knew it – it *is* you! Hello.'

Peter's surprise matched hers; face breaking into a smile, he manoeuvred his handcart around and crossed the road. 'Pip, ain't it?'

'Aye, that's right.'

'You're looking well, lass.'

'Ta, thanks. So are you.' And she meant it. His dishevelled appearance when they'd met that fearful night and he'd selflessly given up his bed for her at the lodging house was gone. Still, he carried the down-at-heel stamp of his station – his coat was threadbare and cheeks sunken from lack of regular meals – but he was neater, cleaner, brighter eyed than before. She nodded to his burden, a rickety contraption that had seen better days, with its large stone grinding wheel that was worked by a treadle. He puffed out his chest proudly and she smiled. 'You peddling, now, aye?'

'That's right. Owd tinker friend of mine, what succumbed to the consumption some weeks gone, passed his here cart on to me, Lord love his soul. It brings me a fair living. I've brass enough for the rent on a dwelling I can call my own. Nice little cellar, I've got, on Angel Street.'

'Eeh, that's gradely.' Remembering the kindness he'd shown her, she motioned behind him. One good turn deserved another. 'You called at Bracken House yet? That one there with the blue door?'

Peter shook his head.

'I'm employed there – ask for Cook, tell her I sent thee. She's sure to find a blunted knife or two what you could sharpen.' And knowing the woman as she did, a plate of something, too, before he left, which he'd surely appreciate. Plying his trade around the streets door-to-door must be hungry work.

'I'll do that, lass, ta.' He touched his cap. 'Take care and God bless.'

'Aye, and the same to thee.'

Smiling, he turned to leave. Then, looking beyond her across the park, he stopped dead in his tracks.

'Peter? What is it?'

It was as though he hadn't heard her. His mouth fell open. He shook his head slowly. 'Nay. Nay, it can't, can't be . . .'

Frowning, she turned. There, up ahead, stood Simon. His incredulous expression matched the man's entirely.

Peter's broken cry rent the air. 'Lad?'

'*Father?*'

Dumbstruck, Pip could only stare from one to the other. He was . . .? They were . . .? My God!

Those stunned seconds seemed to halt time in its tracks. Then suddenly, another noise rang out – a scream of so violent a pitch they all whipped around with a gasp. Horror froze them to the spot at the scene they were met with.

Budd let out another deafening screech. Beside her, Caroline stood mutely. Both were gazing at the lake where, thrashing wildly in the icy waters, they saw Lucy. As her head disappeared beneath the surface, Peter was first to spring into action.

'Get back!' he yelled to Pip and Simon; grabbing the top of the railings, he launched himself over and sprinted full pelt towards the lake. Without hesitation, he dived in. Moments later, his top half emerged. He drew in a huge gulp of air then disappeared once more.

'Fetch Mr Philip, the master,' rasped Pip to Mack, giving him a push. 'Go, go now!'

Seconds seemed like minutes as they waited for the man and girl to reappear. At last they burst to the surface, Peter heaving and spluttering. Lucy lay limp in his arms.

Budd and Simon helped to drag them to the embankment. They plucked Lucy from his outstretched hands and laid her carefully on the grass. Still, Caroline – and what she was even doing here, where she'd appeared from, no one seemed to know – stood statue-like, wordless, wide eyes unseeing.

Shock had rendered Pip into a similar state but now, gazing at Lucy's face, bone-white and lifeless, she snapped from her trance. With a cry, she bolted over and fell to her knees. 'Miss Lucy? Miss Lucy, dear God in heaven above . . . Speak to me! Please!'

Having hauled himself out of the water, Peter crouched, coughing, then staggered to the girl's side. He too dropped to the ground. 'Mind aside, Pip lass.' Bending over the body, he put his mouth to Lucy's blue-tinged lips and blew. Then placing his hands one on top of the other on her chest, he pumped quickly.

With calmness and concentration, he repeated the action twice, three times. As he made to bring his mouth back yet again, Lucy suddenly jolted and a gush of water escaped her on a gargled cough.

'Thank God, thank God!' Pip and Budd chimed, with a sob, and Simon closed his eyes with a relieved sigh.

Quickly, Peter turned Lucy on to her side where a further tide spilled from her on to the grass. Gasping and retching, she opened her eyes.

'It's a miracle! Oh, Miss Lucy, Miss Lucy . . .!' Suddenly, the nursemaid's eyes moved to Caroline. She screwed up her face, her lips atremble. 'You. You did this, you did it, you pushed her. I saw you. Why, Mrs Goldthorpe, would you do such a wicked, *wicked* thing to your own child?'

All heads turned incredulously towards the lady – then behind them at the sound of thundering footsteps.

Philip skidded to a halt. 'My God!' He watched his father rush to the child and wrap her in the thick blanket he'd fetched. Then he turned a murderous gaze on to his wife. 'Caroline? You tried to *murder* our daughter?'

Blinking, she shook her head. 'No, Philip. No.'

'She did, sir, I saw her with my own eyes. She appeared at her bedroom window then, moments later, she was entering the Green. I believed that, spotting Miss Lucy through the pane, she'd decided to come and spend some time with her, thought nothing out of the ordinary when she headed towards her. Miss Lucy had her back to her beside the lake – before she had chance to turn, Mrs Goldthorpe put out her hands and shoved the child straight into the water.'

'Dear God.' Philip's words dropped from his lips on an anguished groan. 'Why, you evil, deranged—!'

'No, no, no, no. My intention was not to murder Lucy.'

My shawl. Realisation smacked Pip full in the face. Lucy had been wearing it. Caroline would have seen this. It could only mean one thing. She'd mistaken her daughter for her. It was *her* she'd meant to push into that lake . . . Oh God! In the next breath, the woman confirmed it:

'It was supposed to be the other girl. That one there.' Caroline's voice was eerily matter-of-fact. She pointed to Pip. '*She* was meant to meet a watery end, to die as she deserves, as she must, not Lucy. No, not Lucy.'

'Wha . . . what are you *talking* about? For God's sake, Caroline—!'

'I know, I know, I made a mistake. It was the shawl, you see. It was careless of me, I admit. I got the wrong child—'

'Listen to yourself! What has *become* of you?'

'As I said, I got the wrong one—'

'That you meant to kill *any* – *any* – child! Can you hear yourself? Can you?' Philip yelled, gripping her by her upper arms and shaking her hard. 'Killing children? Why, *why*?'

'Because it's her, it is. She's the one, she and her friends, who torment me. They must die, Philip. There's no other way.'

The horror-struck party had watched the husband and wife's exchange in numb silence. They were not the only ones. Alerted by the ruckus, several neighbours had emerged from their homes and were standing around, agog.

Albert shattered the spell; his granddaughter in his arms, he rose and walked towards the gate, snapping, 'Make way!' to one or two in his path.

Philip's face was grey. He released his hold on his wife and let his arms fall to his sides. Shoulders slumped, he turned, murmuring over his shoulder to her, 'Come.'

Caroline followed obediently. After some moments, Pip and the others did likewise.

Inside Bracken House, they found that the master had carried Lucy into the drawing room. Weeping softly, she lay shivering on the thick rug before the fire. While Tabby rushed to collect extra blankets, Cook and Josephine knelt beside the girl, cooing broken reassurances to her and stroking her wet hair. Budd hurried in to join them.

'Take your wife upstairs.' Addressing his son in the hall, the master's voice was steely. 'We'll deal with her later. Right now, Lucy is our main concern.'

'Has the doctor been sent for?'

Albert nodded. 'I instructed the housemaid to fetch him. Now,' he added through gritted teeth, his gaze flicking to Caroline, 'get her out of my sight.'

As the master turned back into the drawing room, Pip made to follow but was pulled up short by Simon. Tugging her back, he glared down at her with ravaged eyes.

'How? How the bleedin' hell do you know him?'

Mind dizzy with recent events, Pip was confused. 'What? Who?'

'My father, who d'you bloody well think? I'd have never believed . . . not from thee. How could you *do* this to me?'

She glanced around but Mack was the only other person present. 'Where is Peter?'

'Gone. I sent him packing.'

'But Simon, why?'

'Why?' He shook his head slowly. 'Have you forgot what I told youse, how he let his wife treat me all them years back?'

She did remember. And she couldn't comprehend that the two men could be one and the same. Peter, with his thoughtfulness, kindness . . . capable of neglecting a child in such a callous way? It just didn't make sense.

'What, he thinks he can start afresh with me because he finally saw her true colours? She let slip one day what she'd been about and, so says he, he walked from that house and never returned, reckons he's been searching for me since. Huh! Aye well, his time were wasted, weren't it, good and proper. I want nowt to do with him, nowt.'

'Simon. I believe he's changed. What I've seen of him . . . I think you ought to give him a chance—'

'*What?*'

'At least hear him out.'

'I don't believe I'm hearing this from you!'

357

'Lad, please. All I'm saying is, well, I just think—'

'Listen to me, for it's the last I'll speak on this.' Though his stiff face showed his fury, his eyes glistened with tears. 'That wastrel means nowt to me, less than. And if I ever see his face again, I'll pummel it to a bloody pulp. Right?'

Though her heart told her he was making the wrong decision, she had to respect his wishes. She nodded. 'All right, lad. If it's what you want. Tha must know, I never knew a thing about it, would have never imagined who he were. I'd not hurt thee for the world and am sorry I have. Truly.'

Blinking fiercely, he looked away. 'Me and Bread, we'd best be away back to the kitchen.'

'I'll join you shortly.' Itching to get back to Lucy, after the lads disappeared from sight she hurried into the drawing room. The women were still with her. Along with the blankets, Tabby had collected warm flannels, and with these all were now vigorously rubbing the chilled body. From the window nearby, drawn-faced with worry, the master looked on. He motioned Pip forward when she hesitated.

'Don't be shy. Lucy will want to see you.'

Holding back tears, she headed for the fire. However, the moment the young miss spotted her over the women's heads, and her bottom lip trembled, Pip could quell her emotion no longer. She burst into quiet sobs.

'Oh, Pip, Pip . . .'

'Eeh, Miss Lucy.' She gripped the small hand held out to her. 'So sorry, so sorry . . . This is my fault, me giving thee my shawl, I should never—'

'You are not to blame for a single iota of this,' cut in Albert. 'Do not harbour such thoughts, lass.'

But I do, I must, for ain't I the cause of this one way or another? she responded silently. *Shawl or no, I planted that picture. I've helped to work the woman upstairs into the state she's in. She somehow knew that I – who even to begin with she couldn't stand the very sight of – was involved but was unable to prove it. She wanted revenge. Through me, this girl lying here almost paid the ultimate price. And maybe she will still.*

At the prospect, a swell of panic built in her chest and she struggled to catch her breath. Freezing waters could be deadly. What if Lucy should develop a fever, pneumonia . . .? She gripped the hand she held tighter. It can't happen, it can't. Lucy couldn't leave her. She'd not lose her, not now. *You're my sister and I love you.*

'The doctor, sir.'

Albert turned to the doorway where Cally had appeared. He nodded in relief. 'Doctor Lawley, thank you for coming so quickly. My granddaughter—'

'Your housemaid explained on the way.' His face was grim. 'Your daughter-in-law . . .?'

'Is under lock and key in her room.'

He nodded. 'Show me to the child, Mr Goldthorpe.'

'Here is Lucy, by the fire. We thought it important to try to warm her up.'

'A wise move.' The doctor checked her over briefly, then rose. 'The child needs to be in bed. She must be wrapped up – extra coverings are required. See that a good fire is lit in her room and that it is kept fed. Also,' he added, addressing Cook, 'a mustard poultice applied to her hands, the soles of her feet and insides of her legs, if you please.'

The woman hurried to the door, saying, 'Aye, I'll make one up right away.'

When Albert stooped to lift Lucy into his arms, she whimpered and squeezed Pip's fingers tighter. 'Stay with me, Pip. Don't leave me.'

'I'll not, Miss Lucy, don't fret.'

As the master carried her out and up the stairs, Pip trotted close behind, her fingers entwined in his granddaughter's. However, when they reached the nursery door, the doctor halted Pip by placing a hand on her shoulder. Given what she'd witnessed him do that day to Josephine, she flinched at his touch.

'You may go, now. Miss Lucy must have complete rest—'

'No! Pip is to remain with me.'

'Please, let me go with her. I'll be no bother,' added Pip, tone desperate. The thought of being parted from the girl was every bit as painful to her.

'If Miss Lucy feels up to it, you may pay her a short visit tomorrow.' The doctor made to pull Pip away but, holding on tighter to the hand, she shook her head wildly. 'Nay, nay please—!'

'Away with you!'

'I'll not!' She snatched her arm from him. 'I must stay with her, I must! Nay, nay,' she continued as he tried to draw her to the stairs once more, 'Let go of me! I'll not leave her. I'll not *leave* my sister!'

The world seemed to hold its breath.

With a strangled gasp, Pip turned slowly to the master.

His brow was creased slightly in a frown, his mouth open. He peered at her for an age and the colour visibly drained from his face. 'Dear God in heaven . . .'

She hadn't the words to respond, could never have got them past her lips if she had. Horror had frozen her. When Albert's gaze swivelled behind her, her heart seemed to cease its beating. She sensed without turning who was there.

'What . . . did you say?'

With every ounce of strength she possessed, she forced herself to face Philip. Molten tears blurred his image.

'The child you planted in Lydia May's belly is me. You're my father.'

Chapter 24

'DRINK THIS.'

Cook allowed the master to place a tumbler in her hand, but the amber liquid went untouched. With glazed eyes rooted to Pip's face, her tears ran down her cheeks unchecked.

Philip sat slumped in the chair opposite. He looked as if he'd aged several decades in the course of the hours.

The master, too, was shaken to the core, moved now and then to refill their glasses with brandy as though in a trance. Josephine was the only one who had marginally recovered from the mind-shattering news. She accepted it numbly now, as though she'd always known.

'I need to leave. I should never have told. I'm sorry,' croaked Pip for the dozenth time. However, she didn't move, sat on, head bowed, her hands covering her face.

She'd told them everything. First between uncontrollable sobs when the master, leaving Lucy in the safe hands of the stunned doctor and Budd, had ushered her and Philip into the study. Then again, flatly from sheer exhaustion, when Albert had fetched in Cook.

The servant's reaction had been heart-rending to witness. Disbelief followed by incredulous cries upon being assured it was true, then her wails of anguish when realising her daughter was gone for ever . . . Her white-hot fury at Philip and screamed accusations that his desertion had brought about the untimely death ... Her crushing embrace and noisy weeping and declarations of everlasting love for Pip ... Cook had emptied out every emotion. Now, as though to protect her from feeling anything more, shock appeared to have shut down body and mind. Life had gone out in her.

'Could you leave Pip and me?'

All eyes went to Philip. It was the first time he'd uttered anything throughout.

'Please. I wish to speak with her alone,' he added in a dull murmur. His stare followed Cook across the room. As if feeling it at her back, she turned. Their ravaged eyes locked. 'For everything ...' he told her thickly, 'everything I have done ... I am so very sorry.'

His admission, remorse, *finally*, returned a flicker of life to the woman's features. She'd railed at him something frightful earlier – at one point, Albert had had to hold her back from lunging at her daughter's seducer – and now, Pip expected a repeat performance. It never came. Cook simply peered at him.

'Please. I cannot bear ... If I could only turn back the hands of time ... Please say you can forgive me.'

It was as though Cook saw now the boy she'd once known and loved; her face creased in something akin to remembrance. He'd stripped himself bare before her, shed the display and pomposity, leaving only the man. She swallowed hard. Then she turned and walked from the room. His shoulders sagged.

'Time, lad. Give her time.'

The door clicked shut on Albert's words. Alone with Philip, Pip's heart began to race. For a long moment, he said nothing. Just when she thought she could bear the stifling silence no longer, he lifted his head.

'Lydia's picture. Are you *absolutely* certain—?'

'I'm certain.'

'But, I mean, it is possible you could be mistaken, that you *think* that who you saw—'

'I know my own mother.'

Lifting his face to the ceiling, he heaved a tortured sigh. 'I loved her, whatever people may believe.'

'You abandoned her.' Pip spat out the words. Her fear and anxiety were rapidly diminishing, leaving behind only burning fury.

'You speak the truth. I was young, foolish, believed she wasn't worthy of me. I was blind, too pig-ignorant to see it was the other way around. The memory of my actions . . .' He released a shuddering breath. 'It's a regret I shall carry until my dying day.'

'Good. I pray with all I am that you never know a second's peace.'

'Pip, I'm sorry. So very, very sorry . . .'

To her surprise, he put his face in his hands and burst into tears. She blinked, the venom inside her melting. She was at a loss what to do, think. She'd never seen a man cry. She hadn't expected this, never, and not from him. She bit her lip.

'Tell me what to do.' He came towards her and held out his hands helplessly. 'What do I do, Pip? You're my . . . my *daughter.*' Again, gruff sobs ripped from him. 'I've missed out on your whole life. I *loathe* my weak, disgusting self!'

She rose. Tentatively, she stepped towards him. He'd buried his face again and she gazed at his bowed head. When eventually she spoke, her voice was barely above a whisper.

'I loathe you, too. Least, I thought I did; I don't know. I wanted to hurt you, bad like, as you did my mam, and me.'

He lifted his eyes to look at her. 'And now?'

'I don't know. I don't know what I'm meant to . . . to feel . . . And you're my father. Father,' she repeated, throat thick. 'We *needed* you. Me and Mam, we, we . . .'

The next moment, they were in each other's arms. Rough cheek against smooth, their tears mingling. Of their own accord, her arms tightened. She clung to him.

'Forgive me. Forgive me.'

Her tears fell harder. 'Oh, Mr Philip.'

'Father. Please.'

A fast tide swam through her, warming her from head to toe. 'Oh, Father,' she whispered.

'I don't pretend to be a great husband, nor even a great man. I have wronged more people than I care to dwell upon. However, my child – my *children* – are my all. I vow to do everything in my power to make it up to you, Pip. If you'll let me.'

'There's summat tha must know.'

She had to tell him, must. If they were even to attempt to forge the semblance of a relationship, they had to enter into it with complete honesty. It would never work otherwise, would hang over her for ever like a dark cloud. How he chose to deal with the revelation would be the ultimate test. She pulled back to look at him and took a breath.

'Earlier, when I told you all I'd found Mam's picture on that there desk?' At the time, Miss Josephine hadn't yet been summoned to the drawing room and so the lie that had slipped from Pip's tongue hadn't been questioned. After all, the lady thought she'd discovered it in Cook's possessions . . .

'Yes, Pip?'

'I saw the look of regret in your eyes. You believed you'd been careless, didn't yer, that you'd left the leather carrier out by mistake. You'd not. Nor when I discovered it had I just happened to be in here helping Cally dust because she were behind with her duties. It were the drawer I found it in, had stole the key from your jacket pocket. I sneaked to this room on purpose, had planned it all out.' She paused to gauge his reaction but he simply stared back in silence. Her voice dropped. 'I got the shock of my life when I saw Mam staring back at me from one of the pages. For you see, that weren't the one I'd come seeking. The picture I wanted was the one of Jess Hardman.'

Now, his eyes creased. He shook his head. 'But how . . .? *Why*?'

'Simon, my friend, he spied you looking at it one night when you were the worse for drink. We knew it were just what we needed, thought it would do the trick—' She broke off with a guilty bite of her lip.

Philip spoke grimly. 'What on earth is going on? What have the two of you been doing?'

'Getting our revenge on Mrs Goldthorpe.'

'Revenge? Revenge for what?'

'She murdered Hardman.'

He jerked back as though she'd slapped him. '*What*?'

'She pushed her down those stairs and threatened to pin the blame on me and Simon. We were angry, scared . . . We thought if we made her think the housemaid's spirit were haunting her for what she'd done, her guilt would become too much, that she'd confess—'

'Good God . . .'

'We were wrong, we know, and we stopped it, all of it, when we saw we'd gone too far, that her mind weren't right—!'

'Jess was carrying my child.'

Pip was stunned. She clapped a hand to her mouth in horror.

'She informed me of the fact mere hours before she died.' He cleared his throat. 'Forgive me, I shouldn't, shouldn't be saying—'

'That youse were lovers is no secret.'

His cheeks reddened. He dropped into a chair. 'I'm a man; weak, pathetic where women are concerned. When Jess told me . . . It was Lydia all over again. I was determined to do the right thing this time. Seeing it as an opportunity to make up for past mistakes, I resolved to find Jess a couple of decent rooms in another part of town . . .'

He'd planned to provide for her and their child by keeping her as his mistress. But surely the housemaid wouldn't have been satisfied with that? After all, she'd wanted Caroline out of the way. And it was clear now it must have been Caroline herself on the landing that day who overheard that conversation. The question was, had she got wind of the fact that Hardman was carrying her husband's child? If so, would she still have gone through with the attack? Knowing Caroline, probably so. Pip wouldn't put anything past her – particularly after today's events.

'I've caused this,' Philip said. 'If it had not been for my actions, Jess would be alive today. I drove Caroline to this, it's my doing, mine, as sure as if I had been the one to push her. It's my fault—'

Pip cut through his distress. 'However wronged your wife felt, that's no excuse for taking a life. You had a part in this, aye, there's no denying it. But you weren't to know she'd take the measures she did to exact revenge. The blood shall forever stain her hands, and hers alone.'

'I tried my utmost in the beginning to make our

marriage work,' he muttered as though to himself, 'to make her happy, but her shrewishness . . . She made it impossible. I used to think that surely, somewhere in that twisted head, there must be an ounce of human decency lurking. It appears I was mistaken. I feel I don't know her at all, and that I never have. As for the incident at the lake today . . . The devil's work. She once suspected Josephine, at the height of her illness, to be of demonic possession when all along . . . There can be no denying this to ourselves, nor concealing it any longer. The whole damn street witnessed the extent of her madness. Father was right.' He nodded dully. 'The time has come.'

'Time?'

Philip placed his hands on Pip's shoulders. The softest smile caressed his mouth. 'Don't concern yourself with anything – not now. It's over.' He put his lips to her brow, and the tender feel brought a lump to her throat. 'There are pressing matters that need my attention. Run along, now. We'll speak more, shortly.'

Whether things will be well betwixt us, develop into something resembling a relationship, remains to be seen. It will take time and lots of it, of course it will. But of one thing, Pip was certain as, after giving him a last, lingering look, she slipped from the room:

She wanted it to. Aye, she did. And she'd do all in her power to try and make it happen.

*

The following morning, Pip awoke later than usual to an empty room. The sun was already high above the rooftops and she dressed hurriedly, surprised no one had roused her. What time was it? Where was Miss Josephine?

368

Despite the long rest, she felt anything but refreshed. Yesterday and all that came with it – the crushing turmoil, the emotion – had robbed her of all energy. She felt exhausted, as if she hadn't closed her eyes in weeks.

After leaving Philip the previous evening, she'd crept upstairs to the nursery. She'd found the master sitting beside the bed and Lucy was sleeping peacefully. The sight of her beautiful face, cheeks holding their usual healthy pink hue, the streaming dark hair with its familiar halo of bouncy curls stark against the white pillowslip, had stroked her heart in a healing touch. She knew then the girl would be well, that she'd recover from her ordeal. That, thank the good Lord, she wasn't going to lose her. When Albert beckoned her across, she'd obeyed, head bowed. Dropping to her knees on the floor by Lucy's side and clasping her hands, she'd asked him shyly, 'May I? To thank Him, like, for keeping her safe?'

He'd nodded. Closing her eyes, she'd prayed for several minutes. When she opened them again, she'd found the master watching her, his own eyes bright with tears. Hot ones immediately sprang to hers.

'I believe I sensed . . . something, something about you, shortly after we met,' he'd whispered.

The day in the study when she'd received her Christmas box from him . . . Remembrance had her nodding thoughtfully. For reasons she couldn't fathom at the time, he'd given her that day the queerest stare – similar to Cook's when viewing her properly, clean from the bathing. They were looks of familiarity, she knew now. They had seen something in her they recognised, but didn't know what. Or rather, they had seen someone: Lydia. *Mam.*

'Your smile, it was like stepping into the past. Naturally, at the time, I dismissed it as fanciful thinking, never *ever* imagined . . . We owe you, lass,' he'd added with great sincerity. 'Somehow, we'll make this right.'

When Pip had left Lucy and headed downstairs, Cook's emotion upon seeing her again had been far more intense. Simon and Mack had taken themselves early to bed, Tabby had informed her, barely able to suppress her astonishment at what she clearly knew now regarding Pip's identity, before she and Cally made themselves scarce. Alone with Cook, Pip had sidled to her side.

Having had more time to think on it, the woman's joy had turned bittersweet. Gaining a granddaughter had come with a heavy price – the discovery that she'd lost her only child. Pip wished she could take the woman's pain away. But the truth was out; there was no biting it back, whether she wanted to or not.

'All this time . . . I thought I were seeing in you what my desperate heart wanted to. You are my Lydia as a lass all over.' Eyes glazed from the master's brandy, she'd stared into space. Pip had reached for her hand and, though she appeared in a world of her own, Cook had squeezed back. They had sat like that for a time, neither speaking, locked in their own thoughts. It would take the tortured woman longer than any of them, Pip knew, to come to terms with this.

Now, when she entered the kitchen, Simon sprang to his feet. His face was alive with shock and excitement. She smiled softly. He'd heard, then. One of the servants must have filled him in this morning on the incredible news.

'I would have told you, lad. Honest I would. Only my mind were all of a jumble. Discovering summat like that . . . I couldn't get to grips with it myself—'

'All this time I've been hobnobbing it with the gentry and had no clue.' His amazed grin was infectious; she pushed him playfully. ''Ere, you'll not grow too good for the likes of us commoners, now, will thee?'

'Are we to address thee as Miss Pip, like, now?' added Tabby.

'Eeh, the pair of you – don't talk daft!' Yet Pip's smile wavered when she realised they hadn't spoken as jestingly as she'd assumed. Her heart dipped. 'Nowt changes with this. I'm still who I've allus been: me, Pip. Please don't imagine a single thing otherwise.' Looking around, she frowned. 'Where's Cook?' 'Granny' didn't come naturally to her mind. Would it ever? 'Miss Josephine; she didn't waken me and wasn't in her room just now.'

'Mebbe she reckoned the rest would do thee good, what with everything yesterday. They're up with the master talking, like.'

'Oh?'

Slowly, Simon's eyes widened. He dragged a hand across his mouth. 'You ain't heard, have you?'

'Heard what? What's going on?'

Drawing her aside, he could barely contain his fervour. 'Mrs Goldthorpe passed through Bracken House's door for the last time early today. She's *gone*, Pip.' He nodded rapidly when she simply gazed back. 'Apparently, even Miss Lucy weren't upset to see the back of her, screamed blue murder to Mr Philip to take her mother away when he brought her to the lass's room to say goodbye. And afterwards, when the carriage had driven her away, he himself and the master too appeared nowt but relieved to be rid.'

'I don't . . . Where's she gone, lad?'

'Her husband's had her committed to a private asylum.'

She staggered. For a full minute, she gawped at Simon.

'*Father was right. The time has come.*' The snippet of last night's conversation ran through her mind. She recalled the master's parting words to his son following Caroline's attack on her with the scissors: '*See me in the study once you have her settled. We need to talk . . .*' Had he warned Philip then that further trouble from his daughter-in-law would require them to take drastic action? Had the incident in the Green proven she was no longer herself mentally, that the time to act had come? Lord above . . .

'It's our doing, yours and mine, why her brain's turned,' she finally croaked. Guilt overwhelmed her. *What have we done? God forgive us!* And yet, and yet . . . Appalled at herself as she was, thoughts of Caroline gone for good brought a stirring of relief.

'The bitch has got not nearly as much as she deserves. Even were the truth to come out now, she'd escape the hangman's noose on t' grounds of insanity.'

'But lad—'

'Her mental breakdown, I reckon it would only have been a matter of time, regardless. She can't have been of sound mind *afore* our tricks – she killed a woman, for Christ's sake. That ain't normal behaviour. It ain't.'

Not only Hardman. The secret love child, too . . . 'Mr Philip, he knows what we've been about,' Pip blurted. 'I told him all, last night.'

Simon blanched. 'What did he say?'

'He said not to be concerned, that it were over.'

'Then it sounds like he's in agreement: that woman's head were warped afore we even got to it. She needs the right care and treatment, the like of which only an asylum can give. He couldn't of risked her hurting Lucy again, could he? Or attempting a second shot at thee. God only knows what her reaction would of been had she discovered you're his child. Nay. Nay. She had to be

372

committed to a secure institution for all of our sakes, her own included.'

Numbness chased away a response, until: 'She's really gone, lad?'

'Aye.'

'She brought so much misery ... to so many of us. Didn't she?'

He nodded.

'May God forgive me, I'm glad. I'm *glad*,' she whispered. 'It's over, lad.' They gripped each other's hands tightly.

'Tea and bacon out for you, here, lass,' Tabby called across, bringing them back to the present.

As she ate, Pip's thoughts switched to another strand of the previous day's drama and she scrutinised the lad beside her. Glory be to God, he didn't seem the worse for his own discovery. Then again, Simon was a master at hiding things well, suppressing his emotions. He'd been practising most of his life, after all. The less he allowed himself to feel, the less he hurt. It was a protection of sorts. She understood the need to shield the heart only too well.

'How d'you feel, Pip, about all this?' he asked now. 'Cook and the master are your *grandparents*. God above, I can't fathom it. And *him*. He's your father.'

'I don't know, lad, and that's the truth. My mind's a mess. And Mr Philip ...' She sighed. Still, she was unsure how she felt regarding him. 'He took the news well, considering. Disappointed, that would of been the worst, you know? Yet he weren't. He were ... reet nice. I just, I don't know what to do, to think, can't decide how I ought to feel. It's all a shock still, aye.'

'He's a wrong 'un.' The dislike in Simon's tone was clear. 'Be careful with him, Pip. Will you?'

She couldn't blame the lad for fretting. The man's past was enough to make anyone wary. 'I shall.'

'We still don't know the reasoning behind the desperation to marry off your Miss Josephine to that filth, Sutton-Shaw. Just 'cause Mrs Goldthorpe's gone, it don't mean it's over – Mr Philip's as much involved, ain't he? You see? If he can plan devilment with his own sister's life ... Who's to say he'd not do the same with thee, should he have cause to? He's bad news, I know it.'

'D'you know, with all what's gone on ...' She shook her head. 'How did that business slip my mind?' Disillusionment stabbed. And to think she'd so much as dared to believe, to hope ... Simon was right. Philip was not to be trusted. 'I'll confront him over it next time we meet, you just see if I don't,' she murmured. 'I'll tell him all about what sort of man he's friends with, an' all, to boot. And d'you know what?' She raised her eyes to Simon's. She saw his image through a film of tears. 'If he don't believe me, I'll take my words to the master, I will. He loves his daughter, it's clear. Surely he'll put a stop to the sham of a union?'

'Or not.'

She frowned. 'What d'you mean?'

'Let's just get out of here, Pip,' he burst out on an urgent breath. 'We're free to now, after all; that cow has no hold on us no more. We ain't tethered here, can leave if we wish. Bugger these lot, leave them to their troubles. We owe no one nowt, do we?'

But things have changed, her mind whispered. Thoughts of leaving the members of this household, now, twisted her stomach into tight knots. She realised she didn't want to go it alone, not any more. She was tired of having no one to call hers. She *needed* this. She wanted it more so.

'But if we can get to the truth, put a stop to everything, we'd not need to quit, eh?' she almost pleaded.

'Me and Bread not enough for you now, is that it?'

'Simon, it's not like that. It's just, I've come to realise that having folk around you, who yer can call your very own . . . Well, it's summat to be thankful for. You can't ever have too many, you know. In fact . . . in fact, I reckon you were hasty dismissing Peter as you did. Past is the past. That wife of his is no longer in t' picture. He's come to his senses, realises how you were treated. Despite everything, he's still your father, lad.'

'I'll not listen to this. I told you yesterday—'

'Angel Street.' She nodded when he blinked. 'That's where he's dwelling, some cellar there. So now you know. Choice is yours, lad. I will add this, mind: the master asked of me that address last night, insisted Peter deserved a reward for saving Lucy's life. And d'you know what he found when he went there?'

Simon shook his head.

'Your father refused point blank to accept his brass, insisted he did only what the next fella would've. That there's the action of a moral man. So you see, he don't look to be half the one you once knew.' She rose from the table. Before leaving, she placed her hand on top of his. 'Think of poor young Mack, still without a flesh-and-blood soul in the world to call his. We're the fortunate ones. Don't throw it away, eh? Least not till you can say you tried.'

Leaving him to ponder her advice, Pip headed back to Josephine's room.

Chapter 25

CAROLINE GOLDTHORPE HAD indeed gone. And didn't Bracken House know it.

Once everyone got over the initial shock, they seemed to breathe just that little bit more freely. Now, the air felt cleansed, as if a bad poison had left it. Still, they could barely believe it. It seemed almost too good to be true.

However, shaking off Alexander Sutton-Shaw wasn't as easy.

His visits had increased over the days following her departure. Perhaps he'd become insecure because what had clearly been his main ally had gone? With just weeks until the big day, was he keeping a closer eye on matters, ensuring nothing went wrong?

What he was, *what* he had a fancy for . . . there could be no mistaking that he himself was privy to the plan. Why was still unclear. It certainly wasn't for love. And the one person, now, who could have shed light on it, was as absent as his wife.

Less than an hour after signing Caroline over to the asylum superintendent, Philip had packed a travel case and left to stay with a business acquaintance for a short while 'to clear his thoughts'. By waking late that morning, Pip had missed his departure – the discovery had left her both saddened and hurt. She could understand his need to get away after all he'd had to deal with but surely he could have informed her, said goodbye? Just as she'd found him, she felt she'd lost him again. How could he just leave her like that? Didn't he want her after all, was that it? She fretted continually, plagued with insecurity. It was a heavy blow to take.

The one person who made Pip feel closer to Philip was Lucy. Now, as she headed up to the nursery with Mack to spend a few minutes with her, Pip's smile slowly returned. What she'd do without the girl, she didn't know.

The master had broken the news to his granddaughter concerning Pip's true identity, and she'd accepted it in her simple, sunny way. Given the nature of the astonishing discovery, namely Philip's promiscuity, Albert had given her a watered-down explanation, omitting some things and inventing others that he felt her young mind was able to grasp. Time enough for the complete truth when the girl was grown, he'd explained to Pip, and she'd promised to stick to his version if it meant protecting Lucy. She'd rather die than cause the innocent soul a second's pain.

They entered the pleasant room, where a fire blazed merrily, to find Lucy sitting up in bed playing with her dolls. Catching sight of them, her face spread in a beaming smile.

'Good afternoon, you two! Come, sit yourselves down.' Even she appeared happier since Caroline had gone; a sad fact, really, and proof of her poor ability as a mother.

'How you feeling, lass?'

'Excellent, thank you. I shall feel better still when I'm permitted to leave this rotten bed. But, Grandy and Budd will insist . . .' Throwing her hands in the air, she heaved a theatrical sigh. 'I'm bored silly, I am really, and it's quite unnecessary. I feel perfectly well and fine.'

Perching on the edge of the bed beside Mack, Pip nodded sympathetically. 'They just want to make certain you're properly better. That your lungs are cleared of the lake's contents, like. Plenty of rest is what's needed for that.'

Though physically, Lucy seemed none the worse for her ordeal, mentally it was another matter, Pip suspected – her mention of the lake had smudged the girl's smile. That her own mother was behind the attack must be difficult to process. Little wonder she seemed relieved that she had gone. Pip just hoped the trauma would leave the girl in time. It was, after all, a sound healer.

'Yes, I suppose so,' murmured Lucy.

'That's right, lass. You know it's for the best. 'Ere, remember the master, when he was poorly? He stopped in his sickbed, didn't he, and look at him now; healthy as a fiddle. It'll not be for very much longer, I reckon.'

The girl nodded, then her face creased thoughtfully. 'Pip?'

'Aye?'

'Why do you still address him as Master? Why not Grandfather, or Grandy as do I?'

Eeh, lass, if only it were that simple. The very notion was alien to her; it was doubtful her tongue would ever be able to give life to the terms. She shrugged. 'Mebbe one day, Miss Lucy. *Lucy,*' she amended with a grin when the girl made to protest. 'The Miss part keeps slipping in, don't it? Ay well, I'll grow used to that at least, in time, I'm sure.'

Soon after, the nursemaid informed them kindly that her charge needed to rest and, bidding reluctant goodbyes, Pip and Mack exited the room. They were brought up short when, upon reaching the landing below, they almost collided with Alexander going in the direction they had come from.

Burning protectiveness for the girl upstairs rushed through Pip. She lifted her chin. 'The lass ain't fit to receive further visitors. She's resting.'

Rather than be angry, amusement flickered behind his eyes. 'I merely planned to pop my head inside to enquire about her health – Josephine's idea. No fear of my pouncing on her, fret not.'

Pip's stomach turned over; she shook her head in utter disgust.

'After all,' he continued, voice dropping further, 'she, and you along with her, sadly lack between your legs what I have a liking for. Unlike this one, here.' His gaze smouldered as it fell upon the boy beside her. 'Mm. Peachy,' he murmured.

She willed someone to appear, to overhear him, expose him for who he really was. The master, Josephine, anyone. They didn't. She yanked a smiling Mack behind her, out of Alexander's sight: unaware of the meaning behind the words, young as he was, he'd clearly forgotten his previous encounter with this beast. Her voice trembled: 'You'll leave them both be, him and Lucy.'

'Oh, plain old Lucy, is it, now?' His eyebrow danced. 'Yes, that's right. You're not required to uphold formalities any longer, are you? Josephine has filled me in on the extraordinary developments.' Glancing around, he leaned in close, smirking when she shrank back. 'Bravo. It appears you've successfully reeled the family into your web of deceit. Perhaps we have more in common than I thought.'

'You might be a fake and a fraudster but I ain't.' Her knees shook yet she stood her ground. 'I know your game, aye. You don't love the mistress as you claim, not a bit, do you?'

His hand shot out and she winced; however, the expected blow never came. His long fingers were cold and clammy as he stroked her cheek, making her skin crawl. 'Aha, but *she* adores *me*. And that, young flea-bitten rat, is what matters.'

Sickened to the core by his smug smile, she retorted, 'She'd not were she to learn the dirty truth, what you've a taste for—'

'Alas, proving your wild claim would be akin to wading through thick mud: difficult and very, very messy. You don't honestly imagine for a moment, do you, that Josephine would believe you?' He laughed low in his throat. 'If you were to so much as breathe such an accusation, I'd ensure you were cast from here so fast, your feet wouldn't skim the ground.'

Would the lady call her a liar? Knowing she couldn't answer that with absolute certainty brought frustrated tears to her throat. He'd won and he knew it. For now. She lowered her head.

'Hm. I thought as much. Now, get out of my sight.'

Grabbing Mack's hand, Pip hurried for the kitchen.

'What's wrong?' Simon asked the instant they joined him at the table. Holding back her emotion, Pip gave him a quick account.

His jaw trembled with rage. '*Bastard.*'

'I hate him, hate him. If only Mr Philip were here. He'd believe me, I know it. He'd tell me the truth behind this whole queer set-up.'

'Huh! You reckon?'

Somehow, she did. There was no hesitation this time. 'Aye, I do.'

'I'm going to sort this once and for all,' the lad whispered after a long pause.

'Sort what? How?'

'You'll see. Stay here.'

Before she could question him further, he rose. Shrugging on his jacket, he headed out through the back door.

After some minutes, her curiosity got the better of her and she followed. She scanned the garden but Simon was nowhere to be seen. Wrapping her arms around herself against the cold, she skirted the bushes and made her way to the street.

Pip saw him right away, hovering by the steps of a nearby residence. Frowning, she remained where she was, hidden from view at the side of Bracken House, and continued to watch.

When the opening and closing of her own front door shattered the stillness, she jumped. Alexander sauntered down the steps and turned right – to where, up ahead, Simon stood waiting. *For what? Where was the lad's mind at?* she fretted, biting her lip. She hesitated a moment longer then, seeing Alexander halt at something Simon said, stole in their direction.

'. . . And aye, I've had a bloody bellyful of you and I'm warning yer now for the last time,' Pip heard as she neared, catching the end of Simon's speech. 'Leave us and the rest of the household be or you'll regret it.'

'Is that so?' Alexander clamped a hand to Simon's arm which, with one cruel twist, he forced up his back. The lad flinched in pain as he was dragged into the secluded street corner's shadows. 'I'm willing to let your threat slide,' he hissed. 'In return, I have a proposition of my own that you'd do well to accept.'

'Leave go of him.'

The man glanced over his shoulder at Pip, smirked, and returned his attention to Simon. 'You can thank your friend, here, for this: flaunting the boy in front of me, getting my blood all aflame . . . I've been unable to get him from my thoughts since.'

Mack. Flaunting him? Why the deluded, disgusting . . . 'You make me sick,' she rasped.

'You scuppered me once; there shan't be a repeat of that, I can assure you,' he continued to Simon as though he hadn't heard her. 'I want the boy. A mere hour will suffice. I trust you don't deem that unreasonable? It isn't asking too much, hm?'

Simon puckered his lips to spit in his tormentor's eye, but realising what he meant to do, Alexander grabbed his chin, killing the attempt. He brought Simon's face inches away from his, scrutinised him then shook his head. 'No, you're a little too old for my liking,' he murmured, as though actually contemplating it. 'It must be the other one. It *will* be the other one. I mean to have him eventually, regardless: once you come to live with Josephine and me after the wedding, he will be readily available at all times whether you cooperate or otherwise. In fact, I'll simply dispose of the two of you . . . Yes, yes. Then he'll be mine entirely.'

'And if I say nay?'

Pip's brow creased. What did Simon mean, if? *If* didn't come into it!

'Well, then the girl here will do nicely instead.'

Simon's face fell – Alexander smiled slowly.

'Ah. She's your favourite, I see. What, you had hoped you'd be the first to break her in, is that it?'

Simon's eyes widened with black rage but he remained silent.

'Accept my demands and you still can. How does that sound?'

Trying to shut out the man's hideous words, Pip watched Simon's expression drop even further; she couldn't believe he was swallowing all this! 'He's lying, lad. He told me but minutes since how he's not gorra taste for lasses—'

'Well?' Alexander's interjection sliced the air like the cracking of a whip.

'All right. Tha can have the lad.'

Simon's words struck Pip like a kick to the guts. '*What!*'

'You don't hurt him, mind. And I want paying.'

'Deal.'

'Lad—!'

'Sunday, when the house is away at church. You'll not be disturbed. I'll have him waiting.'

Sinister lust filled the man's eyes. He nodded once. Straightening his tall hat, he struck the ground with his cane and strode away.

Pip could barely get her words past her lips: 'What in God's *name* . . .? How could you? *Why?*'

Slowly, slowly, Simon's face took on an expression she'd seen only once before – the night Caroline had forced his hand with *her* threats. A dark smile pulled at the corner of his mouth. 'One down. One to go.'

Chapter 26

AGAIN, PIP PUT a hand to her mouth as another spoonful of porridge threatened to make its escape. Admitting defeat, she pushed her bowl away.

'All right, lass?' Cook eyed her worriedly. 'You've barely scraped the surface, there. Not too salty for you, is it?'

'Nay, it's lovely, honest. I'm just not that hungry this morning.'

Cook nodded, satisfied, and as she passed Pip's chair, stroked her hair with a brief but tender touch.

Despite the mounting anxiety churning her insides into ribbons, Pip couldn't contain a smile. With each passing day, the woman she'd now come around to viewing as a grandmother was accepting her, too, for who she was. It was difficult, would be so for a while to come, Pip knew, but thankfully they were making steady progress. It was all they could do.

Simon entered and she had to stop herself from running to him lest others became suspicious.

'Did you see the master, then, lad? He weren't too busy to hear thee?' Cook asked him.

'Aye, I saw him. He were all for my suggestions.' He smiled, then turned to Pip, adding, 'I had some ideas to put to him about the garden, wanted to get his permission, like.'

'Oh. Right. That's good,' she said as evenly as she could, though her mind spun with confusion.

She could tell when he was lying, and knew he was doing so now. He'd needed an excuse to leave the kitchen and enter the house proper, that was it; for what? Scheming, sneaking around . . . It was like it had been with Caroline, all over again. But, as then, what choice had they?

When he was seated beside her, she said through the side of her mouth, 'Lad, please. I must know—'

'I told thee, I'll be the one to sort this and me alone. The fewer details you know, the less chance there'll be of you slipping up and him cottoning on that summat's afoot.'

'I understand that, but—' However, there was no shaking him:

'Just do as I said and all will work out.' He picked up his spoon and began to eat, indicating that the conversation was over, and she had no choice but to accept it.

That she could have actually harboured the idea of Simon agreeing to hand over their Mack to that man, even for a second . . . Her cheeks flushed with shame. She should have guessed he was planning something; he'd not see an ounce of hurt come to that lad, never, never. But *what* had he in store for Alexander? One down, one to go, he'd said.

Whatever he was up to, it seemed Simon meant to be rid of him for good. She didn't know whether to be excited or terrified. What if something went wrong – and it could, couldn't it? Look how matters had panned out the last time they took an enemy on. *God above, what will the outcome of this day be?* she asked herself, as she had continually since wakening. Again, no answer was forthcoming. All she, any of them, could do was wait and see.

At the appointed hour, Simon gave Pip a look deep with meaning. Though no one would have guessed he had any other agenda when he followed it up with: 'We'll make our way to the nursery, now, Pip. You an' all, Bread, come on. Everyone will be away to church in a few minutes.'

Pip was surprised the servants couldn't hear her heartbeat as she nodded and followed the lads to the door – it was thumping as hard as a drum. The green baize door closed at their backs and she pulled Simon to a halt. 'What's to happen?'

'I told thee. I managed to arrange for us to sit and keep Miss Lucy company so's we could get out of going to church with the rest. That way, we'll be here when that Sutton-Shaw one arrives—'

'I know all that; I didn't mean what's to happen right now this minute, and you know it. *After* they're away to church, what then?'

'How many more times? You don't need to know, for I've got this. *Trust* me. Please?'

She released a shaky sigh. 'It'll work, whatever it is, won't it? You'll be careful, lad?'

'Aye, yes.' He took a deep breath then squared his shoulders. 'Come on.'

As expected, not long afterwards, the sound of the front door shutting drifted up to where they sat playing a card game with Lucy. Pip and Simon simultaneously stiffened. The latter slipped from where he sat at the bottom of the bed.

'Budd?'

Reading a book by the fire, the nursemaid glanced up. 'Everything all right?'

Simon nodded. 'Me and Pip and the lad here, we'll just nip to the kitchen and fetch back some refreshments. There's them little cakes left what Cook baked yesterday . . .' he added temptingly to Lucy as she made to protest at them leaving her. Eyes lighting up, the girl nodded, placated, and he turned back to the woman. 'You want owt, Budd? A sup of tea? Summat else?'

'Tea would be lovely, thank you. Although you may as well leave the boy here with Miss Lucy. She'll soon grow bored on her own; he can keep her occupied until you return.'

Simon's face fell. He opened and closed his mouth but was at a loss to think up an excuse. Pip saved the moment: 'Nay, we'll need him to help us carry everything. There's the pot, and cups and saucers and whatnot. Then there's the tray, and we'll need to collect a blanket or some such to lay over Lucy's legs so as not to dirty the nice clean bedspread—'

'Yes, all right. I see your point.'

Pip swallowed her relief. 'We'll not be long, 'onest.'

Outside, she turned to Simon. They shook their heads in thankfulness that they had managed to pull that off. It had been a close call for a moment, there. Without Mack, the plan would be ruined.

'Come on. Let's get this over with.' Swinging around, Simon led the way downstairs.

Pip thought he'd continue for the last flight to the ground floor, so frowned in puzzlement when instead he halted on the landing and motioned to Josephine's door.

'You and Bread wait in there.'

'For what?'

'Trust me. Now, when that divil arrives, I'll escort him up then make my excuses and leave.'

387

'Leave? What d'you mean? You can't leave me and Mack alone with him—!'

'*Please*, Pip. Just do as I say. Keep him talking for as long as you can, right? Owt you can think of to distract him a while, to drag the time out, do it. You understand?'

She didn't, not a bit of it, but nodded.

'Remember.' His quiet tone was serious. 'Whatever happens, no matter what, do *not* leave him alone with the lad. Not for a single second. Right?'

Frightened tears stung her eyes. 'Right,' she whispered.

'It'll all be over soon. Now, go on.'

Taking Mack's hand, she led him to the room. Once inside, she closed the door and, looking around the empty space, chewed her thumb, unsure what to do, her nerves shot with worry of the unknown.

'Why we here, Pip? I want to go back to Miss Lucy.'

'Soon, lad.' She pointed across distractedly. 'Sit down on the chaise longue, there.'

'But I want to go, want to get back to our game—'

'Please, lad, just do as you're told!' she snapped, regretting her sharpness instantly when his bottom lip wobbled. 'Eeh, I'm sorry, I am. Please, sit down for just a minute. This'll not take long.'

He crossed the room and perched on the edge of the seat, and she'd just begun pacing the floor when the door opened and there he was. Impeccably groomed, dressed in the most expensive attire money could buy, as always, he cut the perfect image of a true gentleman. How deceiving appearances could be . . . She juddered to a stop.

'Leave us,' he told her coldly, eyes fixed firmly on the boy. 'Your friend is waiting for you upstairs.'

Her voice came out in a squeak. 'Upstairs?'

'That's what I said, isn't it? And you and he had better

388

make sure that Lucy and the hag stay put. One wrong move and I will finish the pair of you without hesitation. Now go. I shall let myself out once I'm done.'

Her mind raced; she fumbled around inside it for something to say, *anything*. 'Done with what?' It was the first thing that came out. Instantly, she regretted it. Alexander's lips bunched in a leering smile.

'Oh, come. You're surely not as green as all that? Slum monkeys like you know all there is to before your age has barely hit double figures.' He tossed his hat and cane on to a chair and removed his frock coat. Then he reached up to undo the buttons of his waistcoat.

Bile was rising in her throat; she groped desperately for something to stall him. All the while, her eyes flicked continually to the door. *Simon, where are you? Help us, please.*

'Listen, do you hear that?' Alexander cupped a hand to his ear.

Hope burst through Pip's chest – had he caught a noise from the landing? Was Simon back? 'Hear what?' she whispered.

'His sweet young flesh is calling me, calling me: *"Alexander. Alexander."*'

Her heart sank. God above, no . . .

Breaths now coming in short gasps, he almost tore the waistcoat from his body. He held out a hand. 'Boy, come here. I must, I must . . .'

Smiling in bemusement, Mack rose.

'You. Leave. *Now.*' Alexander gripped Pip's shoulder and threw her in the direction of the door.

By now, tears were streaming down her cheeks. 'But, but—'

'I won't tell you again. Out!'

'You'll not get away with this! I'll tell, I will!'

'And who do you suppose would believe you? Just take your idle threats and get—'

'Me.'

That one word, delivered by the familiar voice, had the power to render them both immobile. It ricocheted through the room, shattering the air into a million pieces. They turned to the dressing-room door in astonishment.

Albert Goldthorpe stepped out. His eyes raged sheer fire. 'Me,' he repeated, voice like steel. '*I* believe her.'

'And me.' Countenance matching the master's completely, Cook appeared next, to stand beside him.

Alexander, mouth stretched in a perfect O, could do nothing but gaze from one to the other in utter disbelief. Then another figure emerged and he sagged.

They had been hidden in the dressing room the whole time. They had heard everything. Oh, Simon. You clever, clever lad!

Halting in front of the man she meant to marry, Josephine locked her ravaged eyes with his. 'And me.'

'Darling, all of you, what you heard . . .' Alexander attempted a disarming laugh but it jerked from him in a series of odd squeaks. 'It's not, not what you think—'

'Aye, it is.' Simon threw the main door open wide. In his hand, he dangled a small pouch. 'This here brass you handed over as payment is proof aplenty.'

Alexander hadn't time to bluster a denial – suddenly, over Simon's shoulder and taking the room by surprise, Philip appeared.

He took in the scene at a sweeping glance and stepped inside. 'What the boy here has just informed me upon my timely return . . . It's true?'

'Every word,' Josephine affirmed with a croak. 'Simon went to see Father earlier, told him the manner of things. Thus, Father informed Mabel, and the two of them came to break the news to me which, naturally, I didn't at first believe . . . God in heaven, who *would*? I had to witness the truth for myself. Alexander believed us to be at church. We heard it all, *everything.*' She was trembling violently. 'I, I cannot, cannot believe . . . I, I . . .'

'Oh, cease your stuttering, you weak mess.' Alexander's simpering stance had gone. No amount of smooth talk would work this time, and he knew it. Now, his true colours finally surfaced. 'You really are the most pathetic creature I've ever had the misfortune of knowing. You disgust me, do you know that? The unchaperoned meetings we were permitted following our betrothal . . . the holding of hands and chaste kisses I was forced to endure . . .' He shuddered. 'It sickened me to my core.'

'*What*?' yelled Philip.

'You low-down dog – my daughter is worth ten of you!' the master added on a roar, purple with outrage. 'What the hell has this been about, then? Why ask for her hand in the first place?'

'It's your son you should be putting your questions to.' Training his stare across the room, Alexander lifted an eyebrow. 'Isn't that so, Philip?'

Every head turned towards him. He shook his own slowly. 'You claimed you were fond of her.'

'I lied.'

'You *bastard*. We were meant to be friends.' Philip spun around to face his sister and father. 'I swear, I would never have agreed to it had I known . . . He promised me!'

'Agreed to what?' the master asked grimly.

Josephine's words were laced with dread. 'What have you done?'

'When my gambling was at its height, I racked up a hefty debt . . .'

'Don't I already know that? It was I who was forced to drag you out of the mess you'd created, remember?'

'No, Father. This particular instance, you know nothing about. I couldn't come to you, not again. Already, you had begun to look at me with disgust and shame in your eyes, and it hurt. I couldn't bear that look to develop into one of hatred. I *couldn't* tell you.'

'However many more . . . I could never hate you. You're my son.'

Philip gave a hollow laugh. 'Don't honour me with such a title, sir, for I deserve it not. A true son wouldn't treat his parent as I have you.' Turning to Josephine, he took her hand in his and brought it to his heart. 'I was desperate; those I was indebted to were not people a wise man would choose to cross. I, of course, was a fool. The threats were mounting to the extent that I felt I was drowning. Danger to my life was a very real prospect. Then, Alexander offered a silver lining to the black cloud crushing me. He agreed to loan me the sum to get the creditors off my tail. But of course, his generosity came at a price.' Philip dragged his hand through his hair. 'When he put forward his proposition . . . I trusted him, Josephine.'

'Tell me,' she murmured.

'He said if I helped pave the way for the two of you to marry, he'd take the dowry that the union fetched as payment and that we would be even. I asked him, asked him what his feelings towards you were. Though he never claimed love, he did assure me he cared for you. I believed that in time, as do most marriages, it would develop into something deeper. He *lied* to me.'

Her gaze flickered to Alexander and back again. 'It would seem he put on quite the show. I, however, hadn't the need to play-act. My love for him was true.'

'Lord, I know. I know. Had you not taken to him, I

wouldn't have encouraged it. But you did. You appeared so happy. You shone from the inside. I truly thought that the deal would prove satisfactory to us all.'

'I understand. I was already galloping past the age of certain spinsterhood. You pitied me—'

'No. No,' he repeated fiercely. 'I wanted only that you should be happy. Though I seldom demonstrate it, you're my sister and I love you. I would never intentionally do anything to hurt you. I believed that everything would turn out for the best. And Caroline was forever pushing, pushing, terrified at the alternative. The deal must be finalised, she insisted, for just as we hadn't had the means to pay the original debtor, so too it would be with Alexander if a marriage wasn't forthcoming. Who was to say he wouldn't sully my good name and reputation, to whoever would listen? I would be ruined.

'The shame, my wife insisted, would be more than she could bear. Father would refuse to bail me out again, would disown me, sling us on to the street. She'd convinced herself that the fault *lay* with Father. For what was the alternative?' Philip's voice turned bitter. 'Facing the truth that her husband was to blame. And that, she could not do. For it would mean I wasn't the man she'd perceived me to be, which would reflect badly on her own judgement. It was easier for her this way. And being the spineless dog that I was, it was easier for me to have her – and myself – believe it also.

'The marriage . . . I believed we were doing the right thing. I believed it to be the best thing for you. I *believed* that the man standing there was honourable!' In a move that surprised everyone, he threw himself at Alexander. Grabbing him by the shirt front, he pinned him against the wall. 'All these years we've been friends . . . I thought I knew you. Truth is, you've been wearing a mask I never witnessed slip, that's all. Just *who* are you?' His stare travelled to the small, light-haired boy now snuggled in the folds of Cook's arm. 'You are warped, Alexander,' he whispered. 'Degenerate, depraved, *putrid* . . .' Suddenly, understanding smoothed out his face. He nodded into the stiff one close to his.

'My sister was a smokescreen for your true character to hide behind, wasn't she? That was your intention from the off. You required a wife, to avoid arousing suspicion as to your true . . . fancies.' He spat the word as though it tasted acrid on his tongue. 'I ought to kill you.'

'Let him go, son.'

Philip flashed Albert a frown. 'But Father—'

'Let him go,' the older man repeated. He walked forward and removed his son's hands from Alexander. Then he himself stood before the man, who now looked decidedly uneasy. 'You are dead to this family. As is now my son's debt to you.'

'Mr Goldthorpe, you cannot do this. Such a loss would likely ruin *me* – he owes me close to two thousand—!'

'Should I ever see your face again,' Albert continued, steely tone hacking through the protest, 'I shall make it my mission to ensure you can *never* show it to any other in public. Your name in polite society will be dirt. The whole of Manchester and beyond will know exactly who, *what*, you are.'

Alexander glared from one man to the other, his breathing ragged. Swinging on his heel, he snatched up his apparel, cast them a last, murderous look then stalked to the door.

'Wait.'

He paused at the threshold. Turning, he watched stonily as Josephine crossed the floor towards him.

394

With the dignity and grace of a true lady, she calmly eased the ring from her finger and dropped it into his hand. 'Now get out.'

He did. Pip moved to Josephine's side and wrapped her arms around her waist.

Cook's voice was grim. 'Gone from this house he might be, but that'll not halt his filthy ways where poor kiddies are concerned, nay.'

Though the master didn't respond with words, his eyes gave a veiled message of reassurance that Alexander hadn't heard the last of Albert Goldthorpe.

'Thank you, dear girl, Simon. What you two have done today . . . You are the bravest people I know.'

Pip's chest ached for her. 'I'm that sorry.'

A ghost of a smile touched Josephine's lips. 'Don't be. Rather a temporary heartache than a lifetime's worth.'

'Josephine . . .'

She turned to look at her brother. He said no more, his stare conveying the heavy sorrow and regret within him. When she nodded, his eyes filled with grateful tears. And Pip breathed a little easier.

Philip had vowed to his sister weeks ago in this very room that he would ensure she was happy. His sincerity then could not be questioned. Nor could it now. He hadn't meant to cause such pain, she was certain. Weak-willed and foolish he might be. Cruel he wasn't. He'd made a mistake but one she was sure the family could, in time, find it in their hearts to forgive him for. Somehow, everything seemed just a little bit brighter.

'Come on, lovies.' Cook shepherded the children out. 'Let's leave the adults to talk matters through.'

Pip was the last to leave. Before closing the door, she glanced over her shoulder. All three Goldthorpes stared back. Their acceptance and love for her filled the space between them. And now, the unquestionable selfsame feelings spread through her to warm her inside and out, and she knew they would dwell there for ever.

She smiled at each of her family in turn. They were bound as one. Nothing could touch them now.

Chapter 27

December 1861

'ALBERT'S DEAD!'

Cook dropped the ladle she held. It hit the stone floor with a clatter. 'What?' she almost screamed, head swinging wildly, while the rest of the room leapt to their feet, faces pinched in horror.

'It's true!' Tears poured down Cally's cheeks. She sniffed loudly. 'He succumbed to the fever late yesterday evening. Oh, I can't believe it, I can't!'

'Yesterday . . .? The *fever*? What fever?'

'Well, I don't know! Not many took to him, him being a foreigner, like, but I did. Oh, the poor dear man!'

By now, Cook's fear and frustration had reached their limit. 'Foreigner? Girl, what are you blathering about—?' She stopped abruptly. Then she closed her eyes. 'Why, you foolish *bloody* girl. You ain't speaking of the master, after all, are you?'

Now, the housemaid wore the confused expression. 'Him? Nay, the Prince Consort— Oh!' She slapped a hand to her mouth. 'Albert and Albert . . . Eeh, I'm that sorry, I didn't think.'

'You never do, that's your trouble!' Cook snapped, dropping into a chair and pressing a hand to her thumping heart. 'By, you near brought an attack upon me good and proper then. Don't ever do owt like that again.

So *our* Albert, he's fine and well?' she still had to ask, just to be certain.

'Oh aye. He's enjoying a brew in the study, told me to inform the servants of the sad tidings.'

Despite the shock, Pip, Simon, Mack and Tabby couldn't contain a discreet smile to each other. Cally was a law unto herself, she was really!

'Eeh, it's a shame, aye. The poor Queen. 'Ere, them's two words there I never thought I'd utter in the same breath. Just shows you, eh, riches can't buy everything. If you ain't got your health, you've got nowt.'

Half an hour later, the whole household gathered in the drawing room in a rare but fitting moment to partake of a drink to the German's memory. The master raised his glass.

'To Albert, Prince Consort of Great Britain and Ireland.'

'God bless,' everyone chimed.

'Long live the Queen!'

'Long live the Queen!' they repeated with feeling.

Philip crossed to the sofa and patted the spaces either side of him. Pip and Lucy sat down and snuggled into him, and he kissed their brows in turn.

Breathing in his scent, Pip felt tears rise for the princes and princesses now bereft of a father. She couldn't begin to think what heartache they must be feeling, for were it to happen to her . . . She quickly forced the notion away. Never could she imagine a single day, now, without him.

The last nine months had seen life changed, for all of them, beyond recognition. She glanced to the boys who stood talking with her grandparents and smiled. Hearty food and good living were seeing them grow into strapping lads. They had come on so much this last year, were the pictures of health, and any outsider looking in would never guess their harsh past on Manchester's streets. The same was true of herself. Several inches taller and beginning to fill out, as all budding young women do, she was looking to become a beauty, or so her proud grandmother liked to tell her on an almost daily basis.

Once a week, she and the lads now took lessons in the schoolroom with Lucy. Their learning was coming along in leaps and bounds – particularly young Mack's. He'd discovered a love of ancient history, and he and the master would pore over books on the subject in the study for hours. Albert had grown particularly fond of the sweet-natured child, who in turn adored the old man's kind, unconventional ways.

Pip let her gaze linger on Simon. As though sensing he was being watched, he looked across and she saw him take in the father and daughters scene with a wince of pain. He smiled at her, but it was almost forced, before looking away again.

Now and then, she would bring up the subject of his own father but he stuck steadfastly to his decision; nothing she said would make him consider seeking Peter out. It was fear of being hurt again that stopped him, she'd come to realise. Who could blame him? He'd been let down deeply by the one person who should have cared for him above all others. She understood his reluctance completely. However, a niggle in the back of her mind, that Simon should give Peter half a chance to at least explain, for both their sakes, remained with her still. Perhaps, in time, who knew? But the choice had to be his. It wasn't hers to make for him.

Josephine, laughing at something Cook had said, cut through Pip's musings. Again, she smiled. For many months, everyone had secretly feared that the crushing event wrought by Alexander's hand would see her slip into her old illness of shattered nerves and anxious ruin. But, proving what Pip knew all along, she'd shown an inner strength that to dwell on left her brimming with pride. Rather than wither, allow him to grind her progress into the dust, she'd risen from the ordeal like a flower pushing through soil to shine in full bloom. Pip had never met anyone like her. Her aunt was capable of anything, now. She didn't doubt it for a second.

As for relations between the older Goldthorpe members, anyone would be forgiven for assuming that Philip's actions could have easily torn their bond apart. Truth was, it had only united them in a way none had expected. The three were closer now than they had ever been before. Talking was the key. Long-held grievances were aired, feelings were laid bare, and what their honesty and hard work produced was the blossoming of something quite special. They were once more a unit, as it should be. Them against the rest, together. Pip couldn't have been more grateful that the same blood as theirs fed her veins. Her family.

The day after Prince Albert was laid to rest, and a year exactly since three young waifs stumbled upon Bracken House, broke crisp and bright. With the nation in mourning, it was widely acknowledged that Christmas would be a quieter affair than usual as a mark of respect. The male members of the household donned black armbands, the females wore black ribbons in their hair, and preparations began in brisk but sober fashion.

Nevertheless, the air sparked with the magic of the day, and not only for the children, and as the hours passed the mood switched to one of gaiety. By evening, the house had been transformed. Holly and mistletoe greenery livened mantels and tables, lights bedecking the tree twinkled like a thousand holy stars, and easy laughter permeated the warm and cosy rooms.

At the family's insistence, much to the servants' shock and delight, everyone was invited once more to the drawing room, this time to get the Christmas Eve celebrations under way. Cook had surpassed herself – the sideboard, groaning beneath the weight of the mouthwatering buffet, was a sight to behold. Games and entertainment quickly followed, and fun and feasting was had by all.

'If I may, I'd like to say a few words,' Philip announced some time later, rising from his seat. 'This past year has not been the easiest. And I, I'm ashamed to admit, have been at the root of most of the problems. I vowed some time ago to eschew my indulgent and selfish activities, that the person I had come to be was a thing of the past. Not only did I mean it, but I stuck to it. However, I realise I have some way to go yet to prove to you all I can be a good man. My treatment of most of you has been nothing short of appalling.

'Father, Josephine – and you, Mabel.' He smiled sadly when the cook raised her brows in shock that he'd addressed her as he hadn't for many years. 'I've been such a pompous and arrogant fool for so long and I'm sorry.' His voice broke. 'For everything.'

Albert and Josephine murmured acknowledgement with soft smiles. After some seconds, Cook did likewise, eyes bright. 'To the future, eh, lad?'

'To the future,' he repeated thickly. 'Pip, I have wronged you most of all but I hope these past months have gone some small way towards proving how much you mean to me. You, you're our gift. Lydia sent you to us,' he choked. 'You've healed us all.'

She smiled back at this man who had changed

completely. Her father. The term came naturally, now. He was right; they had, in their own ways, been through so much. But they came through it, together. And that's what they would always be. As a family. All of them.

'Charity, goodwill, peace and happiness to all,' Philip finished, inclining his glass to everyone in the room; all did likewise, faces wreathed in contentment. 'Now, enjoy yourselves!'

Breaking from the festivities a little later, Pip scanned the room and found Simon absent. She slipped out and headed for the kitchen. The space was empty but on closer inspection, she saw that the back door was open a few inches. She made her way across and poked her head through.

He glanced up from where he sat on the doorstep. 'All right?'

'Aye, you?' He didn't answer and she shuffled beside him on the cold stone. She linked her arm through his. 'This brings back memories, eh?'

A quiet chuckle left him. 'I couldn't believe our luck that night to find this door unlocked. By, I were bold.'

It was her turn to laugh. 'You were that! But look where it got us, eh?'

Stars shimmered across the black blanket above them. They watched them for a while in easy silence.

'I were thinking, I might call in at Angel Street the morrow.'

She spun around to face him. 'To see Peter? Oh, lad, I'm that happy—!'

'Aye, well. Let's see how it goes.'

Hiding a joyous grin, she nodded.

'Are you really happy, Pip? I mean with everything, like?'

Sighing, she nodded. 'Eeh, who'd have thought it?'

402

'I'm embarrassed, you know.'

'About what?'

'How I used to go on at thee about stopping away from Mr Philip.'

'Ay, lad. You weren't to know – none of us were – who he'd turn out to be—'

'Nay, I don't mean that,' he cut in quietly. 'It didn't matter who it were. It could've been anyone, you know? I wanted thee to myself.'

Flushing, she was glad of the darkness. 'Tha were jealous?'

He nodded. 'Aye.'

Something stirred in her for the lad. A deeper kind of love that she couldn't fully grasp the meaning of. She knew he felt it, too.

'You'll likely wed a nob when you're older, eh? Suppose you'd have to, you being who you are. I ain't grand enough for you, now, am I?'

Her heart fluttered and jumped but her excitement was tinged with sadness. 'Nowt's changed really, lad. Aye, I've a room and bed of my own now instead of Josephine's dressing-room floor, but don't I still sit with you all in the kitchen as I've allus done? I ain't a Goldthorpe in my ways and never shall be, for I've never known it. I'm just Pip. The same one you've allus known. I *like* being me.'

Simon nodded, smiled. 'Aye. I like that Pip, an' all.'

She smiled back then glanced behind them as the door opened.

Without a word, Mack shimmied between them and planted his thumb in his mouth. They shared a contented, completed look over his head.

'All right, Bread?' asked Simon.

'Aye.'

403

'What?' the older lad added to Pip when she shook her head, grinning.

'You'll never let that bloomin' name die, will yer?'

Taking out his thumb, Mack cut through their chuckles. 'I like it.'

'You like being called Bread?'

'Aye.'

'D'you know, no one's ever asked your opinion on it, have they?' She shrugged. 'All right, then. Bread it is, Simon!'

When their laughter had died away, they sat and watched the patches of scudding clouds. This time, they saw far more than cats and horses dancing jigs, and fish sporting top hats.

They saw a future. Here, at Bracken House.

Their home.

A SHILLING FOR A WIFE

Emma Hornby

Sally Swann thought life couldn't get much worse. Then a single coin changed hands.

A dismal cottage in the heart of Bolton, Lancashire, has been Sally's prison since Joseph Goden 'bought' her from the workhouse as his wife. A drunkard and bully, Joseph rules her with a rod of iron, using fists and threats to keep her in check.

When Sally gives birth, however, she knows she must do anything to save her child from her husband's clutches. She manages to escape and, taking her baby, flees for the belching chimneys of Manchester, in search of her only relative.

But with the threat of discovery by Joseph, who will stop at nothing to find her, Sally must fight with every ounce of strength she has to protect herself and her son, and finally be with the man who truly loves her. For a fresh start comes with a price . . .

Available in paperback and ebook now . . .

MANCHESTER MOLL

Emma Hornby

Moll thought she could keep her family safe . . .

Eighteen-year-old Moll Chambers works her fingers to the bone doing all she can to support her family. With an ailing father and a wayward mother, Moll is the only one who can look after her siblings, Bo and Sissy.

But Manchester is an increasingly dangerous place to live, overrun with a ferocious rivalry between gangs of so-called 'scuttlers': young men and women bent on a life of violence and crime. And they have her brother in their sights. Soon even Moll can't protect Bo from the lure of the criminal underworld.

Then the scuttlers looked her way.

When she herself falls for the leader of a rival gang, Moll's choices place her and Bo firmly on opposite sides of the city's turf war.

With her loyalties now torn in two and tragedy lurking round every corner, will Moll be able to rise above the conflict and protect those she loves the most? Or will stepping out with a scuttler spell ruin for them all . . .?

Available in paperback and ebook now . . .

As good as Dilly Court
or your money back

We hope you enjoyed this book as much as we did.
If, however, you don't agree with us that it is as good
as Dilly Court and would like a refund, then please send
your copy of the book with your original receipt, and your
contact details including your full address, together with
the reasons why you don't think it is as good
as Dilly Court to the following address:

Emma Hornby Money-Back Offer
Marketing Department
Transworld Publishers
Penguin Random House UK
61–63 Uxbridge Road
London
W5 5SA